W9-AMY-296

PRAISE FOR *QUIN'S SHANGHAI CIRCUS*

"... a profoundly nutty book full of mysteries, truths, untruths, idiot savants, necrophiliacs, magicians, dwarfs, circus masters, secret agents, and a marvelous recasting of history in our century."
The New York Times Book Review

"... as complex as Pynchon, funnier than Vonnegut."
Barry Hannah

PRAISE FOR THE JERUSALEM QUARTET

"Whittemore's colorful characters wrestle fitfully with meaninglessness, time, and the grim realities of war. *Sinai Tapestry* ends with a portrait of the Turks' 1922 genocidal assault on Smyrna that sobers up the reader like a jack-boot at a sock-hop. As the Quartet progresses, the novels become less playful, their earlier flights of fantasy increasingly tempered by failure and pain into a resigned yet mystic melancholy .... Though the geopolitics of the Middle East always loom in the background, Whittemore is constantly probing for the gaps and loops in time. As in Gabriel Garcia Marquez's *One Hundred Years of Solitude*, characters return in name and shape through their progeny, while people, events, and certain phrases are regularly reintroduced, giving you the feeling that you are wandering through a labyrinth of memory. The Jerusalem Quartet is rich with homegrown theology, and leaves you with a mystic taste for the empty network of all things: 'All lives are secret tapestries that swirl and sweep through the years with souls and strivings as the colors, the threads. And there may be little knots of tangled meaning everywhere beneath the surface, tying the colors and threads together, but the little knots aren't important finally, only the sweep itself, the tapestry as a whole.' "
The Voice Literary Supplement

"The four books which make up the Jerusalem Quartet are among the richest and most profound in imaginative literature. . . and also among the most obscure, out of print for more than ten years. Whittemore has been . . . unfairly neglected and it can only be hoped that his star will rise again in another decade or so. Such a superlative body of work cannot be overlooked forever."
Jeff VanderMeer, *Literature of the Fantastic Newsletter*

SINAI TAPESTRY

"The Sinai tapestry of 'lives that had raged through vast secret wars and been struck dumb by equally vast silences, textures harsh and soft in their guise of colors, a cloak of life' is a work of literature, a 'chaotic' book of life . . . . Whittemore is a deceptively lucid stylist. Were his syntax as cluttered as Pynchon's or as grand as Nabokov's or Fuentes's, his virtually ignored recent novel might have received the attention it deserves, for his imagination of present and alternative worlds is comparable to theirs . . . ."
Anthony Heilbut, *The Nation*

"An epic hashish dream . . . . cosmic . . . . fabulous . . . . droll and moving"
The New York Times Book Review

"Sit back and enjoy an outrageously wild and disparate cast . . . range over the Holy Land and other parts . . . highly original. . . . Sophisticated, surreal fun with a cutting edge"
Publishers Weekly

"Whittemore is to Vonnegut what a tapestry is to a cat's cradle."
Rhoda Lerman

"One of America's best writers . . . an author of seismic talents . . . sets in motion an epic of profound invention, one that promises to be as fascinating and self contained as *Lord of the Rings*."
Harper's

JERUSALEM POKER

"Comedy, horror, wit, tragedy, erudition, and breathtaking imagination . . . and it is romantic, as great fantasy dressed in truth must always be."
Cleveland Plain Dealer

"Whittemore presents himself as one of the last, best arguments against television. He's an author of extraordinary talents, albeit one who eludes comparison with other writers . . . . The milieu is one which readers of espionage novels may think themselves familiar, and yet it's totally transformed—by the writer's wild humour, his mystical bent, and his bicameral perception of history and time . . . .
If Whittemore were no more than an 'entertainer' his novels would be worth their price. But he does something more difficult than intellectual vaudeville. He assassinates the banal, revealing the authentic current of madness that courses through human affairs, reminding us that the fantastic is ubiquitous, invisible only because we've shut our eyes to it."
Harper's

NILE SHADOWS

"One of the most complex and ambitious espionage stories ever written. . . . The deciphering of Stern's past which reveals him to have been an incurable idealist, plunges the reader into a hall-of-mirrors world. . . . By a wave of his storyteller's wand Whittemore turns the whole operation into an exploration of the options for good and evil thrown up in terrifying times."
Publishers Weekly

"On both a human and historical level, _Jericho Mosaic_ makes comprehensible, as no other recent book does, the history of the Middle East since the end of World War II. And that is only one of the novel's multitude of virtues . . . . Like Tolstoy, Whittemore shows us the relation between the large movements of history and their most ordinary human sources . . . . [with] his own idiosyncratic vision, one that enables us to see to the human center of history in a thoroughly original way. The final book in what is one of the most wonderful achievements in 20th-century literature. . . . Without illusion, but with supreme intelligence and a generous heart, Whittemore shows us just how painful, beautiful, and surprising . . . life's reversals can be, and how our struggles with ourselves and others can ultimately seem to change time itself."
The Philadelphia Inquirer

QUIN'S
SHANGHAI
CIRCUS

BY EDWARD WHITTEMORE

Quin's Shanghai Circus (1974)
Sinai Tapestry (1977)
Jerusalem Poker (1978)
Nile Shadows (1983)
Jericho Mosaic (1987)

QUIN'S SHANGHAI CIRCUS

*

BY EDWARD WHITTEMORE

*

Introduction by John Nichols

Foreword by Tom Wallace
Afterword by Judy Karasik

OLD EARTH BOOKS
Baltimore, Maryland
2002

PS
3573
.H557
Q56
2002

QUIN'S SHANGHAI CIRCUS

Copyright © 1974 Edward Whittemore, All Rights Reserved
Copyright Renewed © 2002 Edward Whittemore Estate, All Rights Reserved
Foreword Copyright © 2002 Tom Wallace
Introduction Copyright © 2002 John Nichols
"An Editorial Relationship" Copyright © 2002 Judy Karasik
Photo of Author Copyright © 2002 Carol Martin
Cover Design Copyright @ 2002 Julie Burris

Without limiting the rights under copyright reserved above, no part of
this book may be reproduced in any form or by any electronic or
mechanical means, including information storage and retrieval systems,
without written permission from both the author and copyright holder,
except by a reviewer who may want to quote brief passages in review.

ACKNOWLEDGEMENTS

The essay, "An Editorial Relationship" also appeared in AGNI 55, Spring 2002

Published by
Old Earth Books
Post Office Box 19951
Baltimore, Maryland 21211
www.oldearthbooks.com

Original Interior Book Design by Batten, Friedman and Kreloff

Book Production: Old Earth Books Edition
Garcia Publishing Services
Post Office Box 1059
Woodstock, Illinois 60098
www.american-fantasy.com

10 9 8 7 6 5 4 3 2 1

ISBN: 1-882968-21-2

PRINTED IN THE UNITED STATES OF AMERICA
By Thomson-Shore
Dexter, Michigan

5115 9767

for Brigid

●

Photo by Carol Martin

Edward Whittemore (1933-1995)

"Some twenty years after the end of the war with Japan a freighter arrived in Brooklyn with the largest collection of Japanese pornography ever assembled in a Western tongue. The owner of the collection, a huge, smiling fat man named Geraty, presented a passport to customs officials that showed that he was a native-born American about as old as the century, an exile who had left the United States four decades before." Thus begins *Quin's Shanghai Circus*; it ends with the largest funeral procession held in Asia since the thirteenth century.

The year was 1974, the author Edward Whittemore, a forty-one year-old former American intelligence agent; he and I had been undergraduates at Yale back in the 1950s, but then we had gone our separate ways, he to the CIA and I to a career in book publishing in New York City. Needless to say, I was pleased that my old Yale friend had brought his novel to me and the publishing house of Holt, Rinehart and Winston where I was editor-in-chief of the Trade Department. I was even more delighted when the reviews, mostly favorable, started coming in, capped by Jerome Charyn in *The New York Times Book Review*: "*Quin* was a profoundly nutty book full of mysteries, truths, untruths, idiot savants, necrophiliacs, magicians, dwarfs, circus masters, secret agents . . . a marvelous recasting of history in our century."

In the next fifteen years Whittemore went on to write four more wildly imaginative novels, his Jerusalem Quartet: *Sinai Tapestry, Jerusalem Poker, Nile Shadows*, and *Jericho Mosaic*.

Reviewers and critics compared his work to the novels of Carlos Fuentes, Thomas Pynchon, and Kurt Vonnegut. *Publishers Weekly* called him "our best unknown novelist." Jim Hougan, writing in *Harper's Magazine*, said Whittemore was "one of the last, best arguments against television. . . . He is an author of extraordinary talents. . . . The milieu is one in which readers of espionage novels may think themselves familiar, and yet it is totally transformed by the writer's wild humor, his mystical bent, and his bicameral perception of time and history."

Edward Whittemore died from prostate cancer in the summer of 1995 at the age of sixty-two, not much better known than when he began his short, astonishing writing career in the early 1970s. His novels never sold more than 5000 copies in hard covers, three were briefly available in mass market paperback editions. But the Quartet was published in Great Britain, Holland, and Germany where Whittemore was described on its jacket as the "master American storyteller." The jacket on the Polish edition of *Quin's Shanghai Circus* was a marvelous example of Japanese erotica.

*

Whittemore graduated from Deering High School, Portland, Maine in June 1951 and entered Yale that fall, a member of the Class of 1955. Another Yale classmate, the novelist Ric Frede, labeled Yale undergraduates of the 1950s "members of the Silent Generation." The Fifties were also the "Eisenhower Years," that comfortable period between the Second World War and the radicalism and the campus unrest of the 1960s. Ivy League universities were still dominated by the graduates of New England prep schools. Sons of the East Coast "establishment," they were closer to the Princeton of F. Scott Fitzgerald and the Harvard of John P. Marquand then the worlds of Jack Kerouac and Allen Ginsberg. They were "gentlemen" and athletes but not necessarily scholars. Often after receiving "gentlemanly C's" at Yale and the other Ivys, they went on to careers on Wall Street or in Washington; to the practice of law, medicine, or journalism. They entertained their families and friends on the playing fields of Yale as well as at Mory's. They ran *The*

Yale Daily News, WYBC (the campus radio station), *The Yale Record* (the humor magazine), *The Yale Banner* (the year book), and sang in various Yale music groups. They were usually members of a fraternity and were "tapped" by one of the six secret Senior Societies.

By the Yale standards of the day, Whittemore was a great success, a "high school boy" who made it. Affable, good-looking and trim, he presented a quizzical smile to the world. He casually wore the uniform that was "in": herringbone tweed jacket, preferably with patches at the elbow, rep tie, chinos and scruffy white buck shoes. In a word, he was "shoe" (short for "white shoe," a term of social approval). He was not much of an athlete, but he was a member of Zeta Psi, a fraternity of hard-drinking, socially well-connected undergraduates. At the end of Junior year he was tapped for Scroll and Key.

But his real distinction was that he was the Managing Editor of the 1955 *Yale News* Board at a time when *News* chairmen and managing editors were as popular as football team captains and the leading scholar of the class. During the immediate postwar years and the 1950s the *Yale News* produced such prominent writer-journalists as William F. Buckley, James Claude Thomson, Richard Valeriani, David McCullough, Roger Stone, M. Stanton Evans, Henry S.F. Cooper, Calvin Trillin, Gerald Jonas, Harold Gulliver, Scott Sullivan, and Robert Semple. They would make their mark at *The New York Times*, *The New Yorker*, *Time*, *Newsweek*, *The National Review*, *Harper's*, and the television networks, and go on to write many books.

*

I met Ted early in the spring of Freshman year. We were both "heeling" the first *News* "comp," and as was usually the case with survivors of that fierce "competition" to make the *News*, we remained friends throughout our years at Yale. It was assumed by many of us on the *News* that Ted would head for Wall Street and Brown Brothers Harriman, a blue-chip investment firm where Old Blues from Scroll and Key were more than welcome and where Ted's older brother later worked. Or at the very least, he would get on the journalistic fast-track some-where in the *Time-Life* empire founded by an earlier *News* worthy, Henry Luce.

But we were wrong. Whittemore, after a tour of duty as an officer in the Marines in Japan, was approached there by the CIA, given a crash course in Japanese, and spent more than a decade working for the Agency in the Far East, Europe and the Middle East.

During those years Whittemore would periodically return to New York. "What are you up to?" one would ask. For a while he was running a newspaper in Greece. Then there was the shoe company in Italy and some sort of think-tank in Jerusalem. Even a stint with the New York City drug administration when John Lindsay was mayor. Later, there were rumors that he had a drinking "problem" and that he was taking drugs.

He married and divorced twice while he was with the Marines and the Agency. He and his first wife had two daughters, but under the terms of the divorce agreement he was not permitted to see them. And then there were the women he lived with after the second divorce. There were many; they all seemed to be talented—painters, photographers, sculptors, and dancers, but never writers.

There were more rumors. He had left the Agency, he was living on Crete, he had no money, he was writing. Then silence. Clearly, the "fair-haired" undergraduate had not gone on to fame and glory.

*

It was not until 1972 or 1973 that Ted surfaced in my life. He was back in New York on a visit. On the surface he appeared to be the old Ted. He was a little rumpled, but the wit, the humor, the boyish charm were still there. Yet he seemed more thought-ful, more reflective, and there was Carol, a woman with whom Ted had become involved while in Crete and with whom he seemed to be living. He was more secretive now. And he had the manuscript of a novel he wanted me to read. I thought the novel was wonderful, full of fabulous and exotic characters, brimming with life, history, and the mysteries of the Orient. The novel that came to be called *Quin's Shanghai Circus* went through three more drafts before we published it in 1974. Set in Japan and China before and during the Second World War, two drafts even began in the South Bronx in the 1920s and involved three young Irish brothers named Quin. By the time the novel came out only one Quin remained and the Bronx interlude had shrunk from eighty pages to a couple of paragraphs.

As mentioned, *Quin* was a bigger success with the critics than it was in the bookstores. Readers loved the novel, even though there were not nearly enough of them. But Whittemore was not deterred. Less than two years later he appeared in my office with an even more ambitious novel, *Sinai Tapestry*, the first volume of his Jerusalem Quartet. Set in the heyday of the British Empire, it takes place in Palestine during the middle of the nineteenth century. Foremost among the larger-than-life characters were a tall English aristocrat, the greatest swordsman, botanist, and explorer of Victorian England; a fanatical trappist monk who found the original Sinai Bible, which "denies every religious truth every held by anyone;" and an Irish radical who had fled to Palestine disguised as a nun. My favorite was (and still is) Haj Harun, born three thousand years earlier, an ethereal wanderer through history: now an antiquities dealer dressed in a faded yellow cloak and sporting a Crusaders' rusty helmet while pursuing his mission as defender of the Holy City. He had several previous incarnations: as a stone carver of winged lions during the Assyrian occupation, proprietor of an all-night grocery store under the Greeks, a waiter when the Romans were in power, and a distributor of hashish and goats for the Turks. Before I first went to Israel in 1977, Whittemore, who was then writing in New York, gave me the names of several people in Jerusalem. One was named Mohammed, the owner of an antiquities gallery. When I finally tracked him down in the Old City I saw before me a fey character who, if he had been wearing a faded yellow cloak and a rusty helmet, would have been a dead ringer for Haj Harun.

Clearly Ted had been caught up in a new life in Jerusalem. The immediately preceding years in Crete where he had been living on a modest pension in the early 70s were behind him. He had been sharing a house with friends in Khania, the second

largest city on Crete. In its long history it had been occupied by
the Romans, conquered by the Arabs, Byzantines,and Venetians
before becoming part of the Ottoman Empire in the seventeenth century. Now it was a sprawling Greek city. Athens
without the Parthenon, but with an even richer history. In other
words, a perfect place for a former intelligence agent to take
stock and decide what history was all about, to re-examine what
he had learned as a Yale undergraduate.

*

While in Japan in the 1960s Whittemore had written two
unpublished novels, one about the Japanese game of Go, the
other about a young American expatriate living in Tokyo. In
Crete he began to write again, slowly, awkwardly, experiment-
ing with voice, style,and subject matter, distilling his experience
in the Agency into that sweeping raucous epic, *Quin's Shanghai
Circus.* By the time he embarked on the Quartet, he was more
assured, he was becoming a writer, and he had found a subject
that was to engage him for the rest of his life: Jerusalem and the
world of Christians, Arabs and Jews; faith and belief; mysticism
and religious (and political) fanaticism; nineteenth century;
European imperialism, twentieth century wars and terrorism.
But above all Jerusalem, the City on the Hill, the Holy City. The
novels would still be full of outrageous characters, the humor
was still often grotesque and macabre, and there was violence
aplenty. But there was also a new understanding of the mysteries of life.

The new novel, finally published in 1979, was *Jerusalem
Poker*, the second volume of the Quartet. It involves a twelve-
year poker game begun in the last days of December 1921 when
three men sit down to play. The stakes were nothing less than
the Holy City itself. Where else could a game for the control of
Jerusalem be played but in the antiquities shop of Haj Harun?
Actually, Ted did not come to live permanently (that is "permanently" according to his ways) in Jerusalem until he was well
into writing the Quartet. His knowledge of Jerusalem was based
initially on books, but later on he wandered endlessly through
the crowded, teeming streets and Quarters of the Old City.

Merchants of every kind, butchers, tanners, glass blowers, jewelers, silversmiths,and even iron mongers spoke nearly every known language and dressed in the vibrant and exotic costumes of the Middle East. I once remarked to Ted while we were making our way along a narrow passage in the Arab Quarter, that I fully expected we would run into Sinbad the Sailor coming the other way.

The next time I visited Jerusalem, Ted had settled down with Helen, an American painter, in a spacious apartment in a large, nineteenth-century stone building in the Ethiopian Church compound. The apartment overlooked a courtyard full of flowers and lemon trees. Over one wall there loomed a Cistercian convent, and around the corner there was a synagogue full of Orthodox rabbinical students praying twenty-four hours a-day, or so it seemed to me. And standing or quietly reading in the courtyard were the Ethiopian monks. One morning I woke at six in my sunlit room and heard the Cistercian nuns singing a cappella. They sounded like birds and I thought for a moment I was in heaven.

After a midday nap we usually headed for the Old City, invariably ending up in the same cafe, a pretentious name for what was little more than an outdoor tea garden where hot tea and sticky buns were served. The proprietor sat at one table interminably fingering worry beads and talking to friends, an ever-changing group of local merchants, money changers, students, and some unsavory hard-looking types. They all seemed to have a nodding acquaintance with Ted, who knew as much, if not more, about the Old City as its inhabitants.

*

By 1981, Whittemore was living much of the year in the apartment in the Ethiopian compound, but in the years ahead he also rented a series of rooms in New York, a walk-up on Lexington Avenue, a studio apartment on Third. And he was writing steadily. I had left Holt earlier that spring for another publishing house and Judy Karasik took over the editorial work on Whittemore's new novel, *Nile Shadows*. She has written the epilogue to this book, a eulogy which she should have but didn't give at Whittemore's funeral twelve years after *Nile Shadows* appeared.

Nile Shadows is set in Egypt, it is 1942 and Rommel's powerful Afrika Corps is threatening to overrun Egypt and seize control of the entire Middle East. A group of characters, some old, some new, hold the fate of the world in their hands. At the very beginning of the novel, Stern, an idealistic visionary in *Sinai Tapestry* turned gun-runner a half century later, is killed by a grenade thrown into the doorway of a backstreet bar. Violence as well as mysticism dominates Whittemore's novels. Elsewhere he had described with horrible abandon the "rape" of Nanking and the sack of Smyrna in 1922 when the Turks butchered ten of thousands of Greek men, women, and children. A *Publishers Weekly* reviewer said: "One of the most complex and ambitious espionage stories ever written." And a critic in *The Nation* said: "Whittemore is a deceptively lucid stylist. Were his syntax as cluttered as Pynchon's or as conspicuously grand as Nabokov's or Fuentes', his virtually ignored novels might have received the attention they deserved."

But sales still hadn't caught up with the critics. By the spring of 1985, Ted was finishing the novel that was to be called *Jericho Mosaic*, the fourth of the Jerusalem Quartet. I was in Israel for the biennial Jerusalem International Book Fair. Afterwards, Ted suggested we drive down to Jericho, that oasis to the southeast of Jerusalem from which most of the caravans of Biblical times set out for the Levant, Asia Minor, and Africa. On the way we visited several Greek Orthodox monasteries in the Judean wilderness. Since they were built into solid rock at the bottom of isolated ravines reachable only on narrow paths, we had to leave the car up on the road and scramble down hillsides more suitable for mountain goats than a novelist and a New York editor. However, once we made it safely to the bottom, the monks proved to be extremely hospitable. Whittemore was a frequent visitor and the monks seemed to enjoy his company.

After being shown around the rocky quarters, not much more than elaborate caves, and consuming some dreadful retsina (the monks didn't drink it themselves) we continued to Jericho and a typical lunch of dried figs, a bread-like pastry and melon and hot fragrant tea. Then we made our way to the Negev. Over the years Ted had befriended some of the local Bedouins and we were greeted like old friends at several encampments. We spent one night at an Israeli meteorological center/desert inn near a Nabatean ruin. There seemed to be antennae and electric sensors everywhere, and as we used to say in those days, gray men in London, Washington, Moscow, and Beijing could probably hear every sparrow-fart in the desert. In retrospect, I sometimes wonder if Ted had ever really retired? Was he still, in this case, visiting his "controller," and using me as his "cover?"

Several months later, when Ted sent me a post card urging me to save a spot on an upcoming list for his next novel, the design on the card was a Byzantine mosaic of "the Tree of Life" Ted and I had seen on the stone floor of a ruin in Jericho. I took it to the art director at Norton where I was then a senior editor. He agreed with me that it would make an excellent design for a book jacket. All we needed was a manuscript.

*

Jericho Mosaic arrived before the end of the year, a fitting culmination to Whittemore's marvelous Quartet. In my opinion, *Jericho Mosaic* is the most breathtakingly original espionage story ever written. The novel is based on events that actually took place before the Six Day War and Whittemore demonstrates his total knowledge of the craft of intelligence and its practitioners, his passion for the Middle East, his devotion to the Holy City, and his commitment to peace and understanding among Arabs, Jews, and Christians. The novel and the novelist maintain we can overcome religious, philosophical, and political differences if we are ready to commit ourselves to true understanding for all people and all ideas.

This humanistic message is imbedded in a true story involving Eli Cohen, a Syrian Jew who sacrificed his life (he managed to turn over to Mossad the Syrian plans and maps for the defense of the Golan Heights) in order that Israel might survive. In the novel Whittemore tells the story of Halim (who is clearly based on Eli Cohen) a Syrian businessman who xxii • QUIN'S SHANGHAI CIRCUS

returns to his homeland from Buenos Aires to help forward the Arab revolution. Halim becomes an outspoken advocate for Palestinian rights, he is the conscience of the Arab cause, "the incorruptible one." But Halim is a Jew, an agent for the Mossad; his code name is "the Runner," his assignment to penetrate the heart of the Syrian military establishment. At the same time the novel is a profound meditation on the nature of faith in which an Arab holy man, a Christian mystic, and a former British intelligence officer sit in a garden in Jericho exploring religion and humanity's relation to its various faces.

There were fewer reviews of *Jericho Mosaic* and even fewer sales than before. Arabs and Jews were involved in a bloody confrontation on the West Bank, there were lurid photographs in the newspapers and magazines and on television every day, and even more horrific stories. The times were not propitious for novelists defending the eternal verities, no matter how well they wrote. One critic did, however, proclaim Whittemore's Quartet "the best metaphor for the intelligence business in recent American fiction."

Shortly after *Jericho Mosaic* was published Whittemore left Jerusalem, the Ethiopian compound, and the American painter. He was back in New York living during the winter with Ann, a woman he had met years before when she and her then husband befriended Ted and his first wife. In the summers he would take over the sprawling, white, Victorian family home in Dorset, Vermont. The windows had green shutters, and an acre of lawn in front of the house was bounded by immense stately evergreen trees. Twenty or so rooms were distributed around the house in some arbitrary New England Victorian design, and the furniture dated back to his grandparents, if not great-grandparents. Ted's brothers and sisters by now had their own houses and so Ted was pretty much its sole occupant. It was not winterized and could only be inhabited from May through October. But for Ted it was a haven to which he could retreat and write.

*

In the spring of 1987 I became a literary agent and Ted joined me as a client. American book publishing was gradually being taken over by international conglomerates with corporate offices in Germany and Great Britain. They were proving to be more enamored of commerce than literature and it seemed to me I could do more for writers by representing them to any of a dozen publishers rather than just working for one.

I regularly visited Ted in the fall in Dorset. "The foliage season," late September, early October, is a very special time of year in New England: crisp clear days, wonderfully cool moonlit nights. We walked the woods and fields of southern Vermont by day, sat in front of the house after dinner on solid green Adirondack chairs, drink in hand and smoking. Actually I was the one drinking (usually brandy) because Ted had stopped years ago (his "habit" had become so serious that he had joined Alcoholics Anonymous); while we talked I would smoke a cigar or two, Ted would merely smoke one evil-looking cheroot. Comfortably ensconced on the lawn near the United Church, where his great-grandfather had been a minister, within sight of the Village Green and the Dorset Inn, our talk would turn to books and writing, family and friends. To his family, Ted must have been the "black sheep," the Yalie who had gone off to the CIA, had, so to speak, burned out, had come home via Crete, Jerusalem, and New York as a peripatetic novelist whose books received glowing reviews that resulted in less than glowing sales. But they, and "his women," supported him and continued to believe in him.

It was during these early fall visits that I discovered that his Prentiss great-grandfather had been a Presbyterian minister who had made his way up the Hudson River by boat from New York to Troy and then over to Vermont by train and wagon in the 1860s. In the library of the white, rambling Victorian house in Dorset there were shelves of fading leather-bound volumes of popular romances written by his great-grandmother for shop girls, informing them how to improve themselves, dress, and find suitable husbands. I gathered she was the Danielle Steele of her day, and the family's modest wealth was due to her literary efforts and not the generosity of the church's congregation.

We talked about the new novel. It was to be called *Sister Sally and Billy the Kid* and it was to be Ted's first American novel. It was about an Italian in his twenties from the Chicago of the roaring Twenties. His older brother, a gangster, had helped him buy a flower shop. But there was a shoot-out, the older brother was dead, and Billy has to flee to the West Coast where he meets a faith healer not unlike Aimee Semple McPherson. The real-life McPherson disappeared for a month in 1926, and when she returned claimed she had been kidnapped. The stone house in which Billy and his faith healer spend their month of love (from the beginning it is clear that the idyll must be limited to one month) has a walled garden behind it full of lemon trees and singing birds. Although that house is in southern California, the garden bears a close resemblance to another garden in the Ethiopian compound in Jerusalem with a synagogue on one side and a Cistercian convent on the other.

Then one day in early spring 1995, Ted called me. Could he come by the office that morning? I assumed it was to deliver the long-awaited manuscript. There had been two false starts after *Jericho Mosaic*. Instead Ted told me he was dying. Would I be his literary executor? A year or so earlier Ted had been diagnosed as having prostate cancer. It was too far along for an operation. His doctor had prescribed hormones and other medication and the cancer had gone into remission. But now it had spread. Less than six months later he was dead. They were terrible months for him. However, during those last weeks and days while he slipped in and out of consciousness, he was looked after by "his women," one of whom, Carol, had returned to his life after a nearly two-decade separation.

There was a hushed memorial service in the United Church in Dorset that August. Afterwards, a reception was held on the large lawn in front of the family house. It was there that the disparate parts of Ted's world came together, perhaps for the first time; there was his family, his two sisters and two brothers and their spouses, nieces, and nephews with their own families (but not Ted's wives or the two daughters who had flown to New York to say "good-bye" to the father they hardly knew); there were neighbors, Yale friends, and a couple of colleagues from the Lindsay years. Were there any "spooks" in attendance? One really can't say, but there were eight "spooks" of a different sort from Yale, members of the 1955 Scroll and Key delegation. Ann and Carol, who had become allies while watching over Ted during those last, bitter days, were, of course, there.

Jerusalem and Dorset. The beautiful Holy City on the rocky cliffs overlooking the parched gray-brown desert. A city marked by thousands of years of history, turbulent struggles between great empires and three of the most enduring, vital religions given by God to mankind. And the summer-green valley in Vermont (covered by snow in the winter and by mud in the spring) where Dorset nestled between the ridges of the softly rolling Green Mountains. Once one of the cradles of the American Revolution and American democracy, and later a thriving farming and small manufacturing community, it was a place where time stood still since the beginning of the twentieth century. One was the subject of Whittemore's dreams and books; the other the peaceful retreat in which he dreamt and wrote the last twenty summers of his life.

Ted had finally come home to New England. It had been a long journey: Portland, New Haven, Japan, Italy, New York, Jerusalem, Greece, Crete, Jerusalem, New York, and now Dorset. Along the way he had many friends and companions; he was not a particularly good husband or father and disappointed many. But gradually he had found his voice, written his novels, and fallen in love with Jerusalem. I would like to think that Ted died dreaming of his Holy City. In a sense he was at one with that stone-cutter turned medieval knight, turned antiquities dealer, Haj Harun. For Whittemore was the eternal knight-errant who "made it" at Yale in the 1950s, "lost it" in the CIA in the 1960s, and then made himself into a wonderful novelist with the voice of a mystic. The voice of a mystic who had absorbed the best of Judaism, Christianity, and Islam. His great-grandfather the minister and his great-grandmother the writer would have been equally proud of him. His spirit rests peacefully in Dorset, Vermont.

Tom Wallace
New York City, 2002

INTRODUCTION

Who knows how Ted Whittemore came upon this fabulation? By way of introduction, I just finished reading Philip Short's enormous and compelling biography of Mao Zedong, published in the year 2000. It is so rich, fascinating, and full of history, chicanery, adventure, corruption, and amazing action, that afterwards you need to inhale straight oxygen from a canister for a while simply to recover.

That's the same feeling produced here by Ted Whittemore's first novel (written long before Philip Short put the hammer to Mao), now reissued twenty-six years after it debuted thanks to Holt, Rinehart, and Winston (in 1974). It's a novel as complicated and luridly interesting as a pornographic tattoo parlor, as recondite (in the extreme) as the Kabala, as comic—sometimes!—as the Three Stooges. In short, it is totally amusing (and intriguing) at every twist and turn (of which there are many).

Talk about your inscrutable orient. Whittemore takes us there, and then some. If you like sadistic Japanese gangsters with downright mythical powers, you'll love this book. If fantasmagoric rock and rollers from another age and another country are your bag, *Quin's Shanghai Circus* should be graphically titillating. If you're in love with the mystical tough underside of our absurdist Twentieth Century skullduggeries, you will get it here served up on a silver platter.

Some of the novel is outrageous cartoon, some is exasperating erudition. All of it is crisply written, occasionally with tongue in cheek, often earnestly weighed down with pathos, and not infrequently suffused with a thrilling violence. Whittemore manipulates history (and convoluted plotlines) like a magician who has smoked enough opium to sink a battleship. "Colorful" is hardly the word for this book; "insane" might be more appropriate, except that despite all the surface confusion the author obviously knows exactly what he is about, and everything eventually comes together.

The story takes place "At the onset of an era given to murders and assassinations," says the narrator, "a time when a hunger for human flesh rumbled in men's bowels. Look what happened in Nanking where a sergeant strangled his own commanding general. When he told me that on the beach, I knew I was hearing a voice direct from the rectum of lunacy. No one but me would probably ever believe such a voice, but that doesn't matter now."

That voice "direct from the rectum of lunacy" is manipulated, throughout the story, by chance, strained coincidence, deliberate farce, and melodramatic hyperbole. Here's a passage describing how the enormous clown, Geraty, submits to a grilling by Quin himself:

> "The fat man muttered and swore, laughed, lied when there seemed no reason to lie, and then corrected himself before wandering off on some byway of his four decades of travel through Asia, He recited Manchurian telephone numbers and Chinese addresses, changed costumes, sang circus songs, beat a drum and played a flute, consumed bowls of horseradish and mounds of turnips, sneaked through the black-market district of Mukden late in 1934 and again in 1935, noting discrepancies, brought out all the peeling props and threadbare disguises of an aging clown working his way around the ring. Grinning, weeping, he eventually

revealed how he had discovered thirty years ago that Lamereaux was the head of an espionage network in Japan, a network with such an ingenious communication system it was the most successful spy ring in Asia in the years leading up to the Second World War. The information had come to Geraty by chance because he happened to fall asleep in a Tokyo cemetery . . ."

That's a good enough description of this book and its tone. Whittemore thrives on creating apocalyptic confusion and then setting things straight. He loves spies, and enjoys leading us down one path, and then up a totally different one. Half the time we don't really know where we're at, but that's the fun—and the funhouse—of it. Whittemore, a master of deceptions, doesn't miss a bewildering trick. At one point a character says, "Life is brief and we must listen to every sound." Novels are essentially brief also, but this prose wonderkind certainly listens to every sound.

I don't know much about Ted Whittemore. He's dead. He died in 1995. Rumor has it that he once worked for the CIA, and maybe he was a Russian double agent on the Middle Eastern beat, maybe not. "Whatever," as Kurt Cobain might've said. The fact is, Ted seems to have led a bizarre and complicated and rather mysterious life that fed a bizarre and complicated imagination, and he could write like *hell* . . . *about* hell, and about everything in between.

When you aren't flinching at the pedophiles and the necromancy, you are liable to be chuckling up a storm. In *Quin's Shanghai Circus* all roads lead to the rape of Nanking by the Japanese in 1937, painted—of course—by the alter ego of Ted Whittemore, Hieronymous Bosch. You don't *really* want to go there, girlfriend—but you can't stop from turning such deliciously malevolent pages.

It's grotesque, the whole mordant circus, and sometimes too arcane for words, and often frustrating, and not a little scary (and excessive) and screwball, but it's about what happened (more or less) leading up to World War II, and the author rarely glosses over the horrors, or the brief magnificent euphorias of our tragic human experience.

After this novel, Whittemore went on to distinguish himself with The Jerusalem Quartet, a vibrant stew of richly invented books that would put Lawrence Durrell on notice, and may yet claim for Ted a piece of the immortal action in our groves of academe.

But *Quin's* came first, greased the skids, as they say, and it is a fascinating novel. You can't pigeonhole the thing. It can revulse you as much as anything William H. Burroughs (or Hubert Selby Jr.) ever wrote: *Naked Lunch* meets *Last Exit to Shanghai*. But although there's a lot of disturbing stuff for the queasy stomach to rebel against, there's also a rich and deranged heartbeat that captures the bustling panorama we all call "home."

Abandon all hope, ye who enter here . . . and prepare for a bumpy, yet illuminating, ride. Tennessee Williams once said something to the effect that if it weren't for his devils his angels would have no place to go. Ted Whittemore has angels and devils galore, and their wide range of halos and pitchforks drive this lusty debauch toward its rousing conclusion.

You can't say I didn't warn you . . . but isn't that the point?

John Nichols
Taos, New Mexico 2002

John Nichols is author of *The Sterile Cuckoo* and *The Milagro Beanfield War.* His most recent novel is *The Voice of the Butterfly.*

To remain whole, be twisted.
To become straight, let yourself be bent.
To become full, be hollow.
Be tattered, that you may be renewed.
Those that have little, may get more,
Those that have much, are but perplexed.
The Sage does not show himself, therefore he is seen
   everywhere.
He does not define himself, therefore he is distinct.
He does not boast of what he will do, therefore he
   succeeds.
He is not proud of his work, and therefore it endures.
He does not contend,
And for that very reason no one under heaven can
   contend with him.

                                   —Tao Te Ching

For by grace are ye saved through faith, and that not of
   yourselves. It is the gift of God. Not of works, lest any
   man should boast.

                                       —Ephesians 2

THE IMPOSTOR

i

The suspicious illness and subsequent investigation of a corporal serving in Mukden suggest that an espionage network with astonishing capabilities is operating within the Empire.

The net has access to such important material it must include a member of the General Staff, in addition to whatever foreigners are involved.

The corporal died while undergoing questioning. Just before death, however, he revealed two unrelated facts.

1. The code name of the net is Gobi *(the barbarian name for the great desert in western China).*

2. The unknown disease from which he was suffering is called, phonetically, Lam-ah-row's Lumbago.

—From a secret report submitted in the autumn of 1937 to Baron Kikuchi, Japanese General in charge of intelligence activities in Manchuria.

The report was said to have been seen in the archives of the Imperial Japanese Army immediately after the surrender in 1945. But it never reached Allied intelligence officers, having been either lost or destroyed in the first days of the Occupation.

●

Some twenty years after the end of the war with Japan a freighter arrived in Brooklyn with the largest collection of Japanese pornography ever assembled in a Western tongue. The owner of the collection, a huge, smiling fat man named Geraty, presented a passport to customs that

3

showed he was a native-born American about as old as the century, an exile who had left the United States nearly four decades before.

The collection contained all the pornographic works written in Japan during the last three hundred and fifty years, or since the time when Japan first closed itself to the West. More important, it included rare manuscripts from several thirteenth-century Buddhist monasteries.

According to Geraty, the very existence of these manuscripts had never been suspected. The tales they told began harmlessly, but before the scholar reached the end of the second page he was confronted with astonishingly obscure practices, and by the beginning of the third page he was totally immersed in devices and dreams and masks, all serving the wildest sort of inversions.

The manuscripts were illustrated with ink drawings exquisitely detailed to show every hair. Even the cat hairs could be counted, where cats appeared.

For the officials at the Brooklyn customs house the sudden appearance of Geraty's collection was an uncommon event. Although they frequently handled questionable materials, never in anyone's memory had the pornography to be examined been of such vast scope.

Thus a second official immediately applied himself to the case, and a third soon joined the second. In fact by the end of Geraty's first day in New York there were no less than eight customs officials of differing ranks and seniority, representing a reliable spectrum of American ethnic and racial and cultural backgrounds, lined up behind a row of desks at one end of the spacious customs warehouse in Brooklyn, solemnly listening to Geraty deliver a lecture on the secret merits of his collection.

He noted at random, for example, in order to emphasize the artistry of the drawings, the patina that had been worked into the leather phalluses and the grain that showed in the spiraled ivory finger pieces. Because of these touches, he claimed, a specialist could easily tell whether the leather was cow or pig or whether the ivory was from north or south India.

The women depicted in the illustrations were as numerous as the men, but they were always shown with their own kind. There was no mixing of the sexes.

After pointing out the value of the manuscripts in the fields of animal husbandry, trade, and sociology, Geraty went on to discuss their literary and historical merits.

The manuscripts were invariably told in the first person. Therefore they were source material for modern Japanese fiction, which was also confessional.

The century under study, the thirteenth, was an era of national upheaval in Japan, an age of revolution led by innumerable orders of fanatical monks. Therefore the manuscripts were a record of the unknown thoughts of these warring monks at a time when Zen and the game of *Go*, the tea ceremony, rock gardens, and *No* plays and so many other unique Japanese arts, notorious for their refinement and austerity, first became revered throughout the islands.

Geraty, in short, was able to trace most of modern Japanese history to the pornographic fantasies found in his collection.

The documents had been translated and bound under his personal supervision, a project that had taken forty years of his life. Although reluctant to part with his treasure, he was now returning to the United States to retire. He intended to sell the collection to a university or some other academic institution so that it could be available to scholars.

Or so he claimed.

Finally, with special pride, Geraty discussed his system of annotations. The system was exclusive and comprehensive, his own invention, and could only be understood by using the key or code book. It consisted of numbers in the margins, entered by hand, often as many as sixty-four numbers next to only one line of print. The drawings were thus wedged in between swarms of minute jottings.

These masses of numbers, it seemed, identified and cross-referenced every real or imagined act that took place in all those tens of thousands of pages.

Because he was so fat, Geraty sometimes gave the

impression of being less than a giant. When he was sprawled over a bench in the customs warehouse waiting for his audience to assemble, doing nothing, staring blankly at the ceiling, he looked as if he might be only six and a half feet tall. But the moment he began to gather up his arms and legs, a transformation took place.

He seemed to put on weight as he pulled his parts together. It took several minutes for him to find his balance, but when at last he was standing he filled the room he was in, any room, his immense bulk the equal of three or four large men.

Geraty leaned far back to keep his belly from dragging him over. His feet were splayed to support his body, his chin rested on his chest, his massive arms stood out to the sides. When he moved, his hands hung behind him, stiffly jarred by each step. His white hair was clipped short in outdated military fashion and his face was scarred by pockmarks, or perhaps a combination of pockmarks and poorly treated knife wounds.

When he got to his feet the blood rushed to his head, causing it to expand, opening the pits and scars. After a while this swelling subsided together with the deep purple coloring that had accompanied it.

Geraty arrived in New York toward the end of winter. The unraveled tops of three or four sweaters showed at his neck, which was swathed in a piece of red flannel tied with a string. He wore torn military boots, the type issued to American soldiers during the Second World War, and a black bowler hat that might have belonged to a circus performer in the 1920s. Over everything was a military greatcoat, ancient and spotted and patched, of no recognizable era or campaign. Despite his size the ancient greatcoat covered him completely to the floor.

Before much time had passed the eight customs officials were no longer curious or suspicious or even bored, they were simply dazed with disbelief. For several days Geraty had been lecturing them, and they could no longer pretend to understand what he was talking about, or why. The senior of the eight officials, therefore, interrupted Geraty to ask him if he had a letter from a university, or a document of any kind from any academic institution, expressing interest in his collection.

Geraty had to admit he had nothing to show them.

He was then asked to produce academic credentials from the United States or Japan or any country in the world. Again he had to admit he had nothing to offer but his collection.

Throughout these interviews, or lectures, he continued to address everyone as *nephew*.

The obscenity laws were still strict. Even so, Geraty's case might not have been dismissed as fraudulent had it not been for two facts. First, he never turned up at the customs warehouse even partially sober. Second, it was apparent from his eyes that he was suffering from a long-term addiction to some drug, probably of the stimulant class.

In the midst of a harangue he would suddenly rush away to the toilet, muttering about an incurable Oriental disease acquired in his youth. But later the same day even this pretense would be dropped. Instead of leaving the end of the warehouse where he was lecturing, he would turn around in the middle of an incomprehensible sentence and bury his head in his greatcoat. There would be the unmistakable sound of liquid being sucked through a straw, then a rapid movement of the hands followed by a sneeze and a violent cough.

Geraty turned back to face the eight officials as if nothing had happened, but it was impossible not to smell the fresh alcohol on his breath, or to ignore the unnatural luster of his eyes which were now bulging from his head more prominently than ever.

After these lapses he never failed to make reference to the charity shown to slaves by the founder of the first monastery for women in Ireland, the gently forgiving lady known to history as St. Brigid.

Yet the collection was still an extraordinary effort by someone, and that was the only reason the eight officials spent as much time with him as they did. They took the trouble of sending a report through a special review process, including a senior board that was then in session. To do more Geraty would have had to take his case to court.

All this was explained to him at length one winter morning in the customs warehouse in Brooklyn when the time came to confiscate the collection. Geraty listened gloomily to the decision, then began the long process of getting to his feet. Not until he was standing at full height did he break his silence.

He roared and upended three of the desks. He bellowed and knocked over the other five desks. He shouted that he had no money for lawyers, that America was a lunatic asylum, that the whole country could drink dragon piss down to the day of judgment. When a platoon of guards finally reached the end of the warehouse that Geraty had demolished, they found him struggling to take off his clothes, trying to strip himself naked, either to free himself for a fight or because he was sweating so heavily.

Geraty landed in the street in an Oriental squatting position, perhaps a modification of the lotus, his greatcoat soaking up the snow that had turned to slush in the morning sun. During the next few minutes he was totally immobile, either because he was meditating or because he was stunned, then he abruptly lurched to his feet and staggered down the block shouting the names of saints. He entered the first cheap waterfront bar he came to and was told to shut up or leave. He scratched himself, ordered a double gin, and collapsed in a booth by the window.

For the next thirteen hours he remained in the booth, not leaving even to go to the toilet. He stared at the grimy snow in the gutter, drank gin, and sank into a stupor, all the while carrying on an incoherent dialogue with himself in a variety of Oriental languages and dialects, a journey that began in Japan and moved west and south through Manchuria, from Mukden down the coast of China to Shanghai. From there he took a freighter to the Philippines, snored in the mountains during the Second World

War, took a United States army airplane back to Japan, and began the journey again.

When the sun went down Geraty emptied out the pockets of his greatcoat. In the manner of a fortune-teller he spread the objects across the table in front of him. He tapped each one three times and studied it.

A freighter ticket for the return trip to Yokohama.
His real passport.
An empty pint of gin with a straw twisted around the neck.
Sixty-odd dollars, a few less than the years he had lived.
A small gold cross, a Nestorian relic of incalculable value.
Several tattered passports from the 1930s, forged, stating that the bearer was a Belgian expert in animal husbandry, a Belgian dealer in films, a Canadian dealer in patent drugs. None of these false papers of any use anywhere in the world.
A worthless green paperweight that might have been meant to resemble jade, stolen from one of the desks he had overturned that morning.

Along with a screw-top jar hidden in a recess of his greatcoat, this was all he owned in the world.

●

Late that night Geraty took a subway to the Bowery and knocked on the door of a shelter for homeless alcoholics. Before entering he insisted on presenting his counterfeit Canadian passport with the consular stamp that was thirty years out of date. He was fumigated, given a shower, and sent to bed.

The whole following day he slept. The next day he was able to swallow some soup. On the third day, feeling stronger, he resurrected himself and broke the lock on the closet where his clothes were stored. He made his way to the city bus terminal and found a bus that was journeying north through the Berkshires to a town where there happened to be an orphanage run by an order of Catholic fathers.

Forty-eight hours later he was back in New York without the precious small gold cross or the worthless glass paperweight, his money down to sixteen dollars. As insurance against a robbery attempt he bought a pint of gin, then took a subway to the Bronx, dozing most of the way, occasionally ordering a round of drinks in one Oriental language or another. He found a bar with a steam table and bought three large corned beef sandwiches which he covered with a thick layer of green paste from the screw-top jar hidden in his greatcoat.

He ended the meal with a double gin and a small dab of green paste tucked into each side of his nose. He sneezed and heaved himself out the door, his money now reduced to eight single dollar bills.

Darkness had fallen, the slush was freezing into ice. Geraty picked his way carefully along the sidewalk, his bulging eyes rolling over the buildings and down the alleys. From time to time he stopped under a streetlight to gaze at a fire alarm box, the number on a tenement, the stairs leading down to a basement. Once in the course of every block his hand dipped into the greatcoat and came out with a pinch of green paste which he pushed into his nose absentmindedly.

At last he came to the corner he was looking for, a bar with an old wooden sign in the window. There was a larger neon sign with a different name, but the old-fashioned lettering on the wood, in faded green paint, could still be read beneath the buzzing coils of electric light.

Geraty's.

For several minutes he gazed dully at the sign. He had come to the United States for only two reasons, and when those tasks were accomplished he had intended to return to Japan immediately. In the first he had failed. He had been unable to sell his magical collection of pornography. And in the second he had succeeded. He had returned the mysterious small gold cross to its rightful owner.

But now a third possibility crossed his mind. Instead of just making a nostalgic visit to his family's old neighborhood in the Bronx, he would honor his mother by invoking her memory on the feast day of the saint for whom she had been named.

Geraty crossed himself, the first time he had done so in thirty years. From St. Edward the Confessor he begged forgiveness for what he was about to do, for what it might lead to, for the lost paths that might be opened and the forgotten lives that might be discovered. Then he crossed himself once more and kicked aside the door of the bar, shuffled to the counter, clamped a paw on the bartender.

Dragon piss, nephew.

How's that?

Double gin.

He rested both arms on the counter listening to the noisy conversations around him. Twenty minutes later he was on his way to the toilet at the back, bumping into drinkers as he passed. When he returned he bumped into them again, this time choosing a stool toward one end of the counter next to a younger man whose name was Quin.

Geraty had heard the name soon after coming into the bar. There were two drinkers there with that name, one closer to the right age than the other, but before he approached his man he wanted to be sure the name was spelled correctly. So he had waited until both men were near the counter and picked their pockets as he went to the toilet, replacing their wallets on the way back.

In the years he had spent wandering around Asia he had known only one other man named Quin, a lecherous and violent drunkard who had last been seen in Shanghai before the war, supposedly in a warehouse on the outskirts of the city. There were rumors of a terrible night in that warehouse, but Geraty never knew whether they were true or not. By the time he got to the warehouse the next morning, it was deserted. The only sign that anyone had been there was a discarded hat on a mound of sawdust, the black bowler he himself was now wearing.

Geraty spread his greatcoat over the stool and lowered himself into place.

●

Quin was then about thirty. He had grown up in the Bronx, played stickball and fought in the streets as a boy, spent two years in the navy and one in prison as a man. A short time ago his only relative had died, the woman who had raised him, his father's older sister. The aunt had left him a small amount of money, and he was trying to decide what to do with it the night a fat staggering giant, old and drunk and ragged, wheezing and muttering, lurched into his stool and nearly knocked him to the floor.

A dozen years ago, perhaps even two or three, Quin might have broken a bottle over the old man's head. But at the moment he was paralyzed. A hideous stench had enveloped him, a mixture of rotting wool and rotting cheese, sour wax and decaying skin, all of it overwhelmed and held together by a pervasive smell of mustard.

The fat giant had breathed on him as he settled down on the next stool.

●

Blow it the other way, said Quin.

Double gin, nephew, the fat man called down the bar. Quin swung his elbow and the fat man hiccuped.

You stink, buffalo.

How's that?

You bumped into me just now.

Not me, nephew.

You. Twice.

The fat man rubbed the red flannel around his neck while sneaking a hand under his greatcoat. Quin saw him unscrew the top of a jar. A finger came out with a dab of green paste, the cap was rescrewed, the finger flickered under his nose. It was all done in one quick movement, but Quin recognized the smell.

Hooked on horseradish, buffalo?

A Japanese blend. By far the most effective.

For what?

For the thirty years I've used it which is little enough in the game the Almighty plays. He looks for longer scores and every point is as hard as a dragon's hemorrhoids. I know what I'm talking about, nephew, I've spent most of my life there.

Where?

The other side, the dark side, our own foreign shore. A place so different, saints preserve us, it's whatever you want it to be. Where are the dice? It's time to drink to what we were and are becoming.

Money?

The fat man grumbled and put his eight single dollar bills on the bar. Quin nodded. No one in Geraty's had ever been able to beat him at liar's dice. The fat man rolled and passed the cup. On Quin's second roll the fat man called him.

You win, buffalo. Where did you say that place was?

Where? The old Tokyo and the old Shanghai, cities that don't exist anymore. Cities where people went around in disguises passing themselves off as emperors and Buddhas and dwarfs and precision masturbators. So afraid, some of them, they hid in unlocked cages waiting for the hinges to rust. The Orient, that's where. This is the first time I've been back here in forty years. I've been to Massachusetts and I've seen the Bronx and now I'm leaving.

I spent a year in Massachusetts, said Quin.

Doing what?

Time.

What kind of time?

Mailboxes.

An unworthy cause, nephew. Your mother wouldn't have liked that.

Never knew her.

Your father wouldn't have liked it either.

Never knew him.

I know, muttered the fat man.

What do you know?

The fat man's face suddenly darkened. The scars and pits opened as he fumbled for his gin glass. He emptied the glass and his eyes receded, the hat settled back on his head. He pointed at the cup of dice.

Roll. We need a drink.

Quin lost. The fat man massaged his enormous belly and licked the new glass of gin with a long yellow tongue. Quin's question had turned him into a huge jungle beast crouching beside a path.

What I know is that over there, before the war, everybody was plotting. One day a hundred conspiracies, the next day a hundred new ones. Agents everywhere and all of them changing sides yesterday or tomorrow. From what to what? Why? International networks spent millions of dollars while others were so clandestine they consisted of only one individual, existed in only one man's head. His private fantasy? No. The Almighty had dumped His creatures in a secret bag and put the bag on His back and was dancing over the earth. The thirties, nephew, the Orient. This overcoat I'm wearing belonged to a sergeant who murdered the general responsible for the rape of Nanking. An overcoat? For He hath put down the mighty from their seat. Or the beach just south of Tokyo where four people once sat down to a picnic that only one of them ate. Why? Because the other three were wearing gas masks. The beach was near the estate owned by Baron Kikuchi, the most feared man in the Japanese secret police, and at the end of the afternoon those picnickers had arrived at a decision that kept the Germans from capturing Moscow ten years later. A picnic? Impossible?

For He that is mighty hath done great things to me. Let's have another game.

The fat man scratched his gallbladder with the dice. Once more Quin lost and had to pay for the drinks.

I knew them, the fat man announced abruptly.

Who?

Your parents. Over there of course, before you were born. Your father had a limp, shrapnel in his leg, some kind of hero in the First World War. Left New York in the early 1920s, worked his way to Paris, ended up in Asia. Where? Shanghai? Tokyo? A postcard to your aunt once in a while, the last news from south China in the late 1920s. Canton? In any case nothing after that for eight years. Eight years? Not until 1935 when a missionary couple brought a baby to your aunt. War was coming, China was unsafe. The Quins were to follow in a few months but of course they never did, of course they were never heard from again. Eight years without any news? In those days, out there, a long time.

Quin's glass was in the air. He stared at the fat man.

Or rather I should say I knew of them. About them. We were in the same places but at different times. A friend mentioned that to me. He knew them.

What else did he mention? said Quin, having just heard repeated everything his aunt had ever been able to tell him about his father after he disappeared from New York. About his mother she could tell him nothing, not even having been aware that her younger brother had married. The missionary couple had only been able to add that the woman who came to their ship in Shanghai asking for help was an American about thirty years old, that her papers were genuine and proved both her own and the baby's identity.

The fat man scratched his liver.

What else. What else? Nothing else. He's still alive though, that friend, his name is Father Lamereaux. Lived in Tokyo before the war and still lives there although he never sees anyone, no one at all except a dead cat. Rather a strange man. Too bad you can't write to him but he never touches mail, something to do with a vow he made during the war. A vow? Of course if you were to talk to him that would be different.

Talk to him?

Not that expensive by freighter, nephew, and once you get there you'll be able to taste the finest horseradish in the world. The finest and the best.

The fat man groped behind his back trying to find a kidney to scratch. Quin nodded to himself.

Buffalo. What did you say your name was?

Didn't say. Right? It's the same as that wooden sign in the window.

What? Geraty?

When addressing St. Edward the Confessor I use none other.

All right, Geraty, that's just fine. Now tell me how you knew who I was when you walked in here. And better than that, tell me why you walked in here in the first place.

Geraty's head rolled sideways. He seemed exhausted by the weight he was carrying in flesh and memories. He licked his gin and began reciting in a monotonous voice.

He said Father Lamereaux must have also mentioned the neighborhood in the Bronx where the aunt lived. Tonight he was in the same neighborhood visiting friends.

Who? said Quin.

Geraty ignored the question. He left his friends and passed a bar with his name on it. That intrigued him so he stopped in for a drink. Someone used Quin's name and when he heard it, he didn't know why, Father Lamereaux's long-ago story came back to him. The recollection made him wonder. The neighborhoods were the same, his own name was on the bar, thirty years had passed.

A coincidence?

Or perhaps thirty years didn't matter. He was curious and decided to find out. He picked Quin's pocket to see how he spelled his name, to see if the two Quins were the same.

Quin nodded. The tale was so outrageous and told so matter-of-factly he might have believed it if Geraty had left out the pickpocketing episode. But with the exception of opening and closing his horseradish jar, Geraty seemed too clumsy to do anything covertly.

Quin watched the giant sink closer to the counter.

Come to think of it, nephew, the old man's become such a recluse he might not want to talk to you even if you did go to see him. He wasn't just another priest, Lamereaux, he was quite a rake in his time. He might not want to recall that era at all, I mean not at all. Still there could be a way.

Quin waited, expecting there would turn out to be a way.

Yes, just possibly. Do you know whose feast day you are honoring this evening with your beer? By chance, that of St. Brigid, known for her miraculous powers and particularly for her charity. Charity I said, that may be the clue we're looking for. It so happens that Father Lamereaux was the guardian of a boy, an orphan who was brought to America not long after you were. Father Lamereaux loved that boy dearly but he's never been able to see him because the boy can't make the crossing alone, he's a little simple in the head, and Lamereaux's lumbago is so bad he can't make the crossing either. Lumbago. As I remember a lot of his friends had it before the war. Well it seems to me that if you took the boy with you for a visit the old hermit would be so delighted he'd tell you everything.

Geraty ordered another round. They rolled the dice, Quin lost. The giant's bleary eyes roamed the bar completely out of focus.

Boy isn't right, he's only a few years younger than you are. I only call him that the way I'd call you a boy. Most of the time he's just like anybody else only more so. More so, anybody. Now and then you have to tell him what to do but he's obliging and friendly and kind, kinder than anyone you'll ever meet, saints preserve us. I know because I've just been to see him.

In that case, buffalo, why aren't you taking him to Japan?

Because it wouldn't be for a visit, that's why. My bowels

haven't moved since I left the East, haven't and won't
until I get back where I belong and stay there. I came to
this country to sell a magnificent set of documents on the
sources of Japanese culture, my life's work, intending to
retire on the proceeds in some pine grove and what
happens?

What?

The rich He hath sent empty away.

What happened to the collection?

What do you think happened to it in this hell of stupidity
and violence? They confiscated it.

Why?

Pornography, hard-core pornography, no redeeming social value. Value? Manuscripts written by the monks who
invented rock gardens and tea ceremony and made Zen
famous and made *No* and *Go* famous and everything else
anybody has ever heard of? No value in them? Does that
make sense? Does it? Now does it?

Geraty was raving, yelling, waving his arms. He lost his
balance and fell into the counter, his face coming to rest
in a pool of spilled gin.

He was muttering to himself, Manchurian telephone
numbers and Chinese addresses, the name of a bar in
Mukden where he had gone to get drunk after buying a
supply of films before the war, a description of Bubbling
Well Road early one winter morning when he was on his
way to a warehouse on the outskirts of Shanghai. He
returned to Tokyo, still in the thirties, to make a train
connection to a beach just south of the city. He changed
buses three or four times in the international quarter of
Shanghai before approaching the locked, shuttered room
where he went nightly to set up his movie projector, to
take off his clothes, to whisper silently to himself the
words with which he secretly greeted the wealthy degenerates and drug addicts he was there to entertain, *magnificat anima mea Dominum*, my soul doth magnify the
Lord. He sneaked through the black-market district of
Mukden late in 1934, and again in 1935, noting discrepancies.

Smiling affably during the early months of the Occupation in Japan, having just stolen a secret intelligence report marked with the code name *Gobi*, he ordered drinks for everyone at his favorite Tokyo bar and shouted out yet again the verses from St. Luke that obsessed him.

He hiccuped. Someone was poking him in the ribs.

Wake up, buffalo. What's the boy's name and where do I find him?

Geraty blinked up from the bar. He sneezed, raising a spray.

You were born there and lived here, I was born here and lived there. See the difference? Don't bother, there is none. The truth is I don't know who you are or what you're talking about. Nothing you've told me makes any sense, nothing I've heard in years makes any sense. The truth? The truth is that everything they said about my leprosy drugs before the war was a lie, but then and now and forever He hath scattered the proud in the conceit of their heart. Are you satisfied now? Is that what you wanted to hear?

The boy's address, buffalo. And Lamereaux's address in Tokyo. And yours.

Geraty emptied the gin glass into his mouth without taking his head off the bar. He scribbled the address of the orphanage in Massachusetts, an address in Tokyo, the name of a bar in Tokyo.

Everybody knows the place. They can tell you where to find me.

And the boy's name?

An odd one, I've always thought so. Gobi's his name. Gobi. The same as the desert in western China.

Gobi what?

Nothing. Big Gobi maybe. He seems to like that.

Geraty was struggling to gather up his arms and legs. His face was purple again, his head swollen. With a groan he lurched off the stool and pocketed his eight single dollar bills that had been left untouched on the bar. His hand rummaged inside his greatcoat and made the flickering motion under his nose. He sneezed, coughed once. Quin watched him heave himself out the door.

Quin ordered another beer and looked down at the three

passports he had stolen from the giant's pocket. He had taken them thinking the fat man would have to come back for them, but now he realized they were worthless, the props of a clown.

The nationalities were different, the names were different, the combinations of false eyeglasses and false beards and false moustaches were different in each of them. But there was no mistaking Geraty's huge scarred face in the three disguises.

Three costumes. There might be dozens more. Dozens of hidden pockets in the greatcoat stuffed with forged papers. For the bowler and the greatcoat, the army boots from the Second World War, the layers of sweaters and the red flannel tied with string were the props of an impostor as well as a clown.

Quin nodded to himself. A giant, an impostor, a clown. Yet he knew things, and in the end Quin decided a few facts were reasonably certain.

For one, a recluse named Father Lamereaux must have known his father and mother.

For another, the priest wanted him to bring to Japan a retarded boy who was probably his bastard son.

And third and most intriguing of all, the best player of liar's dice he had ever met bore the name, real or assumed, of the neighborhood bar where he had spent a good part of his life.

BIG
GOBI

·

2

Jade, Quin. Geraty brought it all the way from Japan.
It comes from palaces where princesses live. And
there are dragons there and people who speak a
funny language no one can understand.
But they'll probably understand me sometimes
because I look a little like them. Geraty said so.

●

There was only one other passenger on the Japanese
freighter sailing from Brooklyn, a solitary young student
who had just completed two years of graduate work in
New York. The student was plump and carelessly dressed.
His straight black hair, parted in the middle, hung down
to his shoulders. He also wore false sideburns and a false
moustache, being unable to grow them himself.

The student's name was Hato. Quin and Big Gobi talked
with him only once during the Pacific crossing, on the
evening the ship sailed when he invited them to his cabin
to share a bottle of beer before dinner. The lower berth in
Hato's cabin, the only one made up for use, was strewn
with a thick layer of well-handled movie magazines
pressed down as if someone had been lying on them. The
magazines dated from the 1930s and were stamped with
the name of a student film society from which Hato had
evidently stolen them.

There was also an amazing array of shoeboxes in the
room, neatly piled and arranged, some of the stacks
reaching as high as the porthole. The shoeboxes were
numbered and marked with Japanese characters. When

Quin asked about them the nervous student broke into a short but violent diatribe on the cruelty of Americans to foreigners. He refused to discuss the shoeboxes and a few minutes later they left the cabin in silence, Hato choosing to sit with the Japanese officers rather than with his fellow passengers.

During the next few days Hato spent all his time in the lounge coaxing one or another of the off-duty officers into a game of checkers. On the third day he was caught cheating at checkers, and thereafter no one would play with him. Hato took to his cabin and locked the door, staying there the rest of the voyage. He had his meals brought to him and visited the bathroom only after midnight.

A few months after the freighter docked in Japan, Quin was to spend a long night in the company of Hato. And although Hato subsequently strangled himself while playing a drum in an apartment rented by Quin, having first caused a murder that led to the largest funeral celebration in Asia since the thirteenth century, an anonymous event in which only Quin and three or four other people knew the true identity of the deceased, he was never to connect the strangled Tokyo gangster with the retiring student who had guarded the secret of his shoeboxes across the Pacific. For as soon as Hato set foot in his homeland he abandoned his hairpieces and shaved his head, put on an immaculate dark business suit, and stopped speaking English.

In addition he quickly lost a great deal of weight due to the calisthenics forced on him by his new employer, the cigar-smoking poet who staged the magnificent funeral and saw to it that most of Tokyo's twelve million inhabitants spent an entire day watching the black procession circle the city.

As soon as the ship was out of sight of land Big Gobi sat down on the deck beside Quin's chair and admired the green glass paperweight that had been stolen from the desk of a customs official in New York. Gently he turned the paperweight over and over and held it up to the sky.

Jade, Quin. Geraty brought it all the way from Japan. It comes from palaces where princesses live. And there are dragons there and people speak a funny language no one can understand. But they'll probably understand me sometimes because I look a little like them. Geraty said so.

Big Gobi smiled shyly. He placed the paperweight carefully on the deck and with a deep breath touched the small gold cross that was hanging from his neck. Along with the paperweight it was Big Gobi's most treasured possession. As far as Quin knew these two objects, given him by Geraty, were the only belongings Big Gobi had wanted to take with him when he left the orphanage.

The paperweight was a personal gift from Geraty. The small gold cross was supposedly a gift from Father Lamereaux that Geraty had been asked to deliver. The cross had unusual markings on it. To Big Gobi it was no more important than the paperweight, but Quin had been curious enough to ask one of the priests at the orphanage about it.

I suspect it's very valuable, the priest had said. The markings may be an ancient form of Syrian which means it could be a Nestorian cross. If it's genuine it could go back very far indeed, a thousand years or more, perhaps as much as fifteen hundred years. If you ever have a chance, I suggest you ask the former owner.

I intend to, said Quin. By the way, Father, what can you tell me about Father Lamereaux?

Nothing, answered the priest. He was apparently known by one of the fathers here before he went to Japan, but that was fifty years ago, long before my time. I suppose Father Lamereaux contacted his former acquaintance here when he was trying to find a place for his orphan just before the war.

And by reputation?

Nothing. Nothing whatsoever except that old story they tell in seminaries about him and Aquinas.

What's that?

Well it seems that when Father Lamereaux first began studying Aquinas, he memorized the entire *Summa theo-*

logica. They asked him why and his answer was that the thirteenth century seemed crucial to him in the history of the church. Something of an eccentric, I'd say.

The priest smiled. Quin thanked him and said good-bye.

He had learned a little about Father Lamereaux, less about the small gold cross that in fact was not a gift from Father Lamereaux, who had never seen it although he knew every step of the strange journey that had brought it across central Asia. Yet the small gold cross would turn out to be vital nonetheless, for as Quin eventually discovered, it had belonged at one time or another not only to his mother and Big Gobi's mother but to the two men who had played the most significant roles in his father's life, the one his chief collaborator, the other the Russian linguist who had assembled the vast collection of pornography that Geraty tried unsuccessfully to pass off as his own in the customs house in New York. The ancient Nestorian relic, then, had a long history prior to its arrival in Shanghai during the 1927 Communist uprising, there to entwine the lives of many people before Geraty finally intervened one night, ten years later, to steal it from a drugged woman who came to him with a confession.

Quin was leaning back in his chair, his eyes closed, when Big Gobi suddenly exploded beside him. A lump of seagull droppings had landed in his lap. He was shrieking and beating the deck.

Fuck suck kill, he screamed. *Shit cunt triple sea cocksucker.*

Quin grabbed him by the arm.

Easy, Gobes, remember the cross. It was a present to you. Remember the cross and think about that and forget the other things.

Big Gobi moaned. He lowered his eyes and wiped his hand with the seagull droppings on the back of his shirt. He was glad Quin was holding him by the shoulder because that meant that Quin liked him. Quin liked him and he wanted to do what Quin said, so he kept his head down and he stared at the cross, he didn't look at the sea. But his anger was still so great that one of his hands, the one soiled by the seagull droppings, crept across the deck and took hold of a large metal fixture protruding from the bulkhead.

The hand squeezed, the flesh went white. The metal snapped, the fixture struck the deck. With one twist Big Gobi had ripped apart the thick metal fitting.

Quin watched the hand clutch the jagged edge where the fixture had been. He saw the fingers tighten once more, heard the flesh tear and the bones crack, watched the blood trickle down onto the deck.

He clamped his teeth together and pressed Big Gobi's shoulder as hard as he could, pressed and waited, knowing nothing could be done because Big Gobi's ageless childish brain was trying to save him from an even more impossible pain, trying to protect him from the overwhelming insults he had known in life by making him feel instead the shattering bones and muscles of his hand.

●

When they arrived in Tokyo Quin wrote to Father Lamereaux explaining who he was, who was with him, and why he had come to Japan. Then he went to the bar where Geraty had said he could be found.

Most of the men in the bar were foreigners, several of them long-term residents of the country. Geraty had not been seen there in over six months, not since before his trip to New York, but it seemed this sort of absence was not unusual for him. No one was aware that he had been out of the country. Over drinks Quin learned a good deal about both Geraty and Father Lamereaux.

At the beginning of the war, he was told, Father Lamereaux had been interned in a special prison camp, a former mountain resort where a few Western scholars and missionaries were sent, friends of Japan who were now enemies because of the color of their skin. It was there that the renegade priest had become a drunkard, a minor scandal compared to others he had known.

Before the war, in particular, he had been notorious for

the ever-changing procession of young acolytes who followed him through the streets on Friday at sunset on the
way to his Victorian house, there to be entertained by him
far into the night.

The priest was either a Canadian or a Belgian. He had
arrived in Tokyo so long ago no one was quite sure of his
origins. When he first came to Japan he studied *No* plays
and Buddhism, in the Jesuitical tradition, in order to be
able to wrestle with his theological opponents. He took
instruction for ten years in the Buddhist temples of Kamakura, coming to accept the fact that Gothic steeples were
unsuitable in a land of earthquakes, learning to bend his
beliefs as bamboo bends, again perhaps in the Jesuitical
tradition.

Soon after he went to Kamakura there were rumors that
his love for nature and his appreciation of *No* had lured
him into becoming a practicing Shintoist.

Later there were more serious rumors that he had
deserted his church altogether and taken Buddhist orders
of initiation.

Lastly there was his alleged crime of having col-
laborated with the enemy by informing on his fellow
Westerners.

Throughout the period prior to the war, supposedly, he
had submitted regular reports on foreigners in Tokyo to
the Kempeitai or secret military police, Japan's principal
intelligence and counterespionage agency. The evidence
against him, considered conclusive, had been gathered
over the years by a number of Westerners familiar with
the operating techniques of the Kempeitai.

The story began when Father Lamereaux was called in
for an interview with the Kempeitai.

This in itself was not exceptional. At the time, most
Westerners living in Japan were periodically questioned
or put under surveillance by the Kempeitai. But when
they were questioned it was generally under some other
guise, the Kempeitai officer posing as a civilian in a
government office where the foreigner went on routine
business. Only in the case of a man who had many

government contacts and traveled frequently in and out of the country, such as a journalist, might the interview be conducted by an officer in uniform for purposes of intimidation.

Father Lamereaux never left the country. He traveled no farther than Kamakura and had no government contacts whatsoever. Yet when he was called in by the Kempeitai the interview was conducted not only by an officer in uniform but by a general in uniform, and by no less a general than Baron Kikuchi, the hero of the 1905 Russo-Japanese War who was thought by many to be the most powerful man in the secret police.

Astonished by this, several journalists later asked Father Lamereaux in private to tell them what had happened. The Jesuit spoke directly and succinctly as was his manner, quoting the entire conversation verbatim.

●

Baron Kikuchi was a tiny man. Father Lamereaux was tall, and his gaunt figure gave him an appearance of even greater height. The General had therefore not gotten to his feet when Father Lamereaux entered the room. He stayed behind his massive desk and pointed to a chair. The chair was small and low so that it would be impossible for a guest to arrange himself comfortably. Father Lamereaux had not missed the fact that the desk was bare, the General's way of saying he knew everything he wanted to know about the priest without consulting his dossier.

The General spoke curtly, using the verbs and pronouns that were only appropriate when a man was speaking to his wife, to a child or servant or animal. Father Lamereaux had three choices. He could accept the gross insult and answer as an inferior speaking to a superior. He could use the same forms of speech and return the insult. Or he could ignore the insult and speak as an equal to an equal.

He chose the last to show that he had nothing to hide and to prove that he was in complete command of his emotions no matter what the situation, an approach the General might find slightly humiliating after having adopted a superior pose. The strategem worked, for the General subsequently switched to Lamereaux's idiom.

Sit down.

Thank you.

How long have you been in this country?

Over ten years.

What have you been doing?

Pursuing my Buddhist studies.

Where?

Kamakura.

Why?

In order to gather the skills necessary for my missionary task.

What makes you think you have a missionary task here?

God's task is here and everywhere.

Does it include what happened at your house last Friday night?

There was a meeting for religious instruction.

And the Friday night before that?

Yes.

The Friday night six months ago?

Yes.

How does it include all those Friday nights?

Because the meetings for religious instruction are always held on Friday evenings.

Night I said, not evening. What do you do with these young boys after you have finished your religious instructions early in the evening?

Sometimes we have a discussion on some topic.

What?

Generally some aspect of *No* drama.

Does one or the other of you act out a part?

We may.

Why?

To illustrate a point we are trying to make.

Do you dress up?

We may.

Why?

Because *No* cannot be performed without the proper costumes.

Do you wear masks?

They are part of the costumes.

Do you dance?

In some *No* plays there are dances.

Do you wear the dragon costume?

If that is a scene we are illustrating.

Not *we*, you. Do *you* wear the dragon costume?

If that is a scene I am illustrating.

And who wears the princess costume?

Whoever is illustrating that part.

Always one of the boys?

Not necessarily.

All right, you and the princess are doing your dance. What are the other boys doing at that moment?

They play the part of the chorus and the musicians.

You mean they sit around the room and watch? They make comments? They hum and make some private music of their own?

They sing the verses of the chorus and play the instruments that accompany the drama.

Playing their instruments, are they?

The drum and the flute.

What happens after you finish dancing?

We have refreshments and they go home.

Always?

Yes.

But sometimes it is very late?

It may be.

Dawn?

If the *No* play is a long one.

A long one, hissed the General, leaning forward over the desk. He rested his chin in his hands and stared at Father Lamereaux.

You are an expert on *No*?

I have studied it.

You are one of the leading Western experts on *No*?

I may be.

Then you understand Japanese tradition and you know a Japanese warrior will not allow corruption in his country.

Religious instruction does not corrupt.

And what do you do with one boy while other boys watch?

No drama does not corrupt.

But you corrupt.

If there is anything corrupting Japan today it is the army. It is you and men like you.

Be careful, you know nothing about politics. You are not in this country to advise us on politics. If you were you would be expelled.

I know I love this country, and what you're doing to it is detestable.

We are on good terms with the West. Of course we wish that to continue.

Yes.

So there is no question of a missionary being expelled.

No.

You may remain here as long as you have the sanction of your church.

Yes.

You are naturally free to carry on your religious work.

Yes.

Including religious instruction to young boys.

Yes.

Naturally in the privacy of your home as well.

Yes.

But I am concerned about the fathers of the boys who attend your Friday night meetings. Their sons may be enjoying themselves but their fathers may not be. Is it possible they're in jobs that don't suit them? Perhaps we should release them from their jobs so they can be free to pursue their interests, just as you are free to pursue yours. Of course it is difficult to find work today because of what

Western capitalism has done to my country. The fathers might not be able to find other jobs, but then, they could always go into the army.

And be sent to China?

We will not allow the West to do to us what they have done to China. We will achieve the kind of strength the West appreciates, and at the same time we will save China with our strength. We are of the same race as the Chinese. We understand them whereas Westerners don't.

How could they when they're foreign devils?

You are knowledgeable in *No*, that means you know that devils exist. Evil exists. Do you know it?

I do.

I am sure you do. And would you deny that evil exists in the West? In Westerners? In yourself?

I would agree it moves in the wind although its domain is a minor one.

Good, you agree. Now what I would like you to consider is what Western avarice has done to China, which it will not be allowed to do to Japan. Or consider a more immediate problem, consider the difficulty of finding jobs in Japan because of the collapse of Western capitalism. Consider the fathers of the boys who attend your Friday night dances. You must care a great deal for those boys and you love our country, we know that. It would be unfortunate if these men could not find work and their families had to suffer as a result. Reflect upon this situation for a moment.

The General stared at Father Lamereaux and a completely unexpected interchange began.

The priest was still slumped uncomfortably in the small, low chair. The General was still seated behind his massive desk with his chin resting in his hands. Now the General leaned forward and closed his left eye as if to multiply the acuity of his other eye, to increase his vision by narrowing it. The one open eye, round and unfathomable, stared at Father Lamereaux without blinking.

A minute went by. Father Lamereaux didn't move. He was staring back also without blinking.

Two minutes went by.

A full five minutes according to the ticks of the clock on the wall.

Father Lamereaux kept a large collection of cats in his house. Sometimes to amuse himself he practiced outstaring the cats. Early in life he had discovered he had an unusual talent for concentration, so acute he could perform extraordinary feats of memorization. He could shuffle rapidly through a pack of cards once, and repeat the exact location of every card in the deck. He could memorize a list of random three-digit numbers, up to one hundred of them, in the time it took someone to read them off. He could enter a reading room in a public library, walk once around the room at a normal pace, and immediately upon exit give the title and author of every volume in the room.

Later, when he found his vocation, this talent was made impregnable by the rigors of Jesuitical training. Nothing he had seen or heard was ever lost to him. A cat could stare at him for fifteen minutes or more but eventually it had to turn away, its dumb mind no match for the severity of his intellectual discipline.

Yet he met his match that morning in General Kikuchi's office. He met his match and lost a contest of intellect and will for the first time in his life.

The break came after fifty-nine minutes of silent staring, fifty-nine minutes during which time neither man moved, neither man blinked. At the end of that agonizing period Father Lamereaux could no longer bear it. He knew he was beaten. As the clock struck the hour he blinked. He sighed and looked out the window.

All right, he said.

The General stirred. He opened his other eye.

What did you say?

I said all right. I'll stop holding my Friday night meetings.

It seems the wise thing to do, said the General. One might call it the safer course of action considering who you really are and what you are *really* doing.

Is that all then?

Yes.

Father Lamereaux climbed out of the small, low chair.

Somehow he managed to do it gracefully, not giving the General the pleasure of seeing how stiff he was. He rose to his full height and glared down at the tiny man behind the desk.

You are inhuman, a worm, not a man but a devil. I answer to God for my actions, but you answer to the wind of evil that has captured your soul. I pity the despicable companions of your spirit. May this country be delivered someday from its demons.

You may go.

Thus ended Father Lamereaux's account of the interview. The journalists who heard it knew he was not a man who would lie. They also knew General Kikuchi's reputation for fierce, unwavering attention, but they still could not accept the story the way Father Lamereaux told it. Obviously a part had been left out.

After discussing it among themselves they concluded the General had probably threatened to send Father Lamereaux to jail for corrupting minors unless he agreed to serve the Kempeitai as an informer. That had been the cause of the contest of wills that resulted in a full hour of unblinking silence, the suggestion of a *safer course*, a contest Father Lamereaux had lost.

Further evidence of the priest's traitorous role turned up almost at once. Instead of leading a gay procession of young boys through the streets on Friday evenings, he was now seen in obscure quarters of the city late at night, hovering in doorways. Once he was reported to have been observed sneaking over a cemetery wall at midnight. Another time he was observed sneaking out the back gate of a cemetery at three o'clock in the morning. On both occasions, as the automobile of the observer drew near, he disappeared so quickly it was as if he had evaporated in the night.

Such clandestine behavior was readily explainable. The priest was meeting his contact from the Kempeitai.

Early in the 1930s the Western community in Tokyo succeeded in isolating Father Lamereaux. No one would speak to him. If he appeared on the street or at a public gathering, all backs turned on him. New residents were warned to have nothing to do with him. The tall, gaunt Jesuit who had once been known for his gentle wit, his perceptions, his prodigious memory, his articulate and sympathetic discourses on the subtleties of Japanese culture, became a totally solitary figure, shunned, abandoned, despised.

When Japan went to war with the West he was interned with other scholars and missionaries in a prison camp in the mountains. But even then his former services to the Kempeitai were not forgotten, for at a time when the other prisoners were finding it difficult to eat, Father Lamereaux was getting drunk day after day, alone as always, on genuine Irish whiskey captured by the Japanese army at the British officers' mess in Singapore.

No one who talked to Quin had anything good to say for Father Lamereaux. Those who had known him hated him, everyone else reviled him.

I'm only sorry, said one man, that he wasn't around to face a court after the war. Or at least to face us.

After the war? said Quin.

Yes, he died a few days after Japan surrendered, I'm not sure how. One story has it that he came back to Tokyo and finally succumbed to acute alcoholism. Another was that he returned to Kamakura and went insane, committed suicide by throwing himself under a collapsing wall during a typhoon.

In any case he's gone. A lost curiosity and an ugly one.

●

Geraty's history, by contrast, seemed to begin where the Jesuit's had ended.

Little was known of his life before the war other than that he lived in Tokyo claiming to be the representative of a Canadian firm that manufactured quack leprosy drugs. He was a gloomy man who kept to himself, he was uncommunicative and seldom spoke to Westerners. On the rare occasions when anyone saw him he was always alone. He never tried to peddle his drugs and had no apparent source of income. In fact, he never seemed to do much of anything.

One suggestion was that he had been a criminal wanted in the United States. Another possibility was that he had been smuggling contraband from Mukden to Shanghai, for that was the route he took when he left Tokyo in the 1930s. He appeared to have remained in Shanghai until the coming of the war, when he escaped from China to the Philippines. Trapped there by the Japanese invasion, he went into hiding in the mountains.

As soon as the Japanese surrendered he presented himself to the American forces as a legendary guerrilla figure who had been fighting alone in the mountains for years, an elaborate tale he told with such conviction he was awarded a decoration for valor and recommended for a colonel's commission in the army reserve.

While waiting for his commission to be approved, Geraty talked himself into a flight to Japan on the basis of his knowledge of the language and his long experience both there and in China. He arrived back in Tokyo during the first days of the Occupation and was given a sensitive position doing preliminary research in the archives of the Imperial Army, more specifically the captured Kempeitai files on China.

Geraty was in the job only a month or two when a mysterious fire burned down an entire wing of the warehouse where the Kempeitai files were stored. The American authorities were immediately suspicious because of the absence of paper ashes in the ruins. Furthermore, a blind Japanese beggar who had been sleeping in a gutter near the warehouse reported that he had been awakened by a convoy of passing trucks on the night of the fire.

A few telephone calls revealed that although a number of military trucks were out on various errands at the time of the fire, no one had authorized a convoy anywhere in the Tokyo area.

This information coincided with a report on Geraty's

pending commission. A routine investigation in the Philippines had showed that the giant American was remembered in many mountain villages, but only for his outrageous indolence. Hundreds of peasants were ready to testify that he had done nothing during the war but steal their homemade beer and sleep. It was true he had taught their children to sing *Onward Christian Soldiers* and had urged them to march off and fight the Japanese, but he himself had never left the safety of the remote mountaintop church where his hammock was strung in a dark corner behind the altar.

Geraty was called in and shown the report, which he read without comment. The beggar was brought in to repeat his testimony. Geraty's observation then was that the blind man was starving and therefore probably subject to hallucinations. To prove his point he gave the ravenous beggar a turnip and asked him how it tasted. The shaking old man replied that it had the bouquet of green tea, the flavor of new rice, and the delicate consistency of the finest raw tuna. Geraty patted the old man on the head, offered to buy him a sackful of turnips, and turned back to his accusers grinning broadly.

He was fired on the spot and told he would never be able to work for the American government again, an announcement he accepted with a guffaw and a gesture so insulting he was thrown out the door.

Thereafter he supported himself by conducting lurid after-hour entertainments for American officers and their wives. While stationed in the bar of one of the better Tokyo hotels he would allude to what he called the frightening sexual habits of the everyday man in kimono. Most of the Americans in the Occupation knew nothing about Japan and Geraty obviously knew a great deal. In the course of an evening, besides having his drinks paid for, he generally managed to talk himself into at least one private showing.

Beginning at midnight, he would say, because that's when these demons come alive. These vices sprang up during the era of warring states when the capital was in

Kyoto, saints preserve us, before the devils moved their foul activities to Kamakura. You've seen Kyoto? Then you know the dark alleys I'm talking about, the hidden passageways and trapdoors, the monasteries tucked away up in the hills where even the most hideous screams would go unheard. The boating parties were always set for midnight, and long before dawn, you can be sure, the tortured victims were bound and gagged and weighted and flung into the water so there would be no evidence of the fiendish pleasures witnessed only by the moon. Read the old chronicles, it's all there and has been for a thousand years. There's an awesome legacy, I tell you, behind the blank face and ingratiating manners of the everyday man in kimono. But possibly for a certain sum, if we went about it in the right way, a man and his drinking companion or even a man and his wife might be able to catch a glimpse of these lost lustful aberrations, these age-old sinewy slithering depravities of the Eastern mind. Why come to the Orient and not see the truth? How can we overcome evil unless we see it in all its perverse variations?

Geraty would grow more florid as the evening wore on, his huge head hovering above the bar, his eyes bulging as he intoned the names of his favorite saints.

Atrocities, he would hiss, atrocities a thousand years old, Satanic atrocities sipped and soaked and sating. Cormorants were sent to fish in the Uji just before dawn, and not just for fish. Nobles unmasked their falcons, warrior monks unsheathed their swords, warrior abbots unleashed their spiders and bats, whole battalions of enslaved children screamed from the shadows. What's that you say? A private showing?

Geraty licking his chin and whirling down drinks, staggering off through back streets at midnight with his customers trotting in his steps, stumbling down the stairway to some dingy cellar where he would empty half a bottle and chant verses from the first chapter of St. Luke, the prayer wheel turning in his mind, while bringing on a crowd of hungry, tired performers and lining them up against the wall, while turning the spotlight on himself and undressing as he muttered memories from his childhood, from Mukden and Shanghai and the old Tokyo, a journey that led west and south through Manchuria and China to a long sleep in the mountains of the Philippines before returning to Japan, where he now took off his clothes in order to display his fat massive body to a few dazed, sleepy spectators.

Over the years Geraty's acts deteriorated. After the first postwar months it was difficult for him to find the starving youths who would degrade themselves for so little money. His girls deserted him for cleverer operators, his boys grew older and older. What had begun as a giggling dance by corrupt children ended as a stiff parade of derelicts with nothing to show the audience or each other but collapsed veins and ulcerous sores.

Geraty himself found it increasingly impossible to break out of his alcoholic stupors. There were evenings when his exhibition of the history of Oriental lust consisted entirely of him taking off his clothes. He would stand in the spotlight mumbling the line he always repeated when naked, *magnificat anima mea Dominum*, at the same time as he fought off swarms of imaginary falcons and shouted orders at hordes of invisible children. After a time the whirlpool closed around him and he sank to the floor, collapsed on the immense black barge that was carrying Kyoto and all its ancient monasteries down through the night to the sea, there to begin for the ten thousandth time his incomprehensible recitation of dates and addresses, the journey across Asia that Quin remembered from the bar in the Bronx.

So ended Geraty's first decade after the war. Business dropped off, tourists avoided him. He was thrown out of hotel bars and told not to return. Whenever he got any money he spent it on a drinking bout that lasted until the money was gone. More often he could be seen behind a noodle stand in one of the slums of the city, washing a few dishes in exchange for a pinch of horseradish.

Quin asked about the rare Buddhist manuscripts owned

by Geraty, the extensive collection of pornography he had supposedly annotated.

He found that not only had no one ever heard of the collection, no one believed such manuscripts could really exist. And in any case, it was inconceivable that they had been translated by the old giant with the horseradish habit.

A scholarly exercise so vast it would take a convoy of trucks to transport it?

They shook their heads in the bar and laughed. Obviously Quin had his man confused with someone else.

●

When Quin returned from his wanderings in Tokyo, when he came back to the apartment where Big Gobi was waiting patiently for him, watching television, he always put his arms around Big Gobi and hugged him. That was the way they greeted each other. Quin smiling, Big Gobi grinning with tears in his eyes because he was so happy.

Well, Gobes, I hope I wasn't gone too long.

It was nothing, Quin, nothing at all. You know you never have to worry about leaving me alone. I always know you're coming back.

They hugged again, Big Gobi laughed. Ever since he was a child he had always wanted to touch people and have them touch him. It was the only way he could be sure they were real. But at the orphanage they had never understood that. When he put his huge hands on the other boys they had always backed away from him.

Stop pawing everyone, said the fathers.

Run away when he does that, they told the other boys.

From the beginning Big Gobi's hands had disturbed him, even frightened him. He was never sure what they might do. For that reason he stopped touching the other boys, so they wouldn't dislike him, and instead watched them carefully so he could understand how they acted, what they did and how they did it, so that he could do it the same way. He listened to them and said the same things. He watched their mouths and laughed the same way. He imitated everything about them and made the same silly faces.

But for some reason the faces weren't silly on Big Gobi. And when he laughed it didn't seem funny.

On Sunday nights they had oyster stew at the orphanage. While still young, Big Gobi discovered he loved oysters. He loved the smell of the sea that came from the pale jelly. He loved them because they were shapeless, because they had no hands.

When he was old enough he asked for the job of opening the oysters on Sunday afternoons. They showed him how to do it, and it was his happiest hour of the week. Alone behind the kitchen facing the sky and the fields, the receding ridges of the Berkshires, he slit the cartilage of the shells and peeked into the juicy caves of tides and algae, a calm, quiet place, a home deep and narrow, light brown, sucking and oozing, darker at the edges.

And for Big Gobi there were other sensations hidden in the mysterious oyster, not so much peaceful as ecstatic. Once while he was shucking them, once and no more so that he would never be caught, he sneaked an oyster for himself and held it above his lips, let it slide down slowly and swell in his throat until he grew dizzy and began to shake, felt a numbness in his loins and then a warm sticky wetness there.

An exquisite experience certainly, but for Big Gobi, not unexpected. Strangely similar, in fact, to the wonders the fathers attributed to the act of communion whereby God momentarily possessed the soul.

About the time Big Gobi should have gone to school they discovered his shoulder was malformed. The shoulder was operated on and allowed to heal, broken again and allowed to heal. Throughout his childhood he was operated on every year, and during the recoveries there was nothing to do but watch television.

He didn't care about the programs but he loved the

commercials because they told him what to do. They told him where to go every day. They told him how to get there. They advised him what to buy and what to eat, what to drink, when to drink it. They told him what to do once he was home again, and after that and later and the next time, everything he needed to know about life.

Of course he was an orphan who lived in an orphanage, he had no money, and his shoulder was in a plaster cast so there was no question of going anywhere or doing anything or buying anything. He had to eat and drink what he was given to eat and drink, when he was given it.

But none of that mattered. The commercials were concerned with his welfare. They watched over him. They cared for him the way family and friends might have cared for him had there been family and friends in his life. So he returned the love of the commercials. He loved them as they loved him.

The first time Big Gobi whispered that secret to Quin, Quin didn't laugh or even smile. He just put his arms around Big Gobi and hugged him to show that he understood. Yet even then Big Gobi hadn't been able to bring himself to mention the tuna fish. Instead he had pretended he had gone directly from the orphanage into the army.

●

He told them he didn't want to go, but they said he had to. One afternoon during training he was sitting outside the barracks not doing anything, staring at the sand and thinking of television commercials, humming them, repeating their warnings and instructions, when all at once a corporal kicked him and shouted that he was out of his head, that he'd missed a meal sitting there, that he must be crazy if he didn't know enough to eat.

What's a crazy bastard like you doing in the army? They don't let crazy bastards into the army.

That night Big Gobi was so excited he couldn't sleep. The next morning he sat down on the edge of his cot and refused to go to breakfast. They pushed him and yelled at him and threw him into the shower. After refusing to eat for three days he was taken to see a doctor.

The doctor asked him questions and sent him to another doctor. The second doctor asked him more questions and moved him to a hospital with bars on the windows. Every morning the doctor came to ask the same questions again.

Do you like the army? Are you afraid of the army? Do you like boys? Do you like animals? Are you afraid of men?

Big Gobi smiled and answered all the questions with a different answer every day. The only questions he always answered the same were those about the army.

I like the army very much, he said. I want to spend my life in the army.

Why won't you eat then?

Big Gobi smiled. He wasn't hungry. The doctor pointed at his arms and legs.

Hungry? You're starving.

Big Gobi smiled. He didn't know about that. All he knew was that he wasn't particularly hungry.

One day a nurse came to his bed with a large hypodermic needle. She showed him the thick point of the needle, how long it was, how much fluid the hypodermic held. She made him hold it so he could see how heavy it was.

This is water, she said, and its only effect is pain. If I inject this water into your arm you'll be in pain all afternoon. Just tell me you don't want it and I won't give it to you.

Big Gobi smiled and put out his arm.

That night the nurse came back with the hypodermic. She said the pain would certainly keep him awake all night. But if he didn't want it she wouldn't give it to him. Big Gobi smiled and was still awake when she brought the hypodermic again in the morning.

Big Gobi spent his foodless, sleepless days and nights watching the soldier in the next bed. The soldier took a long time with his meals because he was right-handed and ate with his left hand. He kept a razor in his right hand and even while eating he continued to shave himself, shaving only the right side of his body.

He started with his right foot and shaved his right leg. He shaved the right half of his pubic hair and belly and chest, his right armpit, the right side of his face, his right eyebrow, and the right side of his head. When he had finished he went down to his right big toe and started over again.

Although he worked without water, soap, or mirror, the soldier never cut himself.

Big Gobi took the water injections for two months. He never ate and he never slept, he smiled and told everyone he loved the army. At the end of that time, unable to stand or even raise his head, he was given a medical discharge and taken by ambulance back to the orphanage.

When Big Gobi had regained his strength he was told he would have to leave and support himself. The fathers gave him a bus ticket and a sum of money sufficient for three or four months. The bus ticket was good for thirty days of unlimited travel anywhere in the United States.

Big Gobi was twenty-one years old. He took a bus to Boston and spent almost all his money in three days eating raw oysters. He asked where less expensive oysters could be found and was told the Maine coast. At noon the following day he arrived in Eastport on the Canadian border. By mid-afternoon the last of his money was gone.

He took a bus down the coast to Plymouth, Salem, and Lexington, a few of the sites made famous by the early English colonists. Next he went to Valley Forge, Yorktown, and Mt. Vernon tracing the steps of Washington during and after the War for Independence. He traveled to Atlanta and turned east to Charlestown on the route taken by Sherman during the Civil War. He rode down the section of the Florida coast where Ponce de León had sought the fountain of youth, reached the tip of the

Florida Keys, traversed the Gulf Coast to the delta of the Mississippi. He bisected the country to the headwaters of the Mississippi, viewed the Great Lakes, sped across the plains of the former Sioux nation, and rose through the Rockies on the path favored by the solitary French *voyageurs*. On the far side of the old Northwest Territories he once more found himself standing on the Canadian border, this time with the Pacific beside him instead of the Atlantic.

He crossed railroads built by Chinese and dropped down to the tabernacle of the Mormons on the shores of the shrinking Great Salt Lake. He traveled the Spanish trail of the first European explorers through Santa Fe, surveyed the Rio Grande and the Grand Canyon and Yosemite and Yellowstone and Old Faithful, sweated in Death Valley, reached the Pacific on the Mexican border. In San Francisco, while watching the sunset from Russian Hill, he decided to return to the orphanage. He boarded a bus but the driver ripped up his ticket.

Hey, yelled Big Gobi. Hey that's my ticket.

Thirty days, said the driver.

Big Gobi was bewildered. He wandered down a street vaguely aware that his hands were creeping around in the air. Suddenly remembering that he hadn't eaten in weeks, he got into line outside an office where men were being hired.

In his confusion he didn't understand what they said to him. He signed a paper and found a bus token in his hand. The bus took him to the docks, he was directed to a gangplank. The next day, on his knees chipping paint, Big Gobi sailed under the Golden Gate on a freighter bound for Asia.

From east Asia the ship sailed to India and Africa and South America. Although the other sailors frequently went ashore, Big Gobi missed one port after another. Once he had the watch, another time he took the watch for a sailor who promised to bring him a present. A third time he took the watch for a sailor who said he had relatives ashore, a fourth time for a sailor who said he had to see a dentist.

He had been on the ship about a month when the cook began to slip things into his soup, sometimes broken egg shells, sometimes pieces of a light bulb. He could fish them out, but when lumps of grayish foam began to appear in the bowl he didn't know what to do. The lumps dissolved when he touched them.

Big Gobi spied on the cook and discovered the lumps were seagull droppings. For over a year he ate the contaminated soup without getting angry, reminding himself what had happened with the tuna fish.

Three days before Christmas, during a snowstorm, the freighter docked in another port. To his surprise Big Gobi learned they were in New York.

That night he went ashore for the first time in a year and started running. He ran the length of New York City and reached the suburbs. There he asked directions and set off again cross-country. He ran all day and all night and all the following day and night. On Christmas Eve he found he had made several wrong turns and was still far away from the orphanage. Nevertheless he reached it late on Christmas Day, having run six hundred and forty miles in eighty-eight hours, the entire last stretch through the worst Massachusetts blizzard in several decades.

Big Gobi collapsed on the steps of the orphanage and was admitted once more to his old home, this time as a laborer on the farm run by the orphanage. There he remained until a wheezing giant who said his name was Geraty arrived from Japan some years later to present him with two stolen objects, a worthless green paperweight and a small gold cross that had originated in Malabar around the beginning of the Middle Ages.

●

Oysters. Television. The army. Seagull droppings soup.

While crossing the Pacific Big Gobi had told Quin all his secrets but one. That last one he had put off and put off until all at once it was their last day at sea and he had no

choice. The next morning they were due to dock in Yokohama, and if he were ever going to confess his final secret
he had to do it while they were still out of sight of land.

He didn't know why that was so but all the same he
knew it. He knew he was so ashamed of that secret the
truth of it could only be spoken where flux was all around
him, where space turned without boundaries upon itself,
where time and reach and movement were endless and
indistinguishable. That is, in a desert or at sea.

It was toward the end of the afternoon. Quin sat in his
chair, Big Gobi beside him on the deck. Big Gobi kept his
head down so that Quin wouldn't be able to see his face.
He was pretending to study the small gold cross.

Hey, Quin, sometimes things happen by accident, don't
they? I mean even bad things can be mistakes, can't they?

Right, Gobes, that's the way it is.

Even the worst things? Between people I mean.

Well maybe, but maybe not. The worst things may not
be accidents.

You really think so?

Yes, I guess I do.

Big Gobi turned away. He had always wanted to think
the tuna fish was an accident, a mistake. He had been
only eighteen then, it was the first time he had left the
orphanage. They wanted to see if he could do regular
work, so they found him a job in Boston unloading fish. He
moved to a foundling home near the harbor and went to
work every morning at six. In the evenings he watched
television. On Saturday night he went to the movies.

One Saturday he stayed late to help the foreman. They
worked alone, only the foreman knew he was there and
not at the movies. Big Gobi was moving crates of fish in
the freezer locker, stacking the crates along one wall. He
had to walk around a frozen tuna that was lying in the
middle of the floor, a fish about six feet long. All at once he
realized the eye of the fish was staring at him. He swung
his foot and the foreman yelled.

What the hell?

For a moment Big Gobi didn't know where he was. He

looked down and saw that he had kicked a hole in the fish. A large chunk of flesh had fallen out of its belly.

I'm sorry, he said, I must have slipped.

He got down on his knees and stuffed the chunk of flesh back into the hole in the belly, but when he removed his hand the chunk fell out on the floor.

What the hell, yelled the foreman, what are you doing now?

Don't worry, whispered Big Gobi, I can fix it.

He ran out the door and came back with a bucket of wet fish slops and a piece of rope. The foreman watched him plaster the hole with fish paste, refit the chunk, and tie the rope around the fish.

You'll see, said Big Gobi, we did it all the time at the farm. You cement around the stone and then the cement hardens and the wall's perfect. This slop will freeze in no time, you'll see.

Freak, shouted the foreman.

Like new, whispered Big Gobi. I promise.

Promise your fucking ass off. That's fish, not stone.

I tripped, whispered Big Gobi.

Tripped my ass. You kicked that fish and you're going to pay for it. Don't you know you can't go around destroying things?

The bucket of fish slops was still in Big Gobi's hand. He groaned and his hands came together. The metal snapped, crumpled, fell in a ball at his feet.

A mistake, he whispered.

You idiot freak, yelled the foreman.

Big Gobi remembered telling himself he didn't destroy things. He whispered it and shouted it as loud as he could, shouted so loud his ears were still ringing when he opened his eyes and saw the foreman's head in his hands, blood on the man's mouth, the broken neck twisted away from the body.

Big Gobi dropped the body and ran out of the freezer, ran until he was exhausted, hid in his bed in the foundling home.

The foreman was found in the locker on Monday morning. His neck was broken and the upper part of his body was crushed. Apparently he had returned to the freezer sometime during the weekend and slipped and struck his head, losing consciousness. He had left the door open, which caused the temperature to rise inside the freezer. During the thaw a stack of heavy crates had become dislodged and come crashing down on him.

Shortly after that it was decided at the foundling home that the experiment with Big Gobi had failed. Working with other men seemed to depress him, the traffic in the city frightened him, the noise kept him awake at night. He was better suited to the solitude of the farm where he had grown up. The fathers at the orphanage agreed with the fathers in Boston, and he was sent back to the Berkshires.

The deck beneath his eyes had blurred. Big Gobi had kept his head down so that Quin couldn't see his tears.

You really think so, Quin?

Yes, I guess I do. It just seems that's the way it has to be.

Sure, Big Gobi had whispered. Sure, of course it does. It just has to be, that's all.

He had squeezed his eyes closed then, felt the tears burn, been furious with himself for being too afraid to tell Quin his last secret before they landed in Japan, a mythical land of princesses and palaces and dragons that had been tenderly described to him one winter afternoon and evening by a hulking giant, the ragged clown and impostor who had been his father's closest childhood friend.

Angry with himself and yet sad as well. For if he couldn't tell Quin it meant he could never tell anyone.

No one. Ever. He would have to bear one secret on his own, carry alone and forever one terrible inexplicable mystery.

●

Big Gobi had said nothing about the Japanese crew during the Pacific crossing because he knew all freighter crewmen were ugly regardless of nationality. But the morning the ship docked in Yokohama he clutched Quin by the hand.

What is it, Gobes?

Big Gobi pointed at the official who was stamping his passport, a short, stunted man with narrow, puffy eyes and skin that was sickly and discolored. The official had looked with apparent interest at the glass paperweight Big Gobi claimed was jade, and he had even listened politely while Big Gobi described Geraty's famous emerald palace beneath the sea and asked where it might be found. But when the official opened his mouth he didn't say anything. He only made odd squeaking noises.

What's the matter? said Quin.

Big Gobi gripped his hand and peeked at the other people who were standing around on the pier. They were all making the same queer sounds and they all had the same disease, the same sickly skin, the same half-closed puffy eyes.

Big Gobi was terrified.

Hey, Quin, don't you see what Geraty did? He lied to us. This isn't the emerald kingdom, it's a leper colony.

●

Quin didn't know why Geraty had sought him out that late winter night in the Bronx. He didn't understand how the old buffalo had known which bar to go to, only one of many in the neighborhood but the one where Quin and his friends always happened to do their drinking. Nor even how he had known it was Quin's neighborhood in the first place. And above all, why the fat, muttering giant had lied so outrageously about Father Lamereaux, himself, Quin's parents, everyone and everything.

Quin completely distrusted the old buffoon, but there was nothing to be done now but to find him and to try to get him to reveal some small part of the truth, or some clue that would lead to the truth.

Geraty hadn't been seen in the Tokyo bar he normally

frequented for six months, but Quin was told there was one place he might look, an abandoned empty warehouse in a slum on the outskirts of the city. In the past Geraty had been known to disappear in the vicinity of the warehouse for certain periods of time, a few days or weeks, perhaps even a month, never longer than that. He claimed these disappearances had to do with religious meditation, but of course no one believed that. Obviously Geraty's retreats from society were caused by his basic condition, that is, advancing age, advanced alcoholism, general disability, and total poverty.

Exactly why Geraty had a fondness, or compulsion, for lurking near a warehouse no one knew. There was nothing whatsoever distinctive about the warehouse in question. It was merely an abandoned, empty place, roofless, in a slum on the outskirts of the city. But since he did spend periods of time there, it was probable he had built some sort of shelter for himself next to the warehouse. Quin would have to look for that. A taxi driver was called into the bar and given directions.

They found the small warehouse after nearly an hour of driving back and forth through the tiny alleys of the slum. But as soon as they pulled up before it Quin saw what he was looking for on one side of the warehouse, a shack made out of flattened gasoline cans that had been left behind by the American army after the war.

The shack was about as high as his shoulders. A burlap sack hung across the opening. Quin went up to it and rapped sharply on the roof.

For a minute or two he heard nothing. Then there was a heavy groan, a sneeze, a single violent cough. He pulled aside the burlap and saw the huge fat man sitting on the ground. He was squatting with his legs beneath him in the manner of a giant immobile Buddha, his greatcoat wrapped around him as a blanket. The space was so narrow Geraty could neither lie down nor stretch his legs, yet even in that cramped position his enormous body completely filled the shack.

Quin turned his head away from the stench of sweat

and horseradish. Geraty cursed in several languages, finally in English.

Is this America? Have I died and gone to hell? Why are you disturbing the anchorite in his cave?

Up, buffalo. Outside. We've got some things to talk about.

Geraty scratched his belly. He moaned.

If that's really you, nephew, you might as well know I can't move. I came here to die and I'm staying here. He that is mighty hath done great things to me.

What?

Combined all the maladies known to man and visited them upon me. Laid me low at the end of life with a condition that amounts to general and extreme fatigue of the spirit. In other words I've given up. I'm never going to leave this cave again. So drop the curtain and leave me alone with the saints who have succored me in my years of torment, drop it and good-bye.

A drink, buffalo?

Geraty's arms and legs began to move. A moment later the giant was outside gathering himself together, swatting at the clumps of mud that covered him. Despite the warm weather he still wore the thick layers of clothes Quin had seen in New York. His eyes rolled as he retied the piece of red flannel around his neck.

My condition is delicate, nephew. I have to be careful when exposing myself to the night air, even the air of summer. Did you come here looking for a game of liar's dice?

But Geraty didn't smile, nor did Quin. Quin rocked back on his heels and poked the fat man sharply in the ribs. Geraty hiccuped.

What's this about the priest, buffalo? They tell me he's dead.

No hope of that.

Well, is Big Gobi his son or not?

Him? A son? Are you mad? I don't know who could have given you that idea.

Quin nodded. He rocked on his heels. It had been his

own idea, and he was beginning to realize that with Geraty it was better never to have any ideas of your own.

The truth, buffalo. That's what I want this time.

He hath filled the hungry with good things. Where are my documents?

Quin held them out, the forged Canadian passport and the two forged Belgian passports. As Geraty secreted them in his greatcoat the black bowler hat crept back on his head, his mouth opened, a wheezing cough struck Quin in the face. The fat man was laughing.

That? Just that? But you should have said so before, nephew. Right this way for the illusive dream often sought and seldom found, or to be exact, often found but seldom recognized.

Abruptly Geraty turned away and lurched into an alley, his immense shadow moving surprisingly fast down the narrow passage. As much as it bothered him, Quin had no choice but to trot along behind recalling a scene only recently described to him, Geraty leading one of his customers off at midnight to some interminable obscene performance that existed only in his own mind, if it existed at all.

●

They sat on stools at a pushcart beside a vacant lot where a few vagrants were already asleep on the sand. The pushcart served boiled vegetables and cheap liquor. Geraty ignored the owner and fished in the pan of steaming water with his hands. He threw a bamboo shoot over his shoulder, grunted a few words, wiped his hands on his sweaters.

A bowl of horseradish appeared followed by two glasses of raw sake and a plate of turnips. Geraty dipped a slice of turnip into the horseradish and chewed.

The priest, buffalo.

Geraty swallowed and threw off one of the glasses. His eyes bulged.

Could it be that we are both referring to the hero who shortened the Second World War and thereby saved millions of lives? A man whose vocation is the alleviation of suffering? An elderly drunkard and pederast, now reformed and retired, who once sent reams and reams of valuable secret information to the West? Is this the heroic figure before us at tonight's turnip bar of history? Look now behind you at those wandering Japanese poets curled up on the sand in the spacious urinal they have found for themselves in a slum of the world's largest city. Note that they sleep soundly because of what a frail, gentle man once did for them three decades ago. The sacrifices were his. The courage was his. Save for him they might never have returned from China. Their bones might be bleaching at this very moment on a Pacific atoll. But do they know it? Have they heard his name even once in the waves and the desert and the wind?

The priest, buffalo.

Geraty stuffed horseradish into his nose. He sneezed, coughed once.

An anonymous Jesuit once known for his Friday night performances? Precisely that frail, gentle man who wears the buttons on his coat in a totally personal configuration? Yes, I thought so, I was sure that's who we were talking about. A genuine article and rare. Rare? Rare by God, you never met such a man in the Bronx. When you see him you'll find out for yourself, but I suggest you not expect too much at first. His memory was phenomenal once but now, as I say, he's reformed and retired. To have some idea of what he's done for people in the past, savor the name of St. Brigid. Recall her sanctity and her miraculous powers, above all her hospitality to the poor and the suffering, her charity to slaves. Most of us are slaves of one kind or another, to one thing or another, and the alleviation of suffering, nephew, is the path this Jesuit has followed. But also remember that path has been in Japan for fifty years, fifty years of speaking nothing but Japanese. You'll have to adopt their manner of circumlocution with this rare man, you'll have to talk about nothing at first and sniff the air for clues. Clues? Sniff the air and chat about this and that, whatever comes up, slip from one unrelated and unresolved topic to another, and all the while circle your man the way a puppy circles a wise old hound, waiting for a whiff of his hindquarters, waiting to find out who he is in fact. Backward it may seem to you, coming up from behind it might appear to be, but that's the way it's done over here. Why? For He hath exalted the humble and put down the mighty from their seat. The sergeant who wore this overcoat the day they took Nanking could tell you what that means, could tell you just as he told me years later on a beach south of Tokyo, a beach in Kamakura, the same beach where they put on gas masks and had the picnic that saved Moscow from the Germans.

Lamereaux, buffalo.

That's right, that's our man and none other. Why else would I be talking about the picnic? They were there to recruit Lamereaux of course. That was the whole point.

Who was there?

Adzhar for one. Adzhar the incredible linguist. How did he ever survive the roads where life took him? No matter, he did, and someday I thought those roads would lead me to the pine grove I've always wanted to find, a quiet grove on a hill above the sea, no more than a soul deserves after lurking forty years in the locked, shuttered rooms of Asia. But no. Adzhar in his simplicity was too complex for them, his simple faith in love was beyond their comprehension. The fools were delirious on dragon piss and confiscated everything.

Who was Adzhar?

You're right there, who was Adzhar and who was Lamereaux? And who was Baron Kikuchi for that matter? The picnic was held near his estate after all, saints preserve us. They say he was the most feared man in the Kempeitai and I've no reason not to believe them, but who was I? Who was I then and who am I now? And who was Edward the Confessor? Go ahead, tell me that.

Adzhar, buffalo. Who was he?

A reindeer from Lapland, a dragon from every country in the world. I didn't know him, I only knew him through his work, his legacy to me. Other people knew him that way too. He and Lamereaux were good friends then. Why? Who can say. Who can fathom why people watched those worthless films I bought in Mukden? Who can say why those films led to a cemetery in Tokyo, why the cemetery led to two bottles of Irish whiskey in Lamereaux's Victorian parlor, why two bottles of Irish whiskey led to a picnic on a beach south of Tokyo. A beach? Kamakura of course.

You said there were four people at the picnic.

Exactly four, definitely four. The trinity plus one? Three men and a woman? The trinity in gas masks so the secret conversation could not be overheard? The fourth presence not bothering with a gas mask, instead concerning herself with the blanket and the food and the comfort of the other three? Yes, that's what Lamereaux told me the night we made our suffering journey through two bottles of Irish whiskey.

Adzhar and Lamereaux. Who were the other two?

Ask your man, he would know because he was there. Fools say he became a drunkard when he was interned in the mountains, but that's because they can't sniff a change in the wind, they can't feel it coming, they like to think it happens quickly. An hour ago? Yesterday at the latest? Eight years ago is more like it and fifty years ago is even more like it. And as for those little boys he knew, he loved them like a father. Why not? He was and is so ordained by the Almighty.

Buffalo, when was the picnic?

At the onset of an era given to murders and assassinations, a time when a hunger for human flesh rumbled in men's bowels. Look what happened in Nanking where a sergeant strangled his own commanding general. When he told me that on the beach, I knew I was hearing a voice direct from the rectum of lunacy. No one but me would probably ever believe such a voice, but that doesn't matter now. A long time ago I destroyed the evidence, destroyed the only report the Kempeitai had on it.

On what?

The spy ring. The report was short, no more than a

paragraph or two. That sergeant had gone mucking around in the rectum of his lunacy and killed the courier they caught, beat him to death, murdered the only source of information they had before there was time to get anything worthwhile out of him.

Spy ring. What spy ring?

My God, nephew, isn't that what we're talking about? The spy ring run by Lamereaux? The man who saved Moscow from the Germans? The hero who shortened the war in China and saved millions of lives? Worthless films, a cemetery, two bottles of Irish whiskey, a picnic for the trinity plus one? That's the path Lamereaux and I were on thirty years ago. What path? The path at our feet, nephew, the path that runs from a whiskey bar in the Bronx to a turnip bar in Tokyo, that begins right here beside a vacant lot where dreaming poets pass themselves off as sleeping scavengers. My doctors have warned me to be careful of the night air, my condition is delicate at best. Another glass of dragon piss is what we need now, then perhaps we'll be able to find a barge and float our souls down the river to the sea, through the mist and vapors we see rising from our vessel, not really a pushcart. Steam, you call it? The breath of boiled turnips? Saints preserve us, nephew, you better examine more closely the shores where we pass.

●

Geraty emptied one glass after another. Quin forced him to eat, forced him to answer questions, forced him to sit up when his head sank toward the counter. The fat man muttered and swore, laughed, lied when there seemed no reason to lie, and then corrected himself before wandering off on some byway of his four decades of travel through Asia.

He recited Manchurian telephone numbers and Chinese addresses, changed costumes, sang circus songs, beat a drum and played a flute, consumed bowls of horseradish and mounds of turnips, sneaked through the black-market district of Mukden late in 1934 and again in 1935, noting discrepancies, brought out all the peeling props and threadbare disguises of an aging clown working his way around the ring. Grinning, weeping, he eventually revealed how he had discovered thirty years ago that Lamereaux was the head of an espionage network in Japan, a network with such an ingenious communication system it was the most successful spy ring in Asia in the years leading up to the Second World War.

The information had come to Geraty by chance because he happened to fall asleep in a Tokyo cemetery.

At the time he was planning a trip to the mainland, ostensibly to sell patent drugs. His real interest, however, was in acquiring pornographic movies that could be sold at a large profit in Shanghai. Since the military had come to power in Japan these movies could be found nowhere in the country, but there were rumors that when the Japanese army had seized Manchuria a few years before, they had confiscated a large supply of them, probably from a White Russian entrepreneur.

Geraty made inquiries and was finally introduced to a young Japanese army corporal, on leave in Tokyo, who worked as a film projectionist in a unit stationed near Mukden. The corporal, little more than a boy, said the films could be provided for the right sum of money. The amount named was far more than Geraty had.

At this point Geraty's story became confused. Although he would not admit it outright, it appeared he had stolen the money.

Worse, he was particularly ashamed of the source of the stolen money. He cried uncontrollably in front of Quin and insisted on whispering in a voice so low Quin couldn't hear him. He was talking to his saints, he said. At least half an hour went by before Quin could get him to resume his account.

A meeting between the corporal and Geraty had been arranged for a Tokyo cemetery, one of the few places

where a Japanese and a foreigner could still safely transact illegal business. Geraty was to bring the money, and
the corporal in turn would tell him where the films would
be cached for him in Mukden.

Geraty took a circuitous route through the cemetery and
met the corporal behind a mausoleum. The deal was
settled and the corporal left. Geraty had gotten very drunk
before coming to the cemetery, obviously because of the
stolen money he had just given away. It was a warm
evening. After the corporal left, Geraty leaned against the
mausoleum and wept. A minute later he was asleep on his
feet.

Some time passed. He awoke in a heavy sweat, unable
to remember where he was or how he had gotten there. He
stumbled between the gravestones until he heard a man's
voice, whereupon he dropped behind a stone to hide. He
was lying on his stomach and it was impossible to make
out anything in the darkness.

The clouds suddenly parted. Geraty was astonished to
see the young boy he had just met, the corporal from the
unit near Mukden. In the corporal's hand was the packet
of money Geraty had paid over for the films. The boy was
holding out the packet as if to give it to someone. The
packet disappeared, the corporal turned and dropped his
trousers. He bent over a tombstone, baring a slender
bottom to the moon and whoever else was there.

A tall, gaunt figure stepped forward from the shadows,
his eyes raised to heaven. He had the features of a
Westerner and the clothes of a cleric. A specific deed was
about to be performed.

Geraty stared. Only one man in Asia answered to that
description.

Lamereaux piously crossed himself, but his next action
wasn't at all what Geraty had expected. The priest's hand
shot out and made a flickering motion, a deft and practiced movement much like Geraty's own when he was
inserting a ball of horseradish in his nose. The hand
withdrew, the corporal retrieved his trousers and fled.

Geraty watched Lamereaux drop to his knees. The
Jesuit took hold of his rosary and recited the fifty-three

Hail Marys, curiously omitting both the Credo and the Our Fathers. The clouds closed as suddenly as they had opened. In the darkness Geraty heard the priest begin to sing the Litany of the Saints.

Once more Geraty's narrative broke down. He became incoherent, he sobbed, he hid his face and whispered. He admitted the scene infuriated him, but he wouldn't say why.

Quin had no way of knowing what it meant. Was it because the money Geraty had stolen was now being given to someone else? To someone he knew? Because that person was Father Lamereaux?

Who or what enraged him? The corporal? Lamereaux? A gesture by the priest that mimicked his own?

Or simply himself.

Geraty whispered over his bowl of turnips. He cried. He buried his scarred face in the folds of his greatcoat. Again it took some time before Quin could coax him back to the story.

Fury, hissed Geraty. Overweening wrath was upon me.

His first impulse had been to rush over and give Lamereaux a beating, beat him mercilessly over the head and shoulders as he knelt there in the darkness. But fortunately it had been many years since he'd heard the Litany from beginning to end. The sound of Latin was a nostalgic memory to him, a monotonous chant from his childhood. He knew the chant would last a good thirty minutes, so there seemed no reason to hurry the beating.

He was lying on his stomach. The buzz of Latin was comforting. Long before the Litany ended he had fallen asleep for the second time that night.

The next day he went to see Father Lamereaux, who it turned out had a hangover every bit as bad as his own. The two men drank green tea and swallowed fistfuls of aspirins, but that was no help to either of them. Before long Lamereaux suggested something stronger and broke out a bottle of Irish whiskey.

An hour later they were both feeling better. They got into a discussion on *No* plays and proceeded to lecture each other. Finding words inadequate, Lamereaux got to his feet to illustrate a point by acting out a scene. Geraty watched him, then in answer acted out a scene of his own. They tried a second sequence and discovered they both knew all the movements, all the poses.

When they were drunk Geraty mentioned what he had seen in the cemetery and how Lamereaux's choice of the Litany had probably saved him from a beating. The two exiles laughed so hard they were in tears. Lamereaux broke out a second bottle of Irish whiskey and they began drinking in earnest.

The afternoon turned into the evening. Much of the truth Geraty had already guessed. Father Lamereaux told him the rest.

The Jesuit had always been opposed to Japanese militarism, he wanted to help China and the West if he could. After his friend Adzhar had arranged the meeting on the beach, he had known what to do. The Japanese acolytes who had served him over the years were still loyal to him. By then many of them had good positions in the army, the ministries, the occupied areas of China. Some traveled back and forth throughout the Empire on one mission or another. Their bits and pieces of information could be compiled to form a complete intelligence picture.

The problem was getting the information out of Japan. Some of the ex-acolytes traveled to areas where contact could be made with Allied agents, but how were they to smuggle the reports out of Tokyo? The information was too bulky to be memorized. Everyone was searched both going and coming by the secret police. Father Lamereaux analyzed the problem and found a solution.

The Kempeitai considered itself the defender of the samurai tradition. Its officers and agents prided themselves on their fierceness, their warlike masculinity. Therefore when they searched a young man they only went so far. Their searches were thorough with one exception. As a result, Lamereaux's couriers could always get through with the microfilm they carried in his small bamboo device.

Device? Nothing more than a hollow piece of bamboo sealed at both ends. Among the couriers it was called *Lamereaux's Lumbago* because of the severe backaches it caused when the courier run was a long one, deep into China, say.

Thus had Lamereaux been responsible for the most successful invention in the history of espionage, the living dead drop, revolutionary because it moved where the master spy wanted it to go, because it recognized for the first time the very simple concept that espionage, the collection and storage of information, was based on the principle of man's anus.

Lamereaux asked Geraty to keep the story of his incredible intelligence pipeline a secret, and of course Geraty agreed. He even went so far as to destroy the one vague report on the ring that appeared in the files of the Kempeitai after the war.

And the fire he had started, claimed Geraty, the fire that had burned down an entire wing of the Kempeitai warehouse and lost him his job in the Occupation, the beginning of his downfall and degradation, that fire had been set for no other reason than to conceal the destruction of that one vague report.

True, shouted Geraty. All true. That's how it ended and that's how it began. Awake setting a fire one night after the war, asleep in a cemetery one night a decade earlier. Ended and began it did, and not even Edward the Confessor can tell you more.

Geraty hung his head. He peeked over his shoulder at the bodies lying in the vacant lot. With a shudder he lowered his face into the steam rising from the vegetables boiling on the pushcart. He teetered on his stool. He was whispering.

Asleep and awake, you say? Awake? The time came that night when Lamereaux and I had finished that second bottle of Irish whiskey. Done we were, saints preserve us, and we knew it. The old days were gone and we knew it. We were two drunk butterflies circling a candle, two motionless *No* actors stuck in a pose, two exiles in the secret bag the Almighty was carrying across Asia. War. The Orient thirty years ago.

Geraty's head hung over a bowl of turnips. He stared at the turnips, the steam creeping up along the layers of sweaters, the red flannel tied with string, the black bowler hat pulled down to his bulging eyes. His dark, gloomy face was cut with scars, running with tears.

Quin waited. After five or ten minutes of silence he tapped Geraty on the shoulder.

My father. What about him?

Your father, hissed Geraty, *who's* your father? Who are you?

His fist struck the counter. He waved his arms in the air, fighting off imaginary bats and spiders and falcons. All at once he was on his feet moving away from the pushcart, roaring and shouting curses, shaking his fists at the sky.

Slander, do you hear? They call him a drunkard and a pederast and that's how they've always treated him, with lies and ridicule. Do they know a man of God when they see one? Do they? Just point him out to them, point him out now, point him out where he stands. Point out that Emperor so they can slander him and malign him and drive him where? *Where?*

Geraty crashed into the vacant lot and fell on his back, his greatcoat settling around him. Quin propped the black bowler hat under his head. He felt his pulse and listened to the painful rasp of his snoring. There was no way to move him. He would have to lie there until he awoke.

Quin picked up a handful of sand and nodded to himself. He thought of leaving some money in Geraty's pocket, but then he realized there were already too many scavengers there waiting like Geraty for the night to grow old, some not yet too drunk to go through his pockets before they fell asleep, before they in turn were robbed of all they had.

Another time, thought Quin, not knowing he would meet Geraty only once again in his life, three months from then when he was about to leave Japan on a clear autumn day that happened to be the feast day of the saint Geraty revered above all others, Edward the Confessor, three months that he would spend tracking down the lives of the men and women whose secrets lay encrypted in the code name *Gobi*, perhaps because not until then would Quin be ready to witness the final performance of this raving giant who had spent a lifetime posing as a clown.

●

The year Big Gobi went to sea he heard innumerable accounts of the nights the sailors spent on the beach. There were stories about tattoo parlors and whores, cops and whores, pawnshops and whores, camera stores and whores, whores and bars and whores and special shows and whores jiggling their things in front of jukeboxes that had colored lights. Big Gobi had never left the ship as it went around the world, and that was the reason he was excited the day Quin took him to the beach.

On the train Big Gobi took out his small gold cross and rubbed it against the side of his nose. Polishing the cross helped him when he felt dizzy, he had discovered that as soon as they arrived in Japan. It kept him from being confused, it kept his hands from wandering. Big Gobi continued polishing the cross all the way to Kamakura.

They left the station and began to walk. Quin said they should have looked for a bus but Big Gobi didn't hear him, he was dreaming. After an hour or thirty years, a mile or two or ten thousand miles, they reached the end of the continent, the eastern shore of Asia. Quin was walking across the sand but Big Gobi didn't move. He was staring into the distance.

Hey, he whispered. Hey where are we?

The sand was hot on his feet, his mind was a jumble. Below him there was a nearly deserted cove, ahead only the endless stretch of the sea.

Hey, he whispered. Where is everybody?

●

Big Gobi sifted sand through his fingers. He turned away so that Quin couldn't see his face.

Where are the parlors? he whispered softly.

Quin rubbed himself with a towel.

Which ones, Gobes?

The ones for tattooing, the ones they have on the beach. They were always talking about them when I worked on the freighter.

Liberty port. Yokohama.

I don't know the name of the place, but it's where they have the jukeboxes. You know, the jukeboxes with colored lights where the girls stand around and jiggle their things.

Yokohama.

Well where is this?

Kamakura.

Well what's it for?

How do you mean?

I mean is this a beach or is the other one a beach?

Both of them. One's for swimming and one's for whores and tattoos. Aren't you going to take a swim?

Big Gobi shuffled down to the edge of the water and put his big toe in. Cold water made him feel lonely. He dragged himself along the shore kicking sand, wondering why things never happened the way he wanted them to, never, no matter how long he waited and waited.

His foot touched an oyster. He pried it open, gazed at the pale, swelling meat.

There was a reason why those things never happened, and he knew exactly what it was. He was afraid. That was why he hadn't gone ashore with the other sailors from the freighter, and it would have been the same today if they had gone to the other beach, the one not for swimming. He would have been afraid, too afraid to do anything.

Yokohama. Quin had been there in the navy. Probably he'd been there a hundred times and knew all about it.

Big Gobi sipped the juice from the oyster, poked the soft meat with his nose, sucked, swallowed it. All at once he jumped in the air.

He was running back up the beach, running as fast as he could, running so hard his legs ached. He fell down on his knees near Quin and scooped up a fistful of sand, threw it down, scooped up another. He pawed with both hands, pushing the sand behind him through his legs. He knew Quin was watching him but he was going to say it anyway.

Hey, he shouted. Hey this is a nice place for swimming.

He stopped digging. Why was he yelling like that when Quin was only a few feet away? Quin would think something was wrong. He leaned forward and rested his elbows at the bottom of the hole he had dug. He tried to grin.

I like it, Quin. I like it a lot.

He was whispering now, but Quin smiled and nodded, a warm smile that made him feel better.

Glad you do, Gobes. I was wondering what you were thinking while you were walking down there.

Were you, Quin? That's funny, because I had an idea just then, just now I mean. I was walking along thinking how much I like this beach and that got me thinking about the other beach you were talking about, and then I remembered you'd been there and knew all about it, I mean you know, you're a friend so why shouldn't I ask you?

Big Gobi hung his head.

That was my idea, he whispered.

Right, Gobes. Sure. Let's hear about it.

Well you have to understand it's not much of anything, I mean I even feel kind of silly bringing it up but it's just that I've never done it before, I mean gone right up and said it, said what you have to say, and if there were any misunderstanding I'd feel terrible.

About what?

Me, Quin. Me. I mean just suppose she didn't know what I was talking about, suppose she got frightened or something and started backing away.

Who started backing away?

The girl jiggling her things in the colored lights. I mean what do you say to a girl at a time like that? Let's fuck? Something like that?

Just a minute, Gobes, let me get it straight. Where are we, Yokohama?

That's the place.

All right. We're in Yokohama and we pass a tattoo parlor and come to a bar where there are a lot of whores standing around. One in particular is over by the jukebox keeping time to the music. I mean she's bouncing and they're big ones and you know she's ready the second you walk in. Is that it? Something like that?

Big Gobi whistled.

That's it. That's the place all right, and she's the one I'm talking about.

Quin nodded. His face was serious. Big Gobi leaned on his elbows, his chin on the sand, and waited. When Quin didn't say anything he was afraid he had upset him.

Thinking about Yokohama, Quin? Thinking about the other times you went there?

No, Gobes, but listen. Have you ever had a girl before?

No.

Never?

Well I mean I never left the ship the year I worked on it, you know that. And where else would I have found a girl?

I don't know. On the bus trip maybe.

Well maybe, I mean I suppose I could have if I'd ever left the bus but I didn't. I mean I got off lots of buses lots of times, but I always got right back on another one again. And before that I was in bed with my shoulder and after that I worked on the farm at the orphanage. The only girl I've ever really talked to, I mean the only girl who's ever talked to me, was the nurse who gave me the water injections in the army.

All right, Gobes, that's settled. Done. Finished. Tonight we're going to Yokohama and have a session.

What?

It's on the way home, more or less. We might as well drop in and see what's doing.

Tonight?

Sure.

One of those places?

Sure.

The one jiggling in the colored lights?
Sure.
And maybe you'll help me speak to her?
Sure.
Just like that?
Just like that.
Big Gobi jumped into the air. He yelled, he danced, he spun up and down the beach collecting driftwood from Chinese rivers and Manchurian forests, dancing down a beach on the edge of Asia finding wood for a bonfire in the sun.
Hey, he shouted. Hey hey hey.
Women *hey*.
Oysters *hey*.
Hey hey hey.

●

Late that night, his lips torn and his neck scratched, his back bearing scars, Big Gobi staggered into a train bound for Tokyo, a veteran of the campaigns on the Yokohama waterfront, that narrow strip of land where hordes of invading sailors streamed ashore every night to do battle with a handful of brave whores.

The ferocious adventurers came from every corner of the world. There were Burmans and Chadians and Quechuas and Lapps and Georgians swearing in a hundred tongues and brandishing a thousand varied weapons, every conceivable kind of knife and pick and sword and bludgeon and pike. Between them they were missing every part of the human body. They had warts in every combination supplemented by a multitude of tattoos and moles, birthmarks, miscellaneous discolorings, and wounds both old and new, generally treated but often only recently scabbed. They were a desperate army with only one goal, a night of unlimited plunder after weeks at sea.

Darkness fell, the late sunset of a summer night. Chil-

dren waved good-bye to the pretty ships in the harbor,
crowds moved from the department stores to the movie
theaters. Strollers ate cold noodles. It was a peaceful
evening in downtown Yokohama with a cooling breeze off
the bay.

And yet no more than two miles away the battle was
ready to begin. Some fifty or sixty Japanese heroines were
preparing to defend the homeland against the combined
navies of the world.

The gangplanks came down, the launches sped back
and forth. The first wave of barbarians swarmed into
pawnshops snatching up cameras and silk jackets, raced
down the streets through the whining music, climbed over
the crashing chairs, and hurtled the bottles shattering
in the alleys. The massed squadrons pushed forward,
regrouped, mounted another assault. Heads cracked
on the pavement, bellies spilled out in doorways. The
sailors fought on their backs and rolled over to strike
again from the side, from above, from below, in between, in back, knee level, naval level, chest level, eye
level, from the rooftops and the tops of chairs and toilet
bowls.

But gradually their ranks thinned, their bodies piled up
on the docks and jetties. A few snipers still carried on in
upstairs windows, but long before sunrise the outcome of
the battle was decided.

Here and there a whore lay temporarily unconscious,
but most were walking home on their own sturdy legs,
limping perhaps, certainly exhausted, but with their sea
chests bulging with money from around the world. Behind
them they left carnage and ruin, snoring carcasses from a
hundred distant ports, the broken lust of foreigners. Once
again a handful of heroines had won total victory in the
nightly Yokohama battle, and all over Japan innocent
women and children were able to sleep safely because of
it.

Big Gobi sat in the train with his eyes closed. When he
had first left the princess in the palace, he had felt as if he
had no bones, then for a while he had lost his legs and
been an amputee. Now the numbness was gone and he

was suffering the torture of a thousand cuts. Oriental torture. Time.

He smiled.

Did you see how she walked right up to me, Quin? She never backed away at all. On the freighter they used to say I smelled of seagull droppings, but she didn't say anything like that. She just took me by the hand and then when we were in the room she let me turn on the television set so we could watch it from the bed. Imagine just doing it and watching television at the same time. You know tomorrow I think I'll just stay home and relax and watch television. She said she watches all the time, so I think I'll just sit around tomorrow and think about it. She must have been about sixteen and that was the first night she'd worked there and I was the first one, you know, she'd ever done anything with. Her parents are poor and she doesn't want her little brother to go to an orphanage and that's why she's there. She said I understood a lot about people considering I don't even speak Japanese, the people we were watching I mean, the people on television. She said I could come again and watch television, or watch her while she was watching television, or watch them while they were watching us. Just us, the two of us I mean, and all the others. I mean I've never been with a person like that where there were just the two of us, two of us alone but me not alone at all because she was there. Never. Not since I was born.

Big Gobi smiled as he fell asleep.

Quin looked out the window at the lights flashing by. He was thinking of Geraty then, wondering as always how much of the giant's tale he could believe, not realizing that at that very moment he was returning from the site of the famous picnic on the beach south of Tokyo where Maeve Quin had long ago laid out a blanket for three men in gas masks, her husband and Father Lamereaux and the elderly Adzhar, the wandering Russian linguist whose cross Big Gobi now wore, thereby setting in motion an espionage game that was to last eight years, culminating in Big Gobi's conception in a warehouse on the outskirts of Shanghai on the eve of a doomed circus performance.

FATHER
LAMEREAUX

.
3

*I had to sneak back and forth through the city,
evaporate and materialize, die in doorways and
resurrect myself in the moonlight of the cemetery.*

*There seemed to be only one thing to do, so I
did it. I became a ghost.*

●

Father Lamereaux peered down the corridor. The kitchen
door was closed, a mop slapped the floor. He tiptoed out of
his study. Just before he reached the garden door the mop
stopped.

Master?

He held his breath. The voice spoke again from the
blank wood of the kitchen door.

It's raining, master. Use the toilet.

Father Lamereaux sighed. A little summer drizzle
never hurt anyone. Besides, he had intended to go only as
far as his favorite patch of moss beside the garden wall.

He left the toilet and sank into the chair behind his desk.
Japanese urinals were the worst-smelling in the world,
everyone knew that. They were so bad Japanese men
never used them, which was a sound custom, practical as
well as wise. It kept little boys from associating their
tassels with dark, smelly places. In the West a boy had to
hide in a closet, lock himself in. No wonder he grew up
thinking his body and the demands of his body were
impure.

Yet at the same time the little Western boy was enjoying
himself, he had no choice. Eliminating waste was always
enjoyable.

75

Guilt.

While in Japan, on the other hand, a boy was encouraged from the beginning to do his business out-of-doors. In public. His mother spread him over the gutter when he was a baby. Later, on the train, his older sister urged him to use an empty bottle rather than bother people by pushing up the aisle. Or if there wasn't an empty bottle, she showed him how to stand on the seat and direct his aim downwind.

Women admired him. A natural act naturally performed. A world of sun and rain and men and flowers living together in harmony.

After fifty years in Japan a man couldn't piss in his own garden?

Fifty years, half a century. A life that spanned three-quarters of a century. Nearly one-quarter of a century without a drink.

Father Lamereaux liked to think in terms of centuries, epochs, dynasties. When he first came to Japan it had helped him understand these people. Now it helped him understand himself.

He stirred. Someone was watching him.

He saw his housekeeper standing beside his desk, a tiny woman with a flat face, tangled hair, legs thinner than a man's wrist. She wore yellow cotton trousers rolled up to her knees, a faded yellow blouse that hung open. But there was no sign of a woman there, only a pole of ancient polished wood. The womanly parts had dried up long ago.

Go away, he said. Don't you know I lived half a century without you?

She stood with her arms hanging down to her sides, her eyes fixed on the middle of his forehead. Did she see anything when she stared at him like that? Or had she died at the end of the war as he often suspected, died in a fire bomb raid. So many had died then, almost everyone he knew. When the Americans arrived, there were only two million people living in the charcoal, two million from a city of five million.

He fumbled with the book in his lap, dropped it. A page ripped.

Now look what you've done, Miya. Go away and leave me alone.

You were going to the garden without your hat, she whispered. Without your rubbers.

Father Lamereaux crossed himself. How could he argue with a dead woman? She saw through doors, she saw in the dark. She heard the smallest sound no matter where he was in the house. She had the eyes and ears of a cat and she was always watching him. Listening. Watching. A dead cat.

Miya, leave me at once.

There are visitors.

What? Where?

Here. In the parlor.

Who are they?

Two men. Foreigners.

What do they look like?

Who knows? They all look alike.

But what do they want? Why are they here?

The housekeeper held out a letter. It was written by himself, signed with his name. The letter was addressed to someone named Quin and suggested an hour and a day when this Quin could come to call. The date, in his own hand, showed that he had written the letter several weeks ago.

Father Lamereaux frowned. He had not had a visitor since the war. Who was this man? Why had he come to call? Why had he agreed to let him come to call in the first place?

Father Lamereaux reached out for the sheaf of papers he always kept beside him no matter where he was in the house, whether in his study or his bedroom or the dining room. He never carried them into the parlor, but that was only because he never went into the parlor, because he never had any visitors anymore.

The sheaf of papers was the index to his memoirs, a manuscript on which he had been working for nearly a quarter of a century. The memoirs were not yet finished but the index was complete and up to date. He thumbed through it and found no one by the name of Quin listed there.

I'll tell them you're resting, whispered the housekeeper.

No, don't do that, of course I'll see them. It's just that I can't recall the man's name at the moment.

●

Welcome. It's raining. This house has not seen a caller since the war.

Quin found himself facing a tall, cadaverous priest in his middle seventies. The old man smiled gently. He sat down in a chair with horsehair arms and poured tea from a tray brought by the dwarf who had met them at the door. Quin introduced himself and Big Gobi.

It's raining, repeated Father Lamereaux. Exactly half a century ago I came to Japan on a day much like this. At one time the Emperors of Japan were men of great stature, but all that changed when military dictators seized power and moved the capital to Kamakura. The young Emperor was left behind in Kyoto to barter his autograph for pickles and rice. That was in the thirteenth century. Then in the 1920s I went to Kamakura to study in certain Buddhist temples.

Father Lamereaux unbuttoned his coat. There was something wrong with the movement. Quin looked more closely and saw that the buttons were reversed, buttoning right side over left as with a woman. The priest turned his attention to Big Gobi, who had nervously taken out his small gold cross to polish it on the side of his nose.

Four decades ago, whispered Father Lamereaux, I heard the tale of a cross very much like that one. This other cross was a rare Nestorian Christian relic that had been in the hands of a Malabar trading family for hundreds of years, during which time the family made a fortune in peppercorns. A man named Adzhar married into the family and traveled east with his wife and the cross. Of course Adzhar wasn't his real name, only the name we knew him by. He was a Russian from Georgia and I believe he adopted the name of the province where he had been born. He also died before the war.

Father Lamereaux paused. He looked thoughtful.

I hope we're not disturbing you, said Quin.

Not at all. I was just working on my memoirs as I have been every day for the last quarter of a century. Did you know cannons were placed around the Shinto shrines during the thirties? Decrepit artillery pieces captured from the Russians in 1905?

Father Lamereaux rubbed the horsehair arm of his chair.

An ugly mistake. For me the best years in Japan were the 1920s. I was young and I had just arrived, so everything here appealed to me. My studies were in Kamakura but I came to Tokyo on the weekends, to this very house, which was filled with cats then. In those days Tokyo was constructed entirely of wood and every night there would be a fire within walking distance, the flowers of Tokyo they were called. There's nothing more stimulating than watching a fire when you're young. On Friday nights we had our meetings here, and if we had been to see a fire the discussions we had on *No* drama were always more spirited. Since the war I've been a strict vegetarian, honey and eggs excepted. Rice has a particular effect on the Japanese an hour or two after they've eaten it, which is undoubtedly the principal reason they prefer the out-of-doors.

Quin nodded. He was looking at the legs of Father Lamereaux's chair. They ended in carvings of claws crushing the heads of rodents.

How is your work progressing, Father?

Slowly, a little bit at a time. I want my memoirs to be as nearly perfect as possible. To me it seems unworthy of a human soul to resign itself to imperfection. I think the early fathers made a mistake there, I've always felt it was the Virgin we should be imitating. Christ doubted himself in the end but not the Virgin. We're not enough like her, yet those years in Kamakura were charming all the same. The temples in the hills were beautiful and the views of the sea, the pine groves, the gongs and the rituals and the hours set aside for contemplation. And there was a spring afternoon when I nodded with the flowers while they played the music that had once tempted the sun goddess from her cave, played and also sang the epic of the dragon in a still small voice, a song so strange and soaring it surely was descended from the distant Lapps. A sad tale and yet not so. The shoemaker's son sang it, sang it from his shoemaker's bench. Incredibly, his code name when he was still in the business himself was *The Holy Ghost*. Did you know him? Did you know Elijah or the sun goddess? Did you know Henry Pu Yi?

No, said Quin.

Father Lamereaux leaned forward and rested his long, thin fingers on the stack of papers he had brought with him into the room. The papers were wrinkled and soiled as if often consulted. Slowly, pondering, he ruffled through the stack with his thumb and forefinger. Nothing was written on the papers. They were empty save for the prints of his fingers.

Henry was the last survivor of the Manchu dynasty, whispered the old priest, the last survivor and a very naughty man. We had a chat once, that was when visitors still came to call at this house. For a time he was Emperor of Manchukuo, as the Japanese called the mythical kingdom they pretended they had set up in Manchuria. It didn't last very long, but all the same, Henry was the last Emperor I talked to.

Father, said Quin, it was Geraty who recommended me to you.

The old priest smiled gently.

I see. Well just let me think for a moment, I'm quite certain I can remember him. Names come back to me slowly, but they always come back. Perhaps you could just refresh my memory. What was he doing before the war?

He sold patent drugs. Eventually he left Tokyo and went to Mukden and then to Shanghai.

Mukden and Shanghai? A man who carried a valise for his samples? Yes, I believe I remember him. He came to my Friday night meetings.

Which meetings were those, Father?

The Legion meetings, the Legion of Mary. After the meetings ended there would be a discussion on *No* drama, and if we had happened to have seen a fire earlier in the evening the discussions were exceptionally spirited. I can recall him quite clearly now. He was a spare, large-boned man, very tall and very lanky, quiet, rather pale. Introspective and solemn, sometimes too solemn, I had to warn him not to be morose in his attitude toward religion. After all, it should be a happy part of our lives. Of course he wore stylish suits and flamboyant ties to make himself appear vain and worldly, but that was just to hide the truth about himself. How he suffered, that man. Did you know, by the way, that they placed cannons around the Shinto shrines in the thirties? Decrepit artillery pieces captured from the Russians in 1905?

When did you last see him, Father?

Henry?

No, Geraty.

Oh yes, I see. Well the last time would have been the morning he came here with his valise and was afraid to open it. The day he broke down and cried.

And when was that, Father?

Before the war, naturally. A good thirty years ago. And then before that I had my studies in Kamakura, where the temples in the hills were so beautiful, and the pine groves and the views of the sea, and the gongs and rituals and the hours set aside for contemplation. And then before that in the thirteenth century military dictators seized power and threw the Emperor out in the streets where he had to bugger his autograph and barter his pickle for rice. Since then I've been a strict vegetarian, honey and eggs excepted.

Father?

Henry was the last Emperor I talked to, although of course Manchukuo was only a mythical country. Henry wouldn't admit that naturally, Henry was a very naughty man. But admit it or not, the truth was still the same. There's no escaping the fact that Henry was out in the streets like the rest of us.

●

It took Quin many hours and many trips to the Victorian parlor to gather even a few facts from the old priest, so accustomed had he become to dwelling in the familiar terrain of some faraway kingdom that had long ago become a private domain. But even a few facts were enough to make it clear that Geraty had lied when he claimed he had learned about the espionage network from Father Lamereaux.

The Jesuit had never described the famous picnic on the beach in Kamakura to Geraty, never mentioned Adzhar's name, never told Geraty about the dead-drop device he had invented, never said anything to Geraty about any aspect of the clandestine work in which he was involved.

Yet other parts of Geraty's account were accurate. In fact, there had been a meeting in a Tokyo cemetery one night between Father Lamereaux and a young Japanese army corporal, little more than a boy, who was working for the spy ring as a courier. And the corporal was the same young boy whom Geraty had met earlier in the cemetery, the boy to whom he had given a packet of stolen money in exchange for what he thought would be a valuable cache of pornographic films waiting for him in Mukden. The boy had passed on the money to Father Lamereaux before dropping his trousers and bending over a tombstone to receive the bamboo microfilm device, subsequently traveling to Manchuria where he was caught soon after his arrival in Mukden and beaten to death by the Kempeitai, an incident that had produced the one vague report on the ring to be found in the files of the Kempeitai after the war.

But Father Lamereaux didn't know Geraty had witnessed that scene in the cemetery. He didn't know the source of the money given to him by the corporal. He didn't know Geraty had watched him accept the packet and watched him insert the bamboo device with a deft flickering motion, that he had then fallen asleep listening to Father Lamereaux sing the Litany of the Saints to himself on his knees in the darkness.

On the contrary, it was Geraty who had confessed his secrets over two bottles of Irish whiskey the following day.

The two men first became acquainted when Geraty began attending the Legion meetings the priest held in his home on Friday evenings. Geraty affected the manner and clothes of a successful salesman, but Lamereaux suspected this bluff appearance had nothing to do with his true nature. He soon discovered Geraty was a sensitive man who tormented himself with obscure spiritual concerns that even to a Jesuit seemed remote. Obviously there was a contradiction in his gloomy approach to life. Geraty would never admit it, but the priest felt it had to do with religion. For some reason he sensed that Geraty yearned for a religious vocation yet at the same time could not bring himself to accept his natural inclinations.

Geraty had a great interest in *No* although Lamereaux didn't discover this until the very last time they were together. Lamereaux was the spiritual director of the Tokyo presidium of the Legion of Mary, Geraty became its treasurer. While Lamereaux delivered an exhortation at the Friday night meetings, Geraty passed around under the table the secret-bag for the members' contributions. He then left the house immediately after the meeting, claiming he had work to do. Thus he always missed the discussions on *No* led by Lamereaux.

A regional senatus of the various Asian presidia of the Legion was to be held in Shanghai. Geraty, who said he was due to make a business trip to Shanghai at about that time, was elected to be the Tokyo Legion's delegate to the senatus.

The day before he was scheduled to leave for the mainland he turned up at Lamereaux's house early in the morning. He seemed very agitated. Under his arm was the valise he used to carry his samples. Lamereaux wasn't feeling at all well that day, but when Geraty begged to be allowed to stay for a few hours, to be near a friend as he said, the priest put aside his own concerns to make him welcome.

Geraty drank tea and chewed fistfuls of aspirins. The pain in his face was evident, but it was just as evident that his suffering was more than physical. He was severely troubled.

Lamereaux invited him into the parlor. The moment Geraty laid eyes on the long table at the end of the room, the table where it was his duty to pass the secret-bag to the legionaries on Friday evenings, he buried his head in his hands and began to cry. Lamereaux gently bade him sit down and unburden himself. After sobbing helplessly for ten or fifteen minutes Geraty finally began to whisper.

He spoke first of an inconsequential matter. For some time he had been in the habit of going directly from the Friday night meetings of the Legion to Yoshiwara, the licensed quarter, to proselytize the harlots there. He would stand in the middle of the street facing a row of brothels and deliver a long sermon in a voice loud enough to be heard in every room.

Because he was such a large man, not only a giant but a foreign giant who spoke fluent Japanese, there was considerable curiosity over this spectacle. Often there would be hundreds of faces gazing down at him from the windows. Geraty began his preaching at midnight, when there was more chance the customers would be sleeping and the prostitutes would have time to listen.

Father Lamereaux knew that this was what Geraty had been doing after he left the Friday night meetings of the Legion. Such an activity was too flagrant not to be noticed at once and brought to his attention by his Japanese acquaintances. He had heard about it several years before and he didn't like it. He found it overzealous and unseemly and not at all consonant with Japanese sensibilities. But because it obviously lifted Geraty's spirits he allowed it to continue.

Hesitantly Geraty introduced his subject. He talked about girls from poor families who had to prostitute themselves for money during the first half of the evening and then spend the rest of the night lying beside a snoring man whom they had never seen before and would probably never see again. They were defiled and they knew it. They wanted to be cleansed, but they didn't know how to go about it.

Father Lamereaux listened, fairly certain what would follow. Yet he said nothing. He smiled gently and made no effort to interrupt.

The confession was a long time in coming cut. From midnight until three in the morning Geraty preached to the prostitutes from the street, but as soon as the hour of three was sounded he sneaked around to the back entrances to the brothels, let himself in, and knocked on one door after another, desperately searching for a prostitute whose affections or sympathies he might have aroused with his oratory.

His aims were limited and abject. He wanted to perform cunnilingus on a prostitute, free of charge, at the foot of the bed where her paid customer for the night lay asleep. Geraty could probably have performed this service, without paying, on almost any prostitute in the brothel who was unengaged. Conversely, if he had paid, he could probably have performed it with most of those prostitutes who where engaged but whose partners were already asleep. But Geraty had to have it his own way. The girl's immediate sin had to be evident, and he had to earn her redemption with his eloquence and his apparent conviction.

In the alleys behind the brothels Geraty shuffled his feet, stated his case, and begged for forgiveness. He had spoken forcefully during his three hours in the street, and more than once he was accepted.

When a prostitute agreed he locked the door behind him, got down on all fours and listened to her customer snoring only a few feet away, then insisted she stand over him and quietly insult him while he was at work.

When he had finished he carried her to the large Japanese bath on the premises, locked the door once more, and elaborately washed the girl, using an excessive amount of soap. He dried her and washed her again, using an even larger amount of soap, washed her tenderly a third time, and dried her tenderly a third time. After the third drying he was careful not to touch her with his bare hands. He put on gloves that he had brought with him in his valise and sprayed her with perfume that he had also brought with him in his valise.

Finally he carried her back to her bed and tucked her in beside her snoring, unsuspecting customer. He thanked her with tears and smiles and several quotations from the first chapter of St. Luke before proceeding down the corridor to knock on the next door.

Geraty continued in this manner as long as no hint of light showed through the rice paper sliding doors that served as windows. A peculiarity of this rite carried out under cover of darkness was that he remained fully dressed in his stylish suits and flamboyant neckties, never removing anything even while splashing water and soap over himself and the prostitutes in the bath. The result was that he was thoroughly soaked by the time dawn came.

He always walked home from the brothels as the sun came up, and this meant a perpetual cold in the winter, often amounting to mild pneumonia, and at the very least an annoying catarrhal condition throughout the rest of the year.

Geraty finished the description of his Friday nights in Yoshiwara with a grimace. He was even more agitated than when he had stepped into the Victorian parlor. Father Lamereaux was gently whispering a few consoling words about favors freely given and freely received when Geraty suddenly leapt to his feet. He snatched up his valise, couldn't work the fasteners, sobbed compulsively, and ripped apart the sturdy metal locks with his hands.

The priest knew they were now getting down to the real purpose of Geraty's visit.

●

The valise contained a map of Mukden, a thick wad of colorful neckties, and two unopened bottles of Irish whiskey. Without a word Geraty swung one of the bottles against the table, breaking off its neck. His hands were shaking so badly there was no other way he could have opened the bottle. He took a long drink and passed the bottle to Father Lamereaux.

For an hour or two they drank in silence. Geraty was apparently transfixed by what he had to say. He was paralyzed, an animal facing a torch in the dark.

As for Lamereaux, there was nothing he could be told that would surprise him. He had known suffering himself, but he also knew it wouldn't make any difference for him to say this. He was there to listen, to try to help his friend to speak. Eventually he thought of a way to relieve the tension that was growing more profound between them as time went on.

The priest got to his feet and assumed a pose from a *No* play. He moved from that pose into another, a complex transition that required complete concentration. Geraty studied the movement, he considered it as Lamereaux held the pose, stiff and rigid, not one muscle contracting or expanding.

To anyone who understood *No* such finality and decision could not go unanswered. To his surprise Lamereaux saw Geraty getting to his feet and working himself into a pose from a different *No* play. It was the first time he had known that Geraty was also a devotee of *No*, an expert fully as skilled as he was. This information amazed and delighted him, for he knew there was now a way for him to help his tormented friend. So powerful was the discipline of *No* that it could contain any emotion no matter how painful, no matter how seemingly unbearable.

Lamereaux watched Geraty shift his pose. The giant sat down and the priest stood. The afternoon wore on. At some point they drained the first bottle of Irish whiskey and started on the second.

Night fell. The silent scenes from hundreds of *No* plays followed one upon another.

Late that evening the two actors broke into tears over the unparalleled performance they had staged together that day. Since early morning neither of them had spoken a word. Instead they had communicated through the abrupt, austere attitudes of their arms, their hands, their bodies. Even without masks they had completely understood each other.

Geraty had confessed utterly to stealing all the funds from the secret-bag of the Tokyo presidium of the Legion of Mary.

Lamereaux had reassured him by noting that St. Brigid in her charity had worked a miracle for him, had showed her love for him by already redressing his wrong, for just that previous night a young legionary, wishing to make a last significant contribution before going abroad with the army, had unexpectedly provided a large donation to the secret-bag that easily made up for the missing sum.

And so they embraced and wept and prepared to ᵧ ᵣt. As drunk, as Geraty murmured, as two butterflies circling a candle. For they were exiles far from home and war was coming.

At the end, at the door, they were crying in each other's arms. It was then that the Jesuit whispered into his friend's ear the opening line of the prayer that had sealed the meetings of the Legion and sealed as well Geraty's stolen secret-bag.

Magnificat anima mea Dominum.

Remember it, whispered Father Lamereaux, for in those words you will find an end to your suffering. In them you will find what you seek within yourself just as the Savior was found within the womb of mankind. Go now and remember.

Geraty lurched away from the door knowing that he would remember, knowing also that he would never dare face Lamereaux again because the lesson he had learned that day was to be the travail of his life.

Thus he remembered the words when he escaped to Mukden to acquire a cache of worthless films and again when he escaped to Shanghai, there to undress nightly in a locked, shuttered room while projecting his worthless films on the wall, rendering himself naked night after night as he silently repeated the phrase he had learned at Lamereaux's table, on Lamereaux's motionless *No* stage, the words that were aged in two bottles of Irish whiskey and spun through the magic lamp of a battered Shanghai movie machine thirty years before they led him to his vocation, *my soul doth magnify the Lord.*

●

Again it's raining, whispered Father Lamereaux. Until you came no one had visited this house since the war, and now you've come many times. My housekeeper goes out to do the shopping but I never leave, I stay here and work on my memoirs. Occasionally I sit in the garden, but only when it's warm and only when it's not raining. Are you familiar with the Peram?

No, said Quin.

They're a tribe in central Borneo that has a necronym system. When a man's grandfather dies, for example, the man takes the name *Grandfather Dead.* He keeps that name until another male relative dies, a cousin say, and then he becomes *Cousin Dead.* This continues until he has a son, then his name changes to *Father of So-and-so.* But naturally the son's name will be *Uncle Dead* or some such thing. Thus we find that the brother of the dead man is called *Father of Uncle Dead.* It's an odd way for a man to remember his brother. At first it seems unduly complicated and roundabout for such simple tribesmen. It suggests, in fact, that relationships between people are more complex than we often suspect. It leads one to the conclusion that simple acts may not be simple. That where God's children are concerned, that can never be.

Father Lamereaux rubbed the horsehair arm of the chair. Quin nodded to himself and finally asked the question he had waited so long to ask.

Father, what does the name Quin mean to you?

The old Jesuit sighed.

Yes, I see. I've been thinking about it myself and it seems I'm not quite sure. It seems I've been alone in this house a very long time. This morning, or perhaps it was yesterday or several weeks ago, I looked through the index to my memoirs to see if I could find the name, and it wasn't there. Is that possible? I'm afraid it is, and now I don't know what to tell you.

The priest unbuttoned his coat the wrong way. He stirred. Some image had passed before his eyes.

The first time you came here, he whispered slowly, you had a friend with you who was wearing a small gold cross similar to the one that belonged to Adzhar. He was a most unusual man, Adzhar, he was a man of many surprises. What was the name of your friend? Ordos? Tarim?

No. Gobi.

Yes I see, the desert Adzhar crossed on his way here. Well there's no mistaking it then. Forty years later we have the same three names again, we have Adzhar and we have Gobi and we have Quin. Was he a relative of yours, that other Quin?

He was my father.

I see. I never knew about you, but then I knew very little about his personal life.

Where did you meet him?

Someplace. I can't really recall.

Could it have been at a picnic?

It certainly might have been at a picnic. Adzhar and Lotmann and I used to enjoy having picnics at Kamakura. The pine groves in the hills above the sea are beautiful there.

Father, could this picnic have been by the sea? On a beach near the estate of Baron Kikuchi?

Baron Kikuchi? Which Baron Kikuchi? The first or the second?

The one who was important in the secret police. The Kempeitai, was it called?

It was, whispered Father Lamereaux. Indeed it was.

And could there have been four of you at the picnic? You
and Adzhar and my father and one other? Three of you
wearing gas masks?

Father Lamereaux sighed.

Gas masks, he repeated gently. The Father and the Son
and the Holy Ghost in gas masks. What a curious scene to
remember after all these years.

●

A clear autumn day. The year was 1929. Father Lamereaux had completed his Buddhist studies in Kamakura
and was preparing to move back to Tokyo. Adzhar suggested a picnic and they walked together to the beach.
Lamereaux expected to find Lotmann waiting for them
there, but instead they were greeted by a couple, a young
man and woman, Americans.

Adzhar introduced the couple. The man's name was
Quin. His wife was called Maeve.

Actually Father Lamereaux had met the woman once
before under quite different circumstances. But either he
had forgotten what those circumstances were or else he
chose not to discuss them now, with her son, after all
these years.

It was apparent to Quin that the priest hadn't liked
Maeve. It seemed their previous encounter had left him
with the impression that she was hard and unsympathet-
ic, excessive in some unexplained way, too willful perhaps.

In any case, when they were introduced that day on the
beach the priest pretended it was the first time they had
met. She did the same. Neither Adzhar nor her husband
said anything, so it was unlikely that either one of them
was aware that they already knew each other.

The gas masks were Adzhar's idea. There was no one
within a thousand yards of them, but Adzhar said that
didn't matter. The secret police might be using deaf

people to read lips through binoculars. He had known that to happen elsewhere, he said, and they couldn't afford to have anyone overhear the conversation they were to have that afternoon.

Quin agreed and the three men put on the gas masks Adzhar had seen fit to bring with him in his picnic basket. Maeve laid out the food but took no part in the discussion.

Adzhar began by saying he wanted to help but he knew he was too old for this kind of work. He had come only to make the introductions and offer advice, should any be needed. He then turned to Quin and asked Quin to explain.

Quin talked about Japan and Japanese politics, about the way the military was beginning to take over the country. In a very few years they would be ready to move into Manchuria, and after that they would attack the rest of China. War was inevitable, there was no escaping it, but a great many lives could be saved if the war were shortened. That could be done by sending information to China. Quin had sources who could provide the information. What he needed was a courier system that could secretly transport microfilm to the mainland.

Father Lamereaux was known to have many young Japanese friends who trusted him and would do what he asked. For the good of both the Japanese and the Chinese people would he take on the task of establishing a courier system?

The alleviation of suffering was Lamereaux's vocation. He agreed at once to do what he could. Quin spent the rest of the afternoon explaining the methods they would use.

The information would be turned over to Lamereaux coded, on microfilm, along with instructions on where it was to be delivered in either Mukden or Shanghai. For safety Lamereaux would deal only with Quin, the couriers only with Lamereaux. Quin wouldn't know who the couriers were, Lamereaux wouldn't know the sources from whom Quin obtained his information.

The couriers would deliver the microfilm to places, not people, also for safety. At a certain hour on a certain day the capsule would be wedged behind the mirror in the toilet of a restaurant in Mukden. Or it would be taped under the lid of the water cabinet in the toilet of a bar in Shanghai. There would also be capsules that had to be retrieved in either Mukden or Shanghai and brought back to Tokyo.

The afternoon came to an end. The picnic was over. Young Quin said the only thing left to do was to give their network a code name.

Adzhar spoke up with a smile.

I've done nothing at all here today, he said. At least let me offer a suggestion for that. Don't you think *Gobi* would do nicely?

The three men shook hands and took off their gas masks.

●

Toilets, whispered Father Lamereaux, always toilets. The result of the device I developed for the couriers. All systems have definitions, even the vegetarian system, honey and eggs excepted.

Quin nodded.

Father, did you know that Geraty claims he found a report on the network in the Kempeitai files after the war?

Geraty? Alive after the war? I thought he died in Shanghai.

No, he escaped to the Philippines and later came back here to take a job in the Occupation.

And he's still alive?

Yes.

It's hard to believe. I didn't think anybody was still alive.

But, Father, I don't understand. Geraty destroyed the report so the Americans wouldn't see it, and the Americans had just finished fighting Japan. Why keep it from them?

From them or anybody, what does it matter now? The action in a *No* play occurs when no one is moving. The past reduces emperors to pickles who bugger and barter. Once there was rice beside the road where now there is only a forgotten signature fading on withered parchment, a lost sign on a wayside of the thirteenth century. The 1920s were the best years for me, before all this happened. They played the beautiful music for me then, music so rare it tempted the sun goddess from her cave, played and sang in the still small voice of a shoemaker's son, sang at the shoemaker's bench the epic of a dragon descended from the Lapps. I had my cats and the flowers of Tokyo, but in the 1930s they placed cannons around the shrines, they ignored the effect rice has on the bowels and went to war, and soon the flowers were gone and my cats were gone and the Legion was gone. Did you know Elijah? Did you know the sun goddess or the shoemaker's son? They were gone and there were no more Friday nights. Everything I had ever known was gone.

The old priest turned. He stared at the rain running down the windows.

I could no longer meet the legionaries here, it wasn't safe for them. I had to meet them one at a time for a minute or two behind a tombstone. I had to sneak back and forth through the city, evaporate and materialize, die in doorways and resurrect myself in the moonlight of a cemetery. There seemed to be only one thing to do, so I did it. I became a ghost. And Quin became a ghost as well. The idealist became violent and unsure of himself, I could see it in his eyes. You don't understand, you say?˙ No matter now. There's nothing to understand anymore.

Father Lamereaux rose. He gazed at the windows.

How did it end, Father?

End? How can there be an end when Our Lady's reign is forever? As for Quin, he went to Shanghai and never came back.

When?

Just before total war began, but in retrospect who can say? Artillery pieces were placed around the Shinto shrines in 1905.

Is there someone who might know what happened to him?

There was a woman who once played a thousand-year-old *koto* with indescribable tenderness across the hours of a spring afternoon in Kamakura. She might have been in Shanghai then, I'm not sure. I'll give you her name.

No one else?

Father Lamereaux moved into the hall. He opened the front door and held out his hand. He wrote on a piece of paper, then stared at the drops of rain in his palm. Deep scars formed around his eyes.

In Tsukiji, he whispered. A gangster. Good-bye.

The door closed. Quin moved up the street in the rain reading the piece of paper. On one side *Mama, The Living Room,* an address. On the other side no address, a name, *Kikuchi-Lotmann.*

Kikuchi-Lotmann must be the gangster in Tsukiji, the fish market district of Tokyo. Mama must be the woman who had been in Shanghai. Beside the names two arrows were drawn pointing in opposite directions.

The rain came down and Quin watched the Emperor's autograph dissolve in his fingers.

●

Miya sat in the kitchen slicing turnips. The shopkeepers in the neighborhood, who knew nothing of her forebears, assumed that tuberculosis had stunted her growth as a child and made her into a dwarf. But that wasn't true. The men in her family had been tiny for generations, and they had always been careful to choose tiny women to bear their sons. They were *No* actors who specialized in the difficult role of the princess.

In the tradition of a family devoted to *No,* these severely disciplined men passed their stage name down from one generation to the next. Miya's father had been the thirteenth actor to use it. Thus when she was born in 1905 the stern old man barely noted the fact. He had dedicated his life to *No* and there were no roles on the stage for women.

At the age of sixteen Miya ran away from her home in

Kyoto to marry a painter, an act of abandon that gave her the only moments of happiness she was ever to know in life. Romantically she thought she might become a painter like him in the Western style, using oils rather than charcoal, but as it turned out her young husband never had time to teach her. He was dying and her escape ended within the year. She returned home with the two gifts love had given her, a child and tuberculosis.

Her father wouldn't forgive her act of disobedience but he embraced his grandson, who he assumed would someday be the fourteenth actor in the family to bear the traditional name. Her father stopped speaking to her and never entered her room. A servant brought her meals. From her bed she could hear the old man and her son playing together.

When the boy was a little older her father got him admitted to the Peers' School in Tokyo. At the same time he was enrolled in a *No* theater in Tokyo to receive his initial training.

Miya objected to him being sent so far away, but her objections meant nothing. As she expected, his busy schedule kept him away from Kyoto for all but a few days out of every year. And even when he did come home he spent most of his time away from the house with his grandfather.

As he grew older he was increasingly ill at ease in her presence. He was silent and even sullen, as if embarrassed to be with her. She knew this was because she had always been sick and had never been able to be a mother to him. She also knew this couldn't be helped, but that didn't lessen the bitterness she felt toward the course life had taken.

Her father died suddenly one winter, and to her surprise Miya found herself relieved, perhaps even secretly pleased. Despite her sickness her son would now have to turn to her because she was all he had.

She wrote him a long letter praising his talents and talking about the future. With the letter she sent a small childish self-portrait done by her dead husband, the only memento she had from that short period in her life when both sickness and her son had come to her. The painting had hung by her bed since her husband's death, so she was quite sure her son would understand what she meant by sending it to him.

A few days later she received a telegram from her son's school saying he had disappeared upon learning of his grandfather's death. He had not received her letter. She sent a telegram to his theater and learned that he had not been seen there either.

Miya left her bed and took a train to Tokyo. Her son's classmates could tell her nothing, but at the theater she was given the name of a foreigner, a *No* scholar who had apparently befriended her son. Several hints or suggestions accompanied the information, but Miya was too agitated to hear them.

She went to the address she had been given and found a large Victorian house. The sun had already set. In her confusion she forgot to knock on the door.

Although ice covered the windows the house was insufferably hot, so hot she almost fainted when she stepped into the scene being enacted in the oppressive heat of that Victorian parlor, in near darkness, the outside world invisible beyond the frosted windowpanes.

A tall thin man floated between the pieces of stiff furniture, drifted across the floor in the wavering light of a single candle. He was toying with the folds of his formal kimono, a costume worn by virgins in *No* plays, and toying with the plaits of a black lacquered wig that only partially covered the wisps of graying hair flying in front of his face.

The shadowy figure held a whiskey bottle in one hand, a fan in the other. As he danced around the room he used the fan to reveal his genitals, which were fully exposed through the open kimono.

Near him on a horsehair couch, his middle raised by silk pillows, the candle resting on his belly, lay her son, naked and giggling.

Miya reached the door, the cold air, the icy wind.

Somehow she made her way out of the neighborhood before she collapsed. She was found that night in a snowdrift and taken to a hospital. Weeks later she learned from one of her son's classmates that he had gone to work briefly in a factory that manufactured military overcoats. When he was fired for incompetence he had lied about his age and gone into the army under a false name.

That was in 1935. In 1937, while serving as a corporal in a film unit near Mukden, he was arrested as a spy and beaten to death by the Kempeitai.

Miya had to sell her father's house and her father's valuable collection of *No* masks to pay for her long convalescence. When her disease at last subsided she managed to find a job with the army. She was trained as a film projectionist at a base near Tokyo. The general at the base was a follower of *No* who made her his private projectionist as soon as he discovered the identity of her father. The general was transferred to China and killed, Miya went to work for another general who was transferred to China and killed, then for a third general who was transferred to China and killed. At the end of the war she was working for General Tojo, the Prime Minister who was soon to be hanged as a war criminal.

The winter evening the wind drove her away from the Victorian parlor Miya thought she was entering a Buddhist hell, an infernal, suffocating vision where angry demons forever tortured their victims. She had been a victim before, she was a victim again.

Yet the demons of legend always wore fierce masks. They grimaced and scowled, while the face in the candlelight of the Victorian parlor had been gently smiling, smiling so gently she was curiously reminded in time not of the hate she had felt that night, before she collapsed in the snowdrift, but of the love she had lost in life, all the love she had never known.

During the war as she moved from one tiny cubicle to another the memory of the face in the candlelight was always with her, an expression beyond her comprehension, the mystery of a *No* mask that was not a mask.

And it was still with her in the winter of 1945 when she retraced her steps one night through the ruined city, hungry and cold and alone, making her way back through the snow to the Victorian house eight years after the death of her son, returning to the man who had destroyed him, the only person who had existed for her in the world.

She didn't knock at the door, perhaps because that was the way it had been the other time. But if she had knocked no one would have heard her, for Father Lamereaux was not only alone but unconscious.

She found him on the floor of a back room where he had fallen, delirious and starving. The windows had been open since the previous autumn. Snow blew across the room and piled up in the corners. The thin cotton kimono the priest wore was stiff with frozen vomit and excrement.

Miya covered him with blankets and covered the windows. She heated the room and made a bed for him on the floor, for even though he was a skeleton she was still too small to move him. She sold a piece of furniture and bought medicine. She washed him and dressed him and called in a doctor to give him injections. The doctor told her what to feed him and she prepared it.

Twenty years went by.

Sometimes she was still frightened by the strange love she felt for this aging foreigner who had locked himself behind the darkness and doors of his years. But despite the corridors and eras that separated him from her, he needed her all the same, she knew that. She had saved him once and now she went on saving him, telling him what to do and when to do it, not letting him drink whiskey or eat the foods that upset his stomach, keeping him away from the garden when it was raining.

Long ago her orders had become a habit to him. In twenty years he had not once ventured beyond the grounds of the house.

To Miya this was proof above all else that she had at last succeeded in finding someone to love and serve. For in the end that was the only meaning she had been able to discover in the mysteriously gentle smile from the candle-light, that love was so fleeting a hope it had to be trapped like the expression on a mask and imprisoned.

So she kept watch. She guarded the house and the garden.

A footfall. The door. In the kitchen Miya abruptly raised her head, a movement so commanding it might have been perfected by her fathers, those tiny determined men who for thirteen generations had pursued the role of the princess.

●

Father Lamereaux stood in the middle of the parlor with his back to the windows. His gaze fell on the long table where the Legion had met, on the formal chairs, on the horsehair couch. Miya watched him.

Master?

He turned, looking over her head.

Has he left?

Who?

The visitor.

Yes, he's left.

Did he disturb you?

Father Lamereaux didn't answer.

Would you like to rest?

No. As a matter of fact I want you to go shopping. I've decided I'll have raw tuna for dinner. And rice and the best pickles and whiskey. Irish whiskey.

Why, master?

Father Lamereaux drew himself up. He clasped his hands behind his back and glared over the head of the little woman who was not half his height.

Why? What do you mean why? Those are my instructions. I used to enjoy life and now I want to enjoy it again. Do as I say.

Tuna fish is bad for you, master.

What do I care about that? I'll do what I want. Now go

and buy the whiskey and bring it to me in the garden. You'll find me sitting in the rain beside the patch of moss, but don't interrupt me. Just bring the bottle and a glass and leave me alone.

There are turnips for dinner, master. I'll bring tea to your study.

He watched her leave. Stiffly, slowly, he crossed the room and went into his study. Books were piled up all over his desk. Books and the thick sheaf of papers he called the index to his memoirs. A thick sheaf of blank papers.

Did anyone know that he wasn't really writing his memoirs? That he'd never written a word of them?

No. She knew but of course no one else did. No one else knew anything about his life since the war.

Once, not long after his release from internment in the mountains, he had thought of leaving Japan, Tokyo, this house, leaving everything behind and returning to Canada. He had thought of it for an hour or a day or a year but then he had decided it was already too late. Time moved in epochs and there were no hours or days or years in the life he had lived. He had loved his cats and the flowers of Tokyo, he had loved his legionaries, and now there was nothing left for him but the solitary empire where they roamed as ghosts.

He looked at the windows. The rain was still coming down. He opened the volume that lay in front of him and saw that a page was torn. That wouldn't do.

He turned more pages. They were all torn. That wouldn't do at all.

After dinner he sat in his study repairing books, patiently holding each page in place until the glue cemented itself. He seldom slept anymore. Often he sat up until dawn. So it was late that night, even later than usual, before his memories finally collapsed and led him into despair.

As always he was silent and rigid at that moment. So silent and rigid that even the woman who thought she loved him, who did love him cruelly as best she could, would never have suspected that the cry within him then was rising to a scream.

MAMA

·

4

Life is brief and we must listen to every sound.

●

High above Tokyo, Mama sat in her apartment painting her fingernails. Twenty-four floors below lay the Imperial palace, the swans in the Imperial moat little white dots, the pines on the Imperial slopes no bigger than bonsai. As with the aristocrats of old, she kept her nails long to show that manual labor was beneath her. Mama had last cut her nails in 1938 prior to the labor that brought forth her second son.

It was late morning and Mama had just taken her fifth bath of the day. No matter how late she stayed at her nightclub, Mama always rose at six o'clock in the morning to take her first bath. Then she breakfasted on tea and three raw oysters and arranged herself in front of the window, on a raised dais in the shape of a lotus that sat on the back of an ivory elephant.

Her posture was one of contemplation. Her legs were crossed, with the ankles tucked over the knees. Her hands assumed the attitude of the fist of knowledge.

This *mudra* was Mama's favorite when facing the rising sun. The right hand was curled, with thumb touching forefinger, as if ready to grasp a cylindrical object. The left hand was held directly below, the thumb clasped by the three lower fingers, the forefinger pointing rigidly in the air. When all was in order the forefinger of the left hand slid up into the slot of the right hand.

The cosmic soul enclosed the individual soul, the sun

105

rose in the sky. Thus did she come to terms with the dawning day.

The fist of knowledge also had erotic connotations. The left forefinger that rose with the new sun could be interpreted as a *lingam*, the receptive palm or sky of the right hand as a *yoni*. But Mama was not one to question an ancient Tantric stylization. If the sexual act occurred during meditation, so much the better.

There was another reason why the fist of knowledge appealed to her. In that *mudra* the five senses of the left hand rose and found themselves completed by the sixth sense of the right hand. Physical nature entered into gnosis.

Or in everyday language, the woman took the position above, the man below. Over a period of years Mama had found that men grow heavy. The woman above, the man below, was a pleasing concept to her as well as a comfortable position.

Or as Lao-tzu had said, *seize the way that was so you may ride the things that are now.*

Or in everyday terms, choose the position of childbirth. The woman straddles the man so the manchild can be born, which is what the saga meant when he advised seizing the way that was. When the woman rides on top there will be a spurt of new life, for the couple at that moment is following the way of wisdom.

Complex metaphysical subjects. Mama would not have bothered with them had she considered herself an ordinary woman. As she looked down on the Imperial palace she recalled the words of the ancient Chinese chroniclers, the graybeards of the Han dynasty.

East and south of Korea there lies a kingdom known as Wa. The people are much given to strong drink, respect is shown by squatting. The men tattoo their faces and adorn their bodies with designs, the size and pattern indicating their rank in society.

And as the later graybeards of the Wei dynasty had remarked, *the curious kingdom of Wa is a queen country, curiously ruled by a queen.*

Now Mama was tattooed from neck to ankle and had been since she was a child, so who was to say? It might be that the curious kingdom of Wa had been ruled by one hundred and twenty-four successive generations of male emperors, but the curious question remained, who had ruled curiously in the beginning?

In any case temporal history interested Mama less than spiritual, and the religious situation was much clearer. After years of meditation she could not deny that she and the Kannon Buddha had certain characteristics in common.

First, the Kannon was the only woman in the crowded pantheon of male Buddhism, just as Mama was the only woman who had ever worked in a brothel in Kobe without subsequently getting married. Second, like that goddess, she always followed the path of compassion and mercy.

Among the many males there were chanting and silent Buddhas, laughing and crying Buddhas, Buddhas for every purpose and occasion. But among all the confusing statues to be found in the temples of Japan there was only one woman, and she alone seemed to have a distinct personality.

Of course Mama had never actually seen a statue of the Kannon using the fist of knowledge. But as everyone knew, the statues had all been carved by men. What would have happened if women had been allowed to join the carvers' guild? Would the Kannon always be shown with open hands, passive and accepting?

In addition to the fist of knowledge Mama used twelve other *mudras.*

Sincerity.
The empty heart.
The unopened lotus.
The newly opened lotus.
Intentions clearly made known.
Holding one's water.
Seeking refuge.
The backhand or hindside.

The difficult back to back.

The equally difficult position of middles touching while the rest is held apart and erect.

The variation where middles touch with both hands on their backs.

The final position where both rest in the clasp of covering hands.

One *mudra*, in short, for each stage of the sexual act.

Mama sat on her ivory elephant contemplating the sky until eight o'clock. By then the sun had risen high enough to establish the pattern of the day. She then took a bath every hour on the hour until noon, when she lunched on tea and six raw oysters. Prior to her afternoon meditation she took another bath. At six in the evening she took her eighth and final bath before changing into an evening kimono and going to her nightclub.

One measure of her influence in Japan was her apartment, the only one in the skyscraper where she lived. The Imperial chamberlains had objected strenuously to a skyscraper beside the Imperial moat, and the only way it got built was through a promise that the building would be used strictly for offices, that it would always be empty at night.

The chamberlains felt that the Emperor, although not a god since the end of the war, still deserved some privacy at night. At the beginning of the century, after all, there had been one hundred and thirty-four living gods registered with the relevant ministry in Peking, and of these only the Japanese Emperor still survived as an institution.

Mama had used her business connections to make an exception of herself. Because there could be no lights in the skyscraper after dark, her apartment was furnished with infrared lighting invisible to the naked eye. From below, the immense tower looked deserted but high on the twenty-fourth floor, unknown to the twelve million inhabitants of Tokyo, a small elderly woman in infrared goggles watched over them. Every night she smiled benignly down on the world's largest city as she ate her last meal of the day, tea and twelve raw oysters.

●

Although she was today the most powerful woman in Japan, life had not begun easily for her. She had been born to a peasant couple in the Tohoku, the poor northern district of Japan. Each year thereafter her parents had another child whom they suffocated at birth, the regular practice among farmers living in poverty. Mama was eight years old when the silk market in America collapsed for a season, leaving her parents no choice but to sell her to a brothel.

A house in the licensed quarter of Kobe offered the highest sum, and that was where she went. Her father blamed her mother for the silk disaster in America, since her mother was an Ainu and therefore of Caucasian origin. Before he went off to drink at night he beat her as hard as he could.

The year Mama left home a son was born to the couple. They kept him because their daughter was gone. After the war this man, who had the body hair of his mother, confessed a long list of crimes to Geraty, a heinous record of torture and arson, killing and sexual perversion that stretched from Siberia to Mukden to Shanghai and up the valley of the Yangtze, that included among many atrocities the murder of Miya's son and the murder of the Japanese General responsible for the rape of Nanking. It was from him that Geraty stole the military greatcoat he was wearing the night he first met Quin, not by accident, in the bar in the Bronx once owned by Geraty's father.

As for Mama, she never knew she had a brother, neither then nor years later when the night came for him to murder both her surviving son and Hato, the freighter passenger on the Pacific crossing who had worn a false moustache and false sideburns and so angrily kept the secret of his shoeboxes from Quin and Big Gobi.

Although she was only eight years old when she went to the house in Kobe, Mama soon came to know the customs of the world from the sailors who passed through that busy port. Throughout her childhood she was tattooed a part at a time, as was customary at the beginning of the century for Japanese children entering a serious life of prostitution or crime.

When puberty came her body was entirely covered with tattoos with the exception of her face and her hands and feet. The tattoos recounted the epic story of a dragon. The dragon's tail curled around her waist, its fiery breath licked her stomach, its tongue forked into her crotch, its eyes peered from her nipples.

On her backside, in even more terrifying guises, the theme was repeated with variations.

Thus when a visiting knight sagged in bed, thinking he had met the challenge and triumphed, slain the dragon and earned a night's sleep, Mama had but to whisper to him in the candlelight to prove that facts were always illusionary when compared to myths.

Turn me over, she suggested.

And sure enough, as soon as the tired warrior turned her over the dangers of the night returned and he was faced with a whole new saga of battles and miracles.

The dragon tattoo was a masterpiece, the most intricate anybody had ever seen. Her epic became legendary in the ports of Asia and soon she was in great demand.

In particular she appealed to opium addicts, who were convinced they would never be able to make love to a woman again. But Mama showed them there could be more to puffing the magic dragon than they had ever suspected.

Mama worked first in the Chinese wing of the brothel, since the Chinese were not only the principal opium addicts but also the principal seducers of virgins. The older Chinese men, bent on deflowering the world now that they had reached an advanced age, would pay almost any price if they thought they were getting a virgin. Being small, Mama was able to serve this lust in the Chinese wing for several years.

From there, for seasoning, she was sent to the Korean wing with its rich smells of garlic and fermenting cabbage, then back to the sailors' section to relearn any of the international traits she might have forgotten from her childhood.

Lastly, sixteen years old and fully experienced in all carnal matters, she was certified an apprentice Japanese woman and allowed to enter the Japanese wing on trial.

Mama studied fortune-telling, music, conversation, and especially the match-stick games with which Japanese men were sexually aroused. She learned to arrange stones, to pour water over tea, to fold a piece of paper into the shape of a crane. In return she was given diamonds and emeralds and cameras, which were just then being developed.

When she was twenty she bought her way out of the brothel and established herself as an official second wife available by the year, month, week, or half-hour. Over the following four years an astonishing number of Japan's future leaders passed her way, including, one weekend, an entire graduating class from Tokyo University that eventually produced three prime ministers, forty suicides, and the postwar head of the Communist party.

In 1929, at the age of twenty-four, she finally decided to stabilize her life by forming a permanent liaison. Because of the growing influence of the army in the country, she chose an army general, a man who happened to be not only wealthy but an aristocrat as well.

●

Baron Kikuchi's fortune came from his large landholdings in the Tohoku, the same northern district where Mama had been born in poverty. He was the younger of twin sons, born eight minutes after his brother, so the barony had not originally been his. But when his elder brother converted to Judaism after the First World War, he inherited the title.

The twin boys never knew their father, a famous statesman in the middle of the nineteenth century who was one of the leaders of the Meiji Restoration, the movement that overthrew the military dictatorship that had governed Japan for two and a half centuries and returned the

Emperor to power. The old Baron, a close friend of the Emperor Meiji, was instrumental in opening the country to Western ways. In fact, he was so involved with modernizing the country he didn't marry until his eighty-eighth year, whereupon he fathered twins and died.

The twins were raised by their mother, a gentle, strong-willed aristocrat sixty-four years younger than her famous husband. Unlike him, she took no interest in ships or railroads or Western education. She preferred to occupy herself with the traditional arts, painting and tea ceremony and the *koto* or Japanese harp, and especially with the intricacies of *Go*, an unusual avocation for a woman since the ancient game had military overtones and was always played by men.

During their early years the twins were educated at home on the estate owned by their ancestors since the thirteenth century, another famous statesman in the family having gone to the aid of the warriors in Kamakura at that time and received land in the north as a reward. But although the estate was large and the family's wealth great, the twins and their mother lived austerely in keeping with the practice of the northern Japanese.

Their house was small. Their two or three servants lived with them more like aunts and uncles than retainers. The scroll on the wall might be the gift of an emperor, the *Go* set in the cupboard might be the work of a master craftsman who had made no more than eight such sets in his career, the *koto* in the closet might be a thousand years old, the bowls used in the tea ceremony might be so exquisitely turned as to be of inestimable value.

Yet the room where the scroll was hung, where the *koto* was laid out in the mornings and the *Go* set in the evenings, where the Baroness performed the tea ceremony for her sons every day at sunset, was a small room made of wood and straw and rice paper, as severe in line and simple in design as that of any peasant living on their lands.

And so with the other rooms in the house, with the bare corridors and the plain entrance and the narrow garden where one weathered stone lantern received the blossoms of the fruit trees in spring, the hard sun in summer, the Siberian gales in autumn, and the heavy snows in winter.

The effect the Baroness had on her sons was lasting, particularly the strength they felt in her presence.

From the Baroness the elder twin acquired his passion for painting, to which he devoted the first half of his life, and his love for the *koto*, which was his principal form of relaxation after he returned from Jerusalem as a rabbi.

From her knowledge of the game of *Go* the younger twin evolved his fascination with military maneuvering, while it was the rigorous discipline of her tea ceremony that proved to be his only escape, later in life, from the massive headaches that tormented him.

So excruciating were those headaches they would have made invalids of most men. And in fact when the General eventually revealed the cause of the headaches to Mama, a secret known only to his brother and to a doctor long since dead, he confessed that he would probably have committed suicide years before had it not been for a memory he carried within him, a vision of his mother turning a teacup three times at sunset, gently brushing the green tea into foam, her face utterly calm and at peace.

It was the memory of those moments that gave him the will to live through the attacks that were so blinding they seemed to be the lightning of death itself, an ultimate pain most men might experience only once in their lives but which the General knew would be back with him the next day and the next, next week and next month, a daily ritual of torture and execution that humbled him under a sword and hewed his mind.

The twins grew older, the time came for them to receive their formal education. Together they traveled south, the elder to study fine arts in Kyoto, the younger to enter the military academy. When the younger brother received his commission in the army, the two returned to the Tohoku to spend the holiday with their mother. It was toward the end of the holiday that she died, to them, unexpectedly.

It happened at sunset. The Baroness was performing the tea ceremony as always at that hour, the sliding doors open to the warm summer air. She prepared their bowls and then her own, turned it three times in her hand, sipped, stopped moving.

Three or four minutes went by. Simultaneously the twins rose and knelt beside her. Her eyes were open, her face was calm, the bowl rested in her cupped hands. She was gazing across the garden but she was dead.

That evening the servants told them the truth. Since before her marriage the Baroness had been suffering from an internal disease that kept her in constant pain. She had never told her husband or her sons about the disease because nothing could be done about it. The disease was incurable and in the end would be fatal.

As the twins made arrangements for the funeral of the Baroness they pondered this last lesson of hers, the mystery of pain and peace in life, the manner in which one might overcome the other, a mystery the elder of the two would one day penetrate, the younger never.

After the death of their mother the two young men drifted apart in their separate careers. Although they seldom saw one another, the bond between them remained strong, as Mama eventually discovered.

The elder twin, now Baron Kikuchi, pursued his study of painting both in the Orient and in Europe. The younger twin served routinely at various army posts in Japan until the war with Russia broke out in 1905, when he was sent to Manchuria to command a company of infantry. He was in Manchuria only a short time before he became a national hero.

On a barren plain near Mukden his regiment was surrounded by Cossack cavalry. The fierce horsemen swept repeatedly through the Japanese lines, cutting down the soldiers with their pikes. Kikuchi alone was able to hold his unit intact, a triumph attributed to his decision to use the dead horses of the Cossacks as a barrier against their attacks. Like most of the Japanese officers, his Buddhist background had bred in him an abhorrence of meat, but that didn't stop him from saving his men in the only way open to him.

At the end of three days and three nights Japanese reinforcements broke through the Cossack encirclement to find the lost regiment largely massacred. Only Kikuchi's company had survived, safe behind the walls of rotting meat, eight feet high, that he had erected. The young Captain was awarded Japan's highest combat decoration and singled out as an officer likely to become the youngest general in modern Japanese history.

In any case there was little doubt he would someday sit on the General Staff.

In time Kikuchi fulfilled both these expectations, but not in a way anyone might have expected. It turned out that his decision to defy Buddhist custom on the plains of Manchuria had an immediately harmful effect on him. A fly feeding on the rotting carcass of a horse during the siege had infected his right eye. He was not back in Japan many days before the sight in the eye began to fail.

Kikuchi went to a specialist who was also a family friend. The doctor told him that the infection could be treated and the eye saved but that nearly total blindness was inevitable. He would be left with a gray film over the eye, an ability to distinguish light and darkness but not shapes.

Kikuchi asked if the gray film would make the eye recognizably blind and was told that it would. He then questioned the doctor about removing the eye and replacing it with a glass eye. The doctor said that could be done after they were certain the infection had subsided.

Why not until then? said Kikuchi.

Because if we opened it up before then, answered the doctor, while the infection is still virulent, there could be further damage.

What kind of damage?

To the nerves.

But if we wait it will be apparent to everyone I've lost an eye, and that means I will have to leave the army.

Yes.

Yes, so we won't wait. We will do what we have to do now.

The doctor refused to perform the operation but Kikuchi insisted. Finally the doctor agreed. Kikuchi went on leave and the operation was secretly performed. Three days later a shattering pain burst in his head, a shock so severe the doctor gave him a morphine injection. Thereafter, however, Kikuchi refused the injections, it being inconsistent with *Bushido*, the way of the warrior, for a man to refuse or disguise the pain life brought him.

Kikuchi returned to active duty and continued to rise in rank and power. To avoid suspicion he trained himself never to move his good eye, to stare directly forward and move his whole head when he wanted to shift his gaze. In this way no one would be able to detect the immobility of his false eye.

In the end the daring that had first made him a hero, then blinded him in one eye, brought other rewards. Among regular army officers there was the habit of questioning the patriotism of politicians and industrialists in interminable diatribes, harangues so repetitious that even the most resolute careerist was bound to fall asleep at least once during an evening. When this happened the dozing man propped his head in his hands for an hour or so with his eyes closed, excusing himself when he woke up again.

Not so Kikuchi.

He napped as often as anyone else, but when he did only his good eye closed. The other stared without blinking at the speaker, at a painting on the wall, at the snow or the cherry blossoms falling outside in the garden.

The effect on other officers was uncanny. His juniors were terrified by him, his seniors both terrified and humiliated. The wholly unnatural way he moved his head when he was awake only added to the impression that here was not a man but a demon, unfeeling and remorseless, some sort of determined, bloodless creature the dark powers had placed on earth as their instrument.

The unclosing, unblinking eye was also responsible for the speculation that Major and Colonel and finally General Kikuchi not only never slept but never ate, that he existed on only one cup of water every three days because suspended before him was the vision of a wall of dead Cossack horses eight feet high, because the stench of rotting meat within him was as strong as it had once been on a Manchurian plain.

The General could never admit to his glass eye, and thus a sense of total inhumanity surrounded him, false yet inescapable.

●

He was an older man when Mama met him, a bachelor who had never married, obviously ambitious. This was apparent from the fact that he had chosen to make his career in the Kempeitai. Mama assumed quite naturally that he had selected the Kempeitai because there was more opportunity for plotting there than in any other branch of the army.

The position was sensitive, and there were rumors that Baron Kikuchi made free use of the spies and dossiers of the Kempeitai to further his own interests. But the army was notorious for its cliques and jealousies, and any general would probably have acted in the same manner. At least Baron Kikuchi favored no specific faction in the army and this, together with his family name, made him more acceptable to the other members of the General Staff than any of their fellow officers.

Even for a Japanese of his generation the Baron was small, standing no more than five feet tall. He had always been so devoted to his military life that Mama thought his interest in women would probably be minor. It was likely that he looked on them as someone to relax and joke with and enjoy the traditional arts of music and song. She surmised that either sex would be unimportant to him or that he had long ago sublimated his drives, like so many professional army officers, and become impotent.

Accordingly, the ruse she used to beguile him the first

night was an old one, an artifice that often worked with aging military men who found themselves embarrassed when naked.

After the bath, while giving him a massage, she pretended to find some fluff in the crevice of his bottom, from the towel perhaps. She rolled the fluff into a little ball and bounced it in the air.

She giggled and clapped her hands. The General was delighted. For an hour they played with the little ball of fluff, batting it back and forth and chasing it around the room. The next night the General came back to suggest another bath and another massage. Again Mama clapped her hands at what she had found, again the General was enchanted, again they played ball for an hour or two.

Mama's campaign progressed as she expected. At the end of a month the General asked her to move into one of his villas in the city. Mama acquiesced. Presents followed, diamonds and emeralds and cameras, which were much more sophisticated than they had been ten years before in Kobe.

Despite the simplicity of their first days together Mama quickly sensed the General was different from the other high-ranking military officers she had known. He experienced severe headaches, for example, yet at the same time his bowels moved with vigor.

This was contrary to the usual pattern. As Mama well knew, most general officers never had a headache but they did invariably suffer from constant indigestion, a result of their inability to expel the gases that accumulated in them in the course of a day spent agreeing with everything their superiors said.

Before the war more generals in Japan died from the rupture of a vital organ due to excessive gas than from any other cause. And although the public was unaware of it, having always been given more heroic versions, it was not until the very last stages of the war that the American B-29 bomber replaced indigestion as the leading cause of death among generals on the active duty list.

Baron Kikuchi proved not to be impotent, only inactive. The first year they were together he made love to her as much as once a week, but later this dropped to once a month or less and eventually to not at all. Mama was not bothered by this, however, having had some ten thousand men make love to her in the course of her sixteen years as a prostitute. She had begun early and in that sense she was older than her years.

As time went on there were other changes in the General. He became less interested in the fluff ball games, preferring instead to spend his evenings listening to her play the *koto* while he sat beside her in his black kimono staring into space.

And there were changes in Mama as well, wholly unexpected changes that were all the more powerful because she had never imagined such a thing could happen to her. She was astonished and more than a little mystified, for the truth was that after knowing ten thousand men, after being intimate with every conceivable male combination of spirit and flesh, she had fallen in love with the little General and his gruff, gentle ways, fallen passionately in love for the first time in her life at an age when the love of most women was already turning to the quiet paths of affection and companionship.

She could not explain it to herself, but it was as if he were the first man who had ever touched her and held her, as if she had come to him a virgin at the age of sixteen and all the other years had never existed. She loved him completely, with abandon. More than anything else she wanted to give him a son.

She confided this to the General one night and he admitted it was his own secret wish. He wept then, his head on her shoulder, and whispered that for months he had been trying to arouse himself in bed with her but could not. His work, his age.

Something. He wept. It was too late.

Mama comforted him, less convinced than he that nothing could be done. She knew many ways with men and in time, she thought, she could bring him to do the impossible. In time she might have been able to, but time turned out to be the only thing they no longer shared.

On Mama's thirtieth birthday, the anniversary of their sixth year together, the General announced that he was being transferred to the mainland.

In his new post he would be in charge of all intelligence activities for the Kwangtung army in Manchuria. At the time Manchuria was controlled by the Kwangtung army, the largest and best in the Japanese Empire. Further, it was the center of all the intrigues against China. It was the most powerful political force within the Japanese military, therefore within Japan as a whole. Much as he didn't want to leave her, the position was too important to be turned down.

Mama knew he must feel honored by this great responsibility before him, yet she also sensed something else in his manner, fear perhaps. She knew it couldn't be a fear of failure. The General was too confident for that, too aware of his own competence and discipline. There was no question of his failing.

A fear of success then?

It seemed strange to Mama. Something was out of place.

Later she never forgave herself for missing that opportunity to help him, to give him love in the way he needed it, by sharing with him his terrible secret. If she had pursued her feelings then, the two years that remained before his death might have been quite different for him, less anguished, at least less lonely. But at the moment she could only think of the son he had said he wanted.

She thought giving him a son was the way to make him happy. Not until just before the end did she learn that he needed only her, no one else.

When she had arrived at a scheme she called in the General's chauffeur, a corporal.

The corporal was a man about her own age. Although he came from a family of respected surgeons, he had long ago slipped into degradation. The first step was expulsion from a private school for recurrent masturbation in the classroom. His shame over being expelled from the school was so great that he went directly to his father's clinic and stole a large amount of ether with which to commit suicide.

Being afraid, he took too small a dose. The next day he tried once more, and the third day he tried again. A week or two went by and instead of vindicating his family's honor he ended up becoming an ether addict.

For about ten years following the First World War, a period of relative freedom in Japan, he supported his habit by hiring himself out for masturbation scenes in pornographic movies. During the Depression he blackmailed his relatives into giving him small sums of money by stationing himself in front of their homes and masturbating in full view of the neighbors. More recently he had turned to begging and stealing. He came to the General's notice when he broke into a Kempeitai dispensary in search of gas to support his habit.

Baron Kikuchi recognized his name at once, the young man's father having been the surgeon who operated on his eye in 1905. Out of gratitude to the boy's dead father he decided to help the boy if he could. He took him into the army and gave him medical treatment. He made him swear that he would never masturbate in public again. The corporal responded gratefully, so the General made him his chauffeur. He often had clandestine meetings in his car and the corporal's loyalty to him was both deep and personal.

Mama knew all this. She knew the corporal was an invert incapable of performing the sexual act with a woman. But she also knew he was her only hope. There were no male servants in the house and no other man ever slept there, except the corporal when the General was with her.

She explained to the corporal that the General very much wanted to have a son but that he was unable to do what was necessary. The corporal understood at once. He hung his head and said he had a confession to make.

Mama reassured him. She said that she knew about his

condition but there was still a way he could help if he wanted to. The corporal replied that he would do anything at all that was within his power.

She then asked him certain delicate questions. Somehow, despite his embarrassment, he managed to stammer out the answers.

She thanked him and excused herself, returning with a large photograph. She gave the corporal instructions and told him he had only three days in which to practice. Three days from then would be the right time of the month for Mama and she dared not wait another month.

It was a sign of the man's profound love for Baron Kikuchi that he accepted the task of perfecting a technique, in only three days, that was entirely contrary to the habits of a lifetime.

●

Time was what she and the General lacked, timing was the hope of her scheme.

When the corporal masturbated he became ecstatically dizzy. He sank into a realm of fantasy. But if anything other than his own hand touched his penis while he was masturbating, the dizziness left him. The flight was over, immediately he wilted.

There was one exception to this and that was when his orgasm had already begun. Then his penis could be thumped or encased by any sort of foreign object and it would still remain erect for the two or three seconds the orgasm lasted. The difficulty, of course, was that he never knew when the orgasm was coming. In that other realm his mind was a blur. He was out of control.

These were the facts he had admitted to Mama. Her solution was the large photograph.

It was a formal portrait, the kind a family had taken on some very important occasion. Everyone was dressed in formal kimono, children and grandchildren, aunts and uncles and parents and grandparents, the one surviving great-grandparent, the nurse who had served the family for half a century. The members of the family stood in straight rows, unsmiling, staring into the camera. In the front row was a stiff young boy wearing the same timid expression the corporal had worn at that age.

The corporal knew the photograph well. Everyone in Japan knew it well. It was natural history, the world, existence.

Yet there was something more in this photograph. Another photograph had been superimposed upon it, or perhaps a clever drawing, or perhaps merely the suggestion of an image, vague and undefined. At first the corporal had difficulty making it out, but the longer he stared at the photograph the clearer the vague image became.

It was a ghostly naked boy lying on his back in front of the family. His elbow was bent, he was grinning, his fingers were flying.

Maniacal freedom right at the feet of the solemn, unseeing assembly.

The corporal practiced according to Mama's instructions. He masturbated vigorously while concentrating on the ghost. The dizziness came, the ecstasy, he was out of control.

His prearranged signal was a sound that resembled a clap of the hands, the sharp knock of two blocks of wood made by the man who passed the house sounding the hour. When the corporal heard the clap he shifted his eyes from the reclining ghost to the other boy, himself, the one who wore a formal kimono and stood in the front row of the family, transfixed, timid.

Instantaneously he had an orgasm. It happened just as Mama had said it would. Due to the photograph he could control his fantasies to the second. The corporal practiced at the turn of every hour, day and night, and on the third day he was ready.

Mama had chosen raw oysters to serve the General that night. The basis of her sauce was ambergris, the grayish-white wax secreted from behind the ear of the sperm whale, a well-known aphrodisiac. To this she added musk and rhubarb and cinnamon for flavoring, lastly a dose of phosphorite. She hoped the General would benefit from the aphrodisiac, but if he didn't the phosphorite would constrict his throat muscles, strangling him and thereby producing a sympathetic erection.

For as Lao-tzu had said, *man is soft and weak in life but stiff and hard in death.*

Timing.

The corporal and his family of respected surgeons.

An oyster and a sperm whale.

Poison and its antidote.

The scheme was dangerous because the antidote had to be administered quickly, otherwise the General would not only simulate strangulation but undergo it. And the antidote couldn't be mixed beforehand. She had to do that part while the corporal was doing his.

Timing.

Time.

Mama decorated the platter with seaweed and placed it before the man she loved.

The General covered an oyster with sauce and swallowed. He gripped his throat. As he toppled backward his kimono fell open revealing an erection.

Mama slipped on top of him and moved up and down. The General seemed amazed and happy, but almost immediately his eyes began to close. Perhaps he had ejaculated, perhaps not. She left him unconscious on the floor and rushed into the pantry.

The corporal was waiting beside the medicine cabinet, masturbating, staring at the photograph. Mama raised her kimono and stepped in front of him, sharply clapped her hands, slid him into place. A few minutes later she was running back into the other room with the antidote she had mixed.

There was a smile on the General's face when he fell asleep that evening. At the end of a month, just before he left for Manchuria, she was able to tell him she was going to have a baby.

The last night they stayed up together until very late.

She played the *koto* as he sat with folded hands thinking of what was to come, the life he faced in Mukden. As the evening wore on she saw the signs come over him. She was sorry it had to happen then, for she knew he didn't want her to remember him that way, the hands gripping each other and turning white, the good eye twitching more violently as it filled with water, closing finally under the weight of the sword.

The glass eye gazed at her helplessly, yet even then he still sat erect as she went on playing the quiet music for him.

The headache lasted longer than usual. Somewhere in the course of that intolerable pain the General once thought he heard a sound interrupt the music, a sharp sound, and another, a third, the sound made by a stone being slapped into place on a *Go* board, that ancient game of strategy and daring he had learned as a child. In fact he did hear the sound but it wasn't made by black and white stones striking wood to acquire or lose territory. It was made by a hand on a face, her hand striking her face, a pathetic gesture of hopelessness because she could do so little for the man she loved.

●

The General went abroad early in 1935. In the spring of that year she received an invitation to visit his twin brother in Kamakura. Although she had never met him, she knew the history of this strange man who renounced his title and his wealth in order to become a Jew, whereupon he had at once begun to suffer uncommonly from hunger and thirst, to lose weight, and to pass an excessive amount of urine.

The more superstitious of his teachers in Jerusalem interpreted this as an immediate and sure indication that his conversion was in some peculiar way anathema to the Lord. They therefore inveighed against him to foresake what he had so recently achieved, to give up his dream of being a Jew and to reembrace his own culture where he was unmistakably, by birth and tradition, in the eyes of all who might look upon him, already both an honored man and an aristocrat.

But Rabbi Lotmann refused. He persisted. He had become a Jew and he would remain one. To allay the fears of his teachers he made reference to Elijah, his favorite prophet, and recalled for them that when the Lord had selected Elijah as His instrument and had feared for his life He had told him to turn eastward, to travel eastward, to hide by a brook before the Jordan where the Lord would then command ravens to feed him.

Now Rabbi Lotmann said that in his case, since he was Japanese, the Jordan must be the Pacific and the brook before the Jordan must be the brook that crossed an estate owned by his family in Kamakura. Thus he decided to turn eastward and travel eastward and go to that estate to await the sustenance God would send him, as He had once sent the ravens to Elijah.

As it happened, his reverence for Elijah saved his life. The level of medical practice available to the elite of Tokyo, many of whom lived in Kamakura, was far beyond anything to be found in Palestine. A routine medical examination immediately revealed that he was not suffering from some divine curse but from diabetes mellitus. Insulin injections had recently been discovered to be a totally effective mode of treatment, so he was on the estate in Kamakura, by the brook before his Jordan, but a short time before his hunger and thirst subsided and he ceased to pass excessive amounts of urine.

The General had spoken often of his twin, his elder by eight minutes, and Mama had long looked forward to meeting him. Ostensibly the occasion for the visit was a *koto* recital by Rabbi Lotmann. Mama went and found two other guests, both apparently good friends of the rabbi.

One of them was a priest, tall and gaunt, whom she would go to three years later with a request that was inconceivable to her then. But when the time came for her to go to him for help she knew he would do what she

asked, for she had only to look once into his eyes on that
spring afternoon in Kamakura to know he was a man who
never refused anyone a kindness.

The other guest was also a foreigner, a short old man
with a merry face who said the exotic name he went by,
Adzhar, wasn't his real name. Like the Rabbi, he was
engaged in some massive translation project. After traveling half the world, he said, learning obscure languages
and backing obscure causes, he had more recently turned
his attention to women. And although he was seventy-
eight, he had discovered that he could never be introduced
to a woman without loving her completely and at once. So
the moment the company of a priest and a rabbi proved
tiresome to her he would be overjoyed to take her to his
home and serve her iced vodka and iced caviar, which by
coincidence he had set aside that very morning.

They all laughed as they moved into the garden, where a
beautiful old *koto* and a second slightly larger one lay side
by side on a raised platform.

Do you also play? she said, turning to Father Lamereaux.

In music, he answered, God has given me the ears of an
angel and the hands of an ape. As a child I was so clumsy
on the scales the piano had to be moved out to the barn.

Then you play, she said, turning to Adzhar, who gaily
held up his stubby fingers in front of his face.

With these? There have been too many nails in my life,
too many blows from the hammer. I have a soul but alas, I
was born the son of a shoemaker and a shoemaker's hands
can't make that kind of music.

And so? she said, turning to the General's brother.

When I was young, he answered, my mother and I used
to play every day on these two instruments. You'll forgive
me, but I've been told how well you play and I thought
that perhaps today, for a minute or two, you would join
me. Will you?

She bowed stiffly, color in her face, the first time she had
known embarrassment with a man since she was a girl of
eight. Rabbi Lotmann showed her to her place and she sat
down beside him. She struck a chord, he answered her.

The recital lasted until the shadows of the pine trees beyond the garden reached across the platform. Nor was it merely an afternoon of music wherein the former Baron Kikuchi and the mistress of the present Baron Kikuchi touched the strings of their separate memories, for as the gaunt face of Father Lamereaux swayed gravely with the flowers, the fourth member of the musicale recited a tale, sang an epic poem he had learned somewhere in his travels.

The short old man with the exotic name spoke of wonders and miracles and voyages beneath the sea. He told of the adventures of a boy who was carried on a dolphin's back to the emerald kingdom, where the boy met a princess who described the enchanted life that would be his if he remained there. But the boy elected to return home; he waved to the princess and rose above the waves again, waved to the dolphin and walked along the beach to find the trees moved, the houses gone, the familiar paths now leading elsewhere because one day on the dolphin's back in the emerald kingdom was the same as one hundred years on earth.

Or was it a dolphin? ended Adzhar. Have I been bewitched by my own tale and confused my creatures? Let me ponder for a moment and make sure I have it right. Yes, I'm certain of it now. It wasn't a dolphin at all. Wait.

They waited, the rabbi and Mama playing their music, the Jesuit nodding amid the flowers. Adzhar was staring at the small gold cross that hung from Mama's neck, studying it as he had been all afternoon while recounting his verses. Now she looked up from her *koto* and their eyes met. He smiled and she returned it, plucked a string, knew exactly what his next words would be.

A dragon, announced Adzhar. Dolphins exist and dragons don't. Of course it had to be a dragon.

They played the last chords. She said good-bye to Adzhar and Father Lamereaux in the garden and walked together with Rabbi Lotmann to her car. By the gate he stopped.

Today, he said, you reminded me of the Baroness. When

she married my father she was about the same age you were when you met my brother. Did you know he came to me three years ago to talk to me about marrying you? He was very disturbed that day but not about you, it was something else that bothered him. Shall I tell you about it?

If you wish, she said.

Yes, I'd like to. He spent the weekend here. On Sunday afternoon I played the *koto* for him and then it was time for him to return to Tokyo. It was December and we had snow that year, if you remember. It was snowing that afternoon. Ever since he had returned from his tour of duty in Shanghai I had been aware that he always wore a small gold cross around his neck. Before he gave it to you, as you know, he kept it hidden under his uniform, but when he was staying with me and wearing a kimono he made no effort to hide it. I had never asked him about the cross and he never mentioned it, but when I saw it was gone that weekend I suspected he might have something to tell me. When I finished playing he didn't move, so I sat at the instrument and waited.

I have to leave, he said.

I nodded.

It was a lovely weekend, he said in a low voice. I always enjoy the few hours I can spend here with you. It's a good life you've made for yourself. Does the translation go well?

Yes.

And your health is the same?

Yes. I take my injections.

Of course, we do what we have to do. That's what she taught us, after all, by performing the tea ceremony, turning the bowls at sunset. We do what we have to do.

I waited. He hadn't had a headache all weekend and I could see he was worried he might have one now, before he could say what he wanted to say. But some things can't be hurried. We've always been very close, the two of us, even though we seldom discuss personal matters. It's the way it was in our family, I suppose. When I wrote to him from Jerusalem that I was converting to Judaism, he never asked me to explain myself although it naturally meant trouble for him in the army. He would have to work twice as hard in order to make up for having a brother who had embraced a Western religion, and not only embraced it but been ordained a teacher. Still he never questioned what I had done. His answer was to congratulate me and wish me happiness.

The tea ceremony, he repeated now. She turned the bowl three times because that's the way it's done. Well, brother, there are three of us again.

I'm glad, I said. Who is this woman you love?

She's from a peasant family in the Tohoku.

They know a hard life.

She's nearly thirty years younger than I am. She was a prostitute.

No matter.

From childhood and for many years.

No matter.

She's known ten thousand men.

The number of creatures placed on earth by the Lord. In that case she understands many things and can love you well.

I've thought of asking her to marry me.

If you asked her, of course she would because she loves you, but is that best? She would be doing it only for your sake. If anything happens to you in the army the lands in the north would become her responsibility. Is it fair to make her the Baroness who owns the lands of the tenant farmers from whom she came?

I think not.

Rabbi Lotmann paused. He looked in silence at Mama for a moment.

That was as far as we got that afternoon. A headache struck him and he could say no more. I helped him into his car and he left. Do you remember that soon after that, in January 1932, he was away for a few weeks?

Yes, she answered.

Did he tell you where he went?

No.

It was Shanghai. A cousin of ours who lived in

Shanghai was killed while he was there. It was an accident that he was killed but not an accident that he was attacked. My brother gave the orders, acting on higher orders. That was what he meant that day in December when he kept referring to doing what had to be done. He was thinking about that special assignment in Shanghai the following month. He wanted to tell me about it but couldn't because of the headache.

I don't understand. Surely he could have refused the assignment or even stopped it by saying a cousin of his was involved.

It seems to me he could and that's what worries me.

Did he tell you about this later?

No. I suppose that after it was over he didn't want to talk about it. I know about it because of the nature of his work, and because he had gone to Shanghai secretly, and because of the circumstances of what happened there.

I don't understand any of it.

As far as that one incident is concerned, it doesn't matter. As for the rest, I don't understand it myself. I only have a feeling he may be something more than just an army officer.

I don't know what that means.

Nor do I. But if there is anything I can ever do for you, or anything Adzhar or Lamereaux can ever do for you, you must come to us. They are close friends and you can rely on them as you would on me. That's all. That's why I wanted you to come today. To tell you that.

Thank you, she said. And thank you for what you said when he asked you about marriage.

He knew it himself, said Rabbi Lotmann. It was just his way of telling me the old *koto* had found a baroness again. I'll be sending it to you now. I've had that in mind for a long time, but first I wanted to hear you play it with me. I've always been sentimental, I'm afraid.

He laughed as he opened the car door.

We've heard that tale of Adzhar's many times, you know, many many times. He always has to tell it whenever I'm playing or Lamereaux is doing a scene from a *No* play. He's an active man and it's his way of taking part.

He can't abide being just a spectator. Today it wasn't quite the same, though. For some reason he left out the last line.

And what is that?

A little trick of his that's supposed to prove the tale's authentic. At the end he waits a minute or two and then asks innocently if anyone is inclined to disbelieve him. When neither Lamereaux nor I say anything, he smiles.

Just as well, he says in the small voice of a child. Just as well, my friends. Just as well, as it turns out. For although I'm old now and it happened long ago, the boy on that dragon's back was me.

●

During the next two years she saw the General more than she had expected, for he frequently flew to Tokyo for a meeting of the General Staff. Often he had no more than an hour to be with her but he never failed to come, encouraging her during her confinement and later admiring their son.

Her love for the General continued to grow while he was away. Thus her confusion was complete when she learned that despite the vague suggestion made by his brother in Kamakura, she had never known anything at all about his real life.

The revelation came in the summer of 1937. Although they didn't know it, it was the last time they were to see each other. Once more the General was being transferred, this time to a high command post in central China. He was to lead one of the armies advancing on Nanking.

His visit coincided with *O-bon*, the midsummer Festival of the Dead, the day when dead souls returned to those who loved them to receive prayers and offer blessings in return. Having always been superstitious, she felt uneasy when he suddenly appeared that day.

He seemed restless when she played the *koto* in the evening, so she stopped and encouraged him to talk.

Again she noticed in his manner the inexplicable hint of fear she had seen so briefly the night he told her he was going to Manchuria.

He began curiously. He talked about his childhood in the north, about the suffering he had seen among the tenant farmers who worked his family's estates. He talked about China and the corruption of the Chinese government, the resistance the Japanese army was encountering in China, the power of militarism in Japan. He mentioned a Japanese monk who had been murdered in Shanghai in 1932, immediately reminding her of his brother's reference to a cousin who had been killed there as a result of an order given by the General.

He grew more agitated. He began to pace the floor. He waved his arms, which was unlike him, and his voice broke, which was also unlike him. She wondered what he was trying to say when all at once he stopped in front of her. He took her hands.

I've loved one other woman in my life, he whispered. I loved her very much and we had a son. That was how it all began.

Her face showed no expression. She sat absolutely still. He dropped her hands and resumed his pacing, speaking in a low voice.

Some ten years before he had been sent to Shanghai as a colonel in intelligence. His main task was to gather information on the various Western espionage agencies operating out of Shanghai. An American came to his notice, but before he could learn much about his activities the American left for Canton. Still interested in the case, he arranged an introduction at a reception to the man's wife, who was apparently staying on in Shanghai.

Baron Kikuchi was already middle-aged. The wife turned out to be very young. In those days he tried to cultivate a more open manner with foreigners, he had to for his work, and often he was successful. He talked with the young woman about literature and painting. They met again. She asked him about Japan, its traditions, its art and philosophy.

For his part, what happened was understandable. She

was vivacious and beautiful, passionate about everything. But she was also thirty years younger than he was.
Why had she become attracted to him?

A few weeks, no more, and they were living together.
They had to keep their relationship secret because it
would have damaged his reputation in the army if he were
known to be living with a foreign woman. Perhaps that
was what spoiled their life together, or perhaps she had
only been infatuated with him because of what he could
teach her.

In any case, it didn't last long. When she left him she
was pregnant, but she said she was going to have the child
and she did. It was a boy whom she took to Japan. Later he
heard she had joined her husband in Canton, without the
baby.

During that time he discovered he wasn't the first older
man to have had an affair with her. Several years before,
when she had first arrived in Shanghai, before she was
married, she had lived with a Russian named Adzhar, a
man close to seventy although he was said to look and act
much younger.

Out of jealousy, vanity, a mixture of pains, Baron
Kikuchi had his agents check into the Russian's life. He
found him to be a man devoted entirely to sensuality. Iced
vodka, iced caviar, women. Those were his pursuits and
his only companions. From a former wife, a rich Indian
woman, he had inherited a fortune that allowed him to
indulge in a totally dissolute life. There were still jokes
told about his insatiable appetites and the ease with
which he seduced the women he wanted.

Baron Kikuchi learned that she had become the Russian's mistress an hour after they met. The information
angered him. He was surprised and hurt.

She was gone from Shanghai a little over a year. Baron
Kikuchi, newly promoted to General, was being transferred to Kempeitai headquarters in Tokyo. A few days
before he was to sail she telephoned him. She wanted to
see him. They arranged to meet on Bubbling Well Road
and walk beside the river.

The General stopped in front of Mama.

She talked about our time together, he whispered, about how happy we had been. After a while we came to a houseboat tied to the bank and she said that was where she was living. She asked me on board. I followed her across the gangplank and suddenly a man was welcoming me, shaking my hand.

It was her husband. Quin was his name.

Maeve apologized for the trick, I just stood there. She put her hand on my shoulder and thanked me for coming. She smiled, at me, at her husband. Then she laughed the way she always laughed when she had done something she liked, something she was proud of.

It was an odd sort of laugh, timid in a way, appealing, almost coy, as if she wanted to be praised but would be embarrassed when the praise came. I don't think I'm trying to make excuses for myself when I say there was a hardness in that laugh I hadn't noticed before.

I mentioned that she was passionate about everything, life, people, ideas. But in the year we'd been apart I'd come to suspect that most of that passion had nothing to do with life or people or ideas. Somehow it always seemed directed toward herself, toward proving that she was whoever she thought she was. She was fervent, but what did it mean? Did she really care about people? How they suffered? What was right and wrong in the world? How she could help?

She talked as if she did, but later I wasn't so sure. I had a feeling she was acting without knowing it. All those words and opinions were costumes she wore in order to be able to say, *this* is who I am.

The baby, for example. She had it because she wanted to have the experience, but then she gave it away for someone else to raise, to bother with, to love. She knew she couldn't love the child, yet she brought it into the world, which was selfish and even cruel. Another life was involved, after all, not just her own.

Love. How could she love anyone if she couldn't love her own child? I suppose she did love her husband in a way, but certainly no one else, and certainly not all those abstractions she pretended to care so much about.

And even with him I'm not sure. You could say the way she helped him in his work proved she loved him, but did she, or was that just the ultimate costume, the ultimate role, the one deepest inside her? A final way of saying, I love him and therefore this is who I am. Who *I* am. *Me.*

I don't know. I'm not sure. At the time all I understood was that somehow she wasn't the person I'd thought she was a year before. But of course love does that to us. We hear with different ears and see with different eyes and I'm glad we do. The peace I saw on my mother's face has kept me alive for years. For years, even though I've known for years it wasn't peace but a mask hiding a lifetime of pain. Hiding it from my brother and me because she loved us.

Maeve. She laughed that laugh of hers, and then she went away and left the two of us standing there.

I was bewildered. Quin smiled and asked me to sit down. He poured me a drink and began to talk. Politics, China, Japan. He had a gift with words and he was fascinating to listen to. He had enthusiasm, a well-trained mind, an enormous grasp of history and its movements.

At some point he dismissed my affair with his wife. He said that kind of thing was inevitable when a husband and wife were separated for long periods. He told me it meant nothing to him and I believed him, for he was the kind of man who would have many women himself. He lived too much with ideas to be devoted to her or any woman. Other things were too important to him. She must have been only a small part of his life.

We talked for a long time and I found we agreed on almost everything, as I suppose he knew we would. Maeve and I had talked a lot when we were together. I suppose she had told him how I felt.

The General stopped in front of Mama again. He took her hands.

In other words, I was lying to you a minute ago. I've become so used to lying I do it all the time. Obviously the reason she was interested in me in the beginning, or pretended she was interested, was because she thought I would be useful to him. She loved him enough to do something like that for him. Or loved herself that much. I don't know which it was.

Anyway, none of that matters now. I'll just tell you what happened.

Quin and I became friends on the houseboat that afternoon. Originally, I imagine, he'd asked me there for some minor thing, but the friendship between us was real, we both felt it, we both felt it strongly even though I was old enough to be his father.

So in the end he told me who he was and what he was doing. He was working for Soviet intelligence to protect China and the Soviet Union from Japanese militarism. He asked me to work with him and I said I would. And so I have, giving him all the plans of the General Staff, where they have intended to move and when, months and years before it has happened.

And now more recently the most important information of all, information that may someday save Moscow from the Germans. For the Germans will surely attack the Soviet Union before long, and Japan will go to war before long, which means fighting the West, and then the Soviet Union will face the near impossibility of fighting on two fronts.

Or that is, they would have faced that possibility if we hadn't told them otherwise. If I hadn't been able to tell Quin that when the time comes the Japanese army will move south to seize the oil and rubber of Southeast Asia, not north into Siberia. That when the time comes, therefore, the Soviets can pull back their Far Eastern divisions to use against the Germans and not worry about the Kwangtung army in Manchuria, for although it will still be there in name, its officers and men will be fighting elsewhere and the Soviet Far East will be safe. That much we were able to tell Moscow, perhaps thereby to save it.

But although you don't understand any of this, you mustn't think I'm a traitor. What I've done has been for the good of Japan. I had to make a decision that afternoon and it was the right one. I believed what Quin believed in, I believed it then and I do now. I loved *Go* as a child and that's probably how I got into the army in the first place, but what the army was doing to Japan and beginning to do to China was wrong. Wrong then, now it's much worse.

So no matter what happens I know I made the right decision. I know it. And as for Quin, he's been a brother to me. Whenever I had doubts or was exhausted or thought I couldn't live through another headache, it was his courage that kept me going, his confidence in me, his will, his determination to finish what we had started, what we were doing together to help people, to help the Japanese and the Chinese by ending their horrible, futile war.

There have been terrible times, times I can't forget. And people.

There was the morning I had to call in the gentle Western scholar who has assisted us by handling our courier system. A kindly man, a good man, a man who has taken many risks for the same cause I have. Of course he didn't know who I really was and of course I couldn't tell him, but I had to get him to change his behavior because it might have endangered our security.

So I insulted him. I blackmailed him. I humiliated him in the most despicable way. Humiliated him, my compatriot. Insulted the man whom I knew was one of my brother's most treasured friends.

A small matter. Merely a case of insulting and humiliating a kindly man, a gentle human being. There were worse cases. There were cases of murder.

Once, about five years ago, I had to get to Shanghai to see Quin, to talk to him about the General Staff's plan to invade north China. I absolutely had to get there but there was no way to leave Tokyo. My office was involved in the planning and my absence from Tokyo then, for any reason, would have been impossible to explain. I was desperate.

And then a way turned up. A disgusting, sickening way. It was ghastly.

The plan called for a man to be assassinated in Shanghai, some well-known Japanese. The assassination would appear to be the work of Chinese patriots, and naturally the repercussions would be great. It was to be the first step, the beginning. A year later the Japanese people would be more than ready for the invasion of China.

Someone on the General Staff suggested a certain Japanese monk who lived in Shanghai, a man who was loved by the Chinese and respected by the Japanese, an ideal target. What little remained of the good feelings between our people was the work of him and a few men like him.

That monk was my cousin, descended from my father's younger brother. But no one knew this because his family had been in China since the beginning of the nineteenth century, and because they had adopted a Chinese name, and because I'd destroyed certain parts of the Kempeitai files so that no harm would come to him.

Now not only did I have to agree to the plan but suggest it was such a delicate operation it required my presence in Shanghai. Behind my back I saw them smiling at each other, whispering that the real reason I wanted to go was because I was a killer, a murderer, an executioner who liked to sniff and smell and taste the scene of an execution.

They hated me of course. They'd always hated me because I had the files of the Kempeitai behind me and knew too much about them. They'd have gotten rid of me long ago if they weren't so jealous among themselves about trusting anyone else with my work.

So they smiled at me.

Yes, they said, an excellent idea. Perhaps you should deal with this matter personally. Nothing must go wrong, and with you there it won't. It will be an efficient murder, that is quite certain, given your skill. Quite certain and most reassuring. An excellent suggestion, Kikuchi.

I had to let them smile at me and get up and walk out the door. I went to Shanghai and met with the agents, telling them that the monk was to be superficially wounded, one bullet in the arm and the rest in the air, nothing more. But in the end that little effort came to nothing. They lost their heads and fired indiscriminately.

Five years ago. There have been other things since then and others before then, things you can't explain to yourself or anyone else, things that just sit there and sit there and never go away, wounds that won't heal, wounds open to the wind, wounds that reach to the bone. Once I talked to Quin about it and he nodded to himself. He nodded to himself and said nothing, for there was nothing to say. Nothing. He knew what I was talking about.

The General released her hands. He had finished. He went over to the cupboard and took down an unopened bottle of Irish whiskey that had been left untouched for eight years, a gift from Quin at the end of that afternoon and evening on a houseboat in Shanghai. The General never drank whiskey, but tonight he poured himself a large glass and emptied it.

She watched him refill the glass. He sat down beside her and bowed his head so that she could not see his eyes, neither the one with vision nor the one without.

So tell me what you think, he said.

I think you are a brave man, she answered, and I think you've done what you believe in. And I feel sorry for that other woman who can't love a man the way she wants to love him. And I feel sorry for him, for someday he may discover why.

But most of all I don't think about them at all. I think of my love for you and that's all I think about, when you're with me and when you're not.

●

Four months passed. Mama was preparing the special rice cakes with which to welcome the New Year. Late in the afternoon she was given the name of a caller. She bathed and dressed in her finest kimono. Lastly she looked in on her sleeping son.

It was snowing when she walked down the open corridor that crossed the garden, toward the soft light that lit the rice paper door of the room where she had played the *koto* for the General. She watched the snow for a moment before sliding back the door on its runners.

A haggard figure knelt in front of her, his forehead pressed to the *tatami*. She begged him to rise, to sit by the brazier and warm his hands, surely stiff from the harsh wind of many an unfriendly night. She poured tea and placed the cup before him.

Dead, whispered the corporal.

I know, she said.

But there has been no announcement.

I knew last summer.

The corporal kept his head bowed. He cradled the steaming teacup in his hands.

I feel uncomfortable sitting here, he said. This was his place.

You need not, my friend. You loved him and tried to make him happy. No one can do more.

The corporal shuddered, but not from the cold. The spasm came from the fires that still burned behind his eyes. He was too frightened to go on. He felt a hand touch his arm and looked up to see a very old face, a tiny woman smiling gently in the yellow light.

It's all right, she said. You can tell me. Life is brief and we must listen to every sound.

●

December 1937.

Nanking.

The ancient capital of the south was the only stronghold on the Yangtze River still under Chinese control. The Japanese armies had advanced from victory to victory. Whole Chinese divisions broke ranks, were slaughtered, surrendered. The better regiments had already been isolated or defeated. Radio messages told the General that he was ahead of the other columns. That day, he knew, he could reach Nanking if he pushed his troops hard enough.

The General called in his senior officers at five o'clock in the morning. He told them what he intended to do. His deputy and several colonels disagreed. The men were too exhausted, they had seen too much killing in the last few days. Some had been caught looting, fires were breaking out. It was dangerous. The breakdown in discipline could be contagious.

The General shook his head. He was tired, he no longer wanted to talk to people. He wanted it all to end. In the name of the Emperor he gave them his orders.

The heels clicked, the troops shouldered their packs and began to march. The pace quickened throughout the morning, by noon the forward elements thought they could see the city in the distance. The infantry units swept through the weak resistance, outdistancing their armor, their supplies, their artillery, racing across the frozen paddy fields and the few remaining miles.

Late in the afternoon the lead elements of the General's army were fighting in the outskirts of the city. Their officers tried to slow the advance. Their battle plans called for regrouping, but the soldiers were no longer under their control. All day they had been running and shooting, by nightfall they were no longer an army. They stumbled along in packs, in gangs, numb and hungry, totally worn out. The city was empty of enemy forces. Only women and children and old men were left. The unfit, the helpless, the cripples.

The General had not slept for many nights. During that whole last day he had spoken only once, to curse the fires he could see springing up on the horizon.

The radio in his command car crackled and he ignored it. Motorcycle couriers sped beside the car waving dispatch cases, pointing at the insignia they wore, theater command. The General gazed straight ahead and told the corporal to drive faster. Headquarters would tell him to stop, to hold up his advance until the other Japanese armies were in line. But the General was too tired to stop. He wanted to reach the end.

The sun had just set when they passed through the gates of the city. Again the General remarked on the fires, more apparent now because of the darkness. It was several degrees below zero, the wind was rising.

They entered a large square. The General looked around him and said something strange was happening out there. These were Japanese soldiers, the best disciplined in the world. What were they doing?

The staff car had been tightly sealed against the winter weather. They could neither hear nor see clearly what was going on outside. They could only make out scattered movements in the darkness, shadows, faces flaring in the headlights, torches flickering. The General ordered the corporal to stop. He gripped his sword and stepped down into the square.

The corporal moaned, he hid his face in his hands. Mama listened to the snow falling on Tokyo. She turned her teacup in her hands, revolved it three times before she drank. Then she rested her hand on the corporal's arm again.

Go on, she said. We must hear it all.

The men, moaned the corporal, they weren't even animals. A soldier speared a baby with a bayonet and threw the baby in the air. A soldier stabbed a woman and skinned her legs. A soldier got over the hind quarters of a horse and pushed himself in. A soldier had a belt of human hair and was eating something. A soldier was playing with a little girl, cutting holes in her, pushing himself in. There was a head in the street. There was a whole row of heads beside a building. They were lining people up and shooting them, building fires around them, tying grenades to them. They threw them out the windows, they dropped stones on them. They tied them under trucks. They used machine guns and pistols and blew up rooms and set fires and pushed people into the fires and cut off parts and roasted the parts and ate them. A soldier ran in circles shouting army regulations, shooting people, stabbing people, clawing his own face down to the bone. They raped and raped and then they raped with bayonets, with rifles, firing the rifles. They used grenades that way to blow women up. A soldier sat on a pile of bodies screaming. A soldier held a pistol to a girl's face and made her drink his urine. He made her lie down and did something on her face and crushed her face with his boot. They cut out eyes and buried people and made them crawl through glass. They beat them with their rifle butts. They broke teeth with their rifle butts. They beat them in the face and clubbed them over the head with their rifle butts. They broke fingers and arms and legs with their rifle butts. A soldier rode on an old man's back stabbing him with his knife. The old man fell and the soldier kicked him and hit him in the head and fired bullets into his head and kept on kicking him. They made them kneel and do things to each other. They made them bend over and do things to each other. They held a girl's hand and made her castrate her father. They cut off a boy's nose and made him chew it. They beat him between the legs with their rifle butts and beat his chest with rifle butts and poured gasoline over him and set him afire. They went on shooting people and lining them up and shooting them and there was nothing but screams, shadows and screams and fires and screams, and machine guns and fires and rifle butts and pistols and bayonets and knives and screams, and shadows and bodies and faces and screams, and filth and blood and screams and fires and people being shot and stabbed and clubbed and kicked and beaten and trampled, crawling people, screaming people, old men and children screaming, women screaming, people burning and running and falling in the fires and the shadows and the darkness, soldiers shooting and people screaming, screaming.

The corporal moaned. His head was in his arms. He was crying.

Mama gazed at the rice paper door and saw the frozen fields in the north where she had been born. She saw the poor farmhouses, the barren schoolrooms, the little Japanese boys bent over their books in winter trying to learn a thousand Chinese ideograms so they could read their own history and write their own names. She saw the schoolrooms burn, and the farmhouses, and the pine groves of the temples. She saw the little boys rip up the graceful Chinese characters and shoot them and stab them and defile them, devour them. She saw it all.

He began to shout, whispered the corporal. He was running after them, yelling at them to stop. I tried to keep up with him but there were too many shadows, too many fires, too many screams. I didn't find him until the next morning.

The corporal looked away.

He was naked. Someone had murdered him and pulled off his clothes. His right eye had been ripped from the socket. There was excrement on his epaulets, which lay beside him. His testicles were tied around his neck.

●

That night, after the corporal left, Mama sat up alone meditating. The next day was New Year's, her birthday as it was the birthday for everyone of her race.

The cough struck her son a short time afterward, struck him quickly and violently as if the world could no longer tolerate the passage of time. Its course was brief, nothing could be done. She held him and watched his spirit go, one tiny sacrifice to an era where Nanking was but the first act of the far grander circus that was to follow.

●

She wanted to leave Tokyo and Japan as well. Only one enclave remained on the mainland where a Japanese could still mix with foreigners, Shanghai, an outlaw city where the chaos and despair might equal her own.

She found it all she had expected and more. Among the foreigners who were still there, who had nowhere to go, nothing was left untried. Mama began taking laudanum, the solution of opium in alcohol preferred by many because of its combination of effects.

She spent her time with a group of companions who met nightly to narcotize themselves, to take part in orgies or watch them. Like them she slept during the day and went out only at night. Her nameless companions disappeared regularly, victims of suicides or intrigues, to be replaced by other weary faces who would disappear in turn.

To ease their pain they gave up using each other, or having others used in front of them, and took to watching pornographic movies, a lifeless display of mutilations and fecal sandwiches and tubercular saliva so unreal they could bury themselves in the long nights and dream nothing around them existed.

Of all the people who passed through her life during that period of forgetfulness, only one remained in her memory, the projectionist who showed the movies.

He was a huge man, an American, a giant with a pockmarked face. His body was bloated and his eyes bulged from the quantities of alcohol he consumed. As soon as he arrived in the locked, shuttered room and set up his battered projector there was a sense of relief because the lights could be turned off. The projector whined, the reels rattled, the flickering images crept across the wall as Mama and the others sank into their couches.

The projectionist had a strange habit of taking off his clothes. Apparently this was because the machine he used was an old one that quickly overheated. Or so Mama assumed as she watched him fumbling with his garments during the course of the evening, pulling them off one by one until at midnight he was naked save for a towel over his loins.

Like others in the room, Mama often slipped over to the machine after midnight to whisper to the giant. When she did he listened to her impassively, not commenting, occasionally nodding his head. As the weeks went by Mama found herself telling him more and more about her life, eventually confessing everything.

It was a unique experience for her. At the time she couldn't have said why he had this effect on her, why she felt the need to slip over to him and whisper in the darkness. Perhaps it was because he accepted everything she said, perhaps because the huge shadowy profile cast by the dim light of the projection lamp was totally anonymous.

Or perhaps simply because he was naked. An immobile naked giant who heard everything and saw everything, from whom there was nothing to fear.

Nor was the bloated American merely her confessor in that locked, shuttered room. He was also an impostor and a clown.

For a long time, it seemed to Mama, the images on the wall had been becoming dimmer. One night she asked the huge naked projectionist about this and he waved his arms extravagantly. He said that maybe he couldn't get the proper bulbs. Or maybe the electrical system in the city was failing. Or maybe this and maybe that.

He kept on talking, muttering. He looked down on her with a smile, and all at once she knew the confessor was confessing, confiding some monstrous private joke to her about Shanghai. About the hopelessly despairing men and women who came to whisper to him in the shadows. About life.

She went back to her couch and watched the films more closely. She made a discovery.

There were great numbers of animals and humans in the films, but none of the scenes was remotely pornographic. She couldn't be sure, the films were so scratched they were nearly invisible, but as best she could tell they were documentaries of some kind, crudely done documentaries that seemed to be explaining the basic techniques of animal husbandry. The animals were common barnyard varieties, underfed, the men and women looked like Russian peasants.

Primitive instructive movies from the early days of the Russian Revolution. Where had he found them and why? How was he able to show them and make the depraved people in that room think they were watching a dazzling tableau of debauchery?

A kind and lonely man. As kind and lonely as a clown.

●

A rumor passed among the companions that one night soon there would be a special circus, an entertainment such as no one had ever seen, a performance that in some unknown way would bring ultimate satisfaction to all those who witnessed it. The companions were excited. They could not disguise their longing for the mysterious spectacle.

Only Mama was unsure. The clown's trick had made her think of oysters.

To her the oyster had always been a theological symbol because it was encapsuled and complete, because it resembled the gray jelly of the brain, because Lao-tzu had once spoken of a substanceless image existing before the Yellow Ancestor. To Mama it seemed likely the oyster might be that image. More than once in her despair she had dreamed of becoming an oyster.

But that was before the clown had smiled at her. There was magic in the illusions he worked with his films, a magic so simple it had made her smile for the first time since the death of the General, made her smile and realize she was not yet ready to join these other voyeurs in a circus of death. Instead she decided to visit the circus master alone, before he gave his performance.

She stopped taking laudanum to clear her mind. She meditated, something she hadn't done in a year. The night before the circus she came to the filming room as usual.

The couches were arranged in rows, the windows shuttered, the door bolted. She waited until after midnight before she sneaked out of the room. By then the companions were dazed with opium smoke and the clown was snoring fitfully, his bulk spread over three or four large chairs beside the stalled projector. After years of use the ancient documentary had finally snapped. The machine still purred, a reel flapped around and around, but the frame on the wall remained the same, a peasant hovel with a large indistinct animal pressing at the door. Perhaps two frames had been trapped in the lens when the machine stalled.

No one saw her leave. She slipped into a rickshaw, closed the curtains around her, and began the long ride down Bubbling Well Road.

Her destination was an abandoned warehouse on the outskirts of the city. The building was square, windowless, with tall skylights. A muffled shriek, a squeal drifted to her on the wind.

She passed down a canvas corridor, the draped cages of the sleeping animals. Strange costumes, spangled and hairy, hung from the packing boxes. The warehouse itself turned out to be a vast open space lit by moonlight. The ceiling vaulted toward the sky, the corners were left in darkness. Here echoes could have no end, for the great empty area was no less than a cavern of the mind.

He was standing in the sawdust ring. He wore a black bowler hat, a lavender frock coat. In one hand he held a megaphone, in the other a whip. He was standing with his head back and his arms spread, staring at the sky.

She went up to him and bowed. She told him who she was and why she had come. She said that she was one of the group that had commissioned the circus but that she had decided not to come, despite her misery. So she was here alone to learn from the master the meaning of his final performance.

He broke into a gloomy laugh and began striding around the ring cracking his whip, hissing orders through his megaphone. He talked about faith, deception, disguises. He swept his arms through history gathering up emperors and peasants, barbarians, poets. He sank into a confused monologue on love, love that was and love that might have been.

The words cracked, the whip flew, the megaphone defied an imaginary audience. This man, she realized, had lost his way in a land of strange beasts and savage costumes.

She couldn't understand the nature of his despair, but as she watched him stalk himself in the ring a curious image stirred within her. She saw a naked giant slumped beside a lamp that dimly projected meaningless figures on the wall.

The image was so vivid it startled her. Why had it come to her then? What connected these two anonymous men, a nameless projectionist and a nameless circus master?

She gazed at the skylight, at the invisible corners of the warehouse, at the tiny sawdust ring. She listened to the raving voice of the circus master and heard within it her own voice whispering, whispering night after night to a silent fat man who sat naked and immobile, impassive, oblivious to every horror she recounted, untouched by the terrors she wished upon herself.

Quickly then she slipped off her clothes and went up to the circus master, stopped his pacing, and took from him the megaphone, the whip, emptied his hands, and held him in her arms until the sobbing quieted, until the spasms subsided and he felt in her a blessing that he had lost long ago, a blessing that she had lost as well, forever she thought, not having known until that moment that the gift had been returned to her by the naked giant who nodded forgiveness.

Their act of love lasted until dawn. When she left him she walked for miles, making her plans to return to Japan.

That night she sat by an open window looking at the stars. Midnight passed, the hours wore on. She considered her past grief, she reflected on the torment of the circus master who at that very moment was introducing the ghosts of his years in their terrible costumes, opening the cages of the savage beasts, celebrating his circus of death. But at that very moment, as well, new life was moving within her.

In the course of knowing ten thousand men she had

conceived only once. Now she knew it had happened again. Through the intercession of the naked giant she had learned once more to love, she had loved well, and now she would bear the circus master's son.

●

The boy was born in the General's old villa in Tokyo. Because he was half-Caucasian she could not keep him. War was coming with the West and it would be unfair to have him grow up in Japan. Despite herself, she had to get him out of the country while there was still time.

She went to the one man she felt could help her, the missionary who was a friend of the General's brother. Father Lamereaux listened to her story and agreed to send the baby to America. Sadly she gave him up.

War with the West came, then defeat. Before the war doors were never locked in Japan, but now desperate men stole everything they could find. Her house was broken into nightly, a new gang of starving thieves entering as soon as one had left.

The General's chauffeur, who had come to work for her at the end of the war, suggested hiring one of these gangs of combat veterans to guard the house and keep the others away. But Mama had a different idea, one consonant as always with the Tao. She quoted Lao-tzu.

When there is Tao in the empire, the galloping steeds are turned back to fertilize the ground by their drop-pings.

But what does it mean? asked the corporal.

It means, she said, that these men who were heroes yesterday, who are thieves today, will one day be heroes again. They are galloping steeds, and if we treat them with the wisdom of the Tao their droppings will fertilize the future.

Droppings? said the corporal.

A man has several, answered Mama. There are still

three or four women servants in this house, and I am sure there are other women near here who are lonely after so many years when the men were away fighting. So instead of posting guards we will invite every passing steed into the house. You will see.

The corporal feared what might happen, but the Tao was in Mama and she knew it. Before many years went by a new Japan began to emerge, an ingenious and industrious Japan, energetic, prosperous.

Many of the old ways had changed, but none more noticeably than the tradition Mama had become skilled in as a child, perfected in girlhood, and left as a young woman, the delicate and profound knowledge of men that for centuries had made the entrance to a Japanese brothel, no matter how humble it might appear to the passing stranger, one of the few truly exquisite gateways in the world, a portal unparalleled save by the path of mystics seeking comfort not in this world but another.

The elaborate brothels of the prewar years gave way to the garish bars of the early postwar years, but then the American soldiers left and Japanese men settled down to learning the lessons of the war and the Occupation. Having been defeated in their venture at Asian conquest, the Japanese combat veterans embraced peace and built industries to supply the Americans, who in turn, having been victorious, were now fighting wars all over the continent, bringing a devastation everywhere that required ever more Japanese goods and industries to replenish what was destroyed, bringing a prosperity to Japan that no warlord or ultranationalist could have conceived possible two decades earlier.

But the unexpected turn of history whereby Japan achieved the goals of the war by losing the war, was not without its victims. Somewhere in the hectic confusion of democratic expansion the traditional Japanese brothel disappeared, taking with it the Orient's artistic contribution to originality and one of man's rarest creations, the Japanese whore.

No longer was anyone willing to pay money for a woman's educated body, a woman's aristocratic smile, a woman's subtle remarks and incomparable cleverness at match-stick games. The businessmen in the new Japan were preoccupied with their wares and the wares that were soon to be theirs, so when the hour came for relaxation they preferred lying on their backs in a massage parlor staring through the steam at the ceiling, calculating profits, considering new markets, dreaming alone and grandly as a firm, anonymous hand reached out from the mists to masturbate them with swift efficiency.

Or they preferred a pornographic film parlor, where such individual democratic acts could be recalled and anticipated.

As was necessary, Mama adapted to the times. She remembered the films shown in Shanghai before the war by a naked clown and built The Living Room with those films in mind. And the combat veterans she had entertained after the war, before they had learned the ways of the new democracy and become successful, certainly didn't forget the little woman who had provided for them when they were penniless.

They remembered and they returned, gratefully spending large sums of money at Mama's nightclub, the most famous place of entertainment in Asia, a club that was almost as much of a legend as its mysterious owner, a tiny old woman whose compassion and mercy were so great that many wondered if she might not be a reincarnation of the Kannon Buddha.

War, disaster, turmoil. Despite it all Mama had followed the Tao.

And now more recently in her old age she had acquired the kind of retreat she had always wanted, a quiet shrine where she could contemplate the sunrise high above the Imperial moat and the Imperial palace. From there she descended to the world below only in passing to accrue some minor transitory wealth, some award or honor, before returning to her real home far above the city, a spiritual temple carried on the back of the mythical dragon that had guided her through the years of loss and love.

KIKUCHI-
LOTMANN

.

5

*Now we see him stepping into the ring, the master of
ceremonies dressed in boots and frock coat, carrying
whip and megaphone, a shaman and arbiter of marvels.*

●

Quin came and went. Big Gobi left the apartment with
him once, for the first visit to Father Lamereaux, but he
was so confused by the meeting Quin left him behind
after that. Quin said something about the names Father
Lamereaux had given him. Big Gobi nodded and kept his
eyes on the television screen.

Names are fine, he muttered as Quin closed the door.

The Living Room was an underground bar many levels
below the street. Quin knew the Japanese custom of
referring to all female proprietors of bars as *Mama-san,* so
as soon as he came upon a waiter, after having walked
down several hundred steps, he asked for Mama-san
saying they had a mutual friend, Father Lamereaux.

The suspicious waiter directed him to a corner where
there stood a man of some four hundred pounds, a former
sumo wrestler with a huge mallet resting on his shoulder.
The former *sumo* wrestler held the mallet over Quin's
head until the waiter returned.

The waiter bowed. He apologized for his family and
education, his meanness of spirit, his boorish and crass
behavior, his whining voice, his unsavory appearance and
total incompetence. Mama would see him presently.

In the meantime Quin was invited to be her guest in the
Round Room, reserved for the most honored guests. They

left the wrestler in the shadows and started down an interminable spiral staircase. Occasionally the waiter stopped to ask Quin if he liked Japan, and when Quin reassured him that he did the man sucked air noisily through his teeth out of wonder or gratitude, or simply because nothing else seemed appropriate.

After descending another three or four hundred feet they entered a circular room where a dozen men or more sat at a counter facing the wall, or rather small windows recessed in the wall. Their backs were to him and no one turned when he came in. The waiter directed him to an empty stool, sucked air, and disappeared.

A face peered up at him from the bartenders' runway, which was sunken so the heads of the bartenders would not protrude above the counter. Quin ordered a drink and saw a hand come up over the edge with a glass.

On the counter in front of him there was a console of buttons. *Family portrait*, said one. *Small projection lamp*, said another. *Tattoos. Kobe cameras.* Quin arbitrarily pressed the button for *Nose*.

The screen that Quin had mistaken for a mirror flickered. The screens were built in such a way that only the man directly in front of one could see which private movie he had selected. To everyone else the screens remained mirrors reflecting a distorted view of the small round room.

The first nose was flat and spreading. It grew in size until the screen could no longer contain it. The pores, rich dark holes, were soon big enough to put a fist in, as big as craters in a desert. The rims of the craters were cracked, deep down inside lay heaps of fertile material. The picture continued to expand until there was only one enormous pore on the screen, a volcanic crater not unlike the one to be found on top of Mt. Fuji, the sides of the pore cut by ancient landslides, the center black with dormant bacterial lava.

The frame faded and another nose appeared, life-size, narrower than the first, quivering, and undeniably sensitive. A chrysanthemum or a cherry blossom presented itself to the nose. The nose hesitated and then inhaled deeply, bringing on a multitude of tender sensations.

The third nose moved rapidly. The hairs in the nostrils flapped as a bowl of custard slipped into view. The nose slammed itself into the custard, emerged, rammed itself into the waxy cartilage of an ear.

The same nose moved down a neck, across an armpit, through the crevice made by two pendulant breasts. It nudged a woman's erect nipples, poked the ridges of her rib cage, shook itself vigorously in her navel, pecked at the mound of her smooth belly. It caressed the thighs and burrowed between the toes, sampling, working swiftly.

Quin's head jerked back. For an instant a totally different image had appeared on the screen, or so it seemed. A scene from what looked like a barnyard, healthy animals being cared for by healthy, smiling peasants wearing starched muslin and embroidered blouses, East Europeans of some kind, Slavs perhaps, cheerfully tending their animals under the benign guidance, the approving fatherly gaze of a dashing man with a moustache and a worker's cap, dressed in a loosely fitted black suit and a high celluloid collar.

Lenin?

The image was gone at once and not so much seen as imagined, an effect that made the tale of the nose curiously disturbing. Somehow the suggestion of an actual historical event added authenticity to a film that might otherwise have been merely obsessive and unreal.

The nose lay on its back as a woman's legs opened at the top of the screen. The legs descended, spread wide, bringing down a curtain of wiry hair that ended the film.

Quin's glass was empty. Even the ice was gone. A legend beside the buttons on the counter noted that all the films were changed every third day. It also invited the guest to indulge himself in combinations by pressing several or all of the buttons at once, thereby creating unique themes previously unwitnessed. Quin was about to order another drink when the waiter reappeared, apologizing as before, and invited him to pay a visit to Madame Mama.

Once more they walked down a spiral staircase, but this

one was narrow and plain and neither carpeted nor lit by
chandeliers. It wound down between weathered boards
that formed a square shaft, reinforced at every level by
what appeared to be a roof. In fact, Quin wondered if they
were descending through a pagoda that had been built
under the ground instead of above, narrowing into the
earth instead of the sky.

She sat at the bottom of the well in a bare wooden room,
a tiny white-haired woman in black kimono, her only
decoration an oval emerald resting on her forehead. She
inclined her head as she greeted him, a kindly, aristocratic woman who spoke precise English with a slightly
archaic accent.

The sages like to remind us, she said, that the only life
we know here is as one underground, that we must pass
through many incarnations before we finally see the sun.
A pagoda can also have three or five stories, but mine has
seven. Is Father Lamereaux still alive?

Yes he is, answered Quin.

How strange. I always thought he died during the war.

No, but it seems he's been pretty much of a recluse
since then.

I see. Well he was very kind to me once and we must
never forget a kindness. What may I do for you, Mr. Quin?

Father Lamereaux thought you might have known my
father in Shanghai. He thought you might have been
there when he died.

And when was that?

About 1937 I think.

Mama's face showed no expression.

I was there about then, she said, and I did know many
foreigners, many of whom died, most of them in the end.
But they were all nameless to me. We didn't use names
then. Ever.

And you've never heard of someone called Quin?

Mama frowned. She unfolded her hands, paused, re-
folded them in a different way.

Yes, I believe I have. But it wasn't in Shanghai, it was in
Tokyo. It was in connection with something that had
happened in Shanghai eight years before I lived there.

Mama spoke slowly. She talked of Japan before the war, of Shanghai and the desperation she had known there. She said that to recall the events of that lurid era would be to play an uneasy, painful game with the past. She talked for over an hour and asked him to come to see her again. Meanwhile she offered him the use of an interpreter to help him find the other person Father Lamereaux had mentioned.

Quin left feeling oddly close to the ancient little woman even though she had not discussed the circumstances in which she had heard his father's name. Instead she had talked at length about herself. Why had she avoided his questions?

Quin thought he knew the answer. Geraty had said the espionage ring operated for eight years. If his father had died in Shanghai when Mama was there, then the event she had alluded to, the episode that occurred eight years before that time, might be connected with the beginning of the ring. Mama had said it would be an uneasy, painful game of memory to recall that era and Quin believed her, for the uneasy, painful game could have only one name.

Shanghai.

●

The interpreter, a meek elderly man, suggested they begin their search at once in Tsukiji, the area of Tokyo where Quin had been told to look for the gangster Kikuchi-Lotmann. Since it was the fish market district, Tsukiji had the best *sushi* restaurants in the city. The interpreter led Quin to one on a main street and indicated a table by the window.

If we sit there, he said, we should be able to get our bearings. Shall we?

The interpreter spoke to the waiter and plates of *sushi* began to appear, those for Quin heavy on the cheaper cuts of octopus and squid, those for the interpreter tending toward expensive sea urchin and expensive salmon roe and an extremely expensive northern whitefish that was so rare it was seldom available at any price.

Quin drank beer. The interpreter drank a premium iced *sake* from a brewery in Hiroshima that bottled the special brand only once a year on the Emperor's birthday.

Quin finished his beer waiting to hear the interpreter's plan for finding Kikuchi-Lotmann. The man said nothing, instead he ordered a second plate of *sushi* and a third. Quin found himself paying the bill, which was exorbitantly high, while the interpreter exchanged pleasantries with the man at the cash register. Once outside, the interpreter walked a few steps to a doorway and stopped.

Careful, he whispered. We must act naturally.

They stood on the sidewalk facing the door. The interpreter rolled his eyes to heaven meaningfully, hiccuped, unzipped his trousers. Quin went over to wait by the curb as a stream of urine splashed between the interpreter's legs and slithered across the crowded sidewalk. The elderly man wiped his hands with a newspaper before joining Quin at the curb.

First piece of information, he whispered. There appears to be a houseboat in the neighborhood that everyone is afraid to talk about.

How do you know? said Quin.

The man at the cash register. We had a short discussion about the stores and shops and houses and inns and shacks and restaurants and hotels in Tsukiji, about the storerooms and warehouses and garages and so forth, and he never hesitated. He chatted right along with me. So that leaves only a houseboat, don't you think? I'm quite sure that's what we're looking for. Shall we?

Quin followed the interpreter into a coffee shop, dark and restful after the hot sun in the street. The interpreter asked for the score to the music, a Mozart symphony, and read the score while they were waiting for their coffee to be brought. The beer and the summer heat had made Quin sleepy. Soon he dozed off. His untouched cup of coffee was sitting in front of him when the interpreter tugged his sleeve and woke him up.

The sun's just going down, he whispered, always a good time to gather information. Besides, that's Haydn and they don't have the score. Shall we?

Shall we what? growled Quin.

The interpreter laughed lightly.

Very good, we shall. This is the moment we've been waiting for.

Quin expected the taxi to take them along a canal where a houseboat would be moored, but instead they drove across a wide stretch of reclaimed land to a breakwater. The interpreter strolled leisurely out toward the end of the breakwater while the taxi waited. Quin ran after him. The man stood at the end gazing across Tokyo Bay.

What the hell, said Quin.

I know, mused the interpreter, there's nothing like it at sunset. The bay and the outline of the city and above it all in the distance our noble Fuji-san. I've always been able to think more clearly here. In fact, I have a feeling the next piece of information is almost within our grasp.

The interpreter rolled his eyes toward Mt. Fuji, toward heaven. The wind was behind him so the stream of urine arched a full thirty feet out over the bay.

Lovely, mused the elderly man.

What is?

All of it. Just lovely and here we are.

Where?

Just here, repeated the interpreter, his gaze fixed on either the sacred mountain or some cloud in the sky. But we mustn't tarry now, the moment has come. Shall we?

The taxi returned them to Tsukiji, to another *sushi* restaurant, this one large and noisy. The interpreter elbowed his way through the drunken, shouting men to the counter and used some of Quin's money to bribe a waiter into giving them seats.

Act naturally, whispered the interpreter as they sat down. This is the place, all right. Pretend we just dropped in to have a bite. No one must think we're really looking for information.

Mounds of raw fish piled up in front of them, the

interpreter eating ravenously as if he had not seen food in weeks. He drank heavily and hummed his way through the entire Mozart symphony that had been played in the coffee shop earlier in the afternoon. He laughed, he picked his teeth noisily, he shouted, he sang war songs, ordered more and more *sushi* and more and more *sake* to go with it.

Hours went by. Quin was furious, drunk, dazed from the heat. Some time after midnight he was presented with an enormous bill. He intended to pay it and leave and never see the interpreter again, but as he got up from the counter the elderly man tugged his sleeve and whispered urgently.

That's right, just act naturally. But give me your money roll to pay the bill with, now is absolutely the moment.

Beside the cash register was a set of scales used for weighing fish. The interpreter dropped some money into one side of the scales, the bill into the other. He belched loudly.

A feast, he shouted.

Miserable fare, shouted the elderly man who served as cashier.

The finest restaurant in Japan, shouted the interpreter.

Impossible, shouted the cashier.

I insist upon it, yelled the interpreter.

The grace of Buddha descends upon me, yelled the cashier.

The houseboat, whispered the interpreter.

There is none, whispered the cashier.

The interpreter eased a handful of coins into the scales. He stroked a fistful of notes and let them flutter down one by one on top of the coins.

Snow, he whispered. Gently falling snow that covers the path to the castle.

Much snow must fall, whispered the cashier, to obscure the footprints of the stranger who attempts to sneak up on the castle under cover of darkness.

The interpreter pulled more notes from Quin's money roll and let them fall into the scales.

Might it be, he whispered, that one must be careful because the lord of this castle is so powerful?

He has power beyond power. No one equals him in power.

No one? That is a difficult claim to make. We have our Emperor, after all.

The Emperor has been powerless since the thirteenth century.

True enough. He has been only a figurehead, a god. Real power has long been in the hands of the warlords. Is it not so?

The cashier shrugged. Of remote eras, he whispered, I know nothing.

But do you mean to say then, whispered the interpreter, that the power of this lord in the castle compares to that of the warlords of more recent eras? That it compares to those warriors who a few short decades ago were our leaders in the conquest of China and the Pacific? Could his empire really compare to their Greater East Asia Co-Prosperity Sphere?

Greater Asia what? whispered the cashier. China, you say? The Pacific? East Asia? Spheres of spheres and prosperity? No, this empire does not compare to that one because it is much larger. And it is real, unlike that other one that was only a dream, so flimsy it collapsed in a day or two under the weight of one bomb. No, this empire exists, I tell you.

Then the man who rules it must be a mighty emperor indeed. When does he hold court in his castle, this emper-or of emperors?

The cashier scooped up the money in the scales and rang up a small sum on the cash register. He stopped whispering and spoke in a normal voice.

Fifty grams, he said. That would be a very good white-fish, short and round, but also too powerful a swimmer for any fisherman to catch. I'm afraid we don't have what you're looking for.

The interpreter hiccuped. The cashier sucked air through his teeth. They staggered out of the restaurant and down the street through crowds of men lurching back and forth, spraying each other. At last the interpreter found an unoccupied telephone pole, where he unzipped his trousers in the glare of a streetlight.

That's it, he whispered, we have it all now. First, he said fifty grams and that's half a hundred or half the night. Midnight. That's when this emperor among gangsters shows up at his houseboat. Second, he's a short rotund man. Third, the rackets he controls make up an empire larger than the Japanese empire during the Second World War. Fourth, the rackets aren't confined to the Orient but operate all over the world. Fifth, he is more powerful than General Tojo was twenty years ago. Sixth, I don't know what the cashier meant by calling him white. The Japanese language is very imprecise. Is it possible this gangster is a Westerner? Partly Western?

I suppose so, said Quin. But anyway, where is this houseboat?

Right behind the restaurant we were just in, that's why we went there of course. Most of the canals in Tokyo are sewers today, one of the few that isn't is behind that restaurant. Clean water. Just what you'd want if you lived on a houseboat. I thought of sewers while we were in the coffee shop, which is why we went there of course, then I thought of clean water while we were looking at the clean lines of Fuji-san at sunset, which is why we went down to the bay of course. But it has been a long day and now I think we must be going. Shall we?

Quin took out his money.

Impossible, said the interpreter. I wouldn't think of it. After all, I've done practically nothing for you. And let me thank you for the *sushi* and the *sake* and the Mozart. It was a very relaxing day.

He waved through the back window of the taxi as he drove away, leaving Quin astonished at the ease with which he had uncovered the information. But of course Quin had no way of knowing that he had just spent the day with a former corporal who had once been the chauffeur of a man who was a great master spy and double agent at the time of that other empire, who had observed ten thousand clandestine techniques as he drove the most feared man in the Kempeitai, the little Baron with the glass eye that never closed, through the dangerous streets of Mukden and the intricate alleys of Shanghai, the bewildering plots and deceptions of a Tokyo that had disappeared with the war.

●

Generally Big Gobi moved around and around the apartment while he was watching television. If he saw a clogged sink on the screen he went out to the kitchen to examine their sink. If he saw a clogged stomach he went into the bathroom to see if he could move his bowels.

Late one afternoon Quin went over to the set and turned it off. A minute or two later Big Gobi moaned.

Hey Quin. Hey what's that all about? I was right in the middle of something.

What?

I don't know. Something.

You haven't moved in days.

Haven't I?

Now listen, Gobes, the tube's been out of focus since yesterday. You lost the picture and you didn't even know it. There's been nothing but a hum coming out.

Well hey, maybe I was in the middle of that.

No good, Gobes. Tell me what's bothering you.

Nothing.

Come on.

Do I have to?

Yes.

Big Gobi twisted his hands. He wrung them, pretended to wash them, pretended to dry them.

It's just this. I can't think straight anymore.

What's the matter?

Everything's upside down, that's what's the matter.

Why?

Because everything's changed. I mean all my life there's

always been one thing I could trust. I didn't have much else and it was terribly important, but now it's just gone, I mean just like that. How can you lose something that used to be the whole world to you?

Maybe you don't, Gobes, maybe you don't really lose it. What was it?

Big Gobi went through the ritual of washing his hands again. He rubbed the dent in his shoulder.

What do you want to know for?

Because I care about you.

I know, I know you do, I know that's why you want to know, but what difference does it make when nothing can be done about it anyway? I mean some things are hard to talk about.

What, Gobes?

Well you know what I mean, don't you, I mean you know me, I don't have to come right out and say it.

All right. It's television, isn't it?

Sure.

It doesn't mean as much to you as it used to.

As much? Doesn't mean as much? It means nothing at all, that's what it means. After all these years it's just gone, just as if it had never been there. And it was my family, Quin, it was my home and my friends and you know, everything. It was just plain me and now it's nothing at all.

Maybe not.

But it is, I mean I know it is. I look at the set now and I don't feel a thing. I mean I remember how I used to feel, but that's all. I used to feel I couldn't live without it and now I don't even care. It frightens me. How can things just be gone? How can you just lose them?

I don't know that you can. New things happen though. Something else comes along. What's the new thing, Gobes?

You know. You must know.

Tell me.

All right I'll tell you, I'll tell you tomorrow.

No, now.

Right now?

Yes.

Like that?

Like that.

All right, Quin, I will. I'll tell you just like that.

Well?

Jigglies.

What?

Jigglies. I can't think about anything but jigglies. I look at the set and I see jigglies. The picture goes off and I still see jigglies. When I try to go to sleep I'm thinking of jigglies and that keeps me awake. I think about jigglies when I'm trying to eat and the silly food won't go down. I mean I know that night wasn't anything special to you, I know that, but it was to me and I feel just awful now. It's driving me crazy.

Big Gobi washed and dried his hands. He buried himself in his chair. Quin was thinking of the bar in Yokohama, of Big Gobi marching away from the colored lights of the jukebox behind an aging, shapeless whore, a scarred admiral of a whore who had commanded fleets of Japanese battleships during the war, who had captained half the freighters in the world since then.

Listen, said Quin. I know a place that's supposed to be the best in Asia for girls. How about it?

Where?

Right here.

Tokyo?

Right.

A kind of palace?

Exactly.

With a princess?

She'll be a princess. We'll make sure of it.

When?

Tonight. Right now.

Really?

Sure. You change and we'll be on our way.

Change?

Big Gobi looked down at himself. He was wearing bathing trunks.

Why was he wearing bathing trunks? He tried to remember. It was because he had had them on that night. He had been in a hurry to leave the beach, the dull one for swimming, to get to the other beach where there were tattoo parlors and jukeboxes and jigglies. He had been in such a hurry he hadn't changed, so that was the way he walked into the bar in Yokohama.

Bare feet. No shirt. Bathing trunks.

A life preserver over his shoulder.

But the aging, shapeless admiral standing in the colored lights of the jukebox hadn't laughed at him. In her long career she had scuttled too many battleships and seen too many shipwrecked sailors to be surprised when a man staggered through the door stripped nearly naked, grinning, gripping his life preserver.

Big Gobi smiled shyly.

Sorry, Quin, I'll change right now. As I told you, I've had this one thing on my mind.

●

They passed a sandlot where barefoot boys in white pajamas were beating their hands against trees.

Why, Quin?

Karate. Smash your hand against a tree for three or four years and you have calluses an inch thick. Smash it into a keg of sand for another three or four years and all the fingers are the same length.

Why?

So your hand's shaped like a hoe.

Big Gobi looked at his hands. He saw a woman carrying pieces of chicken wrapped in broad wood shavings. Why didn't they use paper? Girls in short skirts were going to work, and men with towels around their necks were coming from work after stopping at the public bath. Why didn't they bathe at home? Why didn't the girls go to work in the morning?

It was silly. The whole country was silly. He didn't want his hand to look like a hoe.

He felt for the eye in his pocket, the eye he had bought after the accident with the tuna fish in Boston, the weekend the foreman slipped in the freezer locker and was crushed under a load of thawing fish. The whole episode had started with an eye, Big Gobi knew that and he didn't want it to happen again. So a few days later when he had chanced to pass a store that sold surgical supplies and had seen a glass eye in the window he had gone in and bought it. Now he kept it with him always, never playing with it or taking it out except when he had to, saving it for emergencies. Even Quin didn't know about the glass eye. No one knew about it because it had to do with the tuna fish and the foreman's accident.

They went down a long spiral staircase, passed a huge man with a mallet, kept on descending.

Hey, said Big Gobi. Hey what's the name of this palace?

The Living Room.

It was silly. Nothing made any sense anymore. Palaces didn't have living rooms. Palaces were supposed to be up in the sky.

He was even more disappointed when they went into a small, dark room, smaller than the one in Yokohama, lacking a jukebox. They sat down in an alcove hidden behind palm trees. A bucket of ice was brought with a bottle in it. Big Gobi tasted the bubbly ginger ale and found it bitter. The tall, flat glasses held only a mouthful.

He was lonely. An old woman with a silly green jewel in the middle of her forehead came and sat down beside Quin. Was that Quin's idea of a princess? While they talked he peeked between the palm trees. It was dark out there. Where was everyone?

The old woman left and Quin went with her, saying he would be back in a few minutes. Big Gobi shrugged. He didn't care.

He finished the bottle of ginger ale thinking about the girl in Yokohama who had jewels on her slippers, not on her forehead. He tried washing and drying his hands, but that didn't help either. Another bottle came. He drank some more.

All at once a beautiful girl was sitting down beside him, a young girl with black hair to her waist, a princess. She was wearing an evening dress and stroking his arm. The only girl who had ever done that before was the nurse in the army when she gave him water injections. Instinctively he jerked his arm away.

Her hand fell on his knee. She giggled and went on stroking him.

Whatever you want, said her lovely eyes. I love your knee. I love all of you.

Big Gobi suddenly laughed. He was happy. This princess was the most beautiful girl he had ever seen and she was smiling at him, admiring him, loving him.

He began to talk, he couldn't help it. He told her about the orphanage and oysters and the army and the bus trip and the seagull soup on the freighter and running away from the seagulls through a blizzard. He confessed his secrets, all but one of them, and still she smiled at him, loved him, urged him to go on.

Her hand slipped up to his thigh.

Big Gobi was smiling too, giggling, pouring himself more ginger ale. The princess was beautiful, life in the palace was beautiful. She loved him, why not tell her everything? She would understand about the accident in the freezer locker.

She blew in his ear. Her hand moved over and touched him right there, stroked him right there. Big Gobi took the eye out of his pocket so that he wouldn't lose control.

It all happened quickly. She pulled her hand away, her smile was gone, her face a mixture of wonder and doubt. She was staring at his hand on the table, at the eye buried in his palm. The eye was staring back at her, reflecting the dim light in the alcove. Big Gobi didn't want her to take her hand away and he didn't want to stop talking. He wanted to tell her about the tuna fish and the accident with the foreman before it was too late.

He pulled her toward him, she pulled away. She said

something he didn't understand and her dress ripped. She screamed.

The jukebox in Yokohama, the jewels, the beach, oysters. Colored lights went off in Big Gobi's head. What was that eye doing in his hand? Was it really an eye or was it an oyster?

He pushed it into his mouth. Swallowed it.

The girl shrieked. He pulled her again and her dress tore, the jigglies were right in front of him. He squeezed the jigglies, squeezed himself, got his trousers down as the two of them crashed backward through the palm trees into the middle of the room. Waiters tried to hold his arms and legs, the *sumo* wrestler's mallet landed on his head but Big Gobi went on pumping. The mallet rose in the air a second time.

There was no way of knowing whether the second blow from that heavy weapon, by itself, would have stopped him. In any case his orgasm had already begun before the mallet fell. By the time it struck him he was spent, limp, relaxed. The mallet grazed his ear and he rolled over on his back, snoring, a smile on his face, one arm tucked underneath the naked girl.

He awoke on a landing near the street, his ear bandaged, Quin standing over him. He wanted to tell Quin that it had been nobody's fault. Not hers for touching him right there where a princess touches you when she loves you. Not his for taking out the eye because he loved her and didn't want an accident to happen at the table. No one was to blame. Everything had happened out of love.

Big Gobi thought of all the things he wanted to say, but only the same silly words kept coming out.

I'm sorry.

I'm sorry, Quin.

Sorry.

Terribly sorry.

He tried to say more and couldn't, stammered, repeated himself. And then Quin turned on him.

Hold your tongue, he said.

Big Gobi closed his eyes. He didn't say anything after

that because he had heard that voice before. It was the kind of voice a cook on a freighter used, or a nurse in the army, or a bus driver when he took your ticket and tore it up.

Just destroyed it, just like that, and threw it away not caring that you were all alone and had nowhere to go without a ticket.

It was wrong, Big Gobi knew it was wrong. Quin was like a brother to him, but even Quin got angry because he could never say what he wanted to say, could never open his heart and love people the way he wanted to love them, touch them the way he wanted to touch them without some terrible accident happening. Perhaps if he'd told Quin long ago about the mistake with the foreman and the tuna fish, he might have understood this time. But he hadn't told him then and now it was too late. It was all wrong and no one was to blame, but it was too late.

Hold your tongue.

Big Gobi closed his eyes. Those were the last words that would ever cause him pain for when they sank into him a gate clanged shut behind them, a palace gate that would never open again. He tried to live in a world that was strange and frightening, tried to call it silly, tried to pretend he could live the way other people lived. But the gestures had always been clumsy, the acting artless, a jester with a serious face, a buffoon without a smile. Although he was as kind and lonely as a clown, in the end no one laughed.

Thereafter he might walk after Quin, the brother, down this street or that from the past, through the mythical lost cities of Shanghai and Tokyo and there find his mother or father without knowing it, answering questions that went unheard because the dream was gone, because the child within him had fled to the safety of that changeless inner kingdom where neither pain nor insult could be found, nothing in fact but the silent palace where the prince who might have been sat alone in his cell, beyond hope or sadness, patiently waiting for death.

●

Each morning they had the same conversation when Big Gobi came into the living room and sat down with his hands in his lap, there to remain for the rest of the day.

How's the ear, Gobes?

The ear's fine.

Bandage too tight?

The bandage's fine.

Look, I'm sorry I spoke to you that way, I didn't mean it. I just got angry that something like that had to happen in Mama's place.

Anger's fine. That Mama's fine. What happened's fine.

Quin nodded to himself and went into the kitchen, or outside to walk, or back into the bedroom to stare at the floor. Somehow he knew he had to get through to Big Gobi, he had to break his trance. In the end, not knowing how it might help, he decided to take him along to the meeting with the gangster Kikuchi-Lotmann.

Later that evening on the houseboat with Kikuchi-Lotmann would remind him of another meeting on a houseboat, the one Mama had failed to mention in her first conversation with him, the episode that had taken place in Shanghai eight years before she arrived there, the evening when Baron Kikuchi had embraced his convictions and agreed to supply the plans of the General Staff of the Imperial Army to the engaging husband of his former mistress, a man named Quin.

One recollection, a small one.

Soon there would be many more since Quin was unknowingly nearing the center of the espionage ring that had received its code name from an event in the life of the mysterious Adzhar, a clandestine network that had connected his father and the General and Father Lamereaux, and Maeve and Miya and Mama, and through them others as well, in a performance of love and desperation so powerful it could reach out thirty years later to claim both murders and suicides, create a new Kannon Buddha, and bring on the most magnificent funeral in Asia since the death of Kublai Khan.

And all because Quin wanted to help Big Gobi, and in so doing introduced him to his murderer.

Just before midnight they were walking down the canal behind the *sushi* restaurant when a young Japanese stepped out of the shadows with a submachine gun. He was wearing a dark business suit and his hair was cut short, but Quin wouldn't have recognized him anyway without his false moustache and false sideburns. The young Japanese pointed the submachine gun at an alley and moved behind them. There was nothing to do but march ahead.

They came to a blank wall at the end of the alley. A buzzer sounded. The wall rolled away to reveal an enormous hall, a brightly lit area where hundreds of young women in white overalls and white surgical masks sat at benches studying banks of miniature television sets. Behind the sets were computers. The television screens showed scenes from all over the world, shipyards and oil refineries, camera factories, massage parlors, motorcycle assembly lines, bars and restaurants, transistor radio plants, every manner of enterprise and industry.

The guard waved them through a door into another large hall, less well lit, where young men in white overalls and white surgical masks supervised machines that stacked and packaged currencies.

The next door led into darkness. They were outside again facing the canal. A narrow gangplank ran down to a small houseboat.

When they stepped on the gangplank a light went on. A speaker began to play circus music. They passed through a tiny room with a bare canvas cot and one empty coat hanger on the wall beside a whip and megaphone. They walked through another door onto the deck.

The water was black and still. On the far side of the canal the windowless wall of a warehouse stretched for hundreds of yards. A charcoal brazier burned near the edge of the deck, which was covered with sawdust.

Folding canvas chairs were scattered here and there. From one of them rose a short, rotund man who wore steel-rimmed glasses and a lavender frock coat. He smiled as he put out his hand.

Just in time, he said. I'm serving Mongolian mixed grill tonight. Your name please?

Quin.

The short, rotund man shook his hand warmly.

Kikuchi-Lotmann, Mr. Quin, a pleasure. I was beginning to wonder what had happened to you. I expected to see you soon after you made your inquiries. Were you delayed?

Quin pointed at the bandage over Big Gobi's ear. Kikuchi-Lotmann shook his head with concern.

An accident? How unfortunate. But in any case you're here and now we can have our chat. Who was it that sent you to me?

Father Lamereaux.

Ah, such a good man, so gentle and so kind. I haven't seen him since I was a child. Excuse me, please.

The young man with the submachine gun clicked his heels and handed a report to Kikuchi-Lotmann, who glanced through it with no expression on his face. The guard stood at order arms. Kikuchi-Lotmann lit a long cigar and puffed briefly.

That settles it, he said. Sell our Korean textiles, our Kuwait crude, and our Kabul goats. Buy Surabaja brothels and bring down the government in Syria. I'll see the delegation from Bolivia next week. Tell the families in Belgium and Bali to stop feuding or I'll put out contracts. Corner the unrefined sugar market in Burma, via Beirut. Put a hold on South African diamonds until the Venezuelans agree to our pineapple terms. Bring gin, ice, and bitters.

The guard clicked his heels and left. Kikuchi-Lotmann removed a necktie from his pocket and tied it in the place of the one he was wearing.

Not since I was a child, he repeated, in Kamakura before the war. He often used to visit the man who took me in when I was a nameless orphan, Rabbi Lotmann, the former Baron Kikuchi. Lotmann always admired Lamereaux's knowledge of the *No* theater. Are you also interested in *No*?

Quin shook his head.

Nor am I. Performances yes, but of a different kind.

He paused, smiling, as if Quin were supposed to understand something by that. But when Quin said nothing he nodded quickly.

I see, he told you nothing about me. Well what might the name of your friend be?

Gobi.

Gobi? The desert in China? A curious name. In Chinese he would be called Shamo. That's their word for it, it means sandy wastes. Men known as dune-dwellers lived there in prehistoric times. Artifacts have been found along with dinosaur eggs. Would you like a drink before dinner?

They sat down at a folding camp table and Kikuchi-Lotmann mixed pink gins. A servant, a short man with gray hair, appeared with a platter of kidneys and liver, heart, spleen, a section of the large intestine, tongue and hocks and throat. Something about the man reminded Quin of Mama, perhaps his height or the resignation in his eyes. But the servant was thickset whereas Mama was frail, and the compassion in her face was replaced by hardness in his.

Kikuchi-Lotmann inspected the platter and gave instructions for cooking the meat. At the same time he chopped up leeks and watercress and made a salad dressing.

I wonder if I haven't seen him before, said Quin, nodding in the direction of the servant who was now bent over the charcoal brazier.

Unlikely, answered Kikuchi-Lotmann. He's one of my two personal bodyguards and is always with me. The other is the young man who escorted you in. The young one I call the student and the old one the policeman, because that's what they were when I hired them. The student is good at remembering things and the policeman is good at grilling meat. And now, Mr. Quin, let's have our chat. Why are you here?

To try to find out about my father, although I don't see how you could have known him. He died before the war.

I was a child before the war, Mr. Quin, and the only foreigners I knew as a child were two friends of Rabbi Lotmann. One was Father Lamereaux, the other was an elderly Russian linguist by the name of Adzhar who also lived in Kamakura. Adzhar was in his late seventies then, about the time you were being born. Is it possible you later changed your name to something more American?

Kikuchi-Lotmann grinned. Quin smiled and shook his head.

I'm afraid not. It would make a good story, but Adzhar's not the man I'm looking for.

Looking for? You said he was dead. What do you mean?

I mean I know very little about my father or mother, other than that they lived out here. I came to Japan to find out what I could.

But how am I to help if I never knew a Quin and never heard of one?

I don't know. All I know is that Father Lamereaux told me to come to see you and here I am.

Quin smiled. Kikuchi-Lotmann laughed.

I have a feeling, said Kikuchi-Lotmann, that the old Jesuit's up to something. Well he's clever, we know that. I assume he knew your father?

Not well, only in one special way. He saw him occasionally but never for more than a minute or two at a time. He can't tell me much really.

But he did know him, just as he knew Rabbi Lotmann. He knew your father and he knew my guardian, and obviously there's some reason why he wanted us to meet. Do you know what that might be?

No.

Kikuchi-Lotmann removed his glasses to polish them, his eyes shrinking to two solemn dots. The glasses went on again and Quin was faced with two large smiling eyes.

I think I might, said Kikuchi-Lotmann. I think it might have to do with *No* plays. They're stylizations, aren't they? The actors wear masks so there can be no doubt of that, then too the number of roles is quite limited no matter what the play. Only a handful really. The witch, the princess, the old man, the brother, and so forth. Now it happens there's only one thing I know about my parents, and Rabbi Lotmann might have told Father Lamereaux about it just as he told me.

What is it?

Their last circus performance. How they died. Do you know the story of Emperor Taisho opening parliament?

No.

I'll tell it to you, but just excuse me a minute, please.

The bodyguard with the submachine gun came to order arms, clicked his heels, and handed Kikuchi-Lotmann a second report. He lit a new long cigar and glanced over the single sheet of paper.

Just as I expected, he said. Say no to the automobile franchise in Thailand, offer Icelandic fishing grounds instead. Acquire a controlling interest in Ceylonese tea and let it be known that no ships will be unloaded in Malaysia and no opium allowed out of Turkey unless we get all of Bombay's male brothels. Send a letter of condolence to the head of the Burundi family. Also agree to finance the airport in the Sulawesi but not the steel mill in Sikkim. Fix the horse races in Buenos Aires and send the proceeds to our London insurance firm. Switch our arms shipments from the sultans in Sabah to the terrorists. In Somalia do the opposite, withdraw support from the terrorists and send tanks to the sheiks. Buy Austrian skiing, sell Libyan electronics. Take control of the trans-Siberian pipeline.

Oil or natural gas? asked the bodyguard.

Natural gas, said Kikuchi-Lotmann. Use our Geneva and Zurich banks. Liquidate our off-shore rights in Africa, take an option on the Brazilian jungle. Levy an eight percent surcharge on all vessels anchored in the Mediterranean. Build a tourist industry on the Caspian in Iran, emphasis on speed boats and snack bars and fast service. Schedule a coal miners' strike in Finland the day after tomorrow. End the Honduran boycott of Nicaraguan bananas. Put out the order that I want everyone in the organization to get a haircut before the weekend. Don't bring me any more reports tonight.

The bodyguard backed away. Kikuchi-Lotmann took a new necktie from his pocket.

The Emperor Taisho, he said, was on the throne in the 1920s when Father Lamereaux first came to Japan. There was an event then that made a great sensation although nothing was ever printed about it, naturally. Being god in those days, the Emperor didn't have much to do. One of his few duties was to open parliament. The chamberlains were always worried how Taisho would handle himself at the opening because he had never been quite right in the head. Well this time he stood at the podium and didn't seem to be doing anything at all, not even reading his document. He just stood there looking down at the bowed heads, rather a blank expression on his face. After about ten minutes of this had gone by, he smiled suddenly as if an idea had just come to him. All at once he rolled up the document he was supposed to be reading, rolled it up in the shape of a spy glass. He put it to his eye and swept the chamber with it, peeking at one man after another. The chamberlains were rushing to get ahold of him when he yelled out in a high squeaky voice: *Hello down there. I am the Emperor. Who are you?*

Kikuchi-Lotmann laughed.

He wouldn't give up his spy glass, so they had to lead him away and open parliament without the document being read. Well the point is, perhaps that's what Father Lamereaux is doing. Perhaps he's saying, I am the Emperor and it's up to you to answer for yourself. He knew my guardian, he knew your father, he knew the way my parents died. There's a connection somewhere, and it must have to do with that last circus. With that vast unreal warehouse on the outskirts of Shanghai.

Shanghai?

Of course. Where else in Asia could such a circus have been performed?

●

After they finished the meal Kikuchi-Lotmann poured brandy. Big Gobi stared at the fire and dozed. A full moon had risen above the canal. It was well after midnight and the city was quiet. Facing the still water from the houseboat, they seemed far from Tokyo.

Kikuchi-Lotmann removed his necktie and tied in its place one of deep crimson.

The circus, he announced, taking off his glasses. His eyes shrank to dots as he recited the poem.

To know its sawdust,
Its smells and rings and highbars,
Is to remember.

A haiku, he said. Not a very good one, but at least of my own making. Now let us recall that other circus, the circus we knew as children. The sweep of the trapeze acts, the grace of the dangerous cats, the ridiculous clowns, the lumbering elephants, the confusing jugglers, the flying bareback riders. A magical show without end because of the magic in a child's heart.

Yet when we go back years later we see a different performance. The costumes are shoddy, the smells cheap, the clowns not quite so funny, the aerialists not quite so daring. The dream is gone and what we see is crude, even grotesque. Sadness? Yes. Because we know the circus hasn't changed.

So much for the wonders of childhood. Now for the setting of this particular circus, Shanghai in those last days before the war.

Enormous wealth, enormous poverty. Thousands of entrepreneurs and tens of thousands of slaves. The opium rights to a province lost at a game of cards. Women given fortunes in exchange for an evening of pleasure, or thrown into the baggage train of a warlord as a different kind of payment. Peasant boys reigning as queens one day and tortured to death the next. Hundreds of people slaughtered because a Chinese or Japanese general wakes up in the morning with painful hemorrhoids.

In food the favored delicacy is shrimp fed on human flesh. In alcohol and drugs the preferred mixture is laudanum, which combines the two.

These are the simple facts and figures of Shanghai, a city crowded with White Russians and exiles and adventurers of every kind, the halfway point on the east coast of Asia, a terminal for victims of all breeds and races.

Facts and figures. Are they enough, or is it possible that Shanghai was more than this? Not just a city but a state of mind, or to be more precise, an actual part of the mind? A vision we all carry somewhere within us?

It is here that my father finds himself with his circus one winter late in the 1930s. He is the circus master and my mother, in order to be near him, has taught herself to be an aerialist. A group of wealthy degenerates approaches him for a special performance, a private showing, acts to match the times and mock them. He listens to them and agrees, implying a performance unlike any ever staged. He moves his circus to an abandoned warehouse on the outskirts of the city and goes to work alone rigging the high wires, preparing the props and costumes himself.

The night of the circus comes. It is to begin exactly at midnight. The spectators arrive in evening dress and take their places while the band plays ruffles and flourishes. It is cold in the gloomy warehouse, but the excitement is too great for anyone to bother with that.

Trumpets. A drooping clown holds a sign for silence.

The drum rolls. A juggler spins a shadowy web of balls in the air.

Now we see him stepping into the ring dressed in boots and frock coat, carrying a whip and megaphone, the shaman and arbiter of marvels. He raises the megaphone and we hear the acts he will present.

The one-eyed tomb of Semarang.
The sure-footed vine of Mindanao.
The prancing Brunei horse.
The untamed leopard of Irrawaddy.
The Malacca cane.
The one and only Johore jerkin in captivity.

The spectators refuse to acknowledge this list of preposterous acts. Some are stupefied, others angry, a few fearful. They have brought bags of shrimp with them to eat during the performance, and now they begin noisily cracking the tails of the shrimp, peeling them, stuffing the rich meat into their mouths. There is hissing and shouting, stamping, catcalls.

The snare drum rolls again, the juggler plays out his shadowy game. My father continues announcing acts that have never been acted, animals that have never lived. It's nonsense, of course, yet all of it is serious as well as meaningless.

At last he lowers the megaphone. He walks across the sawdust to the side of the ring looking up at my mother who is poised on the highbar, waiting for her trapeze act, a hundred feet above the ground.

Does she understand at the moment what he is doing? What is about to happen?

Perhaps. But it is too late for her or anyone to stop a performance that began long ago. Long ago, yes, and now it is here.

Tuneless, masterless
Come the acts of memory,
A Shanghai circus.

●

Kikuchi-Lotmann untied his necktie. He took a black one from his pocket and knotted it in place.

Poetry is a sauce, he said, and like all good sauces it

should be both sweet and sour. The performance he had prepared that night, you see, was for a very small audience. The wealthy patrons in the stands, the animals and acts and clowns, the band and the jugglers were all props for a private performance he was about to stage for one person and one person alone, the woman on the highbar. To each of us love is a different mixture. To him it meant a ring and a bed.

But before I complicate the tale, let me say that it is really very simple. A man is enamored with the dash and excitement of the circus. He gives his life to it and discovers too late that the love of one woman is more important. Now wasting one's life is commonplace. This man's madness came because he had knowingly refused the gift.

The ring? The circus ring of course, the circle where a confident dissembler struts in his clever costumes sowing shouts and laughter, thinking he will trick life with his acts and disguises by tricking the fools who have come to watch him, which indeed he will one evening after another since spectators are there for that very purpose. The spectators applaud vigorously but after every performance the hall is emptied, and thus at the end of every clever evening the circus master must remember and remove the disguises he has squandered before the trumpets. He is naked then, trapped in the tight silence of the ring that has become his cage, alone with the squeezed tubes of paint and the hollow, worn costumes, standing alone on sawdust strewn with dead footprints that are mere acts of memory. Others come to see and marvel, they leave, and when they are gone he no longer exists.

And the bed? The bed of my mother, all her beds in one. The bed where she was born and slept as a child, a girl, a young woman. Where she took her first lover and her first ten and twenty lovers and many more even after she married because her husband would not receive her love. Because he thought the circus was too important to him. Because he gave his life to become a ring master in the clamor and triumph of a sawdust circle.

Probably he even encouraged her in those transitory affairs in order to be more at ease with himself, in order to think she wasn't lonely, in order to hide from himself the fact that ultimately he could neither accept her love nor return it. Surely they both must have been involved in those acts of life that became decisive through repetition, even though the two of them might never have openly admitted they were making decisions.

And so it went year after year. An ambitious costumed man cleverly performing in the ring. A lonely woman in a bed exchanging love for hope with one passerby after another, exchanging love for flowers, for dinner, for an evening with someone, anyone, so that at least for an evening time could pass finger by finger instead of minute by minute.

The circus had always been his passion. When did its magic begin to slip away? When did he begin to have doubts about the trumpets that sounded when he stepped into the ring night after night? When did he begin to loathe the costumes and disguises? To detest the audiences who cheered only when he followed one act quickly with another? Who hissed when he faltered, hissed when he stumbled, demanded more and more, and then left the moment the performance ended?

There is no way to know. It happened. The ring became a cage. He had to reinforce himself with heavier and heavier doses of alcohol before he could bring himself to put on his costumes, to fix a smile to his face, to step forward and pretend he was still pleased with himself, still in command of the animals, still trying to amuse the spectators, still striving for the applause that was now utterly meaningless to him. He was given to darker and darker moods. He became morose, even violent.

His wife tried to help him but she couldn't. Her kindness infuriated him because it reminded him of what he had lost in life, what he had thrown away. Despite her efforts the only time he could be intimate with her was after he had been drinking for hours. When he thought he could forget.

A woman opens
Her legs with smiles and gestures.
The bed is crowded.

Crowded with the men she had known over the years,
the men he had driven her to. He tried to forget but he
couldn't. The woman he loved and the circus he hated
mixed in his mind, the bed and the ring were entangled.
One became a vision of the other and that vision obsessed
him. When he looked at her now he saw a succession of
vulgar defiling acts, the smiles and gestures of other men
that were a part of her, a performing hell of screeching
animals and leering jugglers, clowns pulling water pumps
out of their trousers, pulling live chickens out of their
baggy trousers as they smirked and worked their tongues.

A man so haunted by her past that a time came when he
could no longer make love to her at all, no matter how
much alcohol he had consumed. And that was the end for
him. He could bear it no longer. Exhausted, totally humiliated, he prepared a last performance and stepped into the
ring in front of a howling Shanghai mob.

Trumpets. Snare drums. The spotlight rises to the ceiling where a tiny figure is crouching under the skylight, a
world-famous dwarf whose high dive will be the opening
act. All heads go back. Silence. The dwarf leaps into space
blindfolded and hurtles down from the black sky.

A thin silk cord, invisible from below, is attached to the
dwarf's ankle. At the last moment the silk cord will catch
him. His fall will be broken a few inches above the floor.
He will go into a long bouncing swing as he removes the
blindfold, grins, waves triumphantly from his upside-
down position.

Except this time the cord is a few inches too long. The
snares roll, the drums boom, and the dwarf's head splat-
ters over the sawdust.

The end of a man who has been my father's friend for
years.

At once the spotlight turns to three clowns approaching
the stands on stilts a full thirteen feet high. The clowns

assume antic poses. Their hands interpret various obscene suggestions. Suddenly there's a sharp crack, one of
the stilts has been sawed through the middle. The clown
comes tumbling down, knocking over the other two as he
falls.

One man rips open his face, another is pierced through
the heart by the broken stilt. The third lies on his back
opening and closing his mouth, unable to move or make a
sound.

Once more the spotlight shifts, this time to a balancing
act. A man with huge biceps is peddling a unicycle while
juggling balls with both hands. On his forehead he sup-
ports a tall metal pole, on top of the pole is a crossbar
where a naked woman bends backward. The man seems
to be peddling more rapidly, the balls drop away. The
heavy pad meant to protect his head has been tampered
with, the end of the pole has been sharpened and is slowly
boring into his head. As the woman on the crossbar
spreads her crotch wide to the audience, the pole splits her
partner's skull in two.

She crashes to the ground. The spotlight shoots into the
air.

An aerial performance. A woman hangs by her knees
from a trapeze, a mouthpiece clamped between her teeth.
From the mouthpiece dangles another trapeze on which
two wiry men, also hanging by their knees, masturbate
each other while cursing their female relatives. The
woman's neck muscles bulge even more than expected,
for the mouthpiece isn't the one she generally uses. This
mouthpiece has been fitted with a spring that gradually
expands in her mouth. Of course she can't spit it out, nor
can she scream. The fellatio comes to an end when the
two ejaculating men follow their sperm toward the ring
together with the lower half of the woman's face, her
hanging tongue showing where she has been severed at
the ears.

These opening acts, meant to set a circus mood, are
quickly over. Now the spotlight dips back and forth,
leaving the ring in darkness. The audience responds to the
darkness by swinging their little red lights.

The flashlights were my father's idea, miniature red lights on a string. He had devised them after long experience with audiences of children.

A circus ring is continually being darkened to prepare for the next act, and it seems that when a large number of children are gathered together in darkness they have a irresistible urge to exert themselves. They shriek, they tear off their clothes, they punch and kick each other and try to urinate on someone's face.

My father introduced the little red lights so the children could amuse themselves when the hall was dark. Then he noticed that the parents of the children also enjoyed swinging the lights. Subsequently he never gave a performance without passing around the little red lights to everyone.

Although sophisticated and wealthy, the Shanghai audience was the same as any other when it came to darkness. While an act was under way they cracked and peeled their shrimps, giggled, nudged one another, and congratulated themselves. But the moment the act ended they desperately swung their little red lights.

A sense of community, perhaps, in that vast and gloomy warehouse?

There was always an undercurrent of fear, you see, in the old Shanghai, fear of a special kind. The city hung by the sea, a dot of land under international control. Beyond it stretched all of China and more, all of Asia. Tens of thousands of miles of interminable mountains and deserts. Tens of millions of nameless people babbling in unknown tongues. Swarming river valleys and uninhabitable mountain ranges. Caravan trails spiraling back into antiquity.

Who were these bewildering peoples? What esoteric fantasies might be the heritage of tribes that had wandered for millennia on the byways of unrecorded languages?

A few travelers had always explored these ancient routes. Learned Arabs, gentle Nestorians, adventurous Greeks. Some even reached the Pacific and lived to pass on their tales to the curious. But the stories they told only hinted at the mysteries to be found out there, the dragon bones of lost and future worlds, the illusions of mystics and madmen.

Shanghai stood on the edge of this hinterland. There were only a few people there, relatively speaking, with only a few days or weeks to live. To them this precarious existence on the edge of China had become man's precarious existence on the edge of sanity. That's what I meant when I said that Shanghai, then, was not only a state of mind but an actual part of mind. Within the narrow bounds of the city, people explored depravity, to be sure, but perhaps that was only because the wastes that lay beyond were too vast to contemplate.

These creatures now swung their little red lights in the warehouse of my father's mind, the circus of his life. The ring was tiny, the warehouse huge, the walls were lost in darkness. There was nothing for them to do but huddle together in front of the master of ceremonies past and present, the magician and lord of the acts.

A Shanghai circus, then, a circus of the mind. My mother still watches from the highbar a hundred feet in the air. My father stands in the middle of the ring with his megaphone and whip, waiting, and at last the audience begins to see the truth. One by one the skilled performers, his oldest friends, are being maimed and killed. Now one by one the spectators cease to nibble the fat shrimps in their laps. Instead they squirm and whine as they swing their little red lights.

My father points his megaphone. The regular performances have ended, he has seen enough of human acts. The time has come for animals. With growing fury he shouts out the names of the beasts he will present.

The Afghan ibis.
The unicorn and centaur and sphinx.
The Cochin mermaid, the humpbacked zebra, the two-legged sheep.
The pregnant tapir, the Sunda sable and purple sail.
The hairless ibex and furry dolphin.

And a dozen more, all the monsters his tortured mind can conjure up. The cages are opened under the spotlight. Save for the circle of little red lights, the warehouse is lost in blackness.

The animals have not been fed in weeks, nor does their trainer give them any commands. His whip is curled around his legs and he watches them without moving. They paw the ground, staring at the little red lights that spin like eyes in a jungle night.

The Siberian tiger is the first to move. His tail swishes, his head goes down.

The leap carries him thirty feet into the stands, little enough for a tiger that size. The beast chews his way through the undergrowth and leaps again, snapping and growling, a head hanging from his maw.

The tiger's roar is a signal to all the animals. The panther moves quickly, then the leopard, the bison, the herd of baboons, the rhinos and horses and monkeys, the hulking elephants. They crawl and swing through the stands chopping and clawing jungle eyes. An elderly woman is caught between a female elephant and an advancing male. Her daughters, products of successive unnatural unions with her twin brothers many years before, are assaulted in several positions by a pack of baboons. A man falls under the thrusts of a rhino's horn, another is straddled by the bison. A horse eats its way into a leg thick with swollen veins and buried abscesses.

The big cats leap from pile to pile, the monkeys root in the rubbish, stealing shoes and eyeglasses and false limbs, especially teeth inlaid with gold. The shiny metal attracts them and whenever they see a victim captured by a larger beast, nuzzling to find a liver that isn't sclerotic, they pull out the pretty teeth before the head is swallowed.

The baboons abandon the two hemorrhaging daughters and go in search of scirrhoid lesions. They had discovered a cancer in one of the girls that was tastier than the undiseased parts, which in that wealthy group tended to be too fat and oversalted. In just such a short time the baboons have also become specialists.

Last comes the jackal, a cautious beast. He circles a body many times before approaching, for he requires a man or woman who is alive yet paralyzed. When he finds one he settles down on his sticky haunches and performs the sexual act on the victim's mouth. He then licks the mouth clean and moves on, a silk evening cloak over his shoulders, earrings dangling from his teeth.

The band plays, the tubas thump, the snares roll. The base drum booms, the horns blare unrelated chords, and the ring master stands alone in the spotlight. Just beyond the circle a juggler tosses an array of torches into the sky, toward the highbar where my mother watches the little red lights disappear.

By now all the animals have found a specialty. The monkeys hide sackfuls of gold teeth. The baboons wear expensive sport clothes and eat only cancerous tissue. The rhinos wallow in women's underwear, the elephants trample eyeglasses into grains of sand. The horses prance in review, the leopard licks its hind quarters, the panther crunches kneecaps and other heavy bones, the Siberian tiger studies the stains left on the seats. The dogs, decorated in ribbons and epaulets, dance on two feet while the jackal pursues his solitary course along the fringe.

My mother saw it all. She saw him descend into the circus where lust and teeth and the wail of a victim are joined together in a single act, where animals run free and bodies pile up while a band plays and a juggler lifts torches end over end. She saw the performance rage and die, saw him step out of the ring and move away from the life where once he had ruled.

A monotonous juggler. A discordant band. A herd of snoring animals.

She shivers from the cold. After so much meat the animals will sleep for days. Even the jackal has closed his eyes. The band is sleeping too, lost in the nirvana of an opium dream. The spotlight still lights the juggler, but less clearly now. The torches give off an oily smoke and burn low as the juggler falls asleep beside them.

The spotlight is gone, the gloom begins to lift. From the skylight above her head dawn dimly falls on the interior of the empty warehouse.

After that? After my father stepped out of the ring he was never seen again. Armies were marching, war was coming. The great circus was beginning in which millions would have a part to play, an act, a specialty. The audience in Shanghai was soon forgotten, as was my father's night in a deserted warehouse.

Those people, you see, would have died soon anyway. They were looking for death, and one way or another they would have found it. They were on the edge, voyeurs a step away waiting for the final spectacle. They must have known they had gone to the warehouse that night to witness their own deaths. After all, there was nothing else left to see.

So it wouldn't be right to say they were victims that night. There were only two victims. The ring and the bed were theirs, the circus was theirs, the sounds and the smells and the horrors were theirs.

Thus when dawn came she gripped the trapeze and took a last breath. She balanced on her toes and the trapeze swung wide as it had many times before. And as she had many times before, she left it and turned the graceful, loving figures in the air.

Turned and turned through three somersaults, hung still where there was no hand to catch her. Still for a moment, one moment before she spiraled down and down.

●

Kikuchi-Lotmann's glasses had fogged. He cleaned them on his necktie, his eyes black dots.

I have never forgotten, he said in a low voice. I have remembered and lived accordingly. How could it be otherwise?

Heaven and water go their opposite ways,
Thus in all transactions the superior man
Carefully considers the beginning.

Not mine and not a haiku either. That one's from the old book. To the ancient Chinese the superior man was the ordinary man, that's what it means. So I have remembered the way they lived and the torment it brought them and done the opposite, doing everyday business in a businesslike way, putting the war and the passions they knew behind me, satisfying myself with the mundane affairs of ordinary business because I have considered my beginning, my father, and where it led him.

Where did it lead him? said Quin.

To the interior of China I suppose, the coastline was already at war. But where exactly would be impossible to say. Wandering the trails of those learned Arabs perhaps, those gentle Nestorians and adventurous Greeks. Or rather I'd like to think that. As with the audience in the warehouse that night, it would be better not to know the end. It would be better to think he's still wandering.

Kikuchi-Lotmann smiled.

And so I do. I prefer to think that somewhere in the vastness of central Asia, beyond those interminable arid wastes where the paths are too old and new for the rest of us, there is a home for a soul such as his. A small resting place beside a stream, under a tree, where a man who has dreamed and failed can surrender his ghost without regrets. I prefer to believe that.

Kikuchi-Lotmann creaked out of his chair and stretched his arms. The shadows were gone. One final time he changed his necktie. When he turned to Quin he was smiling.

Well, have we learned anything tonight? Have we discovered what Father Lamereaux might have had in mind when he sent you here?

I'm not really sure, said Quin, but one thing bothers me. If he knows the story, which he must, why didn't he tell it to me himself?

Perhaps because he's a holy man and a holy man is supposed to guide, not teach. Or it might have been just a whim of his. In any case we followed the holy man's directions and did what was expected of us.

Quin shook Big Gobi by the shoulder and told him it was time to leave. As he stood Kikuchi-Lotmann noticed the cross hanging from his neck.

That's an old piece. Where did it come from?

It was given to him in America, answered Quin.

Once as a boy I saw a cross much like it. It belonged to Rabbi Lotmann's twin brother, who apparently treasured it greatly. He always wore it hidden under his uniform, which was odd for a Japanese who wasn't a Christian, who was an ultranationalist in fact. It wouldn't have gone well for him in the army if anyone had known about it.

Who was he? said Quin.

A very powerful General who was killed in China in 1937. He inherited the title of Baron Kikuchi when Lotmann became a Jew.

THE
POLICEMAN

6

As for where they go and why, we cannot be sure of
such things. There are no tracks in such a barren waste.
The sandstorms blow, the sun sinks, rivers disappear,
and their camels are lost in darkness. Therefore the
truth must be that the routes of such men are untrace-
able, their missions unknowable, their ultimate
destinations as invisible as the wind.

If the Son of Heaven is to continue to rule with
integrity, we must defend our borders at all costs
from such men.

—A Han dynasty account of the caravans in the Gobi Desert

●

The young bodyguard whom Kikuchi-Lotmann called the
student stood in a long line of people waiting for a movie
theater to open. It was his day off and he didn't have to be
back at the dormitory until muster the following morning.

All of the gangsters who worked for Kikuchi-Lotmann
lived together in the company housing project, a large
concrete block of windowless cubicles built around a
central courtyard. Muster came at six o'clock, when a
bugle sounded over the public address system. The gangsters fell in at attention in the courtyard and the roll was
taken. A physical fitness expert then led them through a
rigorous series of push-ups, pull-ups, and rope-skipping.
The calisthenics ended at seven o'clock with the gangsters maneuvering around the courtyard in military fa-

shion singing the company marching song, *Kikuchi-Lotmann Enterprises Forever.*

The supreme present,
Nothing compares to the present.
Unless it's the past.

The lyrics were much too brief for the music, which one of the older employees claimed was similar to a tune he had heard in Singapore before the war, a song known at that time, there, as *Roast Beef of Old England.*

Hato hated calisthenics and he hated the dormitory. He hated the young whore, a mental health specialist, who burst into his cubicle three times a week dressed as an elderly woman, her face lined with gray make-up to give her the semblance of age, her breasts taped down to appear flat, her belly daubed with green chalk, her legs painted with varicose veins. The young woman yanked him to his feet and pushed him away from the door. He had to spend an hour with her.

Up against the wall, mother-fucker, she shouted as she charged.

Hato didn't have any special feelings about his mother, so the therapeutic effect of the session was lost on him. He would have preferred a girl who looked like a movie star.

Hato's father had made his living since the war selling gloves, hairpieces, and empty lipstick tubes that had formerly belonged to female movie stars. Most of these items were bought by girls who worked in massage parlors. The more select imports he auctioned off to industrialists, veterans of the Pacific war, who would pay high prices for anything that had belonged to an American star because America had won the war.

He had begun his career almost by accident when the most famous blond star in America, later a suicide, visited the Imperial Hotel for a few days. On a whim Hato's father bribed the maids to search the sheets each morning to see what they could find.

When the movie star left he had two genuine pubic

hairs in his possession. He framed the hairs under a magnifying glass together with a nude picture of the actress and auctioned off the display, realizing enough profit to set up a business importing less sensational items collected or stolen by maids and garbage men in Los Angeles.

The house where Hato grew up was strewn with movie magazines used by his father to check the authenticity of the gloves, hairpieces, and empty lipstick tubes he imported. As a child Hato was given to spells of dizziness that caused his eyes to roll back in his head. While the spells were upon him he was in danger of biting his tongue.

The best way to deal with the seizures, he discovered, was to lie down at once on a couch covered with movie magazines and stuff whatever was close at hand into his mouth. Generally the nearest available object was either a glove or a hairpiece or an empty lipstick tube.

Later he outgrew these attacks, but one or two of their ancillary aspects remained with him. When he went to the United States for graduate work in mathematics he found he was unable to fall asleep in a foreign country unless the bed was covered with the faces of several dozen actresses of that country. And if someone called him a Jap in the course of the day or made reference to his height, or to his grin or his lack of a grin, it was further necessary for him to fall asleep sucking a glove or a hairpiece or an empty lipstick tube in order to assure a full night's sleep.

The male students at the university in New York wore beards and long hair. Hato let his own hair grow and bought false sideburns and a false moustache to cover his lack of facial hair.

The first weeks in New York were lonely ones. Toward the end of the third month, his hair now plausibly long, he broke out of his isolation and took a subway down to Chinatown. A chow mein restaurant there was said to have whores available. A woman approached him and he followed her to a hotel.

The whore turned out to be different from Japanese whores. She would neither take off her clothes nor masturbate him. Calling him Jappy, she hauled up her skirt and told him to get busy.

A few minutes later Hato was having trouble breathing. His sweat had loosened his false moustache, which was slowly slipping down over his mouth and sealing itself there.

Hato tried to hurry, his head down so that he wouldn't have to see the whore's face or smell her breath. The added effort loosened his false sideburns, sliding them up and in until they were pasted over his eyes. Blind, unable to breathe, he had to leap off the whore just as he was about to have an orgasm.

He staggered into a lamp. His sperm hit the lightbulb, he followed the lamp to the floor and cut his hand on the sticky slivers of glass. Somehow he managed to get to the bathroom and free his eyes and mouth under the hot water tap. When he came back the whore was gone, having taken not only his wallet but his shoes and socks as well so that he couldn't follow her. Hato wrapped his sideburns and moustache around his bleeding hand and walked up the Bowery back to his room, too ashamed to be seen in the subway barefoot.

During the next weeks Hato brooded over the loneliness of life in New York. He realized he needed a project to sustain him, and at last he found one. He decided to become the world's leading authority on airplane disasters.

Early in the morning he bought newspapers and clipped the articles that had to do with crashes. In the afternoon, after finishing his work, he bathed and changed into his kimono. From that time until midnight, his door locked, he worked on his shoebox files.

First he typed the articles on filing cards, then retyped them on other cards to show where the various accounts agreed and disagreed. Lastly he prepared cards under several hundred categories to cross-reference the accident.

His system was so meticulous that the crash of a small private plane could fill half a shoebox, a major disaster as many as eight shoeboxes.

It was demanding work but Hato knew that someday experts from many countries would come to consult his files. His fame would spread, he would be asked to lecture and give his opinions on television.

Near the end of his second and last year of study Hato was invited to a dance sponsored by an evangelical church group. He found himself sitting next to a girl who was a cripple and also couldn't dance. She invited him back to the same hall that following night for a religious discussion. Hato ate cookies and volunteered to proselytize for the group every day from late afternoon to midnight.

The militant sect, of southern origin, provided him with a sign quoting from the Bible and a tambourine. Because he was in love with the crippled girl he was only too glad to stand on streetcorners in the Bowery waving the sign and shaking the tambourine while she sang psalms. He intended to marry her and take her back to Japan.

A weekend came when the girl invited him to her home outside the city. The girl's father watched him suspiciously, Hato grinned. The girl's mother went into the kitchen and stayed there. The first meal at the house consisted of potato soup, potato pancakes, bread and bread pudding, and peppers stuffed with potatoes. Being accustomed to yogurt and a slice of raw fish for lunch, Hato was both dazed and nauseated. Several times during the meal he had to go to the bathroom to vomit noisily.

Afterward the girl's father sat him down in the living room. He made an allusion to American nurses in Manila Bay. Hato grinned, still feeling ill. The father mentioned forced marches, death marches, sneak attacks, mass attacks, regimented ants, national guilt.

Hato fell asleep, awakening a few hours later to a meal of boiled potatoes, baked potatoes, mashed and fried and roasted potatoes, potatoes colored to look like vegetables and shaped to look like meats. By the end of the weekend he knew that he would always hate all Americans and that marrying the crippled girl was out of the question.

When he returned to Tokyo Hato decided to make a lot of money in order to go to Paris and become a movie director. The quickest way to make money was as a gangster. He was interviewed and eventually sat facing a small, rotund man who was rumored to be the director of an enormous criminal syndicate. In exchange for his loyalty, free room and board, and one day off a month, he was offered a substantial sum of money at the end of eight years of service. Hato accepted the offer, trimmed his hair, and bought a business suit.

Working for a criminal syndicate in Japan, however, didn't turn out to be what he had expected. Instead of kicking whores and pistol-whipping shopkeepers, his job consisted of carrying reports from a computer across the gangplank to Kikuchi-Lotmann's houseboat. He stood rigidly at attention while his employer smoked a cigar, changed his necktie, mixed a salad dressing, poured himself a pink gin.

Finally he was given instructions. He recrossed the gangplank and repeated the instructions to a programmer who fed them into a computer.

Despite his advanced mathematical training, his fanatical desire for adventure, and his fanatical willingness to take risks, Hato had been hired for only one reason. He was extraordinarily familiar with world geography. Few people would have recognized all the names that appeared in Kikuchi-Lotmann's reports, so vast were his enterprises. Hato never confused them, however, due entirely to his experience with the airplane clippings.

In addition to crossing the gangplank he had only one other task, to accompany his employer periodically to the secret meetings he held with bereaved grandmothers. On these occasions he guarded the door while his employer and the grandmother discussed the details of a funeral.

Kikuchi-Lotmann's syndicate was the largest criminal organization in greater east Asia. In terms of gross criminal profits it was the third largest in the world. Yet despite his responsibilities he indulged himself in a very curious sideline known as the funeral racket, whereby he would provide a long procession of black limousines and thousands of mourners dressed in black for a man who died unloved and unmissed.

The funeral procession might contain two limousines or many hundreds of limousines, depending on the amount of money paid. In the last limousine would be found the legitimate family, invariably small, presided over by a weeping, triumphant grandmother. The other family members would be unaware of the funeral's fakery. Only the matriarch knew how large a part of her husband's fortune she had used for this immensely expensive deception.

As they drove through the crowds of mourners the grandmother pointed them out and pointed to the line of limousines ahead of them.

Never forget, she said, the day your grandfather was cremated. Remember how he was loved and revered despite the money he made. Remember the thousands who came to do him homage.

Her children nodded, her grandchildren nodded, the mourners returned to Kikuchi-Lotmann's henchmen to collect their wages.

Hato admired the cleverness of the racket. A whore had to spend at least a few minutes with a customer, everyone couldn't take drugs all the time. But the funeral market had no limit, the number of ancestors to be revered was infinite. Hato intended to expose the operation in his first gangster movie. People would come from many countries to interview him. He would be asked to lecture and give his opinions on television.

Paris. Eight years away.

Hato stood in line thinking of the calisthenics he would have to do the next morning at six o'clock. At seven he would march around the courtyard singing a haiku. That night or the next night a young girl disguised in rags would break into his room and call him a mother-fucker.

Hato grinned. There could be more to gangsterism than

gangplanks and funerals. When the movie was over he would go talk to Kikuchi-Lotmann's other bodyguard, the one who was called the policeman.

●

He was a small man, as small as Mama, born to her parents the year they sold her to the brothel in Kobe, the year before the First World War broke out in Europe. His father beat him as regularly as he beat his wife until he was eaten by a dog one winter night.

The father had collapsed in a snow drift on the way home from a drinking bout. A dog found him and sniffed his hot breath. Like every other creature in the Tohoku that winter, the dog was starving. Soon he was not only sniffing the hot breath but chewing it, chewing the lips and tongue that went with it.

All the peasants in the neighborhood had been ordered to line the road the next day at first light, to show their respect for their landowner who was expected to drive past sometime during the morning. The policeman's father was found with a large part of his face gone. He was carried home and treated, but his wife and son were told to wait beside the road until the aristocrat drove by. Thereafter the policeman's father wore a cotton surgical mask and stopped beating his family.

The dreaded Tohoku district was forever given to gray skies and winds and blizzards from Siberia. Half of the family's crop of mulberry leaves had to be turned over as payment for use of the land. With the other half they paid their taxes and tried to subsist.

Their plot of mulberry trees was an hour's walk from the hut where they lived. Centuries ago the hills had been terraced, which gave the Tohoku the look of a land of giants. But for a peasant family such as the policeman's the giant steps went nowhere.

When he was eight years old the silk market in America

collapsed once again. As before, his father blamed the catastrophe on his wife because she was an Ainu and had Caucasian blood. Unable to bear the hatred in his eyes any longer, she finally broke the ice in a rice paddy and drowned herself in three inches of water.

The policeman's father died of stomach cancer, arthritis, and advanced tuberculosis in 1931, the year the Japanese seized Manchuria after one of their railroads was blown up there, apparently by Chinese patriots. In retaliation the international city of Shanghai boycotted all goods of Japanese manufacture, an act that many Japanese army officers found outrageously insolent. That same year the policeman enlisted in the army to escape the misery of the Tohoku.

From the very beginning he liked his new life. The routine was easy enough, he worked hard and did what he was told. At the end of training he was rewarded with an assignment to a Kempeitai unit in Korea.

The country was as poor as the Tohoku, but now the Koreans were the tenant farmers and he was one of the landlords and tax-collectors. The main work of his unit was the interrogation of peasants suspected of withholding rice. While trying to break the peasants, beating them when necessary, he experienced a sense of accomplishment that was new to him. For the first time in his life he learned to smile.

An inexplicable event occurred soon after he was promoted to corporal. He and some other corporals got drunk one night and the talk turned to women. There were no whores in the village where they had arrived that day, but the policeman boasted he could find one anyway. He went away laughing, leaving his friends laughing behind him.

The next day an officer called them in. A village elder had been clubbed while protecting his daughter. It was not the way for a member of the Imperial Army to act with monkeys of an inferior race. The guilty one was ordered to admit his breach of discipline.

The policeman stood stonily at attention, expecting the other corporals to do the same. But to his astonishment he saw them stepping forward one by one to denounce him.

It was spring. Tiny green shoots were just reaching above the water in the rice paddies. The three months of latrine duty meant nothing to him but the betrayal by his fellow corporals, the men he had thought were his comrades, influenced him so profoundly he was never able to trust anyone again, even to the point where the only sexual act of which he was capable thereafter was one involving a dead person, performed with an instrument so that his own body would have no contact with the corpse.

From Korea he was transferred to Manchuria, to the unit of a captain in Mukden who always wore civilian clothes. Although the Captain could read, he was also a peasant from the Tohoku and didn't despise the policeman just because he was illiterate. It was from the Captain he learned that the bombing of the railroad in Manchuria the year before, the incident that led to the Japanese seizure of Manchuria, had not been the work of Chinese patriots but of the Kempeitai itself.

The Captain was the protégé of a Kempeitai general then stationed in Tokyo. To provide the General with information he wanted on various factions in the army, thereby increasing the General's maneuvering power over his fellow officers, the policeman was asked to steal documents from certain units near Mukden. The policeman was so successful in his assignments the Captain took him with him when he flew to Shanghai on a secret mission in January 1932.

For a week the policeman was locked in an apartment memorizing various Chinese patriotic slogans. The Captain came and went and at the end of the week gave him his instructions.

The two of them, dressed as Chinese students, were driven in a closed van to an alley behind Bubbling Well Road. They entered a hallway guarded by Kempeitai agents disguised as shoemakers and took up their places in an abandoned storefront that faced the thoroughfare. Some twenty minutes later when the crowds were thickest, an elderly Japanese monk came into view.

The monk belonged to one of the most famous Japanese families living in China. His great-grandfather had emigrated to Canton at the beginning of the nineteenth century, studied acupuncture, and founded a hospital.

In 1840 the acupuncturist's son joined the Chinese forces that were fighting the British to try to end the opium trade in that city. Two years later he was killed, one of the last patriots to fall before Britain annexed Hong Kong as a base for expanding its opium interests.

The patriot's son became a Buddhist scholar in Nanking. The scholar's son became a monk in Shanghai. On that winter afternoon in 1932 he was walking from his temple to his residence, following the route he had taken every day for fifty years.

When the elderly monk was abreast of them they burst out of the storefront shouting their slogans and firing their revolvers. A few minutes later they had raced back down the alley and were speeding away in their van.

The next day, in retaliation for the murder, a Japanese squadron bombed the Chinese slums in the city, the first time in history that bombing planes had been used against civilians. A Japanese naval garrison clashed with the Nineteenth Chinese Route Army and thus began what became known in Japan as the Shanghai Incident, one more reason for the Japanese invasion of north China a year later.

Just before they left Shanghai an older man in civilian clothes visited them in their apartment. He was furious with the Captain because the monk had been killed rather than wounded in the arm, which was what he had ordered them to do. The terrified Captain replied that it had been impossible to aim carefully. They had been running across the sidewalk and had only a few seconds in which to act.

The claim was true on the Captain's part. Only one of his bullets had struck the monk, and that one in the arm. As for the policeman, he said nothing. He had purposely emptied his revolver into the monk's chest, partly thinking the Captain would be blamed for it, his revenge for the time his comrades had betrayed him in Korea, partly because he was so excited to be on a crowded street with a loaded revolver he had to empty it into someone.

The policeman had expected the captain to be sentenced to three months of latrine duty, but the old man in civilian clothes simply turned away, tears in his eyes, and left.

The episode in the Shanghai apartment was one of three times the policeman was to see the older man over the next five years. The older man was unaware of the second encounter, for despite the precautions he took it was perhaps inevitable that at least once during his eight years of clandestine work he would be observed servicing a dead drop.

The third time, however, they came face to face and that was when the policeman killed him.

After the adventure in Shanghai the policeman's duties in Mukden seemed routine and uninteresting. He still stole files for the Captain and occasionally served as an undercover agent in one of the restaurants where Japanese officers gathered, but most of the time he worked in the icy cellars beneath Kempeitai headquarters.

The Chinese and Japanese and Korean prisoners were always stripped naked before being sent to the cellars. The Manchurian winters were harsh, and often there was no need to beat a man for more than a day or two before he confessed to anything. Those already condemned to die wore the traditional straw hat covering the eyes that was also worn by mendicant Buddhist monks.

The suspects were chained to the wall with their arms and legs spread, hung high enough so that their toes just touched the floor. The policeman's job was to keep the prisoner awake when the interrogating officer grew tired and went upstairs to perform the tea ceremony or practice flower arranging for an hour or two. Because the policeman had always been humiliated by the body hair inherited from his Ainu mother, he particularly enjoyed the nakedness of the prisoners.

He tried slaps, kicks, punches. He squeezed the eyeballs

and stuffed oily rags into the mouth, pinching first one nostril and then the other. He used his blackjack to rap the kneecaps, the elbows, the teeth.

Many methods worked but by far the best was holding the prisoner's testicles in his hand and tapping them with his blackjack. The dull sounds that came out of the man then were unlike any he had ever heard. Only once did he imagine he heard them elsewhere, during an unbearably hot Manchurian summer when he was sitting alone on the plains, bareheaded, dizzily pulling a cricket apart.

The second time he saw the older man from Shanghai was in the autumn of 1937, a few days before he was transferred to an infantry unit in central China. He was on duty in civilian clothes in a restaurant listening to conversations when the older man came in and sat down alone in a corner. Something in the way he moved his head confused the policeman. Curious, he got to his feet and went off to the toilet.

Ever since the months in the Korean latrines the policeman had been able to think more clearly when immersed in an atmosphere of dung and urine. They were not only the smells that reminded him to beware of betrayal, they also brought back an older memory, one of his earliest, the times as a boy when he had carried heavy buckets of nightsoil up the giant steps of the Tohoku toward the mulberry trees.

There were only two stalls, the policeman sat down in one. He was just beginning to feel comfortable with himself when someone entered the other stall and locked the door.

The policeman always had to have privacy in the toilet, otherwise he couldn't concentrate and make the smells that pleased him. He climbed up on the seat to peek over the partition, thinking he might use his blackjack on the intruder, when he saw a hand go up under the lid of the water tank and place something there. The hand withdrew, the door was unlocked, the older man from the Shanghai apartment left the room. What did it mean?

He went into the other stall and found a small length of

bamboo, sealed at both ends, wedged into a niche under the lid of the water tank. He opened the bamboo tube and took out a tiny film. What was it?

He replaced the device and wandered over beside the urinals. He knew he had discovered something but he didn't know what it was. He bent to tie his shoelace. His hand strayed into the urinal and picked up the hard cake of deodorant lying there. The cake was green and looked like candy. Absentmindedly he bit into the crunchy nugget and chewed.

What had he witnessed just now?

Angered that he could not understand what had happened, angered as well by the indistinct passions aroused in him by the older man from Shanghai, the policeman took a long walk that night to the outskirts of the city. The next day an elderly woman was found beaten to death with a blunt instrument, probably made of leather, and sexually violated with an inhuman object, either the same instrument that had caused the death or one similar to it.

Rape with the instrument had occurred after death. The body had then been stripped and the head scalped. Small patches of hair from the head had been crudely attached to the chest and forearms and thighs, a larger amount to the nearly hairless pubic region.

This necrophiliac crime was similar in every respect to others that had gone unsolved in remote areas near Mukden over the last five years, or since the policeman had completed his tour of duty in the Korean latrines. The victims, always of advanced age, included both men and women. Sexual assault was limited to the anus.

Normally the policeman or one of the other corporals in his unit would have been sent to investigate the murder of the elderly woman, but this time everyone on duty at Kempeitai headquarters had been placed on special alert. A Japanese soldier was being held on suspicion of espionage. A crippling backache had led to a doctor's examination, in the course of which the doctor had discovered a microfilm bearing highly sensitive military and political information.

The soldier, also a corporal, tried to commit suicide by jumping out of a window, but a tree broke his fall and he only suffered a broken arm. Now he was being held in a ground-floor room empty save for the cushion on which the interrogating officer sat. Even the glass from the barred window had been removed.

The policeman's Captain questioned the prisoner a full day and night. At the end of that time he retired for a few hours of sleep after learning only two minor facts, the code name for the espionage network and the unknown disease that had caused the corporal's backache. The policeman was told to stay in the room and not take his eyes off the corporal.

The corporal, little more than a boy, had the delicate features and delicate body of a young girl. Dead leaves blew in through the window along with the cool autumn air. The boy asked if he could use the policeman's over-coat, and the policeman gave it to him after first emptying out the pockets.

There was a secret in that overcoat that had tormented the policeman ever since it was issued to him in the winter of 1935, a secret that had to do with size. In the supply shipment received by his unit that year there had been included a monstrous mistake by the manufacturer, an overcoat so large it could have gone around three or four large men.

The policeman, who was small, was given the coat as a joke and told not to cut it but to take it in, a project that had lasted just over a week. During that time he went about in the cold weather unprotected while the other men ridiculed him.

The young corporal now turned the overcoat over before putting it on. He saw where it had been roughly stitched. Suddenly he held it up and laughed.

What's so funny? said the policeman.

This is, said the boy.

Why?

Because I made it. That coat got me fired from the factory. I was thinking about my mother and the coat came out all wrong, so they fired me. I had to do something, so I went into the army. If it weren't for that coat I wouldn't be here today.

The boy stopped laughing. He moaned the name Miya and began to cry.

The policeman didn't hear the name or see the tears, he saw only the jeering faces that had insulted him two years before when he was cold. The Captain came back an hour later to find the prisoner crumpled up in the corner, his head battered out of shape, his face unrecognizable. The policeman was sitting on the cushion by the window watching the dead leaves fall in the yard.

The Captain flipped the safety on his revolver, but at the last moment kept himself from shooting his subordinate in the head.

Soon afterward the Captain was standing in front of the desk of his commanding officer, a General, the man from the apartment in Shanghai who had once been his patron and protector. There was no need for the Captain to be told that the death of so important a prisoner was unpardonable. At the same time as he turned in his report he made a formal request that both he and the policeman be transferred to a front-line infantry unit.

A month later the Captain was killed in a reckless assault on a Chinese machine gun emplacement. The policeman, however, was still carrying his favorite blackjack the December night his regiment broke ranks outside the gates of Nanking.

Fires were everywhere. For a thousand years the policeman stabbed and shot and clubbed Chinese, for ten thousand years he beat victims and mutilated them and burned them. Then all at once he turned a corner and found himself facing the man from the apartment in Shanghai, from the toilet in Mukden, a man he knew from the winter morning when his father had been found with his face gone and he had had to wait beside the road with a bowed head until an automobile passed bearing the powerful Baron who owned his family's land and all the land for miles around.

He had been only eight years old, but he had peeked up and caught a glimpse of the passing face. The man had held his head differently then, not in that stiff, rigid way, and that was what had confused the policeman in the Shanghai apartment and the Mukden toilet. But now in the screams and shadowy firelight of Nanking the policeman was no longer confused, his head cleared, and he knew exactly whom the face belonged to.

He struck him with his blackjack, the General went down. He dragged him out of the alley into a deserted courtyard, stripped off his uniform, rapped his testicles to hear the sounds from the icy Manchurian cellars.

A low moan. A quiet dying moan.

The fires burned and the policeman tapped out the rhythms in his head, the footsteps on the terraced hills of his childhood, the giant steps to nowhere. He tapped and gently tapped until he felt the sack in his hand growing cold. He severed the sack, shredded the testicles, knotted them around the General's neck and squeezed.

One eye was still wide open staring at him. He ripped it out and threw it away.

Screams.

A collapsing burning wall, flames leaping into the air, the General's epaulets shining in the gloom.

He dropped his trousers, squatted over them before loping out of the courtyard and down the alley.

After a month of arson, torture, and murder along the banks of the Yangtze the policeman was given a summary court martial. While racing a truck through a group of children in a village a machine gun mount had fallen from the truck to the ground. Due to the cries of the children he had failed to hear it. He was found guilty of negligent loss of property. The cost of the mount was deducted from his pay and he was transferred out of the war zone back to his old Kempeitai unit in Manchuria.

The next eight years passed without incident. More and more men were shipped out to the Pacific, to the Philippines, to Okinawa. The barracks in Mukden were unheated, food was scarce. Days he spent in the icy cellars, nights he took long walks into the countryside. One hot summer morning the Russians crossed the border and quickly overran what had once been the Kwangtung army.

As a fascist militarist the policeman was sent with the other Japanese prisoners to a labor camp in Siberia and put to work mining salt, which they did with their hands since the Russians had neither picks nor shovels. His eyes became infected from the salt, temporarily blinding him. Daily classes were held in the new order of justice the prisoners were to carry with them back to Japan.

They were encouraged to grow food or otherwise supplement their rations. The policeman's specialty was a kind of beer made from tundra weeds, homemade beer being traditional among the peasants of the Tohoku. The Russian guards liked it so much there was seldom any left for him, but for some reason he seemed happy to let them have it.

The end of the third year came. The prisoners, fully indoctrinated, were now ready to return to Japan to begin their revolutionary work. On the last night there was a banquet where the guards and prisoners embraced, sang, wept, congratulated each other on now being comrades in a common cause. The policeman left the banquet early to check the special batch of beer he had brewed for the celebration.

Around midnight the Russian guards began to arrive, most of them already drunk. In all, eight of them came, although more had been invited and fewer might have turned up. They sat in the pine grove laughing and singing as he poured out the frothy brew.

The *Amanita muscaria* was a mushroom as well known to Siberian peasants as it was to peasants in the Tohoku. When eaten, a cold sweat was followed by stupor, convulsions, delirium. *Death's angel* it was called, because its victims were always young children who had not yet learned to recognize the deadly muscarine.

The policeman watched the guards die and found himself falling under a magical spell, perhaps because eight fates were dying in the pine grove and eight times eight was the number of paths that led to the primeval Oriental hexagram, the ancient figure found in the Book of Changes.

In any case the sky was so clear that night that every eye in the unfathomable darkness could look down upon this little creature who had come to take part, briefly, in a faceless, patternlesss drama that was without beginning or end, who had come to creep with chance through scenery as impenetrable as millennia of fallen pine needles, a creature who understood as much of the winds that moved him as a leaf broken from the branch of a mulberry tree.

●

The prisoner-of-war ship arrived in Yokohama in the spring of 1948. The cherry blossoms were still in bloom. A Japanese government band played the *Washington Post March* and *Stars and Stripes Forever*. Hundreds of mothers and sisters crowded the pier waving white handkerchiefs, trying to hear the chant from the men at the railings. What were they shouting? *Banzai* three times with the arms raised?

The chant grew louder as the ship moved in. They could hear it more clearly now.

Pulverize. Smash. Crush. Exterminate.

The handkerchiefs dropped out of the air, the families were quiet and uneasy. Down came the gangplanks and the men, but none of them stopped to embrace their wives and mothers and sisters. Instead they set up folding camp stools, climbed on top of the stools, and began shouting out interminable lectures on mad dog revanchists and imperialist jackals. The families surged hysterically up and down the pier losing themselves in the confusion.

The policeman pushed his way through the crowds and took a train to the industrial suburb where he had been given an underground assignment by the party. Ostensibly he worked in a factory owned by a secret party member that made novelties for export. He painted souvenir models of the Empire State Building. But his real job was to stand in the front line during antigovernment demonstrations and use a straight razor rolled up in a newspaper to slash the flanks of horses used by the police in controlling riots.

He also used the disguised razor to slash the faces of policemen who were on the ground. This routine continued for several years until war broke out in Korea. That May Day the party issued different orders. Not only were they to attack the police, they were also directed to burn the cars of Americans and steal revolvers from policemen where possible.

Razors. Fires. Clubbings. By ten o'clock in the morning he had his first revolver, by noon he had his third. Toward early evening he had cached several more. His procedure was to stagger out of an alley when a policeman passed and yell that he was being attacked by Communists. When the policeman went into the alley he hit him over the head with his blackjack and stole his revolver, then hurriedly worked over his face with the razor before going off to burn another car.

When the sun went down he found himself sitting in the cellar where the revolvers were hidden. He was tired. He counted and recounted the revolvers and went into a trance that lasted more than an hour. Once more the mystical number had descended upon him.

Upon awakening he went in search of a demonstrator who had been injured in the fighting. He came across a dazed student whose head was bleeding. He brought the boy back to the cellar and knocked him out with the blackjack.

Shortly thereafter a squad of police broke into the cellar,

acting on the information of a concerned citizen. They discovered eight stolen revolvers under the boy's crumpled body. Due to his head wound the boy could remember nothing of what had happened.

The hero responsible for leading the authorities to the cache was given a patriotic award by a police captain. Despite his illiteracy, his application for employment with the metropolitan police force was given priority because he was an unemployed veteran who had spent three years in a Russian slave labor camp. At his own request he was assigned to the special riot detachment that dealt with Communist demonstrations.

Over the next decade he used his blackjack on any demonstrator he saw carrying a rolled-up newspaper. At the same time a series of murders and rapes occurred in the Tokyo area, unsolved, that were identical in every respect to those reported in Mukden before the war.

On New Year's Day, a month before Geraty arrived in New York with the largest collection of Japanese pornography ever assembled in a Western tongue, the policeman got very drunk and took a train to Kamakura. As always when he left the city at night, he was wearing his old Kempeitai overcoat. He found what he was looking for, an isolated hut on the beach, and was about to break in when he saw someone sitting on the sand, a huge, immobile figure in a squatting position.

The giant had a round black hat pulled down to his ears. The sky was black and the policeman couldn't make out his face. He went across the beach and asked the stranger what he was doing.

In answer the giant held out a bottle.

The policeman sat down and had a drink. An hour went by in silence, perhaps two hours. They finished one bottle of the unknown alcohol and the giant opened another. Not once during this time did the stranger turn his eyes away from the sea. A third hour passed or a fourth and the policeman was reminded of his mysterious union with the stars long ago in Siberia.

He began to talk. He spoke of his childhood, the hateful

body hair he had been born with, his father eaten by a dog, his mother drowned in a frozen rice paddy, the giant steps to the mulberry trees, the latrines in Korea, the icy cellars in Manchuria, the abandoned storefront in Shanghai, the tundra weed beer brewed for Russian guards, the first and second and third meetings with Baron Kikuchi.

Mysteriously he came under the spell of the immobile giant, mysteriously repeating on a Kamakura beach the act of confession performed by his unknown sister in a locked, shuttered room a quarter of a century earlier in Shanghai. The giant was impassive. He never stirred. The lapping waves took the place of the humming reels of film. Toward dawn, exhausted, having confessed everything, the policeman fell asleep.

He awoke colder than he had ever been before, naked except for a towel over his lap. The tide was rising, water washed his hairy legs. Beside him lay two empty bottles of Irish whiskey, a jar that smelled of horseradish, the clothes he had taken off during the night while recounting his tale, thereby reversing the nakedness of that other confession in another era.

But the policeman discovered his clothes weren't all there. One garment was missing. For some reason the stranger with the unseen face had stolen his greatcoat and silently carried it away in the darkness.

●

Hato found the policeman sitting on the edge of his cot in his cubicle, an illustrated magazine in his lap. He smiled down at the little man.

Why don't you admit you can't read?

The policeman stared at the floor. Hato laughed and closed the door behind him.

Listen, he whispered, how would you like to make a lot of money?

What?

Money, you idiot.

How?

Easy. We kidnap one of the Americans who was on the houseboat, the dumb one with the bandaged ear, and make his friend pay ransom. But maybe you're afraid because the dumb one, the bodyguard, is carrying a revolver. I saw the bulge in his pocket when they left the houseboat.

The policeman stared at the floor. Didn't this grinning young fool understand anything at all? It wasn't a revolver that had made the bulge in the boy's pocket, it was a slab of grilled meat. He had seen the boy slip the meat off his plate when no one was looking and drop it into his pocket. He had seen him do it and he knew exactly what it meant. More than once he had done the same thing in Siberia, where there was never enough to eat. It meant the boy with the bandaged head had been in prison. He was a criminal. And he had also seen him pick up a bottle of Japanese meat sauce and look at the label with a dull expression in his eyes. The policeman knew what that meant too. The boy with the bandaged head was not only a criminal, he was illiterate.

Of course he's an American, whispered Hato, grinning. Maybe that frightens you.

The policeman stared at the floor and saw his mother face down in a frozen rice paddy because she was an Ainu with Caucasian blood and the silk market had collapsed in America. He took the magazine in his hands and turned the pages until he came to one without any pictures, a page covered with hundreds of minute Chinese characters. He held the page up in his hands scarred from digging salt in Siberia and tore it into long strips, shredded the strips, let the tiny white pieces flutter over his lap to the floor.

Does that mean you're with me?

The policeman nodded.

They talked for a while and then Hato left, dreaming of Paris and the funeral movie he would make there. People would come to interview him, they would ask him to give his opinions on television, and he would tell them the truth about America. Tell them everything and never again do calisthenics or march in haiku parades or put up with young women dressed as hags who broke into his room calling him a mother-fucker.

Behind him the policeman sat on his cot staring at snowflakes.

●

Mama finished painting the nails on her right hand and went on to the left. For days she had been pondering the small gold cross worn by the young man whom Quin had brought with him to her nightclub.

Once Mama had known that cross well. It was the most treasured present the General had ever given her. Later it was stolen in Shanghai while she was under the influence of laudanum, taken from her during one of those evenings spent gazing at the falsely pornographic images projected dimly on the wall by the whirring imagination of a clown.

Kikuchi-Lotmann. Quin. Big Gobi.

What connected these three men? Why had one of them come to possess the General's gift of love to her?

She knew the names Lotmann and Kikuchi, she knew the name Quin. But Gobi was a desert, a remote place in western China, a forsaken place of sandy wastes. To see what it might teach her she consulted the oldest document on the Gobi that she could find, an apocryphal chronicle written two thousand years ago during the Han dynasty.

A region of sudden sandstorms, read the chronicle, *sudden sandstorms and terrifying visions. Rivers disappear overnight, landmarks go with the wind, the sun sinks at midday. A timeless nonexistent land meant to plague the mind with its mirages.*

But the most dangerous thing that must be mentioned is the caravans that appear at any moment on the horizon, there to drift uncertainly for minutes or days or years. Now they are near, now far, now just as assuredly they are gone. The camel drivers are aloof and silent, undistinguishable, men of some distant race. But the men they serve, the leaders of the caravans, are truly frightening. They wear odd costumes, their eyes gleam, they come from every corner of the world.

These men, in sum, are the secret agents who have always given the authorities so much to fear. They represent the princes and despots of a thousand lawless regions.

Or is it perhaps that they represent no one at all? Is that why their aspects make us tremble? In any case we know only that this is their meeting place, the unmarked crossroads where they mingle and separate and wander on their way.

As for where they go and why, we cannot be sure of such things. There are no tracks in such a barren waste. The sandstorms blow, the sun sinks, rivers disappear, and their camels are lost in darkness. Therefore the truth must be that the routes of such men are untraceable, their missions unknowable, their ultimate destinations as invisible as the wind.

If the Son of Heaven is to continue to rule with integrity, we must defend our borders at all costs from such men.

Thus ended the uneasy commentary written two thousand years ago by a Chinese traveler wishing to warn the Sons of Han of the dangers to be found in the desert west of the Central Kingdom. Mama found the allusions evocative but she wanted to know more.

She telephoned the leading Chinese historian in the country, an acquaintance from her early days in the brothel in Kobe. The historian gave her an account of the tribes that had passed through the desert over the last three or four thousand years, a tale of innumerable influxes and exoduses.

Next she called the leading geologist in the country. He

compared the landscape of the Gobi to the surface of the moon. Lastly she called Japan's most famous paleontologist.

Among her many scholarly acquaintances the paleontologist was somewhat special. He had visited her immediately after she arrived in the brothel and had never forgotten the experience, nor had she, for even then he had bizarre tastes having to do with shards and slivers of bone. The paleontologist was very old now and largely deaf, but a hearing aid attached to his telephone made conversation possible.

My dear, he shouted, it's good to talk to you again after all these years. How long has it been, about half a century? Well, we've both come a long way since then, my bones tell me so. What can I do for you?

Mama told him. She said she was trying to find some significance in the word *Gobi* when it was used as a man's name.

A kind of code word? shouted the paleontologist. Well, as you know, the earth's climate has changed a bit over the last million years. Something to do with shifts in the magnetic fields of outer space. That causes the poles on earth to shift, which changes the balance of the globe. Every now and then, in other words, the world goes out of whack. Right off its head. Things just aren't the same anymore. Confusion at the poles, confusion all around. What used to be isn't, what never was is. Areas get mixed up. A place that was a desert becomes fertile. The fertile place becomes a desert. It's almost enough to make a man believe in the Book of Changes, but of course old books are intolerably boring.

Well, a million years ago man was just about getting started, so what we surmise from the paleontological evidence is that he wasn't getting started in the places you might think. Just the opposite, the worst places today being the best places then. Therefore the Gobi was probably one of the original cradles of the race. Where it all began, my work and yours, the origin of man. I suggest you follow that line of reasoning.

And my dear, don't forget to call again. Fifty years is much too long to wait at our age. Which reminds me, someone mentioned that you were tattooed later on. Was it all over? What kinds of tattoos? Describe the part for me. You know the one I mean.

The shouting paleontologist became obscene. Mama skillfully turned the conversation aside and hung up.

She returned to her dais to prepare for the *mudra* of contemplation. The origin of man. That's what the paleontologist had said.

She reflected on the boy who had raped one of her girls in the middle of the floor. Many times in her life she had seen violence, but never violence committed with such an innocent face. She had known then that the boy was a genuine primitive, a child from another age.

As proof there was the object he carried in his pocket, the object that had started all the trouble. This child carried an eye with him the way another man might carry a watch. That night in the club he had taken out the eye to consult it.

Did the man truly exist who could tell time by looking into an eyeball?

Mama focused her thoughts on an imaginary point in the middle of her forehead, the ancient attitude of memory. Her fingers were immobile, she stopped breathing. Recollections and impressions flowed freely in place of breath. Twenty-four floors below, the swans disappeared from the Imperial moat. Her nails dried in the afternoon sun. High above the city Mama floated in the world of her mind.

The time had come to discover Big Gobi's role in the world. Who was he? Where had he come from?

Mama recalled the information gathered by the General's former chauffeur. After taking Quin to Tsukiji he had watched Quin's house for several days as a matter of course.

The big one, he reported, spends all day watching television. He seems to have no other interest, nor does he ever speak. When the other one is there the big one sits with his hands folded in his lap. He does nothing. But as soon as the other one leaves, he takes a piece of meat out of his pocket. The meat is black and crusted and he holds it while he watches television. The sliding door was open while I was there, so I leaned in to get a better look. The meat appears to be a tongue, a common beef tongue that must have been grilled over charcoal, which explains its black crust. After so much handling, and because of the hot spell we've had, it's beginning to fall apart. Another curious fact is that although he watches television all the time, the television screen lacks a picture. There is just grayness and a hum.

Mama had listened to the former corporal's report without surprise. The surprises that men might work were far behind her. In the brothel in Kobe she had known ten thousand men with their ten thousand tricks and fantasies.

But as the sage had said, *although there may be ten thousand creatures, every one of them cannot turn its back to the shade without having the sun on its belly.*

Mama closed her eyes and thought of the tongue the boy held in his hands, the meat filled with white worms the shape of fingernail parings.

That meat was the same kind of flesh horsemen in the Gobi Desert had been carrying under their saddles for thousands of years. These horsemen, who must be the boy's spiritual ancestors, had once been the terror of the world. From their desert they had galloped across the earth conquering the palaces of many civilizations. But then the sandstorms had come and the rivers had gone, the caravans had lost their way and a single horseman was left to ride on alone into the wastes of the desert clutching his meat.

He holds his tongue in his hand, thought Mama, because he knows the destiny of his Mongol tribe and dares not relate it. He knows it is too fearful for others to hear and he knows that a tongue can never fail to speak of the past. It is the umbilical cord of the past and yet it is the strangest of all umbilical cords for it does not nourish, for those who speak do not know and those who know do not speak.

The sage tells us that the soul of man is like a grandee on his travels. When a place is not to his liking he moves on. He consults the time piece of his eye and enters a realm from another era.

And thus, thought Mama, this child we know as Big Gobi is ageless. He is the oldest child in the world, the child who was born a million years ago when the desert was not even a desert. And now he has removed his tongue so that he will not be tempted to walk on the sands of other eras, to recall those sands and converse upon them and reveal thereby secrets unknown to us, secrets he alone can envision with his timeless eye.

The emerald in the middle of Mama's forehead glistened. An insight had come to her from the cross the boy wore, a cross given to her by the General, whose subsequent death brought her to despair and made of the cross, his gift, an unbearable burden. A cross taken from her then in the locked, shuttered room where she had gone to confess her misery, slipped off her neck by an immobile fat man who had listened to her tale *for her sake*, a nameless naked giant in the shadows who thereupon silently lifted the intolerable weight from her shoulders and in so doing bestowed upon her the most precious of gifts, the blessing of hope.

A small gold cross. A crossing of two people in the shadow of a battered projector that later led to another in the Shanghai warehouse where she gave her love in return to the nameless circus master of the acts, *for his sake*, in the last hours of his torment.

Mama opened her eyes. She began to breathe again.

The ivory elephant bearing the lotus had been moved to the far side of the room, to the window facing west. She climbed up the side of the elephant now and arranged herself on the lotus. It was late afternoon, the time to consider the end of the day. She faced the setting sun.

Long ago she had accepted the loss of the General, her

first son, the circus master, her second son. But now as the light fell and the darkness closed around her, as she recalled the distant blessing from the naked giant that had once given her new life, she prayed that it might not yet be too dark for the child known as Big Gobi to see the smile of the Kannon Buddha, to feel the mercy and compassion in her face, to find somewhere in those worn, wrinkled lines a measure of the love that had conceived him in a Shanghai ring soon to be extravagantly crowded with animals and acts, before his circus came to an end and the lone Mongol was left to wander the barren wastes westward, into the desert of sandstorms and mirages where the secret agents of lost caravans conversed in unknowable tongues.

●

The grayness buzzed and Big Gobi watched, unable to align the ten thousand lines in his head with the ten thousand lines in front of him.

Ghosts smiled from the grayness.

He saw the dancing, solemn ghost of a boy on a beach, a boy in an army hospital, a boy on a bus, a boy looking at a frozen tuna fish and a powdery bowl of seagull soup.

In a few weeks the first typhoons of early autumn would come to Japan. Even now violent winds circled each other in the South China Sea waiting to break out of their ring into the Pacific. But for Big Gobi that dangerous season had already passed. The winds that blew over him came from the north, from the Manchurian plains and the Siberian tundra. Where he lived it was winter, a blizzard was forming in his brain.

He sat with a blanket around his shoulders. Quin had gone to find a doctor.

He was shivering, his bad shoulder ached, his legs were numb. He slumped sideways, no longer able to keep himself upright against the wind. The caravan wound toward the horizon and he knew he was lost, losing touch with the world.

He was sorry he had to disappoint Quin and Geraty and the gentle Father and the wise Mama by falling behind. He wanted to stay with them but he was exhausted, the blizzard raged and he could no longer keep up.

Alone and delirious in the desert of his Mongol ancestors, in the solitude of wind and snow, he raised his hand to wave farewell.

●

Hato stuttered that he wanted to leave. The policeman hit him in the stomach and went on working on the window, working slowly because he didn't want the small half-moon of glass above the lock to fall and make a noise. It was hot, they were both sweating. The cutter slid, the suction cup held. The policeman turned the lock and raised the window.

They were in a bedroom at the back of the house. A light showed under the door. Hato was whispering again, stuttering. The policeman hit him across the mouth and forced him up through the window. He followed and stopped to listen at the door. A humming sound. He brought his knee up into Hato's groin, opened the door, pushed him through.

Hato stumbled into the living room where the big foreigner was sitting with a blanket wrapped around him, shaking, sweating. A television set hummed on the far side of the room. Hato smiled weakly and tried to think of the crippled girl in New York, his shoeboxes of airplane disasters, the chow mein whore, movies.

Nothing happened. He had forgotten all his English.

He grinned and then he frowned. He was wetting his pants. He saw the big foreigner wave, and in desperation he waved back.

Hurry, whispered the foreigner. The blizzard's here, we can't wait any longer, we have to begin the ceremony.

He pulled a small table over and wedged it between his legs. He pushed another small table toward Hato.

Beat the drum, he whispered. Hurry, call the tribe.

Hato squatted on the floor watching the big foreigner with the dark face and the slanting eyes and the high cheekbones drum on the table. He drummed for several minutes and then raised his arms to the sky. There were tears in his eyes as he chanted.

Women hey.

Oysters hey.

Hey hey hey.

I've seen it, whispered the big foreigner. I've been to the top of the mountain and seen the palace. I've looked down into the valley.

While the fool and the giant beat their drums the policeman was working his way around the room. He crouched, he loped, he crept on all fours. He prowled the corners and sniffed the air for the stars he had seen in a Siberian pine grove. He came across a translucent green paperweight stolen from the desk of a customs official in New York.

The paperweight reminded him of urinal candy, urinal candy reminded him of Baron Kikuchi and his father's eaten face. He bit into the paperweight and snapped his front teeth, the pain bringing with it a jumble of memories.

A huge overcoat.

Frozen rice paddies.

Mulberry trees.

Landlords and taxes.

Peace.

Riots.

Shredded testicles.

War.

Hair.

A special sound.

Latrines.

Mushrooms.

Icy cellars, scalped heads, razors, a blackjack.

His head was humming, he had to have the silence of that other night under the stars. He picked up the heavy television set and brought it down with all his strength.

Glass broke, metal cracked, wires spun. The foreigner's huge body toppled backward, the box driven down to his shoulders. His eyes were still open but his skull was crushed, his mouth jammed shut. The policeman saw the face in the hole where the screen had been.

Hato was down on his knees, his chin covered with saliva. The policeman kicked him and watched him fall over. He was moaning, twitching, gripped by a seizure he had last experienced as a child on a bed of movie magazines. His hand reached out for the familiar objects, the gloves and hairpieces and empty lipstick tubes, but there was nothing there but the table drum. He bit his lip. Swallowed. Blood frothed over his mouth.

He was strangling on his own tongue.

The policeman undid the cross the foreigner was wearing and tied it around his own neck. He took the piece of meat out of the foreigner's pocket and squeezed it. White worms dribbled through his fingers. He dropped the meat and licked his fingers.

In the kitchen he found some cans of beer and a package of cigarettes. He smoked and drank until the cans were all empty, then he urinated in one of them and put it back in the refrigerator. He shredded the cigarettes that were left and scattered the tobacco around the kitchen.

Hato was no longer twitching. The policeman dropped his trousers to make a pile between the two boys and smell the familiar smell.

At the subway station he bought a newspaper and stood patiently in line waiting to buy his ticket. All the other passengers in the subway were using their newspapers to fan themselves, but he held his in front of him pretending to read. From Tsukiji he walked to Tokyo Bay, to the end of the concrete breakwater where Quin had recently been with Baron Kikuchi's former chauffeur.

Steps led down to the water. The lights of the city hid most of the stairs. The water was very black as he approached the giant steps of the Tohoku and descended them for the last time.

Around his neck hung the small gold cross that had

been revered for thirteen centuries by traders crossing central Asia, a cross that had once been given to Adzhar by his wife and subsequently worn by Maeve and the General and Mama before a naked giant stole it in Shanghai, stole it for safekeeping, and kept it for thirty years until he could return it to the doomed son of the Shanghai circus, a lonely Mongol horseman from whom it might have been taken in order to bring to an end the last invisible caravans hidden in the code name *Gobi*, carried at last to a dark resting place in the waters where its glittering lines could no longer cross and recross the lives of those who had worn it over the years in honor of love and the memory of love.

HIMSELF, HERSELF

•

7

Move. March.
Where?
What does it matter? All good roads are within.
Mine has been a long one and perhaps your march
must be long as well.

—Adzhar to a leader of the 1927 Communist uprising in
Shanghai

●

One September morning shortly before dawn a procession
of black limousines was seen approaching Tokyo from
some point to the south, perhaps Kamakura, where they
had apparently gathered during the hours of darkness.
The limousines entered the city and moved slowly down a
main thoroughfare keeping themselves bumper to bumper, all of them empty save for a driver.

The funeral procession crept around the streets in a
wide curve until by mid-morning the entire center of the
city was blocked off in a gigantic circle of mourning. By
then the first limousine had come up behind the last to
form an unbroken chain, making it impossible to estimate
how many thousands of vehicles there might be in the
solemn parade.

Since neither traffic nor pedestrians could pass through
the mysterious black ring, the stores and offices of Tokyo
eventually closed and the government declared an unof-
ficial holiday. Twelve million people came out to watch
the unannounced and nameless event while around the
world many millions more pondered the total inscrutabili-

ty of the Orient, bewildered that the death of one unknown person could cause a funeral of such magnitude. In fact it was the most magnificent funeral celebrated in Asia since the death of Kublai Khan, but only one man understood this completely, that other wanderer from the thirteenth century who called himself Father Lamereaux.

From the lawn of an elegant inn, amid stone lanterns and stone paths, twisted pines and miniature bridges, the two surviving half-brothers watched the procession. Kikuchi-Lotmann knew now that the woman he had described on the highbar in the abandoned warehouse was indeed his mother, but that his father had not been the circus master of that story but of another, one that began on a houseboat in Shanghai when his father and Quin's father had been introduced to each other by the woman they both loved eight years before their deaths, eight years before the circus and Nanking, eight years before the conception of the third half-brother, whose funeral was now being celebrated in the world's largest city, the cause of the black ring around Tokyo twenty years after the end of the war known only to them and the Kannon Buddha and the aging Emperor who had long ago found homes for the sons of Maeve and Mama.

Quin nodded to himself, Kikuchi-Lotmann changed his necktie. They watched the procession until sunset, when a servant appeared with a picnic basket and spread a tablecloth on the grass with lox and winter sable, whitefish, pickled herring and herring in cream, rollmops, pickled tomatoes, cream cheese and chives, olives, chopped liver, a tray of bagels.

In front of the array of food two small figures in ice were set up, the one a man in frock coat with whip and megaphone, the other a boy with a dented shoulder.

At the foot of the hill the procession of limousines was at last coming to an end, and although it was cold for September the two ice figures were already beginning to melt. Kikuchi-Lotmann gazed at the sun sinking out of sight.

A little of this, he said, and a little of that. Or put

another way, we sit in the East and watch the sun go down in the West. But if we were to reverse ourselves?

The ice figures were pools of water. Kikuchi-Lotmann's head wagged. He blew the water and sprayed it over the grass, fogging his glasses. A sad smile came to his face as he spread a slice of fish on a bagel.

Mixed buffet, he said in the half-light. Help yourself.

●

The elderly Emperor sat thin and erect in his ornate Victorian parlor, one hand gripping each horsehair arm of his throne. His black habit hung loosely around him, the cloth worn, the celluloid collar unstudded and awry. On the table in front of him stood a bottle of Irish whiskey.

Uncertain weather, he whispered. I've always enjoyed the latter part of September here. The air is uneasy as if hiding some secret, yet we all know typhoons are in the natural order of things. Is that bottle what it appears to be?

Yes, said Quin.

Father Lamereaux sighed.

It's been a long time since I've tasted that, nearly a quarter of a century. When I first came to Japan I had my cats and the Legion and the flowers of Tokyo, and there were the temples in the lovely hills above Kamakura with their gongs and rituals and the periods set aside for contemplation. The Legion met at that long table behind you and we had discussions on *No* plays after the closing prayer and the passing of the secret-bag. But then in the 1930s they took those ugly cannons they captured from the Russians in 1905 and placed them around the shrines. How did that bottle get there?

It's a present for you, said Quin. I'll be leaving soon and we might not meet again. I thought we might have a drink together.

No, we probably won't meet again.

I remembered that Geraty said you and he had a glass of Irish whiskey together the last time he saw you, when he left for China before the war.

Did he say that? Perhaps we did, I've forgotten. After that I lost the cats and the legionaries. The flowers of Tokyo weren't so beautiful during the war when the whole city was burning down. Since then I've been a strict vegetarian, honey and eggs excepted. Rice has a peculiar effect on the bowels of the Japanese, which is one reason they prefer the out-of-doors. I prefer it myself, especially my own garden, but I can't do it when it's raining.

Can I pour you a drink?

I think so. I think I just might have one today because there's going to be a typhoon and because I lost everything a quarter of a century ago, too long a time to have nothing. I believe we should emulate the Virgin, a human soul must not resign itself to imperfection. The Emperors of Japan were great men until military dictators forced them into retirement in the thirteenth century. The Emperor was simply thrown out in the streets and told to barter pickles and bugger his autograph for rice. Then in the 1920s I went to study in Kamakura. Once on a spring afternoon there I heard the music that had tempted the sun goddess from her cave, exquisite music played on a *koto* a thousand years old. Elijah and the sun goddess played it for me as I nodded with the flowers, as the shoemaker's son sat at his shoemaker's bench and sang a dragon's epic so strange and sanctifying it surely must have been a gift from the distant Lapps. Did you know Elijah or the shoemaker's son? Did you know Henry Pu Yi? He was a very naughty man and his mythical country never really existed. But for all that, he was still the last emperor I had an opportunity to talk to. I suppose I've already mentioned the Peram and their necronym system, *Father of Uncle Dead* and the rest. Even among simple tribesmen relationships can be quite complex. Quite complex when we look into it.

The old priest unbuttoned his coat the wrong way. He took the glass of whiskey and studied it. The windows were rattling violently. Gusts of air shot across the room. Although it was only early afternoon the sky was already dark. The whole house seemed to be swaying in the wind.

Father Lamereaux drank. He raised the glass again and emptied it. His hands relaxed and he smiled gently. All at once his eyes sparkled.

I think that's better, he said. I think that's much better.

Father, I wonder if you could tell me why you named the child Gobi? I assume that was your doing.

Yes, it was, although I haven't thought about it in many years. Sometimes we forget certain things when we go into retirement. I believe I'd like another, please.

Quin refilled the glass.

Not in years. Didn't remember it at all, but now I do.

How did you happen to choose the name?

First of all because the infant was brought to me nameless. Hasn't it always been so? The Emperor arrives in the world nameless, yet centuries later we know the era by his name and no other. It's an old custom and an important one. No other name will do.

And what did the name *Gobi* mean?

Ultimately who is to say? We know it was the name of an espionage network that once existed here and in China. We know that Adzhar suggested it that afternoon we had the picnic on the beach, he and I and your parents, the time we wore gas masks. We know your father said our group should have a name and Adzhar said it should be *Gobi*. We know the four of us laughed and that was that.

And who was Adzhar?

I'm not sure. Marco Polo perhaps? I'll have another, please.

Quin poured. Father Lamereaux smiled.

Do you know I'm beginning to think I might come out of retirement? This would be an appropriate day to do it, during a typhoon.

And Adzhar?

Yes indeed, a very dear friend. He and I and Lotmann were inseparable in those days. Have you ever heard of him? Do you know anything at all about this unique little man who had such a miraculous way with languages?

No I don't, Father. Nothing at all.

Well, then you should. It would be folly to visit the East and not know something about the man who spent his whole life getting here. Lotmann never drank, but Adzhar certainly did. Well, I think I'll just have one more before I go on. One or possibly two in memory of both of them.

Quin filled the Jesuit's glass. Father Lamereaux sipped. He smiled gently and began to whisper.

●

He was born the son of a shoemaker in Gori, a town in Georgia, a few years before Alexander II freed the serfs. He was sent to a seminary in Tiflis to study for the Orthodox priesthood but was soon expelled as an anarchist and a nihilist. He was a restless man, Adzhar or whatever his real name was, once he hinted it might be Dzugashvili. In any case, when he was expelled from the seminary he went to St. Petersburg to study chemistry. A few years later, in the spring of 1880, he fell in love with a beautiful woman.

Sophia was a member of the nobility, the daughter of the governor of St. Petersburg. When she was a baby her autocratic father cast off his wife and sent her to Switzerland so that he would be better able to carry on his many affairs with women.

Sophia grew up not knowing she had a mother. When she discovered the truth about her father she decided to kill the Czar.

She visited her mother in Geneva and there contacted the Russian nihilist exiles who were also plotting to assassinate the Czar. With her beauty and her position she was a valuable asset to them. She moved in court circles, and her hatred for her father was so great she was more than willing to use her body to obtain information on the Czar's security arrangements. It wasn't long before the Czar's courtiers, in bed in her arms, had told her everything the plotters needed to know.

Sophia brought Adzhar into the plot because of his knowledge of chemistry. She didn't love him and he knew it, her obsession with humiliating her father left no room for loving anyone. But when she asked him to design the bombs for the group he agreed. Sophia took his prescriptions to Geneva and smuggled the materials back in a suitcase. Adzhar then put the bombs together in a shoemaker's shop he had rented on the route through St. Petersburg that the Czar would be using during the first week of March 1881. In all there were eight men and two women in the plot.

On March 1, near the shoemaker's shop, a bomb was thrown at the Czar's carriage. The Czar was dazed and stepped down into the street. A second man ran forward and threw a bomb at their feet, killing himself and the Czar but no one else.

Of the plotters one man was killed in the explosion, one shot himself, two escaped, and the remaining men and women were sentenced to death. Because of Sophia's rank Alexander III himself had to sign her death warrant. He was reluctant to do so, but his courtiers persuaded him out of fear that she might reveal their indiscretions with her. As it turned out she said nothing. She had disgraced her father and that was enough. She was hanged without betraying anyone.

Adzhar, one of the two men who had escaped, was then in his early twenties. The news of Sophia's execution reached him in Helsinki, where he had gone into hiding. He also learned that the Russian government was sending agents abroad to try to catch him and the other man.

Adzhar knew he had to find as remote a spot as possible, so he went north to the land of the Lapps. For the next half-dozen years he lived with the Lapps in isolation, wandering with them and their reindeer herds across the wastes of the Arctic Circle. When he left them he went to

Iceland and worked as a shoemaker. While with the Lapps he had learned Lappish, an Asian language, as well as the Scandinavian tongues. Now he learned Icelandic. He still had not forgotten Sophia, and the discipline of learning languages, he discovered, was a way of putting aside his unhappiness.

After a half-dozen years reading the Icelandic sagas he went to the Faroe Islands and learned Faroese, then to the Isle of Man to learn Manx. During this period he also acquired Gaelic, Scottish Gaelic, Welsh, and English. With English behind him he went to America, as did so many East Europeans at that time.

The St. Petersburg uprising of 1905 came and went, as did the artillery pieces later placed around the Shinto shrines in Japan. In New York he met Trotsky, the hero of the 1905 uprising who was now traveling to various countries soliciting aid for his cause. Although Trotsky was nearly twenty years younger than Adzhar, he revived Adzhar's political idealism.

One evening there was a famous encounter between the two men that resulted in Adzhar delivering his incredible prophecy, a prophecy that later caused Trotsky to give him his remarkable code name.

It happened in the Bronx. Trotsky had gone to Adzhar's shoemaker's shop for blintzes and borscht. Trotsky was in a bad temper that evening because he had spent the day working on his history of the 1905 failure. He refused to eat anything, and all the food, which Adzhar had spent the day preparing, seemed about to go to waste. Adzhar decided to enliven the gathering with a story. Trotsky replied that there wasn't a story in the world that could lift his gloom at that moment. Adzhar smiled and answered in an unknown tongue.

What's that? asked Trotsky.

Passamaquoddy, said Adzhar.

What?

An Indian tribe, a branch of the Algonquins. I lived with them for a few weeks one winter in order to pick up their language.

And what did you learn in this useless tongue?

How the world was created.

How?

Like this.

Adzhar recounted the epic. He told it first in Russian and then in the original Passamaquoddy. As related by Adzhar, the exploits of the central character strongly resembled Trotsky's life up until then. Trotsky listened more and more intently, delighted to hear his struggles described in such an odd-sounding language. Although he didn't believe for a moment that Adzhar's version was authentic, he still found it amusing to imagine that a half-naked Indian with a bow and arrow and a feather in his hair had once experienced in North America the same struggles he was now undergoing in Russia. He laughed and joked and ate quantities of blintzes and borscht. By the end of the evening he had forgotten all about 1905 and was talking enthusiastically about the next uprising, which he was certain would succeed.

When will it come? asked someone.

Trotsky frowned. He calculated. He searched for obscure quotations from the holy books of revolutions. He was about to squeeze all of history into one ironbound Marxist harangue when his gaze happened to fall on Adzhar. What stopped him then? The mischief in Adzhar's eyes? The slight smile that was always hovering around the little man's mouth?

The harangue never came. The frown flew from Trotsky's face and he burst into wild laughter, the kind of unrestrained, totally goodhumored laughter seldom heard from a dedicated revolutionary whose work, like that of God's, leans heavily on the serious side of life.

Adzhar, he said, your blintzes were superb tonight. Your borscht was excellent, and what's more you've already answered that question for me, for mother Russia and the world. How long did you say your brave Passamaquoddy labored in his act of creation?

A dozen years.

Just so. Well we failed in 1905 and that means we will succeed in 1917.

Adzhar winked. Once more Trotsky went off into a burst

of wild laughter. In revolutionary circles around the world Trotsky was often called *The Pen* because of the power of his writing. He made reference to this now.

Adzhar, he said, on the basis of that epic you told us tonight you should always be known as *The Holy Ghost*, and if you ever join us that's what your code name will have to be.

The two men embraced, Trotsky insisting that a photograph be taken in order to memorialize the evening of Adzhar's prophecy.

When the Third International was founded in 1919 *The Holy Ghost* was in Paris working for Trotsky, using his knowledge of French and German and Italian and Spanish, Hebrew, Hungarian, Lithuanian, Lettish, Flemish, Dutch, Romansh, Slovak, Serbo-Croatian, and several other tongues to recruit European agents and pass information from one movement to another. A Guatemalan, for example, spoke only his native Tzotzil dialect, and if Adzhar hadn't learned Tzotzil in a cafe one afternoon in order to talk to the man the Comintern would never have known of the existence of this potentially valuable agent in Central America.

An innovation of his in Paris was a unit of *moles*, Jewish tailors he brought from Odessa and taught to make clothes characteristic of various regions in the world, and to plant ticket stubs and tobacco and other items in the linings of the pockets, so that Comintern agents could travel freely without fear of being recognized.

In 1919 he returned briefly to Russia to see Trotsky and was almost shot at the border as a White Russian. Fortunately he had with him the photograph taken at the shoemaker's shop in the Bronx that showed him and Trotsky arm in arm beaming at the camera. He presented it to the guards and it saved his life.

Back in Paris one of his many new recruits was a young American who had been wounded in the First World War and wanted to end all wars. Quin, shall we call him? Adzhar even knew the neighborhood in the Bronx where the young man had grown up, for it happened to be the same as that of the shoemaker's shop in the photograph.

He found Quin an intelligent young man, confident of himself, eager to learn, and eager to put his skills to work. He also found his enthusiasm naïve perhaps, but Adzhar wasn't so old that he couldn't remember his own feelings when he left Tiflis and went to St. Petersburg.

He gave Quin some training and received orders to send him on to Moscow. It was not until several years later in Shanghai, after Adzhar had removed himself from espionage work, that he learned from a young American woman that his former pupil Quin had received intensive training at the school outside Moscow and been assigned to a mission in China.

Adzhar was disturbed by Lenin's New Economic Policy after the Russian civil war. When Lenin died in 1924 he decided to give up his clandestine activities and return to the study of languages. He was then over sixty. The time had come to retire, he felt.

Thus he severed forever all connections with the Comintern.

From Paris he went to the Middle East, intending to learn Punic and Ugaritic, Mandaean and Nuzi Akkadian. He did learn them, but while in Jerusalem he met for the second time a man he had known five years before in France, a man he admired exceedingly, a Japanese diabetic who had converted to Judaism since they had last seen each other.

This man was Rabbi Lotmann, formerly Baron Kikuchi of the powerful landowning clan in northern Japan. Lotmann discussed the Orient with Adzhar, and it was because of him that Adzhar decided not to tarry in the Middle East but to continue his journey as far east as one could go.

In Malabar, where he stopped briefly to acquire fluency in Kulu and Kota and Toda, he fell in love with a young woman of wealth and married her, the only time he ever married, so long had it taken him to recover from the loss of Sophia.

His wife was a Nestorian Christian, a member of that nearly extinct sect that had flourished in the early Middle Ages. As a child she had fed her horse from a helmet that had been worn by a soldier in Tamerlane's army. Either that experience or the trading traditions of her fathers, who had sold their peppercorns to both East and West, had caused the young woman to dream of someday going to Samarkand to visit the tomb of Tamerlane, from where she hoped to follow the silk route of antiquity through central Asia, perhaps as far as Peking. In the thirteenth century, after all, a Nestorian monk from Peking had traveled west to discuss theology with the pope and had continued on to Bordeaux, where he gave communion to Edward I of England. Why not reverse the journey? Lastly there was the inducement of a pilgrimage to the famous monument that Chinese Nestorians had erected at Hsian-fu in the eighth century.

Adzhar was delighted when he heard all of this. He and his wife went to Goa to organize a caravan and there found an omen of the misfortune to come.

Goa is built on hills and the sewerage system consisted of open drains cleaned by pigs that wandered the city. At the time they arrived there a band of Arabs had just sailed into port with a shipload of powerful drugs, some suspected of being from as far away as Mexico. The Portuguese were celebrating Easter with these drugs, the Arabs were celebrating Ramadan, and the Indians were supplicating their usual multitude of spring deities.

The problem was that the drugs were much stronger than anyone suspected. They were so lasting that many of their properties passed right through the body of the user, causing a phenomenon known as the high hogs of Goa. For several weeks the entire population had to remain locked indoors on their hills, without food or water, terrorized by marauding hordes of tipsy, careening pigs driven mad by the sewerage in the open drains.

Finally Adzhar and his young wife and the infant daughter recently born to them were able to set out in their caravan. They reached Samarkand without incident and turned east to cross central Asia. Along the trail of the ancient silk route Adzhar continued to acquire new languages, Kashgarian and Yakandian, Taranchi, Uzbek and Sart, Harachin, Chanar. All went well until they sighted the Gobi Desert. At an oasis on the fringe of the desert they were attacked without warning by a tribe of bandits appearing from nowhere.

Adzhar was away from the camp at the time. His daughter was playing under a blanket and escaped notice, but his wife and all the bearers were decapitated. Adzhar shouldered his daughter and crossed the Gobi on foot, his daughter dying of thirst before he reached another oasis.

At last he arrived in Shanghai in 1927, the year the Communist uprising failed there, the same year Trotsky fell from power in Russia.

●

Father Lamereaux paused to pour himself another glass of whiskey.

As it happened, he whispered, a remark Adzhar made during his first days in Shanghai had an enormous influence on modern Chinese history.

When he arrived in the city his only interest was in learning the Kiangsi and Hakka dialects, to go with those he already knew, so that he could read the regional commentaries on the Chinese classics before continuing on to Japan. But at the same time, remembering his own experiences with the czarist police, he could not help but be sympathetic with the revolutionaries who were being hunted down in Shanghai and shot. Consequently he hid a number of them in his home until a way could be found for them to escape from the city.

One of these Chinese was an urbane scholarly man who had studied in Europe and had been one of the leaders of the uprising. He and Adzhar got into the habit of having long philosophical discussions to pass the hours. Not sur-

prisingly, like Trotsky in the Bronx, the Chinese was
depressed over the recent disaster to his cause.

Sometimes, he said one evening, despair paralyzes us.
We become like an animal in the dark that can neither see
nor hear nor smell.

I know that despair, said Adzhar. On one occasion I
knew it particularly well. I was living with the Lapps and
it seemed I would never escape those frozen regions
where the darkness closes around you and closes in. But
then the Lapps with their reindeer taught me what to do
and taught me well, for remember no one knows such a
night as they do above the Arctic Circle.

And what did they tell you?

What I've done all my life since then. Move.
March.

Where?

What does it matter? All good roads are within. Mine
has been a long one and perhaps your march must be long
as well.

The scholarly Chinese smiled at Adzhar, for as they
both knew, the Lapp proverb he had quoted was nothing
more than the way of the Tao. He smiled at Adzhar, but he
remembered the wisdom of the remark because it came
from a man who had known many strange corners of the
world.

A few days later the Chinese was able to escape from
Shanghai. During the next few years he knew many more
disasters, until finally a moment came when he and his
comrades were completely surrounded by armies that far
outnumbered them.

By then the scholarly revolutionary had risen high in the
ranks of the party. Each night after a day of hopeless
warfare the weary leaders sat down on the ground to
discuss their desperate situation, and each night Adzhar's
friend argued with the others to accept the advice he had
heard while hiding in Shanghai.

Almost all the other leaders disagreed with him. What
he was proposing was failure and defeat. They still controlled this one area of the country, and the peasants there

were loyal to them. If they left it they would have nothing. They would be nothing.

So they argued, but Adzhar's friend was clever and eventually he won them over. The order was given to march and they did, six thousand miles in all, a march that saved them from extinction and became a mystical unifying force that brought them to power in the end.

A long voyage? Perhaps. Yet not as long as the voyage of a shoemaker's son from Georgia.

Adzhar busied himself with Chinese dialects, but very soon he was experiencing a new kind of restlessness, the most profound he had ever known. He used to speculate that it had come to him because he had crossed the Gobi Desert on foot, although frankly I see no connection whatsoever between the two. Then at other times he claimed the original cause of the restlessness might have been more general and unspecified than one would expect, perhaps merely a routine result of having arrived in the East after so many decades of wandering. Lotmann favored the latter explanation and as proof quoted the story of Elijah and the ravens, which had saved his own life, but in the end who is to say? In any case the restlessness amounted to this.

Adzhar had loved only two women in his life, his wife and before that Sophia. Now he asked himself why the way of the Lapps should only be applied to geography. People were more important than places, and hadn't he wasted too many years moving from place to place remembering or anticipating love?

He decided he had. He decided that in the years he had left to live, it would be criminal not to make up for the loss, to add an overall balance to his life. Once more he went on the march, only now it was from embrace to embrace.

They must be a vigorous people, the Georgians. Adzhar was over seventy when he became converted to love in Shanghai, yet he began a round of activities that would have exhausted a man fifty years younger. Of course there was no question about his being successful. He had charm learned in a thousand settlements, he could quote poems from any language in the world. Although old and small, his years of lonely wandering had given him an ability to appreciate women that few men have ever possessed. The linguistic genius formerly applied to words now expressed itself through his heart. No matter whether a woman was young or old or short or fat, beautiful or ugly or thin or tall, the moment he saw her he loved her with a genuine and boundless love that completely overwhelmed him.

Could any woman resist such warmth? She could not. Adzhar's lovemaking became a legend and hundreds of women sought him out.

One affair he had then, more significant than the others, was with a young American woman to whom he gave the Nestorian relic treasured in his wife's family for thirteen centuries. Maeve, we might call her.

The reason the affair was significant to him is easy to understand. Maeve was young and beautiful and passionate, to be sure, but more specifically there was a quality in her that reminded him of someone else, a woman he had known half a century before, a quality that often fascinates but seldom brings happiness. As he was ready to admit, that young American woman reminded him of Sophia.

I was there when he met her again at the picnic on the beach in Kamakura. He asked her what had become of the small gold cross, and she told him that she had given it to a Japanese General, a later lover of hers. Adzhar smiled when he heard that. He was glad, he said.

As soon as he learned his old friend Lotmann was returning from the Middle East, to retire in Kamakura, Adzhar moved there to be near him. Lotmann was engaged in translating the Talmud into Japanese, an enterprise that interested Adzhar so much he decided to undertake a major project of his own, a traditional Oriental practice.

Toward the end of life it is customary for an emperor to retire to some spot that pleases him and there write the poetry that will memorialize his reign. This poetic compendium is the means by which future generations can know the name and nature of his era. In Adzhar's case one might have expected a history of all the languages in the world, or perhaps a dictionary of all the languages in the world, so that a scholar ten thousand years from now could know what everything meant.

But no, his great work took quite a different form.

Two factors influenced him. First, Lotmann was doing a translation and that made sense to Adzhar, since it seemed likely that anything worth writing had already been written somewhere.

Second, he decided his subject should deal with the revolution he himself had recently undergone, his insatiable new love of lovemaking.

In the monasteries in the hills above Kamakura he found certain manuscripts to his liking. These manuscripts had been compiled in the thirteenth century by vast armies of monks and were not only whimsical and fantastic but totally pornographic. Originally Adzhar had thought of rendering them into his native Russian, but he realized he was still too disgusted with Lenin's New Economic Policy to do that. On the other hand, Roosevelt had just announced his New Deal in America and a new deal always appealed to Adzhar. For this reason and no other the most stupendous pornographic collection in modern times happened to be rendered into English.

Day and night the retired Emperor could be found laboring in his pavilion to complete the prodigious task he had assigned himself. In addition to translating tens of thousands of documents, he cross-referenced them with an eccentric system of his own invention, numbers written into the margins. These swarming clouds of numbers had overwhelming implications, for the real task Adzhar had set himself was no less than a total description of love by way of endless enumeration, an Oriental concept whereby one blank face turns into an infinite array of masks, a process so unfamiliar in the West it is called inscrutable.

In 1937, in honor of his eightieth birthday, Adzhar

planned an extraordinary fortnight of unlimited libertinism. Both Lotmann and I warned him against it, but he was adamant. He wouldn't listen to us.

Early that summer, you see, a party of Kempeitai plainclothesmen had visited his house as they periodically did with foreigners. They perused his manuscripts and were shocked by what they found. In their view the very existence of such documents in English was a clear and present danger to the state, since mountains of ancient Japanese pornography compiled by monks tended to belie the official position that the Japanese were now and always had been morally superior to all races everywhere.

Adzhar argued that he had no intention of showing his collection to anyone. He even offered to destroy the key or code book to his annotations, without which no one could hope to grasp the ultimate significance of the translations.

But the Kempeitai confiscated the collection all the same. They brought a truck convoy down to Kamakura and carted the manuscripts away to their warehouse in Tokyo, where for some obscure reason they were stored in the wing containing secret files on China, perhaps because it was hoped that if the manuscripts were ever discovered they would be considered of Chinese rather than Japanese origin.

Adzhar was outraged. Thus the strenuous abandon with which he planned his eightieth birthday. He called together all the women he had known in Japan over the last eight years, at least several thousand, and rented hotels thoughout the Tokyo area to accommodate them. During the fortnight preceding his birthday he shuttled back and forth between these hotels satisfying all of his former mistresses.

It was July and the weather was sultry, dangerous for a man of his years. Still he would not let up. The day before his birthday he returned to his home in Kamakura, to bathe prior to having tea with Lotmann and me. In the bath, however, he came across his housekeeper giving her great-granddaughter a shampoo.

The housekeeper was eighty-eight. Her great-granddaughter was sixteen. Adzhar knew the girl because she sometimes came to clean, but he had always kept away from both her and her great-grandmother out of a notion that it was somehow better not to involve his home life with his sexual affairs.

I'm sure it wasn't part of his plan. Adzhar was a sensualist but he also had a philosophical turn of mind. I'm sure that after tea with Lotmann and me he intended to return home and spend the evening alone quietly welcoming in his birthday. But since his conversion in the Gobi Desert he had taught himself to let his smile fall where it might. Later, when the old woman and the young girl had recovered some of their strength, they told us what had happened.

Adzhar surprised them. He smiled and said he would like to finish shampooing the young girl's hair himself. This he did. He then shampooed the old woman's hair, his own, and suggested they all three get into the large bathing pool together. Immediately he dove underwater and stayed there so long they might have feared he was drowning had they not known otherwise. Every so often he surfaced only to go under again at once, causing both of them to swoon a dozen times before he emerged for another gulp of air.

These vigorous water games lasted for perhaps an hour. Adzhar then tucked one of them under each arm and carried them into the living room. Adzhar lived in Japanese fashion, so the entire room could serve as a bed if one were used to lying on *tatami*, which of course all three were. The great-grandmother was afraid the hot water might have weakened him, and urged him to rest while she gave him a massage. Adzhar agreed to the massage but found it impossible to rest. While she walked on his back he busied himself with the great-granddaughter.

And so it went for hours and hours as the weather grew hotter and hotter. Adzhar never slackened, never stopped making love. Sometime in the course of the evening, small as he was, he managed to carry the two of them out to the kitchen, making love all the while, and get a bottle

of iced vodka and a jar of iced caviar out of the refrigerator. These he consumed back in the living room without
interrupting himself.

At midnight, while copulating with both of them in
alternate thrusts, the heart attack struck.

They heard him groan, naturally they were groaning
themselves. The three simultaneous orgasms lasted
throughout the twelve chimes of the clock, at which time
Adzhar turned eighty and died.

Hours passed before the old woman and the young girl
had the energy to crawl over to the telephone. They were
too weak to speak, but we understood from the panting
over the phone that something had happened. Lotmann
and I hurried over and found Adzhar lying on his back, his
member still erect, the same grateful smile on his face
that he had worn that morning when he walked into the
bath and found his housekeeper and her great-
granddaughter there by chance.

Lotmann and I pronounced our various Catholic and
Buddhist and Jewish and Shinto prayers over the little old
man. We carried him up to a pine grove on a hill behind
Kamakura and there, as he had wanted, buried him in an
unmarked grave with his head pointing to the east.

A strange and restless journey? Could he have been that
man who traveled out of the west to visit the court of
Kublai Khan in the thirteenth century?

I don't know. I only know that on the day Adzhar
reached the end of his remarkable wanderings Japanese
troops crossed the Marco Polo Bridge outside of Peking
and brought war to all of China.

●

Quin poured the last of the whiskey into Father Lamereaux's glass. The Jesuit's hand shook a little as he stiffly
buttoned his coat the wrong way, but the only effect of the
alcohol still seemed to be to recall a small part of that

brilliance of memory that had once allowed him to memorize the entire *Summa theologica*, that in its day had reinforced an inner vision so unwavering it had been stared down only once, by the glass eye of a sleeping man, and even then only after a full hour of unblinking silence.

Father Lamereaux sipped.

And the other one? said Quin. The one known as Rabbi Lotmann?

Yes, whispered the priest, there had been three of us who were friends in Kamakura before the war and now there were only two. Lotmann, as it turned out, like Adzhar, was also affected late in life by the founding of the Third International.

As a young man at the beginning of the century his interests were archery and the paintings of the Impressionists. Because he had the vast Kikuchi landholdings behind him, he could indulge himself and did, making frequent trips to Paris before the First World War to increase his collection of paintings. In 1919, already middle-aged, he was off again.

A fellow passenger on the Trans-Siberian Express was Katayama Sen, who was on his way to Moscow to become a founding member of the Comintern. Baron Kikuchi was too much of an aesthete to care for politics, but his countryman's zeal impressed him so much on the long trip that when he arrived in Paris he cabled for his collection to be sold and turned over the proceeds, as prearranged, to a Comintern representative in Paris. The address he was sent to was a shoemaker's shop. The agent, of course, was Adzhar. They took an immediate liking to each other.

Customarily the Baron stopped in Egypt to rest for a month or two before continuing on his voyage home from Europe. As an aesthete he enjoyed contemplating both the symmetry of the pyramids and the regularities of the Temple of Karnak. This time, however, he chose to tarry in Jerusalem rather than in Cairo. There he toured the normal spectacular sights, the Via Dolorosa, the garden of St. Ann's, the Dome of the Rock, the Wall. Not only did he find himself remaining longer in the Middle East than usual but he also found himself, gradually, falling under the spell of Judaism.

What is inevitable appears to be inevitable. Baron Kikuchi converted and began his training as a rabbi. At that point his title and his holdings in Japan automatically passed to his younger twin brother, younger by eight minutes, at that time a Colonel in the army but soon to become a member of the General Staff.

Before long Lotmann left Palestine and returned to Japan. There are two contradictory, or perhaps complementary, stories to explain it. One says that he was expelled from Palestine for excessive Zionist activities. The other says he was passing excessive urine at the time and had the good sense to know that medical advice in Kamakura would be vastly superior to anything available in Jerusalem.

No matter which explanation is applicable, we find the former Baron Kikuchi, now Rabbi Lotmann, taking up residence in the early 1920s on a corner of the large estate in Kamakura formerly owned by him, now the property of his brother.

By nature he was a delicate man. Just as Adzhar grew more sensual in his old age, an ineluctable process, Lotmann grew more ethereal. His favorite prophet was Elijah and he used to claim he heard the same still, small voice in his garden in Kamakura that Elijah had heard on Mt. Horeb.

So perhaps his death, after all, wasn't the accident it appeared to be.

In the spring of 1945 the Americans were burning down Tokyo with their fire bombs. Lotmann was working on his Talmudic translations in the garden, as usual, when he heard a raid beginning over Tokyo. But the Americans never bombed Kamakura, so there was nothing to fear. Lotmann went on writing under the cloudy spring sky.

At noon the sun suddenly broke through the clouds, an unusually bright sun for a spring day. Either one of the American bombardiers was momentarily blinded by the rich colors of the earth thus revealed, or else the sudden heat of the sun stirred a current of wind in some peculiar fashion. In any case one small cluster of bombs missed Tokyo by twenty miles and fell exactly on Lotmann's garden, instantly consuming him and all his translations in a ball of fire.

The fire burned so intensely it was out in a matter of seconds. The house and grounds were untouched. There was a black patch in the garden, otherwise nothing.

Since the death of Adzhar there had been only the two of us. Save for Lotmann and his sweet music there was no one else to comfort me. And now?

And now it came to pass as they still went on and talked that, behold, there appeared a chariot of fire and horses of fire and parted them both asunder. And Elijah went up by a whirlwind into heaven.

●

Father Lamereaux tipped his empty glass. He picked up the bottle and saw that it too was empty. He turned to face the window, scars appearing around his eyes.

We'll have no second bottle today, he whispered, we'll have no second chance in life. That other day of acting is gone, the *No* masks are gone and the music and the poem, gone along with all I knew, gone with all I've known. Once I asked myself these questions. Why does Elijah call himself Lotmann? Why does the dragon call himself Adzhar? Why is the tea bowl turned three times? Why is the *koto* played only once in a thousand years?

I examined these questions and many others when I was abandoned and left alone. In my solitude I looked for the mysteries that stir the facts of life. I looked but now the wind is rising. The typhoon will be here soon, and mysteries and facts alike will be of no avail when it comes. They are the driftwood on the shore to be found by you or another after the storm has passed. Gather them together if you wish and build a fire on the beach against the night. Watch the smoke rise into the darkness and wonder if those are stars you see up there. Listen to the rumble of the sea then, listen to the waves turn three times and turn a thousand years, listen and let your mind wander.

Father Lamereaux sadly lowered his head. He gripped the horsehair arms of his chair.

Even in the thirteenth century there was often confusion in the capital, which is to say we've made a mistake following Christ rather than the Virgin. Without a mother there would be no son and women who have children, even virgins, are seldom bothered by constipation. In the old days this house was filled with cats and there were always fires to watch, the flowers of Tokyo they were called. If we happened to see a flower before a meeting of the Legion, the conversation afterward was always exceptionally spirited.

Turnips. For over two decades nothing but turnips. Half a century in this country. Three-quarters of a century of life.

Father Lamereaux bent his head. His long white hair swung free. A blast of wind shook the house and then there was utter silence. For a minute or two he listened to the silence.

Do you hear it? Do you know it? It is the eye of heaven and we are in it. But there is but a short time to wait, eternity is brief. Soon the wind will be with us again, stronger than before, and the Emperor will pass unrecognized through the byways of his capital, his mark on the gate mistaken for the scratchings of a peasant, the palace a graveyard where his ghost drifts between the stones. There are so many shrines one Emperor cannot visit them all, sooner or later he must retire to his prayer wheels. And now I am afraid there is nothing more this court can do for you. The thirteenth century is coming to an end. Adzhar is gone, Lotmann is gone, I must join them. Our moment is over. The eye of the storm is about to close.

Father Lamereaux stood. His hair streamed around his shoulders.

Quin tried to thank him, but his words were lost in the wind. He reached out, but there was no hand there to take. The old priest's gaze was fixed on an ancient domain bequeathed to poets and musicians. The door closed as Quin ran up the street looking for shelter.

●

Father Lamereaux returned to his study. His walls were lined with books. On his desk lay the manuscript he had never begun, the history of his reign, a work so massive there was no way to record it. The Emperor had ruled from his throne for seven hundred years and now his era was over. Time moved in epochs.

A petitioner.

A dwarf staring at the middle of his forehead.

Master, I have closed the shutters. Go down to the cellar and stay there until the typhoon passes.

Father Lamereaux listened to the temple bells tolling the stages of his soul. Certainly he could retire to the pine grove above the sea where he had long ago received instructions in the mysteries. Certainly he could grant her petition if first he resigned himself to imperfection.

Go down, master. Go down. Do it now.

My life, he whispered, has been devoted to the alleviation of suffering. In the years allotted me by Our Lady I have sought no other justification for life.

His face tightened. The scars around his eyes deepened. His cheeks sank, the skin shrank into the bone. He reached out and put both hands around Miya's neck, strangling her, letting her body fall to the floor.

A window crashed. The front door blew open. He walked slowly down the corridor and paused at the kitchen. It was empty, the Emperor was alone in his palace. Even the princess had fled.

Leaves and branches and earth, the whole world had been set loose in the air. Five thousand people would die in Japan that afternoon and Father Lamereaux was but one of them, a forgotten priest whose kindness had soothed the lives of many.

The wind knocked him down. With the last of his strength, he crawled across the garden to where the moss grew, to where there would be flowers and cats and tombstones for the boys he had loved in cemeteries, where the gong of the wind sounded down through the longest reign in the history of Asia.

His head rested on the moss. He looked up at the sky, stared into the eye of heaven as the thick garden wall came apart, as the prison walls opened and he was crushed piece by piece under the smooth, weathered stones.

●

There were only two buttons in the private elevator, one marked *up* and one marked *down*. The little woman met him when he stepped off on the twenty-fourth floor.

The whole city is at your feet, said Quin. Is Fuji-san always that clear from here?

Only at this time of the year, she said. Just after the typhoon season the air is peculiarly transparent. Distance seems not to count. The rest of the year the mountain is cloudy and mysterious, or dim and mysterious, or invisible and mysterious.

He slipped off his shoes and followed her into a spacious room with *tatami* on the floor, empty of furniture, bare save for a primitive structure by the window. The Japanese shrine was raised on stilts, the thatched roof slanting sharply up to where the roof beams, two on each end, crossed in the air. The interior of the shrine was hidden by thin straw mats hanging on all four sides.

When I was younger, she said, it puzzled me how that design found its way to Japan. The heavy roof and open sides suggest a tropical climate of rain and heat, a land of monsoons, thus the stilts. Yet Japan is a northern country and mountainous. Why fear coastal floods in the mountains? Why build without walls and foundations when the winters are severe? Why use thatch rather than earth and stone like other northern peoples? The Ainu, the first people on these islands, built quite differently. They fought quite differently as well, on foot with short weapons, which seems suitable to a mountain land. Yet the oldest objects of the Yamato peoples from whom we are descended are clay grave figures that show warriors on horseback with long swords. Horsemen with long swords in a tropical jungle? No. That would have to suggest the plains of Manchuria and Mongolia.

Mama smiled.

Northern yet southern. Our ancestors, after all, are a paradox. The house and the people in it contradict each other. Their three holy symbols were a round disk of polished metal, a curved piece of jade, a sword. The sun and the new moon and the lightning of fate. What plans do you have now?

I leave in a few days on a freighter.

Well, then it is over, whatever you hoped to do.

She was dressed in a black kimono. An emerald hung in the middle of her forehead. She touched the jewel now with a slender finger.

I didn't know the name of the circus master then.

I didn't know what became of the son your mother had by the General, nor what became of the son I had by your father. I didn't know then, but no matter. What has been remains in our emerald world, the jewels of our minds where the circus of the past is never forgotten. The man I knew wanted to control his destiny. But lives cross, the sun and the moon contradict each other, we are enmeshed in a network of doing and feeling. Others become part of us and the pasts of others are beyond us. He sacrificed everything to build his own network of destiny. I met him only once for a few hours, yet it changed my life. Why is that?

He didn't do it alone, he did it with another. When I went to the warehouse that night I thought my life was over, but when I listened to the words of the circus master I discovered this wasn't so. An anonymous giant had already returned life to me although I didn't know it until that moment. But then I knew it and knew that even then I had something to give in return, so I did.

Long ago they changed my life, those two anonymous men. The one by listening, the other by speaking. And although now I know the name of one of them, the one who was your father, the other is still unknown to me after all these years. Is this best? Perhaps. Perhaps it can be no other way with us. Perhaps that kind of mercy must always remain a mystery.

Yes, she added, it seems so.

She went on to speak of the General and his death, her flight to China, the year in a narcotized Shanghai dream watching false images being projected on the wall. She spoke of the night a rickshaw carried her down Bubbling Well Road to the outskirts of the city, to the gloomy cavern of the circus master's last performance.

She took his hand.

When he was gone she went to her shrine and drew back the straw curtains. On the platform stood the ivory elephant supporting the dais in the shape of a lotus. The shrine faced west. She climbed up to the lotus and seated herself as the sun dropped over the city.

She sat in *za-zen*, her hands forming the *mudra* of knowledge. The first part of her life had been given to the ten thousand men who had come to explore her tattoo, the mythical epic of the dragon, the last part to the General and the circus master, so unalike and yet so similar in the grotesque ways in which they died.

She recalled the apocryphal chronicle from the Han dynasty that had described the terrors of the Gobi Desert. The chronicler had feared the sandstorms and the disappearing rivers, the mirages, above all the secret agents who represented the princes and despots of a thousand lawless regions, a danger thereby to the rule of the Son of Heaven.

He claimed this was his concern, but then he asked a

question that revealed the true nature of the fear that had made him tremble when the caravans passed, a possibility far more frightening than the massed armies that might be sent by a thousand lawless princes and despots, a vision that horrified him because it was the ultimate threat to the Son of Heaven and the integrity of his rule.

Or is it perhaps that they represent no one at all?

Mama sat in her thatched hut raised on stilts, a structure still used by peasants in the countryside in the tradition of a shrine first built in Japan two thousand years ago on a peninsula in the south.

The sacred object in that shrine was a round metal disk, the mirror that had belonged to the sun goddess before she was enticed from her cave by music, thereafter to become the ancestress of Japan's emperors. For two thousand years, at the end of every second decade, the shrine of the sun goddess had been torn down and rebuilt exactly as it was before, thus to survive unchanged through the reigns of one hundred and twenty-four emperors.

And so it was with men who were destroyed in order that the shrine might never grow old, through change to remain the same, destroyed and resurrected by ten thousand men or by two men who painted tattoos on their minds, followed the tale of the dragon, joined a caravan that yet again was setting out across the desert in search of a fabled kingdom.

The tiny woman bowed her head. Fate had taken her sons and she had nothing else to give, but still there were no tears in the emerald eye that gathered together the final light of that autumn day above the Imperial moat.

NICHIREN

8

*No, they will not believe you but you must tell them
the truth all the same. You must say that once a man
dreamed a wind would come, he dreamed it and willed
it, and because he did the wind came.*

—The monk Nichiren speaking to his disciples after he
destroyed the fleet of Kublai Khan

●

The day before his ship sailed Quin received a postcard at
his hotel across from Tokyo station. The postmark showed
that it had been sent to his old address at the time of Big
Gobi's funeral. There was a picture of a fishing village, an
illegible message, and a scrawled signature.

Geraty.

Quin asked about the village and was told it was three
hours away by train, on the coast south of Kamakura. For
weeks he had been trying to find Geraty, but the answer
everywhere was the same. No one had seen the giant with
the bulging eyes since early in the summer. It was assumed that he had either died or left Tokyo.

There was only one train to the village and it left in a
few minutes. Another returned late at night. Quin ran
across the street to the station and found the train just as
it was beginning to move.

They reached the tiny village early in the afternoon.
Quin went first to the police box on the square. After that
he intended to try the post office, the inn, lastly the shops
that sold horseradish.

267

The policeman seemed to understand a few words of English. Quin used his hands to describe his man.

A foreigner. Also an American but much taller, much fatter. A long, filthy overcoat, a black hat pulled down to the ears. Layers of sweaters and a swath of red flannel at the neck. Alcohol. Horseradish. Head shaved, white stubble. Purple veins in the face. A gigantic nose, sacks for arms. A belly this far out. Eyes a skull could not hold.

The policeman watched him politely. When Quin finished he asked questions with his hands and his few words of English.

Huge? Yes, he understood.

Whiskey? *Sake*? He frowned. Impossible.

Prominent eyes? He smiled. Certainly.

A shaved head? The policeman looked confused.

An overcoat? No, nothing like that.

A hat? A black hat? Nobody wore hats anymore, not even foreigners.

Layers of sweaters? A red scarf? A hat like that and an overcoat that big?

The policeman hid his smile. Not even an American would dress so strangely. For a moment he had thought he knew whom they were talking about but obviously it wasn't the same person. He shook his head. Unfortunately he couldn't help.

Geraty, said Quin. *Ger-a-ty*. He must have been here.

Suddenly the policeman's face was serious. The word came out with a hiss.

Galatiiii?

That's him, said Quin. Was he here?

The policeman laughed. He clapped his hands three times.

Galatiiii, he hissed triumphantly.

He lowered his eyes solemnly.

Galati-ti-ti, he whispered, rocking back and forth as he repeated the name. The first time he had said it with his head thrown back, smiling. The second time he pronounced the syllables respectfully with his head bowed.

Where? said Quin. Where?

The policeman pointed toward the square. He waved his hand for Quin to follow and started down a narrow street that led to the waterfront. There were a few small piers with fishing boats clustered around them. Although it was a cool October day the shops along the harbor were open to the sun. The policeman marched stiffly along the quay swinging his arms.

Galatiiii, he chanted. *Galati-ti-ti*.

A group of children playing in the street dropped their ball and ran up behind Quin. An elderly crone, her back bent into a question mark by a lifetime of planting rice, hobbled up to him and clutched his sleeve. She tugged, grinned, kept pace with him over the cobblestones tapping her cane. Women came out of the shops and fishermen left their nets to join the procession.

Galatiiii, hissed the policeman.

Galati-ti-ti, sang the marching crowd.

The procession stretched the length of the waterfront. First came the strutting policeman, then Quin with the dwarf hanging from his sleeve, the children, the fishermen and their wives and mothers.

They left the harbor and followed a road along the shore. Ahead lay a high, rocky point, perhaps a half-mile away, that formed the bay of the village. The point ended in pine trees and cliffs. The sandy road became an uphill path.

Someone had brought a crude set of chimes. Someone else had brought a drum. The chimes clanged and the drum boomed as they climbed through the rice paddies into a pine grove, along a ledge above the sea, through a defile in the rocks that led to an open clearing. Two hundred feet away a small Japanese house stood on the very edge of the promontory.

The policeman waited until the entire procession had wound through the rocks and entered the field. When everyone was standing along the fringe of the forest he bowed his head and clapped three times.

Galatiiii, he shouted.

Galati-ti-ti, chanted the congregation.

The policeman turned and went to stand with the rest of the crowd. The dwarf gave Quin's sleeve a final tug and hobbled off on her cane. The crowd waited. Quin was alone in the middle of the clearing.

At last the door to the little house opened. A huge figure dressed in kimono wallowed out into the sun. He was enormous, his white hair long and silky. He smiled and benignly raised his arms. The multitude bowed.

Three claps from the giant. One hand went up, the forefinger and middle finger pointing skyward, the medicine and little fingers held down by the thumb to make the pillar and the circle, the symbol of life, the sign of the preacher.

A deep and resonant prayer in Japanese, a short sermon, a rousing benediction. Three loud claps again to end the ceremony. The crowd laughed happily.

Galatiiii, whispered a reverent voice.

Galati-ti-ti, shouted the multitude.

Chimes tinkled, the drum struck a beat. The villagers began to file out of the clearing, the old men rocking on the even ground, the women cackling noisily, the children pushing and pulling, the ancient dwarf rattling the stones with her cane. Quin stared at the huge fat man in kimono.

Buffalo. What in God's name is going on here?

The giant tossed his head, his hair flew, he burst into laughter. Tears ran down his face, he choked, his massive belly heaved up and down. He howled and his feet broke into a clumsy dance that carried him across the clearing, an enormous Buddha prancing in the afternoon sun. He crashed into the trees and came thundering back grunting and wheezing, gurgling, spinning in circles. He staggered, caught himself, hiccuped.

In God's name, he moaned. That's what you said, nephew, don't deny it. That's what you said, and as it happens the work that goes on here is no more and no less.

●

They sat on the narrow terrace of the house, the sea breaking on the cliff a hundred feet below. Behind Geraty lay the bay, the harbor, on the far side the fishing village.

He was wearing a formal black kimono and the short black jacket that went with it. A layer of immaculate white undergarments showed at his chest. The pockmarks had all but disappeared, his eyes no longer bulged from his head. He was heavier than ever, but his deeply tanned face and long, flowing hair gave him a robust appearance. A seagull glided over the house and dipped down the cliff. Geraty followed its flight.

Buffalo. Why did you really walk into the bar that night in the Bronx?

Geraty stirred. He turned away from the sea and gazed at Quin.

Because of my mother. Because I hated to think of her being forgotten after the way she died.

How did she die?

In more agony than you'll ever see. We watched her. The old man insisted she be sterilized and took her to a quack doctor. He and the quack had some drinks and by the time the quack opened her up he was drunk. Instead of tying the fallopian tubes he tied a part of the intestines. She lasted three days.

How old was Maeve?

Eight. Only eight, saints preserve us. There were just the two of us, and I was old enough to take it but she wasn't.

What happened to her?

A couple of years later the old man was locking up the bar one night. Drunk? Stinking as usual. He saw a light in the pool hall across the street and let himself in the back door to see what was going on. What was going on was three of his customers fucking Maeve on a pool table. He laid them out and then beat her until she was unconscious. The next day, when he saw what her face looked like, he locked himself in the cellar with a case of gin and swallowed the key. Planned to starve himself to death but it was winter, too cold for him down there. He died in that cellar all right, but not the way he expected. He ruptured his bowels digging for the key.

Then what? The war?

The war, the Great War. Eddy Quin signs up to be a hero and comes home with his leg full of shrapnel. I didn't see much of him then, I was traveling for a drug company.

How did Maeve get to Shanghai?

Delicate fingers. Somehow she got mixed up with an Indian after the war who had delicate fingers. He was passing himself off as a Hindu prince fighting for the motherland. He talked her into joining the cause and coming back to India with him, but when they got there it turned out the prince's father was a half-caste, mostly white, a butcher who made his living slaughtering sacred cows and selling the beef to the English. Maeve got back on the freighter and ran out of money in Shanghai.

Where she met Adzhar?

Where she met Adzhar. She was hysterical and conceited but she appealed to men, some men, young ones who liked her looks or older ones who liked the way she believed in things, tried to believe in things. Adzhar took care of her and got her going, even bought her a bookstore so she could make a living. If he hadn't been so kind, maybe she would have grown up and stopped talking about causes and heroes with delicate fingers. Adzhar's friends used to come to the bookstore, revolutionary exiles most of them. One of them was a young man he'd recruited back in Paris when he was still working for Trotsky, the hero with the shrapnel in his leg who used to play stickball with me as a kid. Maeve hadn't known him before really, she was too young, but she got to know him then.

Did he tell you what he was doing?

No, she did. She told me all about it and how she was helping him, she was proud of that. A year or two after she went to Shanghai, there were some investigations in the drug business in the States and I had to get out of the country. I went to Canada, and the only job I could find was with a company that had just decided there was a fortune to be made peddling leprosy drugs in Asia. Leprosy drugs? For some reason they thought Asia was full of lepers waiting to buy an American cure. But I needed credentials, so I took the job and got sent to Tokyo. A little later Maeve showed up with the baby she'd had by Kikuchi. She told me all the wonderful things she was doing for the world and then she mentioned the baby. She wanted to get rid of it and asked me to help. I went to Lamereaux.

Did he know who the father was?

Of course. I told him.

Well, when he took the child to Lotmann to raise, did he tell Lotmann who the father was?

No. Buddhist custom doesn't work that way. You're not supposed to know who the child belongs to. You take it as an act of charity.

One of them was a Catholic priest and one of them was a Jewish rabbi. What's Buddhist custom got to do with it?

Japan. They were both living in Japan.

I got it, buffalo. Charity. That's the word, isn't it? Well, that brings us up to the *Gobi* network and the end of the *Gobi* network. You weren't working then, were you? During the eight years the net was running?

No, I had money saved from the States.

Sure you did. Sure.

Quin sat a minute or two in silence. When he got to his feet he moved slowly. It was something he hadn't done in a long time, measuring that kind of distance. He pushed his left shoulder out and swung from far back, putting all his weight behind the fist.

He caught Geraty full in the face. Geraty went over, toppled backward, sprawled on his back across the terrace. Blood ran from his nose and mouth. Quin took a handkerchief out of his pocket and wrapped it around his hand. He was shaking.

Like it, buffalo? Feel right? That was for a guy with a gimp leg who tried to make it and went crazy and a woman who tried to make it and took a high dive. And a broken-down Jesuit and a girl who was working as a whore as a kid and your fucking Marco Polo and your fucking Elijah and all those other poor fucking ticket-buyers who were trying to do something, anything, what does it matter, while you were loping around the edges of the circus whacked out on booze and horseradish, doing your jackal number on booze and horseradish, sneezing and scratching and whacked out in your damn fake costumes playing the impostor. But most of all, buffalo, it's for Little Gobi, let's call him that, not Big but Little, a guy who never tried to do anything at all and never hurt anyone. Those are people you're talking about, don't you know that? So she was conceited and hysterical and he thought he was going to be a hero, so fucking what? What the hell do you think you've done with your life? The gimp finds out he's not a hero and his woman finds out she's made a mess of it, the General tries and gets strung out and Lamereaux tries and gets strung out, and Little Gobi does nothing at all and gets his head knocked in and what the hell are you doing all that time? You didn't do what Lamereaux did or what the General did or the gimp and his woman, you just sat on your ass doing nothing, not trying, doing nothing at all. You make me sick, buffalo. You and your shit. You and your liar's dice. You and your arrogance and your stench and your fat ass and your speeches and your saints and your lies. You talk about other people after the way you've lived? Sitting on top of that kind of garbage? Just where do you get off thinking you can do something like that? Who the fuck do you think you are, going around faking everything in sight? A clown playing God?

Geraty, flat on his back, hiccuped. He licked his lips and rubbed the blood off his nose. He tried to raise himself on an elbow.

Quin spat on him.

Say it, you slobbering fat man. Say it.

No.

No what?

Nothing.

What do you mean, nothing?

I'm sorry, nephew. I'm sorry about that.

You're damn right you're sorry. You're the sorriest bag of secret shit I've ever seen.

No, that's not it, nephew. You don't understand. I'm not sorry that way, I'm sorry you can't have an answer. I'm sorry your questions don't make any sense.

What the hell, you must have something to say for yourself.

No.

Nothing?

Nothing.

What do you mean, *nothing*? Nothing at all? Just nothing? You live sixty-five years and you're noplace? You've got nothing to say? Not a damn thing?

No.

Why the fuck not?

Because a toad and a uterus have the same shape. It's too early now, but when you're a little older take a look at the skin on the back of your hands. Take a look at the pan of gray water after you wash your hair.

What are you trying to say, buffalo?

I'll tell you. First I have something to give you.

Geraty groaned. He pulled in his arms and legs, struggled to get to his feet. A moment later he was lumbering into the house and returning with a black bowler hat. He handed it to Quin, who spun around and scaled it out over the sea. The hat rose on a gust of wind, stopped, slipped down the cliff to the waves with a swarm of seagulls chasing it. Quin rocked back and forth nodding to himself.

Sit down, ordered Geraty.

What?

I said sit down.

Quin sat down. His hand hurt. He was still shaking, but what bothered him most was that Geraty had remained so calm. His uncle jerked his thumb over his shoulder.

That's a fishing village.

I know what the hell it is.

You do, do you? Then you know *O-bon*. You know Nichiren.

Quin said nothing.

What? Do you?

No.

You mean you didn't learn everything there was to know in that Bronx bar of yours? Well, listen to me then. Fishing nets are spread and mended, storms and tides come and go. That's the way it is here most of the year, that's all people think about because that's all they have to think about. But once a year it's different. In midsummer there's a day known as *O-bon*, the Festival of the Dead, a time of the moon when ghosts come back to the world they knew. The villagers welcome them with rice and *sake*, they rejoice, for the ghosts are lost friends and relatives. They talk together, reminisce, the day passes. All goes well until nightfall and then not a light shows in the village. Why? Because the ghosts are in that darkness. They're there and they want to stay there. They don't want to leave.

The villagers gather on the shore. The young men raise the shrine on their backs and carry it out into the water. The old men launch small paper boats and set them afire, set them adrift so they can carry away the restless memories.

The shrine begins to shake violently. The spirits have turned away from the flimsy craft they have been offered. They would rather linger in the village, in the darkness of the homes they once knew as their own. Not willingly will they submit themselves again to the deep.

In front of the shrine stands a man immersed in water to his chest, an intercessor who must face the sea and demand a domain for the living with a voice that can overcome the dirge of ten thousand suffering souls. This voice must be stronger than the wails of the dead, louder than the wind, more insistent than the wishes of all the ghosts ever known to the men and women of this village. He must find that voice and speak with it, and when he does it must prevail.

Geraty spread wide his arms. He fixed his gaze on a seagull suspended in the air. A powerful, monotonous chant rose from the terrace, an unintelligible Buddhist incantation that steadily gathered in force and rhythm.

The pines creaked, the breakers hummed. Abruptly the chant ended and the seagull broke free on the wind.

Geraty dropped his arms to his sides.

What is done is undone, he whispered. The shrine no longer trembles on the backs of the young men. The burning boats cast adrift by the old men float away on the dark waters. The dead sleep, the living set their sails and fish their seas. The dangerous rite is over.

And Nichiren? An unknown monk who lived in the thirteenth century. Who lived alone and unnoticed in a corner of these islands at a time when a Prince of princes ruled in Asia, a Prince of all the tribes, a warrior horseman so fearless and unbending his was the will of the desert itself.

One day the Prince surveyed his empire and decided these few small islands off the coast of Asia should be conquered, not because they would enrich him but for the sake of the symmetry of his maps.

So Kublai Khan commanded that a fleet be built, a fleet to carry one hundred thousand of his finest horsemen. Who but a man of the desert would build the greatest fleet in history for the sake of symmetry?

In Japan there is no hope of combating the army of the largest empire the world has ever known. The Emperor retires to compose a poem, his Generals polish their swords and dictate love letters. Rice dealers bury gold, peasants give birth and die, ladies sigh over their wardrobes.

A nameless monk tirelessly trudges the dusty road toward the south, toward the shore where the unconquerable Khan's horsemen will begin their conquest.

The afternoon comes when the fleet appears on the horizon. Briefly the Japanese forces group and regroup before scattering. The Generals honorably commit suicide. The Emperor observes sunset from his temple in the mountains. Fires and looting break out in the capital. The shoreline is deserted. For many miles inland the countryside is deserted.

Except for one man, one figure toiling through the last

light of day. It is well after dark before he reaches the beach, before he stumbles across the sands and sits down by the water, the first time he has rested in many days. But now he does not rest. He lays his hands in his lap and bows his head, a small man invisible in the gloom facing a forest of masts.

In the deep of night a wind comes. The ships tug at their anchors and the wind shapes itself, grows in fury and in nightmare until it becomes the intolerable world given birth by one man's mind.

In the morning the sky is clear, the horizon empty. Once more the sea is a desert. A divine wind, a *kamikaze,* has destroyed utterly the magnificent fleet of Kublai Khan and all his magnificent horsemen.

Years later Nichiren's disciples ask him how they can ever explain such a miracle. They will not believe us, say the disciples.

No, they will not, answers Nichiren, but you must tell them the truth all the same. You must say that once a man dreamed a wind would come, he dreamed it and willed it, and because he did the wind came.

●

Winter, said Geraty. Last winter, perhaps?

The man in question is no longer young. In fact he's old, he's tired. He has bad habits and he's poor. In the course of sixty-five years of lying and cheating and stealing he has accrued only two things of value, both gifts from the dragon. One is a small gold cross. The other is a collection of rare manuscripts in translation.

The cross was taken from a woman who was falling under its weight. That was in Shanghai before the war.

The collection of manuscripts he found in the Chinese wing of the warehouse where the Kempeitai kept its files. One night he organized a convoy of trucks to carry the manuscripts away for safekeeping, then he set fire to the wing. That was in Tokyo right after the war.

Let twenty years go by. Let them simply pass.

It is winter. Last winter or one like it. Our man puts two bottles of Irish whiskey in a valise and takes the train to Kamakura. He walks to a certain beach and sits down on the sand.

Why? To remember an evening long ago when he shared two bottles of Irish whiskey with a forgotten *No* actor? To recall the four people who once held a picnic on this beach?

Perhaps. In any case he sits down on the sand and opens the first bottle.

An hour goes by, or two hours, or less than an hour. Our man is watching the waves and takes no notice of time. From somewhere in the darkness a stranger appears and sits down. He accepts a drink, mutters, stares vacantly at the stars. After a while he begins to talk.

He mentions mulberry trees, pine groves, giant steps that lead nowhere, blackjacks and urinal candy, a face eaten by a dog, mushrooms, a night in Nanking.

Our man listens to this phantasmagoria and is appalled. For He hath scattered the proud in the conceit of their heart. Must the chaos of the world be infinite? Is this voice from the waves recounting a history of the twentieth century? The thirteenth century? A century that lies a million years in the past?

The stranger is a tiny man. Is it the movement of his hands? His eyes? The way he holds his head?

For some reason our man is reminded of the little woman in Shanghai. He thinks of her, and all at once he knows this little man and that little woman are related. Why? How? There's no explanation, no way to comprehend it. They are, that's all.

The stranger drinks, he talks, he stares at the stars. Just before dawn he falls asleep, naked except for a towel over his loins. It seems that as he talked he felt compelled to take off his clothes. Our man quietly gets to his feet and leaves, but not empty-handed. No, he takes the stranger's greatcoat with him because he has made a decision. Two decisions.

First, he will take the collection of manuscripts to America and sell them for a large amount of money so that he can live his last days in peace.

Second, he will return the small gold cross to its rightful owner.

Both actions are for the same purpose. He wants to assure himself that the insane tale told by the stranger on the beach won't end the way it began. He wants to prove to himself that even an account of history as grotesque as that can have some small measure of order behind it. Above all he wants to believe there has been some meaning in the pathetic parade of events and people he calls his life.

He acts. He goes to America and the collection is confiscated. It's taken away from him but those who take it, who store it in a New York warehouse, don't realize what they have is useless. Useless because he has kept the key, the code book to the annotations, the dragon's secret, the keys to the kingdom.

Failure? No, total disaster. He's sick and old and there's no way he can support himself now. He came to New York thinking he was a rich man, rich at the end of life, but the rich He hath sent empty away.

Our man collapses in a hostel for vagrant alcoholics. Three days later he staggers north to return the small gold cross to its rightful owner. The day he arrives back in New York happens to be the feast day of the saint for whom his mother is named, Brigid. He goes back to the neighborhood where he grew up. He staggers into the bar once owned by and named for his father, another Eddy, like all bartenders a profane confessor. After rolling the dice he boards a freighter and returns to Japan. In his pocket is the secret code book, all he has left.

Summer.

A summer evening. Last summer or one like it. Drunk, dazed from horseradish, our man finds himself lying on his back in a vacant lot in Tokyo, in a slum, on sand that is damp because he has come to rest in a gigantic urinal along with other scavenging alcoholics. The men in the urinal are dying, they're all dying, and before the night is over they'll be robbed of all they have. What else can he do but sleep and forget? He sleeps.

Sleeps and snores and raves, for of course he can't forget yet, the time hasn't come, he must sink lower still. While he sleeps fitfully a horde of faces hovers over him, crowds around him in the urinal. All the experiences he has known in forty years in the Orient come back to him.

In his dream he begins to visit these people, apparently to renew old friendships and share a mild anecdote or two in order to recall the nostalgia of other days, actually to beg something from them that will keep him alive.

For now it's come down to that. He has no excuse for living anymore. Either he finds an excuse or he's finished.

He makes a list and starts at the top of the list. That night and every night over the summer he lies on the damp sand of the urinal working his way down the list of names and faces. When he meets one of these people he smiles pleasantly. He nods at their eccentricities, ingratiates himself in whatever manner seems appropriate, apologizes, agrees enthusiastically with everything they have ever done.

He flatters them, admires them, mentions their goodness and their strength, their tenderness, their humility. He invokes the saints in praise of them. He grins. He wrings his hands hopefully.

Thinking it might amuse them, he shuffles his feet in a little dance. He asks for pity, begs for it.

He gets down on his knees and cries, sobs, admits to all acts real and imagined. He takes off his clothes and displays himself naked so they will see he is hiding nothing. He covers his face with his hands and peeks between the fingers.

Ridiculous. Is anyone going to be fooled by this absurd performance?

Of course not. There's no chance of it and he knows it, but he does it anyway because his pride is gone. Gone. He's desperate to find an excuse for living.

He snatches up the articles they discard. No matter how

worthless they are, he snatches them up and presses them to his chest, clutches them, squeezes them with his thumbs, licks them, wets them with his tears, buries them in his greatcoat.

A greatcoat stuffed with the debris of life.

There's a glass paperweight meant to resemble jade, a forged Canadian passport and two forged Belgian passports, a screw-top jar, the Litany of the Saints, a battered movie projector, a secret-bag, layers of sweaters, a cache of animal husbandry documentaries made during the early days of the Russian Revolution, a piece of red flannel tied with string, two bottles of Irish whiskey, a journey that goes south and west from Tokyo and pauses for a snooze in the mountains of the Philippines before returning to Tokyo, a spotlight, an exhibition, the depraved legacy locked behind the smile of the everyday man in kimono, a pushcart, steam rising from a pan of boiling turnips.

Victorian horsehair chairs, cannons captured in the 1905 Russo-Japanese War, a gentle smile, three gas masks, bamboo tubes, flowers of Tokyo, evaporating doorways, materializing cemeteries, midnight tombstones, dead cats, bartered rice, buggered pickles, an autograph, a vegetarian diet that excludes honey and eggs, a coat that buttons the wrong way, cracked *No* masks and torn *No* costumes, a piss in the moss, the kimono of the princess, a manuscript never begun, a complete index to the manuscript that therefore lists nothing, again two bottles of Irish whiskey, claws crushing the heads of rodents, turnips again, nothing but turnips for nearly a quarter of a century, a reign that lasts seven hundred years, a collapsed garden wall.

A tea bowl turned three times, a game of *Go*, *koto* music, a wall of rotting Cossack horses, a glass eye, headaches, a ball of fluff, a container of ether, a houseboat in Shanghai, a monk, a mirror in a Mukden toilet, the third bottle of Irish whiskey, a fire in Nanking.

A limp, a megaphone and whip and frock coat, again three gas masks, again a spotlight, a ring and a bed, the one-eyed tomb of Semarang and the sure-footed vine of

Mindanao, plump shrimp tails, the highwire, little red swinging lights, sawdust, tubas, the shadowy juggler with his torches, the wastes of central Asia.

A pool table, delicate fingers, a sudden laugh, again a ring and a bed, the highbar, the triple somersault.

Cigars and computers and salad dressings, reports, mixed Mongolian grills, steel mills in Borneo, new governments in South America, massage parlors in Africa, bagels and smoked salmon, folding camp chairs, an endless procession of black limousines, a houseboat in Tokyo, pink gin, fogged glasses, neckties, haiku marching music, once more the megaphone and whip and frock coat.

A tattoo of a dragon, sauce flavored with ambergris and phosphorite, the small lamp of a battered movie projector, a photograph superimposed upon another, the fist of knowledge, oysters, laudanum, a pagoda deep in the ground, a mirror in a shrine high above the city.

More oysters, another glass eye but this one from the Boston waterfront, a nurse with a hypodermic of water, a bus ticket good for thirty days' travel in the United States, seagull soup, another glass paperweight, a life preserver, a jukebox with colored lights, jigglies, frozen tuna fish, a television set, a hunk of rotting meat, a beach by the sea.

Movie magazines and epileptic fits, gloves and hairpieces and empty lipstick tubes, false sideburns and a false moustache, a chow mein whore, shoeboxes.

Korean latrines, icy Manchurian cellars, familiar smells, a breakwater that leads to the dark waters of the bay.

A shoemaker's son at a shoemaker's bench, Lapp proverbs and Malabar peppercorns, high hogs, a final three gas masks, a final transformation, love poems in all the languages of the world, a final bottle of iced vodka, a final jar of iced caviar, a final bath in the morning, a final erection at midnight.

And another *koto*, another gentle smile, another hypodermic but this one for insulin, the Talmud in Japanese, a black spot in the garden.

An end.

The day finally comes when there are no names left on his list, no debris left in his life. He is empty, he has picked himself clean.

He empties out the pockets of his greatcoat and finds only the dragon's code book, his last possession, that small notebook wherein the alchemist Adzhar recorded the ultimate secrets of a treatise on love. When he has returned this to its rightful owner, as he did with the cross, he will be ready to die.

Now Adzhar has been gone for many years, but there was a Japanese who knew him well, who was a close friend and will certainly receive the code book in his name. Our man is so poor he can't take the train to Kamakura, he has to walk. Thousands witness this hulking bundle of rags slowly making his way south down the highway. He walks and walks, each step a torment, and at last reaches the town, finds the house, learns to his dismay that Rabbi Lotmann has been dead for twenty years, killed in a fire bomb raid at the end of the war.

A fire bomb raid in Kamakura? Impossible. Some unique fate existed here, perhaps still exists here.

Vague recollections. Dim intimations.

Our man is too exhausted to think clearly. He's delirious from lack of food and the craving of his powerful addiction. The housekeeper explains the nature of the rabbi's death and also explains that the house is being maintained as a shrine in perpetuity by the dead man's adopted son, an operator who is not only the richest gangster in greater east Asia but the third richest gangster in the world.

Weak from the long walk, raving in a whisper, our man faints in the doorway. The housekeeper rushes away to buy smelling salts. After she leaves, almost at once, our man curiously regains consciousness and lets himself into the house.

He is amazed or perhaps not amazed to find the living room filled with heavy silver objects. There is a large menorah, a silver-embossed Haggadah, a silver-embossed siddur, a silver-plated tallith, a silver-plated tsistsis, an unusual tvillin made of silver rather than wood and leather, a heavy solid silver plaque engraved with the legend *mene, mene, tekel, upharsin.*

What is to be done? Is silver any longer of use to a man who has ascended to heaven in a whirlwind?

Quickly our man gathers up all the silver objects he can lay his hands on and stuffs them into a sack. As payment he leaves behind in a prominent place the secret code book, the keys to the kingdom. They belong to Elijah because he has lived a life that will turn the lock, lived so meekly his push will swing wide the gate.

The sack of loot on his back, our man opens the front door.

A memory.

The holy man whose altar he has desecrated was a diabetic. A diabetic? Dimly there stirs in his tired brain scenes he has witnessed in a locked, shuttered room in Shanghai, even more remote scenes witnessed on rooftops in the Bronx. He makes his way to the medicine cabinet and finds there what he is looking for, the large hypodermic needle used by the rabbi for injecting insulin. He has recalled that before Elijah ascended to heaven he passed on his mantle to his successor.

This then will be the mantle our man receives from the prophet. A hypodermic needle.

He flees. He staggers into the nearest pawnshop and stumbles into the back room, there to empty out his sack. His loathing for what he has done is so great he will accept no more than a ten-thousandth part of the real value of the heavy silver. He leaves sack and silver behind and runs from the pawnshop with his miserable fist of coins.

He buys a cheap valise and stuffs it with bottles of cheap gin. At the railroad station he throws down his few remaining coins and says he wants a ticket down the coast. He will go as far as those coins will take him.

It's over now and he knows it. He has robbed the grave of the prophet. He intends to sit by the sea until the gin bottles are empty, then piss one final time into the wind and drown himself.

The train lets him off at a fishing village. He limps down

to the beach, ignoring the astonished stares of the villagers, and sits down on the sand. A wind has begun to blow, but no matter. First he takes off the black bowler hat he has worn for nearly thirty years, ever since that morning he picked it up in a deserted warehouse on the outskirts of Shanghai and went away to hide and eat horseradish, the first of many times he would eat horseradish to try to quell the stink of his own soul, a stench that had first overpowered him that morning when he went to the warehouse to help his sister, to help the man who had been a boyhood friend, and discovered he was too late.

Too late. The night before the circus his projector had broken down. Two frames had stuck together in the lens and hypnotized him, put him to sleep. And so the next day he began eating horseradish, he put the black bowler hat on his head and never took it off in order to remember always the hatred he felt for his own black soul.

Now he removes that black hat and in its place he ties a large one made of straw, so low it covers his face, a hat worn in the Orient only by men condemned to death and by mendicant monks, those two alone, for it is traditional wisdom in the Orient not to look upon the face of a man about to die or the face of a man who begs in the name of Buddha.

The straw hat is affixed, the greatcoat is wrapped around him. He takes the mantle of Elijah and opens the first bottle of gin, pours, fills the hypodermic, recaps it. As he has seen others do, he ties a cord around the upper part of his arm. He touches a bulging vein. He plunges the needle into the vein and pushes the gin into his bloodstream.

A scream. Is this the still, small voice Elijah heard in the desert?

The needle falls from his hand and he's a long time in finding it. Slowly he cleans the needle on the red flannel wrapped around his neck, cumbersome work because he can't see what he's doing, because he's already incapable of untying the string around the flannel and holding the flannel in front of him.

Finally the needle is free from sand or more or less free

from sand. Once more he pours gin, fills the needle, stabs his vein.

Shoots gin.

Shooting up a valise of gin.

Night comes. He has finished one bottle and started on another. The wind lashes him, the waves whirl high in the air. By morning he has emptied all the bottles and the sea has carried them away, carried away the valise and the needle as well, for now the typhoon is blowing full force.

A man sits on the sand in the eye of chaos and he neither sees nor hears. His legs are crossed, his chin rests on his chest, he is oblivious to all that passes in the world. Even if the princes and despots of a thousand lawless regions were to attack him it would be useless. Nor could the entire assembly of man attract his attention with their pleas, their dreams, their follies. He is invulnerable to everyone and everything, beyond sensation, alone at the end of the earth, alone on the far side of the moon, the dark side, with only the void as companion and parent and child.

The typhoon blows three days and three nights. As it subsides our man awakes at the bottom of the sea, on the floor of the ocean, where the typhoon has draped him with seaweed. Seaweed hangs from his straw hat, encrusts his arms, embraces his shoulders and his belly. The entire lower half of his body is hidden beneath the slippery fingers of rich iodine matter.

His legs are numb and his bad shoulder aches. He is cold, wet, devastated, totally ravaged. His mind is dazed and his eyes are two slim, slanting pools of nothingness. It is as if he were thinking thoughts too profound to be uttered.

On the ocean floor our man sees in front of him a line of gnarled, sturdy ancients, village elders, men who have known a life at sea. Their faces are the bows of ships, their hands are fish hooks. It is a scarred and weathered delegation, an embassy from some distant land above the sea. He watches them fall to their knees and press their foreheads to the sand.

The sands around him are stained with excrement and vomit and urine. A smell of putrid flesh hangs in the air, a stink of decay given off by layers of rotting clothing soaked under seaweed. Yet this foreign embassy seems unaware of the foul odors rising from the foul sands. They are bewitched by the immense, immobile figure dressed in seaweed.

He sees them gaze in awe at his straw hat and he realizes they have mistaken it. To them it is not the sign of the condemned man, it is the mark of the monk who traces the merciful steps and begs in the name of Buddha. Yes, obviously they have mistaken it.

Or is it he who has mistaken it?

For it seems that during the last three days and nights much of the Japanese coast has been destroyed. Above and below the village fishing fleets are wrecked, houses washed away, friends and relatives drowned. This village alone among hundreds has been spared. And how can that be unless the stranger who arrived mysteriously at the onset of the storm and took up his place by the sea, remaining there for three days and nights oblivious to wind and rain and waves, unless the stranger is a reincarnation of Nichiren, that militant holy man of the thirteenth century?

The village elders press their heads to the sand. They offer prayers to their patron saint and beg him to have mercy on them always, to protect them and stay with them forever, to honor them by living on the food they will provide in the temple they will provide.

Our man shakes loose the seaweed that encumbers him and rises to the surface of the water. He looks at the sun. He looks at the house in the pine grove on the cliff above the sea. He removes the straw hat that covers his face and recalls the words learned long ago in a *No* play, the words taught to him by a thin erect *No* actor of incomparable skill and subtlety, *magnificat anima mea Dominum*, my soul doth magnify the Lord.

Thus he bows and accepts the vocation that has come to him at last. Gravely he raises his head and greets the embassy of that small empire you see across the bay.

●

It was dark on the terrace. Geraty lit a candle and placed it between them in a glass chimney. His massive, solemn face hung over the railing searching for something below, a seagull or a rock or a wave.

The candle flickered. Briefly Geraty raised his hand to preach to the invisible seagulls, the invisible rocks, the invisible waves.

When do you leave?

Tomorrow. My ship sails from Yokohama.

Quite so.

Do you ever think of any of them anymore? Of America?

No. Never. There is no America here inside me, no Tokyo and no Shanghai either.

Geraty loomed up in front of Quin. His presence swelled until he filled the shadows of the terrace, his breathing noisier than the waves on the sides of the cliff. He was frowning. His white hair swirled over his face.

It may be, nephew, that you don't quite understand it yet. It's true that a monk ruled in the thirteenth century, a monk and not the Emperor or the great General or even the reckless circus master with his desperate, clever acts. Of course I'm not sure who you are, we can never be sure with another, but that doesn't matter. The fishermen of this village believe I have the powers of Nichiren. They might even believe I'm a reincarnation of his strange spirit. But how could that be? Is that really the way it is?

Geraty stared hard at Quin. Far back in those huge eyes Quin saw a smile begin, and precisely at that moment the candle flame came to rest. The light was somber, still. The wind had stopped.

Not enough, whispered Geraty. Not just his powers and his will. What they perhaps don't know is what you perhaps don't know. It's the final truth of the final scene, and it may be that no one knows it except me. Yet it's simple enough, simpler than anyone would suspect.

I am Nichiren.

Geraty exploded in laughter. His hand struck his belly, and as it did a wind came. The dancing flame of the candle leapt and went out. The pine trees shivered, the seagulls shrieked, the sea surged above the rocks. In the darkness of a minute or an hour or all the years of his life Quin listened to the echoes of Geraty's booming laughter.

●

He found the crevice under the pine trees and crept along the cliff to where the path became less steep. The wind was cold and he walked with his collar up, his back hunched. Halfway to the village he stopped and looked back.

The house was hidden. Did the Buddha sit with a candle? Did he peer through the blackness at the seagulls, the rocks, the waves?

Quin trudged along with his caravan, the lean Emperor and the small General marching to a silent stony drum, the animals in their cages, the jugglers wafting painted flutes and mingling torches in the air. Lotmann played his music, Adzhar spoke in a still, small voice, Lamereaux stroked the moss in his monastery, and Mama prayed on the lotus of her ivory elephant. The aerialist turned a somersault, the Siberian tiger pawed the ground. A brother solemnly changed his necktie, another sang across the sand.

It was a long parade and Quin walked ahead of it wearing the frock coat, carrying the megaphone, no announcement too extreme between the rice paddies and the beach, no costume too bizarre, no act of memory too daring.

He left the waterfront and climbed up the narrow street to the square beside the station. There an itinerant storyteller was setting up his stage. Children clustered in front of the empty frame.

The storyteller was so old his head shook. His tiny stage stood on three poles. He fitted a cardboard painting into the open frame, then assumed the voices of those who were shown.

First came a boy and his parents. The boy wandered along the beach and met a dragon who carried him to the emerald kingdom beneath the sea. A Princess spoke of the enchanted life that would be his if he remained there, but the boy elected to return to his home. He waved to the Princess and rose above the waves again, waved to the dragon and walked along the beach to find the trees moved, the houses gone, the familiar paths now leading elsewhere.

The boy sat down beside the road and cried.

An old man appeared who looked very much like the storyteller. He leaned on his cane in the middle of the road listening to the boy's account of his wondrous journey. Then he explained the sad truth. One day in the emerald kingdom was the same as one hundred years on earth.

But I didn't know, cried the boy.

No, said the old man. No, you didn't.

The children in the square huddled beneath the stage. The tale seemed over. Now the boy stopped crying, the storyteller removed the last cardboard picture and stepped in front of the empty stage, into the frame of stars and darkness.

He was smiling. Leaning on his cane.

A true tale, he whispered. I know because once I was that boy and now I am that old man.

He nodded, the children smiled. They laughed. They shouted. They pushed back and forth and chased each other around the square as Quin walked into the station and left behind the old man with his extravagant cardboard pictures, his empty stage that had framed a shadowy figure in Mukden and Shanghai and Tokyo, in the Bronx, a clown once called Geraty.

An Editorial Relationship

Many years ago when I was a young assistant editor at a New York publishing house, a stroke of fortune led me into an editorial relationship that was to last a long time, until after the writer's death. Our entanglement, like many between writers and editors, was muddied by friendship on the one hand and by the desire to publish on the other.

The relationship began when the editor-in-chief, Tom Wallace, who was leaving the house for another, handed me the file of an author named Edward P. Whittemore.

He was called Ted. He had gone to school with Tom in the 1950s, they were old buddies from Yale, and there the resemblance ended. Tom was a classic Yale type—sentimental yet incapable of expressing emotion, good-hearted and highly principled, and completely stuck in his ways. Ted, by contrast, was completely out of the loop. He defied the loop. Ted had lived all around the world, been in the CIA (in fact, nobody knew for sure if he was really *out* of the CIA), written several crazy novels that were sort of about espionage and sort of about the mammoth course of history, its large brutish atrocities and the small moments of goodness, books that were compared to Fuentes and Pynchon and Nabokov.

Tom described the books by saying they were really all about poker.

Ted was famous to about six thousand people who thought he was a genius; nobody else had ever heard of him at all. He

293

had two marriages that hadn't worked out, and a girlfriend he was breaking up with, and a strong Maine accent. He was a recovering alcoholic who once had been the kind of drinker who wanted to crawl inside the fifth to lick it completely clean, and a chain-smoker, and he lived on the East side of town.

As it turned out, of all the places he *could* have lived in the city of New York, he lived on Third Avenue and 24th Street, while I lived on 24th Street and Sixth Avenue. This is the kind of magical coincidence that populates the novels of Edward Whittemore and it seemed strangely appropriate that our domestic routines were performed in locations that were exactly parallel, yet existed a precise and unbreachable distance apart, as though we were two matching magnets with the contrary ends facing one another.

In 1981, I was handed the manuscript of *Nile Shadows*, which was third in a projected quartet of Jerusalem novels. This quartet followed his first, and possibly his splashiest novel, *Quin's Shanghai Circus*, which we had published seven years earlier.

Ted had also written several that we did *not* publish. I was told both that Ted was a genius *and* that it was possible that the manuscript was not publishable or needed a great deal of cutting. I knew almost nothing about editing fiction; I had never worked on anything remotely this serious, which meant that I was going to have to concentrate very hard. Once I opened it and began there was no question but that this was what they call the real thing. For me, how terrifying and how thrilling.

The first time I read it slowly, almost without thinking, submitting to it, letting it sink in. The book was both domestic and fantastic, its settings shabby and arcane, and doom was everywhere. Ted understood the big and how it depended on the little. Centuries of conspiracy pivoted on a chance encounter. Friendship was everything, and utterly ephemeral. A shaft of light illuminated horror, then a sweet timeless calm, then slapstick. Words kept it going, words and talk and more talk: chatter, letters writ in stone, a scream in an emergency, a late afternoon's long slow story, a coded telegram.

The editor's job was to be inside it and yet float above it, to see where it wasn't true to its own internal logic, to love the characters and expect them to be themselves, to applaud every song—but to mark the slightly flat note—to be sure the plot had all its small signals straight. The second time I read it I tried to remember every word, every gesture, every motion.

My editorial letter advised—but most of all it paid attention. It is not so much the comments made by a careful editor that help a writer revise, I think, but the simpler fact that these comments show the writer that he is being watched. He is being watched intently by someone who tells him, in as many ways as possible, that this *matters*. And so he thinks harder, he reaches in all directions — plot, character, gesture, sequence, tone, echo — and, so doing, activates the deeper and shadowed part of the brain where music and feeling are stashed. The place where stories begin.

Ted lived in a tiny apartment very high up above Third Avenue. He had a big window and a dark-floored single room, a small kitchen—the refrigerator contained only a pint container of milk and a plastic tub of tofu—and a bathroom with a towel. In his room were a double bed, a desk, a writing chair, a second chair, a television, and an ashtray. Just the setting for a former spy.

I went over there on my way home from the office several times, to drop off the edited manuscript, to look at his changes, to explain the copy editing. I gave Ted more personal attention because the novel demanded it, and also, although without saying a word, somehow Ted expected it. The desk was occupied by his typewriter and a few completely neat stacks of typing paper and previous drafts, so instead of interrupting his work space, I laid the box of manuscript on the bed, cracking it open and leafing through the pages, tracing the progress of one detail or another, the intricate traces of his threads. We bent over the manuscript together.

The revisions took place in the winter, so when I stopped by it was always dark out. I was working long hours, partly to get over a disappointment with a man that had happened at the time; work was a secure place for me in the middle of this unhappiness. One night it snowed and we went to the window to marvel. The snow flew in specks outside the window, tiny furry points of light in the darkness, cold dusty sisters to the lights flickering on Third Avenue below and the many apartments winking on the other side of the canyon. We stood next to the glass and watched the snow swirl, high in the heavens of New York, so far away, it seemed, from the rest of my life.

As we stood there looking at the snow in that night sky, that winter night in New York, Ted Whittemore, quite unexpectedly, ran his hand lightly down my back. Tentatively. I did not move, and he did not touch me a second time.

We went back to being an editor and a writer.

Ted left the country after the manuscript went through copyediting, but before we published the book. He took a freighter to Jerusalem. Ted said that it was a bad idea to fly to the Middle East, because you were traveling through so much time that it should take a long time to make the journey. Also a freighter was cheaper than flying, and Ted never had any money.

He read his galleys in Jerusalem, where he lived in an apartment in the courtyard of the Ethiopian Church. In the early mornings, on one side of the courtyard wall, a flock of French Nuns sang their devotions. All day, around the circular Ethiopian Church, a school of monks walked and murmured their prayers. And Ted read his galleys in July and we published in the Fall.

When I pitched the book at sales conference, I got applause, which usually doesn't happen at a sales conference, certainly not for a novel that will advance fewer than seven thousand copies. But the sales reps, those cynical hard eggs, put their hands together, not so much for my performance as for what Ted meant to the house as a whole. His books were the books we published that proved to us that publishing could be about good writing and fearless imagination and vision.

Before he moved from New York, Ted sent me a note. "I'm glad you're part of the Quartet," he wrote. And so I became connected to Ted Whittemore, connected forever.

*

The book, as it turned out, did not sell well. It had some good reviews, but the machine of publishing did not kick in for Whittemore. The reps applauded at sales conference, but the machine did not kick in.

Great fiction is hard to sell. What happens to a person who reads a book—if it's any good—is a profoundly private and irrational process, and the more distinctive the novel, the more private and irrational the process. That's where the trouble with publishing begins.

*

Two and a half years later, I left the industry. I was frustrated by the limitations of the business end and I had fallen in love, this time, I thought, for keeps, to a man who lived in Western Massachusetts who had three kids and joint custody and who was very persuasive. Love to me was more important than work, so I moved to Massachusetts and married. But I discovered that I was not as nice, not as accommodating, as I had thought I was. Even though I had always believed that I was able to make anything succeed if I just worked hard enough at it, I was not able to respond to my husband's demands, and he was very far from being able to help me mend my unhappiness. We were soon miserable.

After two years we divorced. Although the marriage had been horrible, still divorce was like suddenly falling into nothing.

The summer after, I got a call from Ted. I had heard from him from time to time. He had heard about my romance and my departure from New York, and now he'd heard about my divorce.

At my end, over the years, I'd also had reports of Ted back from Tom, who visited Ted in Jerusalem. Ted was with a wonderful woman, a painter named Helen, Tom reported. A year or two after that news, Tom told me that Ted had broken up with

Helen, abruptly. Without so much as a day's notice, said Tom, Ted had packed up and left Helen and left Jerusalem. Tom said Helen was heart-broken. Tom disapproved and so did I.

Although I disapproved I was still glad to hear Ted's voice. He was back in the country and writing, up at the family home in Dorset, Vermont for the season. Would I come up to see him?

I did, twice. Dorset is beautiful in the summer, green and leafy and a good ten degrees cooler than Western Massachusetts. Ted showed me everything and how much he loved it and how much he wanted me to love it, too. We talked a little about the book he was working on, but mostly we didn't. The Whittemore family home was big and rambling; late after-noon we sat on white Adirondack chairs on the great lawn, slop-ing into a meadow, and watched the young girls from the danc-ing school down the road mince like birds into the middle of town, to buy their sweets. Beyond, the mountains misted with blue, and flowers of all shapes and colors and sizes waved in the breeze.

We swam in the Dorset Quarry. The Dorset Quarry is a writer's dream, because when you swim in the Dorset Quarry you are swimming in the space left by the stone that now is the New York Public Library, the great lion library at 42nd Street. The quarry's stone walls rise high and flat, gray streaked with white. Boys in baggy bathing suits jump off the high walls screaming. Women paddle quietly. Children sit on low ledges and dip in their feet. At the far end is an island of stone; birch trees rise skinny and white from its nooks.

After we had spent some time in the water, Ted got out, but I stayed in. He threw me my swimming goggles and I went exploring around the shallower end of the quarry. Looking for what kind of gunk grew down there, where the New York Public Library used to be.

I saw something green. I went to the surface, got a big gasp of air, dove down and swam, down and down and down. I reached for the green and headed back up.

It was a twenty-dollar bill. I swam over to Ted and gave it to him. We were both amazed. "Are you coming out?" he asked.

"In a little," I replied. I went back to see what else was down there. Again, I took a big gasp of air, dove down and swam, down and down and down. Something green. I grabbed it and headed back up.

"Ted," I said. I waved the bill. Ten dollars.

The next time down, I found a five. And that was it. I looked, but nothing else was down there. I shook the water out of my hair and we spent the money on dinner.

It was not surprising to me that magic like this would happen around Ted. It seemed almost predictable. Ted Whittemore was a magician, not only of words, but of moments. He marveled, and any sensation, of light or sound or character or scent, was ratcheted up another notch. We walked past swaying meadows and through the graveyard where all the Whittemores are buried. We drove down roads, looked at the cows, stopped the car near a stream and took off our shoes and hopped from rock to rock and stood in the running water, listening to the leaves rustle and the water bubble, smelling the good air.

Ted put his arms around me and kissed me. I kissed him back, but then I said no.

He could not imagine why I would not grasp this good thing. He could see it so clearly, something between the two of us, he could see it and he wanted it. *The world is full of possibilities*, he said. I could see it, too, when he talked about it, because Ted always made me see whatever he saw, but I still said no.

I came back, however, the next weekend, and I told him I would sleep with him, but only one time, and then it would be over and he had to understand that this was the only way it would happen.

I told myself this was because I was a woman who recently had been hurt, and that Ted was, after all, the man who had left Helen, but my true motives weren't so attractive. Ted's proposal appealed to me a lot—I had a particular weakness for writers (the man who had broken my heart that long-ago winter and the ex-husband were both writers)—but I had no intention of getting tangled up with Whittemore. Like a spoiled child, I wanted to play out this flattering scenario but without accepting responsibility for what would follow. Crazily enough, Ted agreed to my counter-proposition, and so, only once it was.

Afterwards, back in Massachusetts, I spoke to Ted occasionally, but finally, I stopped returning his calls, his persistent, baffled, loving, persuasive, tempting calls.

*

That was 1988. In February of 1994, I was planning on visiting friends in New York (from Washington, DC, where I had moved four years earlier), and so I called Tom Wallace to see if he wanted to have lunch. Tom had become a literary agent, but he was the same Tom, solid as a rock. He gave you a sense that the important things still mattered and that history counted for something. It was a good thing I had called.

"By the way," he said, "I meant to phone you and ask—have you talked to Ted Whittemore lately? You might want to give him a ring. He's back in New York. Ted's had some tough times, I'm afraid, and now there's bad news. He's very sick."

Ted had been diagnosed with a very lethal, inoperable prostate cancer. He was working on a new book and living with a woman named Annie, who had a brownstone on the upper West side, right off the park in the 90's.

Whittemore was completely happy to hear my voice. Yes, he was well; how was I doing? We arranged to meet at Tom's office at 2:30 on Friday, if I could manage to get Tom back by then. We agreed that Tom could talk a person's ear off and lunch was bound to go on forever.

I hadn't seen Ted for so long. Tom's receptionist buzzed him in and he walked into the reception area and took off his knit cap, holding it in both hands, twisting it slightly. His face was puffier than before, but his smile was the same, a smile of such colossal affection that I practically fell down looking at him. He turned his head slightly to the side when he smiled, and the edges of his thin, wide mouth turned up in delighted mystification and complete charm.

He put out his arms; I fell into them. We hugged, hard.

It was snowy and cold. Ted and I walked through Central Park, ice crunching beneath our feet, the same way we had walked down the dusty roads of Vermont, talking, talking, talking. We stopped at a food stand for tea and sat on a patio, in a corner protected from the wind, looking out across an oval frozen pond. Although his attention seemed to be entirely on the beauty of the day, the moment, and the happiness of being together again, Ted still managed to read the notes and over-hear the conversation of the man sitting next to him. Once a spook, always a spook. As we headed up the hill away from the tea shop, he told me the man had been writing poetry. Bad poetry, he said, but not as bad as it might be.

That first long walk, he never mentioned his illness. I saw him again the next afternoon and we walked in the blistering cold wind over by the Hudson. He still didn't talk about it. We just walked, often with our arms around one another, to be close and to keep from slipping on the ice, trooping down the streets that became Ted's because of what he saw. "See that fellow at the corner, in front of the shop?" he'd say, giving a friendly salute to a rangy, beaten-up, leather-faced man. "Been here for years. Turkish, you know." And then he'd explain how the junk in the guy's store told you everything you needed to know to understand some invasion in the seventeenth century, and it would all make perfect sense.

He didn't talk about his illness, but we did agree that I would read his novel when it was done. He was very pleased. And so we fell back into the role of editor and writer, but of course we were something else, too, after all of this time. Time makes friendship in a way that no single action possibly can. That, after all, is what Ted's novels are about—time, friendship, and history, the real history.

At one point, but only once, Ted asked me about the events in Dorset, and afterwards, and how I had stopped being in touch. I didn't have much to say about it.

"Bad timing," I said. He nodded.

That summer Ted and Annie went to Italy, and I saw Ted again in the Fall. I had dinner with him and Annie, but before, he and I took a walk. That's when he told me.

He sat me down on a park bench, over by the wading pool where children sail their boats. It was November and getting cold. We were warm enough, though, in hats and scarves and gloves. He had something to tell me, and spoke very clearly and simply and straight. He had cancer and it could not be cured or permanently halted. He was in remission thanks to heavy doses of hormones; they had left him impotent, but that was better than being dead.

"The trouble is, that I can go out of remission at any time," Ted told me. "And the docs say that if that happens, I can go in as fast as three weeks." He paused. "It changes how you view things. Some things, like politics and what's in the newspaper, become utterly unimportant. And things like friends, family, especially friends, become the most important things in the world."

Ted looked at me. He reached for my hand, and held it fast. "So you see, having you come back into my life, now, all of a sudden, well it couldn't make me happier."

I wrapped myself around him. My arms and also one leg hooked over his lap — actually we probably looked fairly ludicrous there on the bench—but it was a moment where it didn't matter how we looked or what we were doing with our bodies. Ted held on tight. Nothing could change what was, the bad or the good. I said I loved him and then we said no more, just held on.

As we walked back to the house, and Annie, and dinner, we talked. He wanted very much to finish the draft of the novel, the last book he would ever write. I wanted very much to read it.

*

When Ted was still in remission, it seemed to me there were some things going on that were suspicious. Ted had always had a bad back, but it had gotten worse, why he wasn't sure. My assumption was that this was the cancer, he just didn't want to dignify it with the name. That would be giving it too much ground.

I called him one Sunday, from my apartment in Washington. Annie said he was out and she didn't know why he hadn't returned. Several hours later, Ted called and told me the story.

"The most amazing thing happened," he said.

He had gone to a hotel to meet a man who was going to do his taxes; the place was way over west on 58th Street, practically in the river. He walked down the hall to meet the man and heard some music coming out from behind a door; the hotel rented larger halls as well as rooms for people who had business to transact. After getting the tax stuff taken care of, he passed by the door again.

This time it was open. And he could hear the music more clearly. It was gospel. There was plenty of gospel, Ted had explained to me, in the book he was working on, but he had never actually been to a live service. A woman standing by the door saw his interest, and pulled him in. He sat in the rear.

"The music was wonderful," he said, "just what I'd imagined. So full of feeling and passion and emotion and all the good things of being human. The sound just rolled over me. Everyone was singing and the sound was immense." It went on for a long time, and then there was quiet. A small woman came to the front of the room Several people stood up, in no apparent pattern.

Ted's back was hurting him, so he stood up, too.

He hadn't understood. All of the people who had stood up were brought to the front of the room.

The woman prayed over them. She prayed for strength and health. Calls of reassurance and encouragement came from all corners of the room. She prayed in front of Ted. And then she knocked him down.

"I could see what was going to happen, because it happened with the other people," Ted told me. "She stood in front of you, and behind you stood this immense black guy, and she knocked you down, and you had to fall right back. Where the man would catch you. You had to trust her, you see. You had to *let yourself go*, just completely."

"And did you?" I asked.

"I did," said Ted. "I can't tell you how marvelous I feel."

*

Ted finished the novel in March 1995. I was working for the federal government at the time. It arrived in my office on Monday and I took the day off on Thursday and edited it and had it back to him on Saturday.

"Don't rush," he had said, wanting not to inconvenience me. "Take your time."

But I knew we had no time. I read it once, all the way through. I could see the shape. The first time through, I began to understand who the people were. I read it again, slowly, and edited it, page by page, I listened to its sounds, word by word.

I was not young, not then. I was no longer a confused and anxious assistant editor at a New York publishing house. I was no longer a damaged woman who did not know her own heart. I had no questions about who Ted Whittemore was to me; I understood in many ways what was important about his work. I concentrated.

This book was not about espionage. It was about a healer. Ted began the book three months before he got his diagnosis, but still the book was about a healer. And, also, for the first time, Whittemore's main character was female. Her name was Sister Sally and she was unlike any of his other characters; the man with whom she has a brief love affair, Billy the Kid, however, resembled characters in the earlier books and also resembled Ted.

I wrote that I was going to push him very hard. "I think you have a bit further to travel with Sally and Billy. So let's go." I started by telling him that I didn't think the verb in his first sentence was in the right tense. This was a brutal and ridiculous way to start an editorial letter, but I had no choice. I had to be thorough. I told my dear friend what my thoughts were as I read. I tried to remember where everything was and to see when things worked together and when they did not. I commented, I queried words, I flirted with him, I reminded him of old successes and other moments we'd both loved in other Whittemore books, I cheered, I wondered out loud about the characters so he would see how they appeared to someone else, I suggested, I doubted, I applauded, I reflected, I pushed and pushed and pushed.

Ted told me the letter was helpful. Very helpful. He was excited about getting back to work. I sent a copy of the editorial letter to Tom, who had become Ted's agent. Tom called me up. He thought my comments were good.

And, in his old-fashioned manner, Tom said, "You know, the letter you wrote—it's a *love* letter, in a way."

A real writer puts his heart and soul and all his intelligence on the page. Any book can be the last one. Every one of the writer's words, every small motive, counts. The editor must attend as though *nothing* else matters.

*

Ted went out of remission a few weeks after he completed the draft. Although his levels of pain increased and increased in the weeks and months that followed, he was able to do some revisions.

I told him that his revisions were more than I could have hoped for. I came to New York from Washington several times, working on the pages and leaving notes with him, telling him every doubt, but most of all I told him how wonderful the book was, and how each revision made me more convinced that the book was complete and perfect inside of him and our only task was to ask the right questions and bring it all to light.

I called Ted every other day, sometimes every day, until that became too difficult. He told me things about himself, so that in those last months I was allowed to understand more about him and how he'd lived his life.

Combined with my love for Ted was a certain brutality which I tried to keep in check. I tried not to push him too hard.

I tried not to let my disappointment show on the phone when he said he was just too tired from the pain, too sick from the drugs, to be able to write.

There was one section in the book that I really wanted him to revise. It was the scene where Sally and Billy fall in love. The woman in this novel was nothing like the women he'd written about before, who quite frankly had always struck me as a little pale. Sally was a real powerhouse, a force, a tragic mess. One day he called me at the office and told me he'd spent three hours writing the day before, and he felt like hell but he'd revised that scene, which was central to the love story, the scene I was sure he had inside him. He told me—but I did not see the pages. I did not see the fix.

Of course, it is dangerous when an editor has a favorite fix. It's not your book.

Because there was so little time, however, I let myself want it. In part, I just wanted what I wanted, and used the drama of death to cover up my presumptuousness and greed—but in part, I felt unconsciously that my desire for the fix would encourage Ted to fight harder, to slow down the illness for the sake of the writing.

Underneath this I must have believed that writing was more important to Ted than everything else, that he had no more powerful motive for staying alive. Was I crazy?

Meanwhile, he was in and out of the hospital. Annie left to go to Italy, alone, to get some time away from cancer, on a holiday Ted told her she needed to take. Carol came to take care of Ted.

Years back, Carol had been with Ted, longer than anyone else. She had ridden motorcycles all around Crete with Ted. She had been with him the day when, discouraged about ever writing anything worthwhile, he spotted a scarab in a dusty British glass case in the British Museum and the whole idea of the Quartet was born. Carol showed up when things took a turn for the worse. From early until late, she moved hospital beds and nurses in and out of Annie's house, not sleeping much if at all.

One night, when I hadn't been able to talk to Ted for ten days—I had been out of the country—I called him from my younger brother's house, where I was visiting.

Ted told me that he felt, suddenly, he had enough energy to really finish the book. Carol would read it, too, and Ted would mark places to cut, which I would then execute, leaving him the time to write the revisions he wanted to do.

My brother came into his bedroom where I was using the phone. So did my sister-in-law, so I moved out to the unfinished porch out their bedroom, carrying the portable phone, which was taped together with gaffer's tape from the results of abuse by children. As my brother and his wife lay together, sleeping, preparing for another day of work and family, I stood on the deck in the black night and schemed with Ted.

"Yes," I said. "Yes you can do it. Yes," I said. "We've had some great breaks already. You finished the draft before you went out of remission. Remember? Now we have another big break."

The night was wide. "This is what you can fix," I said. "With the time left. I'll come to New York. We'll talk about the cuts."

"Isn't it marvelous," said Ted to Carol, "that just when we need her, just like magic, Miss Judy appears. I hadn't heard from her. Wondered where she was. And here she appears. Stage Left. Enter Miss Judy."

"Yes," agreed Carol, wanly. "It's a good sign." I could hear the humoring in her tone, although I did not know, I could not see what she could see.

Instead, I egged him on. One more piece of luck, I said. One more good break. When so much has gone badly, one more piece of good luck. It's a wonder I didn't ask him to sit down at the desk then and there and write me a scene.

I never knew whether I was important to him for anything but the books. And I never knew if he would have been important to me if it weren't for the books. That was where we connected.

Ted had his own brutality. He had his ambition, which resulted in modest living and ruthlessness. He told me once that women were simply more generous than men, that they were better people, and although I never doubted that Ted had deeply loved the women in his life, and made them feel deeply loved, I wondered if that was an excuse for his bad behavior. He had two daughters, who didn't speak to him for years, although they visited him during his final illness. He said he had been a very bad husband, and a very selfish man. He knew what he was and he knew that as a result of how he had behaved, he had lost his daughters. But he had written his books. Ted had two granddaughters; one is named after his sister, as though his family got his children, but he didn't.

*

Six days after I returned from my brother's house to Washington, at 6:20 on a Sunday morning, my phone rang.

"Judy. It's Ted. Listen," he said, speaking urgently, "I'm in terrible trouble and you have to help me."

"Okay," I said. "Tell me what's wrong."

"I don't know where I am. And you have to come and find me."

"Of course," I replied. I paused.

Ted didn't know where he was, but I knew. He was lying in a hospital bed in his bedroom. He was too sick to be anywhere else. He was there, he just didn't know he was there. So I had to get him to bring himself back.

Suddenly my bedroom seemed very big and empty and the telephone cord a slender tie to the voice at the other end.

"Can you tell me where you *might* be, Ted?" I asked. "Can you tell me where you think you are?"

"Certainly," said Ted, practical, sure of himself. "I seem to be somewhere near Annie's. So you can start looking there."

We talked for a while, and got into a conversation about other things that were going on where he was. Some things confused him, like the workmen who were lifting big sections of pipe onto the roof of a nearby building (they might have been there or might not have been there). When we talked about it, he thought of some reasons why they were there and seemed to grow easier in his mind. And so we said goodbye.

One or two minutes later, the phone rang again.

"Judy, it's Ted." He seemed in a hurry. Or anxious. It was hard to tell.

"I just looked at the clock. It's six thirty in the morning. You must think I'm crazy." He sounded a little frightened.

"No," I answered honestly. "I don't think you're crazy. I just think you're on a lot of drugs, Ted. You're probably on a lot of morphine. That can mess you up. Besides," I added, looking out at the pale summer morning sky, "it's already light here. You probably looked out the window and saw how light it was and figured it was okay to call. Is it light where you are?"

Ted was reassured, and again we talked for a few minutes before he became tired and distracted. I couldn't go back to sleep after we hung up the phone, so I made some coffee and tried to read the Sunday papers. But he was much on my mind.

That evening, I came home around nine thirty or ten from a family picnic at the house of one of my older brothers, in Baltimore. I was afraid for the blinking light on my answering machine. My machine tells callers to wait for the famous beep. Ted had waited and left this message. I listened.

"Judy. It's *Ted*." He spoke very fast, slurring one or two words. "Calling on your famous number that you can't make a call since you're waiting for my beep.

"Judy. I've got some great news from you today. For you today. With you today. And the news is: is that I'm no longer *mad!* And don't you think that it would be nice to know that Ted Whittemore is no longer *mad?* Wouldn't that be fun! I hope it would be! Nice for a change anyway.

"Your number is still the change. Change. Still hasn't changed. My number hasn't either. What changed is that I'm no longer crazy!

"So listen. If you could call me sometime. At that number you know *all* about. And we could talk on *that* number.

"There are a lot of things . . . that are going to become clear — which never were!"

At this moment, Ted's voice, rising in excitement and joy, is abruptly cut off As though he simply went *spinning* off the face of the world. I think I knew then that I would never talk to him again, never hear his voice again.

Of course he did not go, spinning. It was not that simple, that easy, or that much fun. He continued for another month, increasingly disoriented, consumed by pain, pumped with drugs. He soon had nurses around the clock at home, he went in and out of the hospital, and finally went into a hospice. Several years earlier, I had helped to care for someone through the end of a terminal illness, so when my phone calls to New York were not returned by family and by the two women who, at different times, had shared his life and now had the honor and burden of seeing him through his final passage, I knew what this meant. They had too much on their hands to bother calling back concerned but peripheral friends. They were doing the hard work, and the least I could do was stay out of the way.

When it was all over, I knew, I would be handed the manuscript, for Tom was one of the literary executors and he would vouch for me. I would see if Ted had revised that love scene. I would make sure that all the changes in his hand were faithfully entered. I would see if any of the cuts we'd discussed were possible, but be cautious in my acts, just cleaning things up.

Then I would pass the pages to Tom and he would try to sell the story. Tom, however, never was able to make that sale. The novel felt unfinished.

*

The family held a memorial service in Dorset on August 12th. I flew to Hartford, rented a car, and drove north.

The day alternated between brilliant sun and showers. Dorset, in rain or shine, was as beautiful as ever. Tom spoke at the service. He said that Ted had *compartmentalized* his life, that different parts of Ted's life didn't touch. The parts that were represented in Dorset—his family, his true and good friends from Yale, who had supported him during his illness, who spoke of the powerful love they had felt from Ted during that time—were strangers to me.

After the service we were all invited back to the house. It had been renovated, but some parts of it were as I remembered. It was strange to stand there and see those same rooms. Time passed and the house emptied of visitors. Even the family disappeared, for a family meeting that may or may not have had to do with Ted; maybe they were burying him in the old graveyard with the other family members. The house was empty, except for a woman who went from room to room, clearing away food and drink.

I sat in a rocker on the back veranda and had a glass of wine. The rain came and went, yet again, spattering the tall meadow grasses behind the house. And then the sun shone bright. I took my empty glass to the kitchen and then I went to an upstairs bathroom, put on my bathing suit, and headed to the Dorset Quarry.

It was as ever. Young men went screaming over the high cliffs, cannon balling into the water. Two women paddled at the shallower end, near where I had found all the money. Children dabbled their feet, sitting on the ledge.

The water was cool. The birches tossed their leafy arms in the sky. Life contains these perfect afternoons. I swam from one end of the quarry to the other. And then I put on my goggles and dove down, deep.

The rain had left the depths murky, however, so there was nothing I could see.

Judy Karasik
Silver Spring, Maryland and Vitolini, Italy, 2002

Edward Whittemore (1933-1995) attended Yale University before serving as a Marine officer in Japan and spending ten years as a CIA operative in the Far East, Europe, and the Middle East. Among his other occupations, he managed a newspaper in Greece, was employed by a shoe company in Italy, and worked in New York City's narcotics control office during the Lindsay administration.

8744